Sefira and Other Betrayals

Sefira
and Other Betrayals

John Langan

Hippocampus Press

New York

Published by Hippocampus Press
P.O. Box 641, New York, NY 10156.
www.hippocampuspress.com

Cover art © 2019 by Santiago Caruso, santiagocaruso.com.ar
Cover design by Daniel V. Sauer, dansauerdesign.com
Hippocampus Press logo designed by Anastasia Damianakos.

First Edition
1 3 5 7 9 8 6 4 2

ISBN 978-1-61498-239-5 limited cloth
ISBN 978-1-61498-192-3 trade paper
ISBN 978-1-61498-265-4 ebook

For Fiona

Contents

Introduction

Stories within Stories

"When I arrange everything into a story, it seems as if it would have been so easy for the situation to have been settled with a couple of well-timed, honest conversations."

Over the course of two novels, two previous collections, and now with *Sefira and Other Betrayals* and its brilliantly horrific, complex, and thematically entwined stories, John Langan has established himself as one of the premier voices in literary horror. I mean both literary and horror with their attendant baggage and glory, and with all the love in my heart.

In John's earlier work and within this collection, John often employs nested narratives. The aunt in the painfully personal "The Third Always Beside You" gives her second-and-third-hand tale of a couple's relationship woes and infidelity to their shocked and dutiful daughter. There are ancient myths within the myths of the noir-tinged "In Paris, in the Mouth of Kronos" and the terrifying tale of double-cross and sorcery "Renfrew's Course." John tinkers with postmodern narrative techniques as well with the twisted and playful "The Unbearable Proximity of Mr. Dunn's Balloons," spotted with diary entries and an encyclopedic footnote.

Of course, there are more stories, more layers within *Sefira*'s stories: personal and social revelations upon which he smartly builds his plots, characters, and a palpable sense of dread. These great and terrible secrets, and the secrets within secrets, are made more terrible by their familiarity, their painstakingly observed veracity, and the effect of the reveal haunts his characters and his readers.

With John's narrative flair, his intelligence, integrity, and sense of humanity, his extensive classical knowledge and references, his layering, his envy-inducing sentences, I am not the first nor will I be the last to refer to John's work as *Jamesian* or *Straubian*. In a recent conversation with Simon Strantzas, he described a Straubian story as having deep secrets that slowly tease out over the course of the story shedding light upon the characters and ourselves. The Straub comparison is more than apt, but John is in no way derivative of Straub or of the many classic and current writers he admires. John is very much his own writer, one who ultimately builds each and every story toward a reveal and a revel; a revel of emotional catharsis that is as ecstatic as it is disturbing. It's a uniquely, dizzying, *Langanian* affect.

Monsters

"Whatever it was, he hoped it wouldn't be hungry."

John Langan isn't afraid of monsters. One could say that he revels (if I'm allowed to use the word yet again) in the monstrous. Whether gluttonous legends and titans or otherworldly creatures found in the most unexpected, seemingly innocuous containers (including, yes, the human heart: *"There was only the great animal baying inside me, a torrent of emotion"*), all these stories explore monsters and/or the monstrous.

Lesser writers (myself included here) too often lazily use ambiguity as a kind of safety net, afraid to commit fully to the supernatural. Perhaps it's a way to handle perceived suspension-of-disbelief issues. Maybe the ambiguity is mere coyness, a shameless attempt by the author to duck the genre label. Or maybe the ambiguity is a confession, admitting that the monster is essentially toothless.

John employs his monsters fearlessly as living, breathing, and nuanced story components with roles both simple and complex. Often juxtaposed with the harsh and unflinching realism of the human characters' relationships, their everyday lives, and their interior lives, his monsters are made no less real or dangerous. John has the integrity to commit fully to the supernatural. By the end of each story there is little ambiguity in regard to whether or not there really was a monster or an intrusion of the supernatural. Yes, his monsters are quite real, and they are also allegories and metaphors and mirrors and warnings. John's monsters arise from everyday situations, from characters' yearnings and their heartbreaking flaws, pushing already fractious relationships into crisis, past their tipping points, with one of the horrors being that the tipping point cannot be recognized as such until well after the inexorable downward spiral has begun.

That all said, the most frightening monster in this book (no it's not Grover . . . sorry, I couldn't resist one random pop cultural reference; it's what I do) is betrayal. And betrayal is always hungry.

Betrayals

"In nothing I did did I go too far, say words that could not be forgotten, commit acts that could not be forgiven."

Is there another act that feels as intimate and as psychically wounding as the act of betrayal? The breaking of vows and whispered promises are as gutting and gory as a knife twist.

Whether it's the older, unhappily married the couple in "The Third Always Beside You," or the young husband and wife who succumb to their many infections in the relentless "Bloom," or the dissatisfied husband confronting a raging beast and storms outside and from within in the tour de force "Bor Urus," you feel John's characters' pain, shame, and terror. These betrayals do not originate from recrimination, but from a more personal place. They spring from a longing for perfection within their partners, their union, themselves. These characters often betray the other while at the same time attempting to salvage themselves, still hoping their faulty sum will somehow become greater than the broken parts.

Those yearnings for more, for better, and for love are cunningly and authentically rendered and are what make this collection of stories so powerful and unforgettable. What pushes the stories into sublimity and horror is the personal betrayals placed within the wider context of the social and the infinite, vast indifference. We are wired to betray because we are born into a constant state of betrayal no matter how we may attempt to propagate the great lies: *it'll work out, it'll be okay, things happen for a reason.* John humanizes his cosmic horrors by acknowledging that our state of betrayal is the horror. At the same time, John somehow manages to wrest a dark but meaningful affirmation from the meaninglessness. These stories, as all the greatest stories do, will make you feel the spirit of Samuel Beckett's last lines from *The Unnamable:* "I can't go on, I'll go on."

Betrayal is *Sefira's* battery, fully charged and sparking dangerous and beautiful blue arcs of electricity.

—PAUL TREMBLAY

10 November 2016

Sefira and Other Betrayals

Sefira

I

Lisa looked in the rearview mirror and saw that her eyes had turned black.

The process had started a week ago, her second day on the road. She'd been washing her hands in the ladies' room of a rest stop on I-80, somewhere in the sprawling middle of Pennsylvania, and when she glanced at the mirror for a spot-check, saw the black rings around her pupils. Heart beating hard against her sternum, she leaned forward. Her pupils were rimmed by black dark as squid ink. She drew closer. The black appeared to be moving, flowing sluggishly out of her pupil onto the green expanse of her iris. She pressed her nose toward the mirror, trying to distinguish more detail, but her eyes teared, her vision blurred. Reflection fractured, she pushed away and hurried out of the restroom. She forgot to dry her hands, which she didn't notice until she was gripping the wheel of her Accord.

For the next five hours, as evening faded into night and she continued on 80, until the fatigue drawing her lids down forced her to pull off at a truck stop outside Pittsburgh, Lisa checked her vision every ten minutes, closing first the left eye, then the right, in an attempt to determine the full extent of whatever was happening to her. As far as she was able to tell, the change to her eyes was chiefly cosmetic. Her vision didn't seem any worse, her eyes any more sensitive to light, nor was there any pain.

Which didn't make what happened to them over the following days any less unsettling. Days two and three brought the steady darkening of her irises, until even she could no longer say where the pupil ended and the iris began. The effect was both unnerving and noticeable enough for her to retrieve the Ray-Bans in the glove compartment and slide them on. On day four, another mirror, this one in a Day's

Inn in Paducah, Kentucky, showed what appeared to be tiny black clouds churning over her eyes. When, up unexpectedly early, she entered the bathroom, she was considering an extra hour in bed, the prospect of which evaporated as she studied this latest development. The blackness that had spread across her irises was venting up into the humor beneath her corneas, like smoke rising from some internal conflagration. As before, she couldn't detect any impairment to her vision, so after her shower, she slid on the sunglasses to which her reflection had become accustomed—it looked more than naked, it looked incomplete without the chunky tortoise shell frames—and headed out under the sky that was just beginning to fill with light.

At several instants, as she sped up and down Illinois, she saw the white "H" indicating a hospital off the next exit and debated turning from whatever road the Honda's wheels hummed across and steering straight for the emergency room. It wasn't a question of whether whatever was changing in her was something to be concerned about: how could it be anything but? It was a matter of being twenty-four, at most thirty-six hours behind Sefira, and a detour to the E.R. would consume days, because they would have to admit her, run tests, treat her—try, at least. What would happen when their efforts failed, as she guessed they would? Specialists would be called in, experts consulted, she would be transferred to a regional medical center, a university hospital. They wouldn't be able to let her go, would they? Not that she blamed them. They wouldn't want to risk her infecting others with her disease, whose long-term effects might be more severe than she'd yet experienced.

And all the while, Sefira would keep moving farther and farther away, first—assuming Madame Sosostris was correct—to the motel in Montana, and after that, who could say? There was the chance—slim, but not so much it could be discounted entirely—she would overtake Sefira, catch her unawares at some all-night truck stop, surprise her on her way back to that ridiculous van. Even if, as appeared likely, Sefira maintained her lead, Lisa would arrive in time to confront her at the motel. According to Madame Sosostris, she would rest there for at minimum three days, possibly a couple of weeks. All of that, however, was contingent on Lisa keeping her foot pressed on the gas pedal, the car in 5th. Lose a few days, lose Sefira.

By this point, Lisa had cycled three times through the assortment of CDs scattered on the passenger's seat and was beginning a fourth. At first, driving north through the Adirondacks, she hadn't felt much like music, to put it mildly, and had passed the hours imagining arguments with Gary, switching the radio on to NPR when she grew tired of the sound of her voice. The following day, she roamed among the radio stations of upstate New York and the width of Pennsylvania, her finger pressing the radio's scan button almost compulsively, abandoning a song she didn't like only to return to it after a circuit of the local offerings turned up nothing better. She did the same thing the next morning, until sudden annoyance at the static caused by West Virginia's mountains prompted her to reach for the CDs on her right. With irony sharp as a scalpel's blade, her hand came up with Alanis Morissette's *Jagged Little Pill*. She had obsessed over the album in middle school, enjoying its defiant lyrics without understanding the raw emotions informing them. Suffice it to say, that had changed. She sang along to the tracks full-throated, and once it was done, played it again. Alanis was followed by Rihanna, then Luscious Jackson (another blast from the past), then Pink, Lady Gaga, and her guilty pleasures, Dolly Parton and Loretta Lynn.

She'd come by her appreciation for the last two through her job. One of her physical therapy clients was a late-middle-aged woman suffering from Parkinson's who had spent thirty years as a public-school music teacher before the disease forced her into early retirement. At the beginning of each of their sessions, Mrs. Mueller insisted on an album to serve as the accompaniment to her efforts. Her tastes were eclectic, ranging from Beethoven's later symphonies to Frank Sinatra's middle period. The day she put on *Jolene*, Lisa had wrinkled her nose at the album cover of Dolly Parton in her beaded green dress, her thick hair swept up and hair-sprayed in a blond elaboration. Mrs. Mueller tsked as if Lisa were one of her students. "Don't you dare frown at Dolly," she said, her eyes fierce, "the woman's a genius." To her surprise, Lisa agreed with her client, and on subsequent visits, had asked the music teacher if they could listen to another of the singer's albums. "I told you," Mrs. Mueller said. With each new session, she had taken Lisa through Dolly's catalogue, branching out to include Loretta Lynn and Patsy Cline. Gary had been annoyed by her newfound enthusiasm for, as he put it, his parents' music. He preferred electronica, long trains of sound that merged into one another. "It's for my job," she said, more defensive than she should have been. At Rhino Records in Huguenot, she discovered a four-disc compilation of Dolly's greatest hits, along with a two-disc set of Loretta Lynn's best songs. She purchased both and kept them in her car, where they joined the music that accompanied her as she drove from client to client. Hearing Dolly's high, rich voice now was oddly comforting, although the opening lines of "Jolene," with their plea to the protagonist to leave the singer's beloved, made Lisa wince.

Day five of her journey, she awoke with her eyes burning. She stumbled past the frowns of the counter staff at the McDonald's in whose parking lot she'd been sleeping, into the bathroom. Her sunglasses clattered in the sink. The woman in the mirror might have had the mother of all hangovers, or a virulent case of pinkeye, except that the blood vessels crisscrossing the whites of her eyes were black, as if someone had drawn on her sclerae with a fine-tipped pen.

Throat tight, she splashed cold water in her eyes, which helped the burning for a moment, but had no effect whatsoever beyond that—as if it would have, as if she could have cleaned her eyes of whatever was staining them. She bought a bottle of sterile saline and a bottle of Visine at the CVS next to the McDonald's, then returned to the restaurant's bathroom to rinse her eyes with the saline and douse them with the drops. The treatment brought some measure of relief. She ordered a large coffee to go and returned to the road. On the car stereo, Dolly sang about drowning in an endless sea of tears. For the rest of the day, as she first crossed Missouri and then Kansas, her eyes were too dry, gritty, her eyelids scraping across them every time she blinked. She had to pull over what felt like every ten minutes to use the Visine. She was annoyed. The time it took her to roll to a stop, remove the Ray-Bans, tilt her head, pull down her lower lid, and squeeze the eye drop in was time slipping through her fingers. Immediately under the irritation, like dark water under a scrim of ice, was fear, anxiety that the process under way in her eyes had entered a new phase, that this was the start of something worse, something she'd missed whatever window she'd had to address. The fear seeped into her annoyance, until finally, on the other side of Topeka, Lisa went so far as to take the next exit with a hospital nearby. She navigated within sight of it, only to have an emotion she couldn't name make her foot press the gas, her hands steer for signs leading back to the interstate.

When her eyes felt better the next morning, she told herself that she'd made the right decision. The black capillaries crosshatching the whites of her eyes had multiplied to the point the whiteness seemed the oddity, the results of a child's careless coloring. Within another twenty-four hours, only a couple of pale spots would remain across her eyes, like spattered paint. By then, she would have crossed into Montana, and whatever concern had swelled at the penultimate phase of her eyes' transformation was swallowed by the sensation that jolted her when she saw the sign welcoming her to Big Sky Country. It was as if the yellow line delineating the state's margin in her frayed and dog-eared Rand McNally were an actual border, as if in crossing it, she had passed into something else, analogue to the shift in the map's colors from the blue edge of Wyoming to the white expanse of Montana. It was like having had a bad cold, nose blocked, head fuzzy, and then taking a drug that cleared the symptoms instantly. The landscape streaming by her window wasn't especially different from what had flown past the last few hours in Wyoming—land like rumpled sheets on a bed, thick with yellow grass, the occasional house or gas station or farm like a set for a movie—yet it seemed brighter, as if lit from within by millions of tiny, brilliant lights. Thinking the phenomenon was attributable to something on the lenses of her sunglasses, she removed the Ray-Bans, but the impression remained.

Nor had it abated when a glance in the rearview mirror showed her eyes completely black. Despite everything, the catastrophe that was the last week-plus, what Gary had done and what had been done to him, what she intended for Sefira with the butcher knife wrapped in a towel and stuffed under the spare tire, Lisa was startled, jerked the car to the left, earning an angry honk from the eighteen-wheeler rumbling past her. She steered away from the truck, back into her lane. Loretta Lynn was singing about the Devil getting his due. The difference in her eyes was of the slightest degree, but she could not stop staring at them. After a second truck behind her, a pickup, beeped because she had failed to notice herself slowing from seventy to forty-five, she decided it was time to pull off. She hoped there was a McDonald's at the next exit. The drive-thru window meant she didn't have to worry about the teenager working the register staring at her because she was wearing her sunglasses inside.

Not to mention her mouth—there was no disguising that, either.

II

Lisa Murray, née Martinez, never thought her husband would cheat on her. Foolish statement, she knew. Unless you had married someone you knew was promiscuous, or you were part of an open marriage, you expected fidelity. Although her teenaged self would have rolled her eyes hard enough to have knocked her off her feet, now that she was on the other side of thirty, Lisa increasingly looked to her parents' marriage as a model worth aspiring to. They had come to the Hudson Valley, to Newburgh, not long after their wedding in Guadalajara, so her dad could work in his cousin's garage. After having her sister and her, Lisa's mom had found a job as a secretary at the local high school. They had bought a house in the city, which they had traded for a house in the country the summer before Lisa started middle school. Her dad opened his own garage, specializing in Mercedes and other high-end vehicles because, as he said, it was as easy to fix a rich man's car as it was a poor man's, and you could charge him more. Her mom retired from her school job to help him manage the garage. That was the way it was with her parents: as their years together increased, they drew closer to one another. During her childhood and adolescence, so many of her friends had come from families whose parents led pleasant but parallel lives, meeting once a week for Sunday dinner before heading off in separate directions, again. The same was true of a number of her current friends and their spouses. However happy they might appear—or at least, not unhappy—Lisa wanted a marriage that consisted of something more than a shared living space and a weekly meal. She wanted the sense of being partners in a joint enterprise, her marriage a project she and Gary would continue to work on, with lots of dirty sex in the mix.

That Gary would continue to notice other women, even to look at particularly attractive ones, she had no doubt. He was a guy, after all. On top of her karate class, she spent several hours a week at the gym, and she was not averse to evaluating the men on display around her. Just because you were married didn't mean you were dead; as long as you ate at home, who cared where you got your appetite? Just because you were on a diet didn't mean you couldn't look at the menu. Choose your cliché, as long as your selection was followed by one more: you can look, but you'd better not touch.

In seven years of marriage, eight and a half of being together, she had made one exception, bent the rules for Gary's brother Tim's bachelor party, which one May night had taken them and a dozen of Tim's friends from IBM to The Cusp, the strip club on the outskirts of Huguenot. The next morning, when Gary had related the night's events to her, he swore he had no idea the party was going to wind up there, which she almost could accept. Tim was fervently religious, a mainstay of the local Catholic Church. (Although, what were the stereotypes about the devout?) Whether Tim was seething with repressed desire or not, his friends had decided they couldn't allow him to cross the threshold into married life without a last debauch, so after burgers and beers at Pete's Corner Pub, they'd piled into someone's SUV and someone else's SUV and made for The Cusp. Gary claimed he'd had just enough to drink for the idea to seem inspired. The lot of them had been at the club until well past midnight, when the steady parade of naked women finally wore down Tim's resistance, and he consented to his friends' buying him fifteen minutes in the VIP lounge. Lisa had had to admit, the picture of her dreadfully earnest brother-in-law, as buttoned down as his white polyester dress shirts, gazing wide-eyed and slack-jawed as a tattooed dancer with a stage name like Lilith or Isis gyrated in front of him was more than a little amusing.

Her smile had faded, though, when Gary added that he, too, had agreed to a quarter hour in the VIP lounge. Tim's friends had insisted, as had Tim, himself, which she also almost could believe. If Gary were there with him, then it wouldn't look as bad, would it? In case word got back to Robin, or in case his conscience compelled him to confess, there would be someone to vouch that he hadn't really gotten up to anything with Lilith or Isis. And vice-versa, of course. She succeeded in keeping her voice light, level, as she said, "Oh?"

"Yeah," Gary said, cheeks and forehead flushing, rubbing his hands together the way he did when he was nervous. "I'm sorry. I mean, nothing happened or anything. This girl just danced around in front of me for a while; that was it. I shouldn't have let them talk me into it, I know. It was just—Tim, he looked so desperate—"

"How was his fifteen minutes?"

"I think he has some new ideas about heaven." When she laughed, he added, "No, seriously, it was fine. It was nothing."

She raised an eyebrow.

"What?"

"I didn't know you were into strippers. You learn something new every day."

"I'm not—I don't—"

"Maybe I should start taking a pole-dancing class."

"You—really?" he said, catching on to the joke.

That was how she dealt with her husband's disclosure of his fifteen minutes in the VIP lounge at The Cusp, with humor, by acting as if the situation were too ridiculous to bother being upset about. For the next couple of weeks, she teased him about it. Driving past The Cusp on the way to Gary's mother over in Hyde Park, she said, "Sure you don't want to stop in? They're offering a special on lap dances, two for the price of one." Looking over from the TV Guide channel, she said, "Hey, CNN's doing a special report on strippers. We should watch it. Maybe you'll see someone you know." Holding up boxes of hair coloring in the aisle in ShopRite, she said, "Which one would you say is more exotic dancer, cherry Kool-Aid or bleach?" If her jokes were passive-aggressive—or aggressive-aggressive—they kept her from pursuing certain lines of inquiry. She didn't ask him the girl's name (because it would have been a false name). She didn't ask him to describe her (because suppose she was Lisa's opposite, or worse, her double?). And she most certainly did not ask him for the gory details (because he had said nothing happened).

Throughout, Gary continued to blush, continued to apologize, continued to act, she thought, more like someone who was deeply embarrassed than someone who was deeply guilty. The circumstantial evidence supported his version of events. Tim was his only brother. The rest of his guy friends were happily married. He swore he had no desire to return to the Cusp's dimly lit interior. So in the end, Lisa decided to give her husband a pass. Not quite a free one, because she reserved the right to mock him about it should the mood strike her, but one that was heavily discounted.

To any of her friends to whom she told the story, that was the matter over and done with. Most of them were good enough to allow her that ending. Janice, her older sister, had a few acid remarks, but there was no situation for which she did not. If her questions about why Gary had done the laundry that morning before he had made his admission to her—and had she checked their bank balance to be sure he hadn't paid for the dancer, himself—and was she positive he stayed at home writing his computer manuals while she was out working with PT clients—if these questions and what they none-too-subtly implied stuck in her brain, stingers whose barbs anchored them too securely for her to remove easily, then it was because her big sister had a sixth sense for her weak spots, always had. Lisa resisted the urge to call Gary while she was on her way from one client to another. She refused to pore over that month's bank statement. She noticed that her husband did the laundry approximately every five days. She didn't talk to Janice again for a week.

The only thing Lisa could not stop herself from doing was picturing the girl. She made every effort not to, to think about something else, but apparently, her neuroses demanded this tidbit in exchange for lying low. From the start, she knew what the dancer had looked like, which surprised her. She would have expected more debate with herself, more wondering, Would Gary prefer tall or short? blonde or brunette? busty or leggy? Instead, from the moment she thought of the stripper, she *saw* her with hyper-real clarity. Busty *and* leggy: breasts a double-d, legs not as slim as they could be because of the hips needed to balance the boobs, but long enough to look full rather than chunky. Thick, shoulder-length hair dyed blond (badly) then hair-sprayed into a mane that would have done an '80s singer proud. Not as tall as the hair and legs made her seem, maybe five three, five four, but with good shoulders, good posture, and a pair of platform shoes that boosted her height. She was tan, tattooed with a bee above and to the left of her shaven crotch, and wore a navel ring. She began her act in a hot pink short dress, which was more of a long t-shirt, and which she wasted no time peeling off as she undulated to the music blasting from the speakers (something metal: Lisa wasn't sure of this detail). Once the dress was gone and now in a G-string the same neon pink, the girl roamed the stage, slipping one hand under the G-string and sliding her palm around her hip, pulling the tight pink fabric even tighter. She would draw out this part of her performance, ease one side of the G-string down, then let it stay there for a while. And throughout, Gary sitting beside the stage, rapt.

Strangely enough, when at last she told someone about this, it was Janice. More strange, her sister didn't kick her when she was down, didn't say, "I told you so." No, for once, Janice said what Lisa would have wanted her to, that there was no sense in tormenting herself, what was done was done, and anyway, Gary had said it wasn't his idea, hadn't he? And nothing happened, right? Hearing Lisa's description of the hypothetical stripper, Janice said, "She's your opposite, that's all. You're tall and thin; she's short and full. You're brunette and dark; she's a *güera.*" (This was after Janice had, as she put it, embraced her heritage, peppering the high school Spanish she remembered with vocabulary and expressions drawn from Google searches.) "You're what? an a-cup?"

"Har-har," Lisa said, smiling despite herself.

"I'll take that as a yes. She's got tits to die for—and the back problems to prove it. She's all your anxieties in a G-string and platform shoes."

Lisa wasn't so dense she hadn't realized this herself, but hearing Janice saying it in her no-nonsense voice gave the explanation a force and solidity it hadn't possessed inside her head. She waited for the other shoe to drop, for Janice to add, "Not that Gary wouldn't climb all over this kind of girl," but if Janice held another pump, she kept her fingers tightly around it. Although it amazed her to think it, Lisa's sister was the one who allowed the pass she'd given Gary to remain in effect.

This said, had you asked her to speculate on the type of woman with whom her husband might forget his marriage vows, the image of that dancer would have leapt in front of her mind's eye before she'd had time to formulate an answer, an ongoing symbol of her insecurities. Perhaps that was why, the following September, when reports of Gary seen with another woman flooded in (there was no beginning trickle, only an immediate deluge), she was slow to credit them, as the woman they described in no way fit the picture Lisa had of Gary's fantasy. After her friend Karen called to ask about the woman she'd seen with Gary leaving Pete's the other day around lunchtime—freakishly tall, stick-insect thin, black hair, huge sunglasses, wearing some kind of white lace sheath thing that covered her from neck to ankle like Morticia Adams's prom dress—Lisa had been surprised (Gary hadn't mentioned any lunch plans; though there was no reason for him to have done so), but not especially alarmed. Gary had a lot of female friends, probably more than his male friends. He'd been that way for as long as she'd known him, and while the person Karen had detailed didn't match any of her husband's friends, probably it was someone from undergrad passing through town, or someone she knew of who'd gotten in touch with her inner Goth (not that the description otherwise matched anyone she recognized). Making light of Karen's concerned tone, she said, "Oh, her. That's Gary's new girlfriend. Yeah, we decided to go the open-marriage route. I'm doing my gynecologist. He knows where to put his hands, let me tell you." Karen responded with shocked silence, then nervous laughter.

Over dinner that night, Lisa asked Gary about the woman. "Hey. Who's this lunch date I heard about?"

Frequently, these types of questions brought a blush to Gary's forehead, cheeks. This time, he looked up from his salad with his pallor unchanged. If anything, it seemed slightly yellow, as if showing the early signs of jaundice—no doubt a trick of the kitchen light. He didn't bother asking what she was talking about. It was as if he'd been waiting to deliver his answer. Through a mouthful of half-chewed tomato, he said, "Her name's Sefira."

"Sefira, huh? Old friend?"

"She's someone I met online. She e-mailed me about helping her set up a website. She wanted to meet to discuss it."

In addition to his job as a tech writer, Gary had a side-business in web-design, small enough to be microscopic. She could count on two fingers the number of sites he'd built, and that was including the one for her physical therapy practice. "How did she hear about you?"

"Your site," he said. "She has a sister who needs PT, and when she came across your page, she was impressed enough to contact me."

That sounded reasonable. "What kind of business is she in?"

"New Age stuff. Tarot, crystals, demonology."

"Demonology?"

"Yeah. It has to do with getting in touch with hidden forces. She explained it to me, but to be honest, most of it went in one ear and out the other. No big deal. I don't need to understand it to build the site."

"Just as long as you don't wind up with your head spinning around and pea soup shooting out of your mouth."

He smirked. "Don't worry, I'll keep my crucifix handy."

And that was that. The night brought calls from two more friends, one of whom had witnessed Gary and the woman at lunch at Pete's, the other of whom had seen the two of them standing talking on Main Street beside his car, both of whom tried as subtly as they were able to say that Gary and this woman had appeared awfully . . . close, and to ask if everything was all right between her and her husband. Lisa had no difficulty reassuring them that her marriage was fine, they had seen Gary with a new client, that was all.

She was able to repeat the same or similar sentiments the following day, to the three friends who left messages for her on her cell, and to the two more who phoned her at home, one at nine, the other at ten thirty. All five were checking in with additional reports of Gary and Sefira, spotted drinking coffee at Starbuck's, crossing Main Street (him with his hand on her elbow), and sharing another lunch at Pete's. Again, Sefira had been wearing the outsized sunglasses, this time with a red dress slit thigh-high and a pair of long black boots.

Lisa's friend Liz, a painter, couldn't decide precisely what shade of red the dress was, only that it was dark. She was also the one who remarked of Sefira's figure, "God, have you seen this woman? She's—I mean, it isn't that she's thin, no, thin would be fat compared by comparison. *This* is beyond supermodel anorexia. It's beyond skeletal. She's like a collection of lines, a stick-figure from a game of hangman. I don't know if you've ever seen anyone in that state, but it's like, you have this physical response to them, this . . . revulsion. For all that," she added, "and I realize how bizarre this is going to sound, coming after what I just said, I think this woman may be the sexiest woman—the sexiest *thing* I've ever laid eyes on."

"You're right," Lisa said. "How can a skeleton be sexy?"

"No, you don't understand. She isn't even a skeleton. Put two of her one behind the other, and you'd have maybe half a skeleton. It is, it's disgusting."

"But she's sexy."

"Yes, my God, yes. This woman—she doesn't ooze sex. Sex pours off her. She's radioactive with sex. Sex is a highly contagious disease and she's Typhoid Mary. I think of myself as pretty straight. I can admire the aesthetics of the female form, its beauty, but it doesn't turn my motor over. Let me tell you, one look at this woman, and I was ready to strip naked, slather myself with whipped cream, and invite her to lick it off."

"And yet she's repulsive."

"I know, I know, it's completely nonsensical. There it is, though. All I can say is, you must trust Gary way beyond an awful lot to let him spend so much time with her. I wouldn't trust myself, let alone Brian."

To greater and lesser degrees, the rest of Lisa's friends echoed Liz's assessment. Body like a wire sculpture; erotic as a tongue tracing an upper lip. It was the intensity of the latter impression that sent her friends speed-dialing her number. By the third time she heard one of her girlfriends describing the woman as sex incarnate, Lisa was amused by the coincidence, albeit, amused in a way that was more uncomfortable than she cared to admit. Her discomfort increased after caller number four (Liz) and by the time she hung up from talking to Victoria at quarter after eleven, she was wondering if Gary were still awake, so that she could seek further reassurance from him. She rinsed her glass, shut off the downstairs lights, and went up to bed.

As it turned out, Gary was awake—or, not so deeply asleep that, when she slid in under the covers beside him, he couldn't roll over to greet her. Somewhat to her surprise, he was naked, his cock not yet standing at attention, but sufficiently full to signal its readiness to be so. She wasn't displeased, not exactly, but after a day of reports of him and the goddess of sex, it was difficult not to think of his arousal as having another inspiration than his wife in her blue mermaid pajamas. There was no time for a clever remark, or an earnest question, because he pressed himself against her, his hands sliding over and under her pajamas, his lips searching out hers. Gary was a good kisser, but it had been literally years since he'd kissed her like this, his mouth electric on hers. His hands cupped her breasts, his fingertips sparking her nipples, as if his fingers were charged. Everywhere he touched, her neck, her back, her ass, flared with sensation, with pleasure. His sex was ripe and

rich between them; her panties were soaked. Hot—his skin was burning, feverish, the space under the sheets a sauna. She kicked the covers
from the bed, felt no cooler. She pulled her pajama top over her head,
pushed her bottoms and panties down and flicked them away with her
foot. If anything, she was hotter. She turned to Gary, lying on his back,
cock bouncing ever-so-slightly with his pulse. She felt herself open for
him, her cunt tingling with anticipation. Taking his member in one
hand, Gary gasping at her fingers grasping him, she swung her leg up
and over, angling his cock upwards as she lowered herself onto and
around him. She exhaled sharply. He was as big as he'd ever been, bigger, engorged. She was full of him, the spot where their pelvises
ground against one another throwing off bolts of pleasure that shot up
her belly, down her thighs, along her spine. Gary caught her breasts as
she moved forward, easing him halfway, three-quarters, almost all the
way out of her, then backward, taking him in again all at once. When
she did so a second time, he raised his hips to meet her. Another, and
another, and another, his hands on her breasts, her ribs, her ass, and
another, her breath faster, her teeth on her lower lip, half-moaning as
each thrust brought her closer to the moment the bubble of pleasure
building in her was going to burst, and another, and her nerves sang as
if she'd been struck by lightning, as if raw current were pouring
through them, lighting her up from the inside out. The orgasm rolled
over her in waves, one right after the other, each forcing a cry from
her lips. Nerves aglow, she rolled off Gary and flopped onto the bed, a
sigh the best her mouth could manage.

Before she could invite Gary for Round Two, he was kneeling beside her, urging her to turn over. She smiled drunkenly, mumbling,
"Woof-woof," and raised herself on her hands and knees. The mattress shifted as he positioned himself behind her. She felt his cock, hot
and wet against the left cheek of her ass, and reached between her legs
to guide him. He pushed forward, she backward, and she was around
him. He drew almost all the way out, then plunged back in. As he did,
he leaned over her, reaching with his right hand to stroke between her
thighs. Neurons she would have sworn were shorted, fried, flickered
and glowed. From I'm-good-you-do-what-you-have-to, she went to
meeting his thrusts, sliding her knees to either side to take him in
deeper, stretching her hand back to find the weight of his balls and

drag her nails over them. Gary inhaled sharply and increased the tempo, pistoning in and out of her while she caressed his balls and his fingers moved in ever-quicker circles. She was almost there—she was there, pleasure detonating on top of itself, reverberating up and down her. She shuddered, calling, "Oh, oh God," and, shouting, Gary came, spilling himself inside her in a series of hot jets. Some of his semen streamed down her leg, and her own orgasm must have made her more sensitive, because his cum was hot, so much she could picture it steaming.

Afterward, lying tangled with Gary under the sheets he had retrieved, all concerns about Sefira, if not banished, then sent to a distant province, she allowed herself to drift to the sleep lapping the shores of her consciousness. Out and down, down, deep into darkness, into warm blankness.

III

Her third day of driving, Lisa noticed that her teeth hurt. She had turned off I-80 for a series of local roads that led her into West Virginia via its northern spur, then down its heaped mountains. At a convenience store perched on a ledge beside a rushing stream, she bought a pre-made ham and cheese sandwich, a packet of Twinkies, and an extra-large coffee, over which she held the glass sugar-dispenser until the surface of the drink had risen to the cup's lip. She bent to taste it, and decided she had added enough sugar to render the bitter, oily brew drinkable. By the time she was nearing the bottom of the cup, the bland sandwich and dessert cakes long gone, their bunched wrappers rolling on the passenger side floor as she steered the curves of an especially convoluted road, her teeth had started to ache. The pain was dull, distant, rooted somewhere beneath the enamel, in the pulp. It spread through her mouth, as if she'd bitten into a scoop of ice cream straight from the freezer. She rolled her tongue around the inside of her cheek, tasted sugar gritty on her teeth, reviewed the past few days' diet of heavily sweetened coffee, snack cakes, any kind of soda so long as the label mentioned caffeine, and candy bars. *Terrific*, she thought, *not only is something wrong with my eyes, I'm going to need a root canal or three.* One more thing to thank Gary and Sefira for. On the car stereo, Pink sang that she was still a rock star. "Oh, fuck off," Lisa said, and hit the power.

That night, in a gas station near the Kentucky border, Lisa dug the toothbrush and toothpaste for which she'd run into a Wal-Mart two hours earlier out of their plastic bag and set to work cleaning her teeth. Once she was finished, she rinsed her mouth with iron-flavored tap water and brushed again. After she spat a second mouthful of foaming water into the sink, her teeth still hurt. She considered a third pass around her gums, decided her mouth felt sufficiently scoured for further brushing to be more obsessive-compulsive than hygienic. At least the pain wasn't any worse.

She cleaned her teeth in the motel bathroom as soon as she awoke the following morning, and again after her vending-machine breakfast of stale frosted cherry Pop-Tarts and blisteringly hot tasteless coffee. Compared to the steady blackening of her pupils, the discomfort of her teeth was of minor concern, but it was sufficiently distracting for her to buy a bottle of Extra Strength Tylenol at the rest area she stopped at for lunch and wash three chunky tablets down with a swallow of Coke. If the acetaminophen helped, it was to such a minute degree as to make no practical difference, which didn't stop her from taking another three that night between brushing her teeth and falling into the bed she'd taken at the Day's Inn in Paducah. She was too exhausted for the pain to prevent her sleeping; nor was it strong enough to follow her into her dreams.

Were her teeth really that yellow? she asked herself the next day, in the bathroom of the Cracker Barrel where she was waiting for her dinner to be served. She'd gone in to check her eyes and while gazing in the mirror had noticed her teeth, which continued their background ache, and which she continued to treat ineffectually with the Tylenol, telling herself that the pain might be worse without it. No doubt she should search out a dentist, but if she weren't tending to her eyes, then she wasn't likely to do anything for her teeth, which were jaundiced, as if she'd been using coffee as a mouthwash. Which she just about had been. She drew back her lips and dragged her index finger left to right across them, from canine to canine. Her skin squeaked on the enamel, but the color remained unchanged. She sighed, resumed her sunglasses, and returned to her table, where her dinner was waiting for her. After she was done, she ordered a large coffee to go—she had far enough to drive tonight not to—but grimaced as she did.

Her eyes were in too much discomfort the proceeding morning for her to worry over the state of her mouth. At one point, vision swimming with Visine, she glanced in the rearview mirror and thought that her teeth looked more yellow in the middle, as if their discoloration were spreading up and out from the soft spaces where they continued to ache. Not until the day after brought her eyes relief, however, did she devote any time to a closer inspection of her mouth. In the ladies room of a Burger King on the outskirts of Denver whose heavy stink of piss gave the lie to the cleaning schedule posted on the door, Lisa tugged the corners of her lips up and away with her fingers. The tooth enamel was the yellow of daffodils left to rot in a vase of stagnant water. The color concentrated down the center of each tooth, where it described irregular lines, zig-zags, lightning bolts. Toward the edges, her teeth grew paler, to the point of translucency. She traced a finger over them, and was surprised to feel them rough as sandpaper in places. Leaning into the mirror, she saw that the roughest spots matched where the yellow was most dense. She slid her fingers along the contours of her bite, top then bottom. Her teeth were sharper, more jagged, tugging her fingertips.

She wasn't sure when she made the connection between the blackness overtaking her eyes and the hurt daily filling her mouth. Almost from the start, she supposed. It must have been the second day her teeth ached that she knew (didn't realize, *knew*) the two were related, joint symptoms of something she wasn't prepared to contemplate, the straw that, dropped on top of everything else, Gary, that house, was going to leave the camel a quadriplegic.

So she clenched that straw in her hand and held it there as eastern Kentucky and its domed mountains smoothed into the western reach of the state and its long swells of earth, rows of dark green tobacco rippling like spokes on a wheel as she sped past them on local roads that finally released her into Paducah. She held that straw tightly the following day, when she was back on the highway and heading north up the length of Illinois, through the flattest land she'd ever seen, the only disturbances in it man-made, overpasses for local roads, until she reached Champagne-Urbana and Sefira's trail looped back south and

Lisa weighed continuing north, picking up 90 and trying to reach Montana ahead of her, to set up some kind of ambush, versus pulling off at the next exit so she could pursue Sefira down the state. (She heard Madame Sosostris saying, "You must adhere to the path she is making.") She opted not to break off her chase and drove through a thunderstorm that took up the entire early-evening sky, lightning like bright seams in the clouds, rain crackling on the windshield.

By the time she was crossing the broad Mississippi into St. Louis, the gray ribbon of the Arch on her right appeared to be slowly rotating as she stole glances at it, which she was reasonably sure it wasn't meant to do, so she drove to the outskirts of the city, found the parking lot of a McDonald's, and let unconsciousness take her.

Yet she never released her hold on that crippling straw, not that night and not the next day, as she made her slow way across Missouri to eastern Kansas, with its surprisingly steep gullies, and on to the state's western flatlands, despite her eyes feeling as if someone had poured coarse sand into them. When she detoured through Topeka in search of a hospital, she almost lost her grip on the straw, could feel the camel's legs trembling, but she recovered herself and turned in the direction of the interstate.

Nor did the straw come as close to slipping from her again, as the grasslands of western Kansas thinned to the arid waves of eastern Colorado, day bleeding into night. She took a room at a Day's Inn overlooking a reach of brown grass at the center of which a gray, single-story farmhouse listed toward a dead tree. The next day, the first part of her journey led her along a series of local roads past long barbed wire fences strung on tilting posts, lots crowded with cattle, a row of towers carrying power lines above the landscape like metal giants. She wondered when she'd see the Rockies and then there they were, huge even through the distance and haze, nothing at all like the Appalachians. Those mountains shouldered age, history so ancient most of it had been ground off them. These peaks leaned against the sky as if reclining on it, monuments to unimaginable gods, or those gods themselves. Not until she was standing in the ammoniac air of a restroom in Denver did Lisa relax her palm, and in so doing discover that she had squeezed the straw with such force for enough time that it had slipped under her skin, dissolved into her blood, infiltrated the nooks and crannies of her brain to the point its burden of dread had dissipated. Of course the blackening of her eyes, the yellowing of her teeth, were related. It would be far stranger if they weren't.

Braced, if not cheered, by her truth-telling, Lisa ordered a bacon double-cheeseburger, large onion rings, and large Coke to go, watching from behind her sunglasses the cashier's attempt to limit her glances at her mouth. Meal in hand, she flashed the server a smile that made her jump. *If you can't have fun with your monstrous transformation*, she thought, crossing to her car, *what can you have fun with?*

She waited until Denver was clustered in her rearview mirror before rustling through the paper bag in search of her burger. After avoiding fast food for literally the last decade—since, as a college junior, she had decided that, if she was planning on a career in physical therapy, she should model the healthy lifestyle she would be recommending to her clients—the past seven days had seen her diet switch to the all-junk-food plan pretty much overnight. She might as well have been fourteen again, pimpled and drastically unhappy and deadly to any plastic-wrapped confection to cross her path. At scattered moments, she could hear Janice's reproach: "Just because your idiot husband's flushed his life down the toilet doesn't mean you're required to follow his example. I'm pretty sure any obligation you had to him ceased the moment he started boning that skanky *puta*." True, needless to say, but God how she loved the taste of it, from the chalky sweetness of a Hershey bar to the mealy saltiness of a can of Pringles, from the battered blandness of a box of McNuggets to the charcoaled bite of a Whopper. Not to mention soda, Coke, Pepsi, Mountain Dew, Dr. Pepper—pick your beverage, there was none of it that tasted in any way natural. Fuel, she told herself, this stuff was a quick source of the sugar, the protein, the caffeine, the carbs she needed to maintain her pursuit of Sefira. So what if she liked it?

Her fingers freed the bacon double-cheeseburger from its wrapper. Mouth thick with saliva, she raised the sandwich to her lips and took a generous bite of it.

And nearly lost hold of the wheel as pain roared through her mouth. This was not the dull-but-persistent-ache of the last several days, this was the dentist's drill skating across the open nerve before the Novocain has finished working. It was a Fourth of July's worth of fireworks, detonating up and down her teeth, her gums, her jaw, her skull. She tried to move her mouth, to spit out the lump of burger balanced on her tongue, and her eyes flashed with the pain, white bursts wiping the other cars on the road from her view. If she didn't pull over immediately, her pursuit of Sefira was going to end in a tangle of metal and glass, which, even if she survived, would lead straight to the hospital, do not pass go, do not go anywhere. She slapped the turn signal and eased her foot off the gas, steering for the shoulder through a chorus of complaining horns. For what couldn't have been more than ten seconds, but stretched into what felt like minutes, she hunched her shoulders, tensing in anticipation of the car or truck whose collision with her she was certain was imminent. Only when she had guided the Honda as close to the guardrail as she could, shifted to neutral, and yanked the parking brake, did Lisa relax in her seat. After which she opened her door, leaned out, and let the soggy mass of meat and bun fall from her open mouth to the pavement. Even that lit up her skull.

Every last one of her teeth felt loose. It was a sensation she would have assumed archived on the long shelves of her childhood memories, the kind of dusty artifact you retrieved when one of your nieces or nephews was expecting her or his first payment from the Tooth Fairy. A half-pleasant ache, a spot in your mouth your tongue couldn't stop testing, worrying, a space opening as enamel parted from gum. Not this: her teeth seemed to shift with the slightest movement of her jaw, no two in exactly the same direction, each tooth still threaded to its socket by a nerve that flared with the least provocation.

To the extent that she could think with so much pain, Lisa was certain that the next five or ten minutes would bring the sight of a Colorado state police cruiser, roof rack stuttering red and white, to her rearview mirror. If the trooper didn't take one look at her and radio for an ambulance, he might assume she was on some kind of drug (didn't meth rot the teeth?) and order her out of the car, in order to search it for her stash. Which he wouldn't find, of course, but his investigation would lead him to the trunk, and the rolled towel under the spare tire. She could picture the cop lifting the bundle out of the tire well, setting it on the trunk floor, and unrolling it. She could see his features tightening from anticipating to consternation as the cream terrycloth revealed not baggies green with pot, or a white brick of cocaine, but a broad-bladed butcher knife, the kind of implement that comes as part of a set, twelve knives and a pair of meat scissors, slotted into a block of blond wood. It said, wedding present, which it was, or housewarming gift; although the rubber bands wrapped around the black plastic handle to ensure a better grip, and the symbols scratched onto the blade's matte silver finish were more recent modifications. Who knew if the cop would recognize any of the writing, let alone be able to translate it, but if he identified the row of characters closest to the hilt as Arabic—even though those symbols represented one language among many, including Hebrew, Greek, Latin, and Norse—the situation would become exponentially more complicated. Under normal circumstances, she would have trusted her ability to talk her way out of worse trouble than this, especially with a male cop, but with her brain jammed by all the reports of agony trying to force their way into it, she didn't expect she'd be up to more than a blank stare at the cop as he displayed the knife to her and asked if she could explain it to him. Jail would slow her as much as a hospital.

She had to get off the highway, take the next exit and find a place to lay low until the worst of the hurt passed (if at all). The words she employed for her difficult clients, the ones at the beginning of a long course of therapy to restore mobility and strength to an arm withered by a stroke, a leg after hip surgery, or the ones whose fear of the difficulties to come brought curses to their lips the moment they saw her, or the ones who had no hope of regaining the use of their legs or arms, but needed to exercise them to prevent further compromise of their health: those words whispered over her eardrums. *Okay. All right. We're going to take this slowly, all right? Nice and slowly. There we go. Yes, I know it hurts. Okay. But that's all right. It means the muscle's working. Easy. And if it's working, that means it can get better. Okay. Keep going. All right. Almost there. Easy, easy. Nice and slowly. I know, I know. It hurts. I know. Okay. Almost there. Almost.* The soundtrack was barely audible over the pain playing the *1812 Overture*, complete with cannon, in the rest of her skull, but she listened for it, tuned into it the way she told her clients to. *My voice is a station on the radio, okay? And the pain you're feeling, that's static. I want you to tune out the static, and tune in my station, Station Lisa, all right?* This was like trying to bring in a signal from three states over on your clock radio, but she could make out just enough to permit her to set the blinker, release the parking brake, shift into first, and, hands tight on the steering wheel, let out the clutch.

Were she looking for evidence of divine sanction for her mission, the next quarter hour might have provided it. Either that, or it was proof of the operations of a principle of chance so utterly random it could allow the conjunction of unlikely events necessary to deliver her from the spot beside the guardrail, onto the highway, into the path of a double tractor-trailer that somehow swerved around her, the slip-stream buffeting the Accord, past the first exit, which she was speed-ing past before it registered, off onto the next exit, which approached too soon and which she took too fast, tires shrieking as she held the wheel against a ramp that curved back on itself, through a traffic light she watched flip to red as she sped under it, along a road lined with big-box stores, to the parking lot of yet another Wal-Mart—the entire journey, her mouth roaring, white spots flickering in front of her eyes, as if her vision were a movie surrendering to the projector's heat. Nor did the hurt abate once she was safely parked and reclining in her seat, doing her best to remain completely still, the rise of her chest, the thrum of her pulse, motion enough to trigger her nerves.

On top of everything else, she was starving. The interior of the car was thick with the heavy smell of beef, the crisp odor of bacon, the sweet reek of onion rings in their batter. She could practically pick out the milky effusions of the melted cheese, the briny greenness of the pickle, the salt tang of the smeared ketchup. Her stomach didn't just growl, it wailed. Drool spilled over her lower lip. Although doing so made her gums feel as if someone was jabbing pins into them, she wiped her mouth with the back of her hand.

A sip of her Coke did nothing to blunt her hunger, and the rush of icy sweetness on her teeth dissolved them into a burning mass. Too much, it was too much. She was sliding into panic; she struggled not to throw open the car door, leap out, and run around the parking lot screaming. All she could do was let the pain wash over her, try to draw it into her, another instruction she gave her clients; albeit, one she'd never had great faith in. There was no need for her to close her eyes to visualize it. She could see it twisting around her, a roiling fog dense as taffy, the sickly yellow of sulfur, of a bruise three days old, of snow spoiled with piss. She had—it wasn't a coherent thought as much as an impression that this wasn't her imagining, wasn't *only* her imagining, but that was as far as the impression extended.

She opened her mouth, not wide, as much as she would to talk, and took a deep breath, inhaling the sulfur cloud, letting it pour over her tongue, down her throat, into her lungs, out to the rest of her body. Even the rush of air over her teeth stung. The pain wavered, subsiding the slightest fraction, then spiking, then spiking from there, then subsiding, then plummeting, then rising. If there was a pattern to its oscillations, she was in no state to discern it. Instead, she continued breathing in the yellow fog, which was full of black flecks, ash, as if it had vented from a volcano, from one of the earth's fiery arteries. The pain rose and fell and rose and rose. Within the furnace that was her mouth, her teeth were losing coherence, melting. She inhaled the fog coiled around her. The flecks of ash blew up from and dipped back into the churning yellow. Did they—did she see wings on some of them? She maintained her breathing.

The pain didn't subside as much as it submerged. The sulfur cloud swirled and seethed within her, from the peak of her scalp to the soles of her feet. She could swear that the skin on her hands, her arms, had gained a yellow cast. Her teeth were soft as putty. She rode the frothing crest of agony until it dropped, draining away from and into her, as if her body at last had discovered secret reservoirs capable of holding this pain and opened them all at once. She could still sense the hurt, but as something bottled, the yellow fog trapped in a great glass tank.

She didn't faint; rather, everything receded, carried away by the tide of relief that swept her. She was aware of the air dimming, of the day's gradual bleed into night, of cars coming and going around her, of an empty shopping cart clattering its slow way across the parking lot until it crashed into a concrete barrier. But it was all news from a distant country. Her insides were charred. Heat poured from her open mouth. Her teeth—something was wrong with her teeth. They were different, no longer soft, but as if they'd hardened into a new configuration, one her lips sat over uneasily. Her brow creased. Her tongue edged forward—then jerked away as something sliced it. Eyes wide, Lisa sat up, one hand rising to her mouth, the other twisting the rearview mirror toward her. A bright line of pain shone red at the end of her tongue. She parted her lips to inspect this latest insult, only to leap back with a shriek at what awaited her in the mirror. Her teeth—she couldn't have seen that, could she?

A second nick of her tongue returned her to the mirror. She stared at eyes so given over to black it was difficult to distinguish the exact places where the green rims of her irises had curved against the whites of her sclerae. Why should this be any more surprising or terrible than what was already happening to her? She raised her upper lip, flared the bottom lip, and saw gums full of broken glass. The straight white rows it had cost her the extraction of two teeth and eighteen months of braces to purchase during her early teens had been replaced by a mess of dirty yellow shards. No two were the same, nor did any protrude at exactly the same angle as its neighbors. All were sharp as razors, which her tongue regretted and which her index finger verified when she traced the uneven tops of the lower set and felt her skin part. She tilted her head this way and that, examining her gums, stretched and tortured by their new occupants, and groaning at the spectacle. Her tongue tore itself a third time, and the mirror shimmered and dissolved in the tears that flooded out from beneath her eyelids, streaming over her lashes. Her breath caught, hitched, and she was crying, sobbing, a single, shouted question, "What the FUCK?!" holding place for a dozen others.

Your monstrous transformation, she thought after a moment of her tear ducts emptying themselves, her nose streaming, her tongue cutting itself yet again. "Many a truth is spoken in jest," her grandmother had never missed the opportunity to declare. *Thanks, Tita*. She sniffed, blotted her eyes with a napkin. Her mouth tasted copper with her blood. She dried her cheeks. Her stomach growled. The remainder of her uneaten meal was sitting on the passenger's seat. Before she could think better of it, she seized the rest of her bacon double-cheeseburger and devoured it in three ravenous bites. She nicked one of her fingers in the process, not to mention, her tongue, but she barely noticed, cramming onion rings after the burger, pulling the lid off her soda so she could gulp it down, crunching the ice cubes that slid into her mouth between her new teeth. There was no pain. There was only waiting for her hunger to catch up to the food she had sent its way. Even though doing so sliced another three fingers, she sucked ketchup and grease from them.

Fed if not full, she was calmer, ready for a new round of state-the-obvious. What had changed her teeth and what was changing her eyes was Sefira. Who could say if finding and dealing with her would have any effect on either of them, but really, what else was there for her to do? She reached for the key and started the car. The stereo blared, Lady Gaga declaring herself a freak bitch, baby. "You and me both," Lisa said. As she eased forward out of the parking space, she stretched her lips back from her mouth and tried to pronounce, "Double cheeseburger," as clearly as the new arrangement in her mouth would allow. She managed well enough for the drive-through window at McDonald's, she figured. The kids who worked those positions had to be accustomed to all manner of accents.

Talking to Gary, though, was going to be a challenge.

IV

Only when a blurry glance at the clock radio showed the numbers turning to 8:40 did Lisa sit up in bed, wincing at the pain that flared behind her eyes as she did. "Shit." It was late, and her head felt as if a hangover had moved into it, a consequence of oversleeping. No doubt, when the alarm had beeped and she'd slapped at the radio, she'd turned it off instead of hitting the snooze button. There was barely enough time for a shower, coffee, and Greek yogurt if she wanted to make her 9:30 in Gardner. She turned to prod Gary. His side of the bed was empty. He must be up already, probably engrossed in whatever his latest tech writing project was. Or constructing Sefira's website. *Shut up*, she told herself, and slid out of bed.

When she descended the stairs after a quick shower, though, her husband was nowhere to be found. Not seated at the kitchen table revising his latest project with an extra-fine blue pen, the way he liked to begin his mornings; not seated at his desk, either, typing his corrections into the desktop, NPR droning on the old transistor radio balanced on top of the bookcase; not even in the living room, watching TV, or sitting on the rocking chair on the front porch, his preferred locations if he was taking a break from working. Nor was there any coffee waiting in the pot; instead, she found a post-it note on the coffee maker. "Hey Sex Goddess," Gary had written, "Gone to Dunkin Donuts for morning treats. Back in a flash." There was no time indicated on the small yellow square. He could have written his message anywhere from ten minutes ago, when he'd heard her stagger into the upstairs bathroom, to an hour or two before, when he'd decided to surprise her with coffee and a toasted coconut donut. Whichever, he hadn't returned, while if she left in the next five minutes, she could stop at Stewart's for coffee and an apple fritter on her way to Mrs. Sanders's. She plucked the post-it from the coffee maker, reversed it, and wrote, "Hey Sex God—9:30 in Gardner—Couldn't wait—Sorry! See you tonight! Love, L" with the pen she kept in her front jeans pocket. Leaving the note on the kitchen table, she took her purse and keys and headed out the door.

She was expecting Gary to call her at some point during the morning, some version of, "I'm sorry, I completely forgot about your first appointment," likely in combination with, "The service at D&D was shit," and possibly, "You'll never guess who I ran into." But while her cell continued to trill throughout the day, it was not Gary, nor was his voice among those which left messages on her voice mail. Instead, she heard from every one of the eight women who'd called her over the past two days, as well as four others, pretty much the circumference of her circle of friends. The first couple arose from a delay in communication. They'd only been informed of Gary's previous rendezvous with Sefira this morning and had decided to go straight to Lisa. Especially with the space between her legs still pleasantly sensitive from last night's exertions, it was easy enough to repeat yesterday's explanation. The remaining conversations proved more difficult to manage. For a second day, Gary had been spotted with Sefira.

Her friend, Liz, called while Lisa was driving from one appointment to another. She put the phone on speaker. "You bitch," Liz said.

Lisa half-laughed. "I'm sorry?"

"I thought we were friends."

"We are. What are you talking about?"

"I mean, I realize we haven't seen that much of each other since Brian moved in, but I've been really busy, honestly. I know it probably looked like I was blowing you off, but I wasn't, I swear."

"Liz, I—could you slow down? Please?"

"I was at your wedding, for Christ's sake. I designed your invitations. Didn't you think I deserved to know—for you to tell me, personally?"

"You lost me," Lisa said. "You completely lost me. I have no idea what you're saying."

"Gary," Liz said. "Gary and that—what did you say her name was? Cythera? Whatever. I had to go into town this morning to pick up canvases. I parked in the municipal lot, the one beside Prospero's. As I'm getting out of my car, I notice this couple a few cars over. They're making out like they're sixteen and their hormones are set on eleven. Except they aren't sixteen. For about a millisecond, I'm like, Okay, nice to see someone our age show a little passion. Right? Then I recognize them."

Already, Lisa had understood what Liz was telling her, the tone of her friend's voice, the gist of her questions turning Lisa's blood to ice water. She didn't need Liz to say any more, did she? But it was as if she were an actor in a made-for-TV movie about a wife whose husband betrays her, and this was her next line. She said, "What are you saying?"

"Seriously?"

"You saw Gary," she said, "with Sefira."

"It was like they were eating each other. I mean, get a room— which I'm sure they were about to, if they didn't do it right there on the blacktop."

"Huh."

"I just—how could you not tell me? When I talked to you the other night, I believed you."

"Yes."

"I was—I felt so embarrassed."

"Sorry," Lisa said.

All at once, she had to get off the phone. She told Liz she would have to talk to her later, she was at her next client, and disconnected before Liz could protest. The lie was white. She had another ten minutes before she turned into Mr. Spungeon's driveway. She spent them gauging her reaction to Liz's news. There had been three calls before Liz's, none of them as damning, all confirming further contact between her husband and his client. They'd brunched at the Main Street Bistro (which, Liz had told her once, was where you went on Sunday morning to find out who had left the bars together Saturday night), window-shopped Main Street, and apparently browsed the erotica section at Prospero's. Lisa had learned the day's outfit, a loose white blouse, with skintight pants that Karen said looked like snakeskin, or alligator skin, some kind of reptile skin, and brown cowboy boots. Oversized sunglasses. She'd listened to a fresh round of opinions concerning how close Gary and Sefira had appeared (the consensus was very); although, mindful of her previous explanation, her friends had prefaced their observations with, "If you hadn't told me there's nothing going on," and, "It's a good thing I talked to you, because if I hadn't," and, "If I didn't know better." You couldn't say that the trio of calls had in any way prepared her for Liz's—you could not—it was more that the first one had sounded a note, something off-key, whose discord the subsequent calls had echoed and amplified, the vibrations of that collapsing note telegraphing a message she couldn't decipher until Liz translated it for her. Liz, however, had leapt to an interpretation that, while reasonable, might yet be premature. Granted, Gary had been kissing Sefira. There was no point pretending otherwise. But there was no evidence that he had made the first move. It was possible that he had turned around and there she was. If she was as supercharged with sex as Lisa's friends had testified, could she blame her husband if he responded to her?

This was perhaps the biggest surprise, that she would be so ready, so willing, to excuse Gary's behavior, to write him another pass. Had you asked her—well, this morning, sitting in the bed whose sheets were rich with the smell of sex, scenes from last night playing in her memory like her very own X-rated feature, she would have told you flat-out that there was no way Gary would even think about doing anything with Sefira, let alone actually putting his mouth on hers. Please. Nor would her sentiments have been appreciably different following the first report of Gary and Sefira lunching at the Bistro. Even when her cell was trilling a fourth time, after those additional descriptions of Gary and Sefira's further activities—even when she was pressing the answer icon on the phone's screen—while she would have allowed the possibility of Gary's attraction to Sefira, this woman who apparently walked around in a cloud of desire, she would have insisted the chances of that attraction morphing into action were so small as to be not worth consideration; albeit, with a stridency that would have betrayed her growing unease. Now that she was in possession of evidence that

directly contradicted such an insistence, she still was not ready to assume the worst, a worst that threatened so much more than any lap
dance ever had.

The day's remaining toll of messages and conversations made her
hesitation seem less prudent reserve and more desperate denial. No
one else had quite as incriminating evidence to offer, but there were
two sightings of Sefira hanging on Gary's arm, and one of him with his
arm around her shoulders, as well as a less-than-reliable glimpse of the
two of them driving east out of town in Gary's green Subaru (the same
direction as all five of the town's motels, not to mention, the Cusp).
Though she could feel the emotions darting around her on insect
wings, neither pain, nor anger, nor grief had descended on her by the
time she had finished with her last client and started home. Instead,
she was as confused as she ever had been, as if each successive call had
cast another veil over the situation, the kind of thing you'd expect if
you flipped to the back of an advanced calculus textbook. From the
way it was written, the layout of the numbers and symbols on the page,
you knew generally what it was and what it was intended to do, but try
to solve it, and you might as well use your pencil and paper for doo-
dling. There were way too many blank spots in your knowledge for
you to have any hope of figuring it out. She could hear Janice deriding
her naïveté, but she couldn't conceive that, after last night, Gary could
go out this morning to be with someone else. As far as she was concerned, one event precluded the other.

If she was hoping for clarification from her husband, however, she
was disappointed. The moment she turned up Farber, she saw their
driveway was empty. Of course, there was nothing wrong with his car.
Of course, she was not going to find him waiting in the living room
with an explanation that would reconcile last night with today. But she
called out, "I'm home," as she opened the front door, anyway, and
when there was no reply, went from room to room saying, "Gary?
Honey?" Only her voice, ringing on the walls, met her. Her search finished upstairs, in the bedroom, and at the sight of the bed, its tangled
and stained sheets like an abstract painting of last night's passion, a
tremendous sadness coalesced inside her, just below her heart, as if
there were a heavy rock there, pulling her down, onto the bed. The
pain, anger, grief that had flitted around her were caught in the sad-

ness, encased in it, as were most of her thoughts. She sat on the edge of the bed as the air flared with the sun's last light. She sat there as the air charred, grew gray and dim. She sat there as gray darkened to almost-black, as the room lost form and definition around her. She sat with that rock in her chest pulling everything into itself, every stray memory, excerpt of conversation, fragment of image. Gary said, "Hey, dirty girl." The wedding cake smeared her fingers as she wiped it across his mouth. "It's on Farber, in town." The roller climbed the wall, leaving a trail of white paint. "I think he has some new ideas about heaven." His cheeks reddened.

When the house phone rang in the kitchen, she was off the bed and down the stairs two and three at a time, nearly losing her footing as she skidded into the kitchen. Blood pounding in her ears, she seized the receiver. "Hello?"

So prepared was she for the caller to be Gary that, for a moment, she could not understand what she was hearing. A deep, soft sound, intimate as a breath blown in the ear: a woman, saying, "Hello? Gary? Is Gary there?"

And she knew, from that voice like honey cloying the tongue, she knew. The stone in her chest fractured with an almost audible crack. She said, "Who is this?" but it was a formality, a line to advance the dialogue.

"No," the woman said, "he isn't there, is he?"

"No."

"He hasn't been there all day, has he? All day, and alllllllll night."

What time was it? From where she was standing, Lisa couldn't see the coffeemaker's red digital numbers. "Who is this?" she said. "Sefira?"

The voice inhaled. "Why, you know my name."

"Yeah," Lisa said, "I've heard all about you."

"From Gary?"

"Among others."

"I see. Your hubby didn't tell me he'd shared so much with you."

"He's a regular font of information."

"Does that mean he told you how he fucked me until he was raw and red? And how, even then, when the skin on his cock was peeled and bleeding, he bent me over one more time?"

The fragments below her heart ground together. Mouth dry, she said, "No—he neglected to mention that charming detail."

"Did he? Would you like me to fill you in?"

"I'll pass, thanks. It sounds like there's been enough filling in, already."

Sefira laughed, molasses bubbling in a saucepan. "You are clever," she said. "I like that."

Great, Lisa thought, *she'll be trying to seduce me, next. Two for the price of one.* "Why am I talking to you?"

"Because your husband's in no fit state to drive. He needs you to come get him."

"Why would I want to do that?"

"That isn't for me to say, my dear. Perhaps you don't. Perhaps you'd prefer him to stay where he is."

"With you."

"For the moment."

"Oh? Done so soon?"

"Yes, actually. Gary's been a lot of fun. The things your hubby did to me—really, they're nothing compared to the things I've done to him, but he is a *nasty* boy, and I appreciate that. I'm sure you do, too. Nasty or not, though, I have other appointments to keep. So many men and all that."

The fragments had turned to lava; suddenly, she was gripping the phone so tightly she heard the plastic creak. "Why don't you stay there, so I can kick your ass?"

"That's cute. You'll beat me black and blue and then what? Throw your husband over your shoulder and ride off into the sunset. All forgiven and forgotten; boys will be boys?"

"Why don't you let me worry about that?"

"Oh you poor, sweet thing. Shall I tell you what would happen? The next time you fucked—sorry, *made love*—you wouldn't be able to stop thinking about him and me, wondering, *Was he like this with her? Did he grab her ass like that? Did she teach him to do that with his tongue?* And the answer to all those questions would be, *Yes.* Yes, yes, and yes. It doesn't matter if you hang up the phone and do your best to forget you were ever married, or if you and Gary were to have a miraculous reconciliation. I will always be in your bed. You will never escape me."

"Who are you? Why did you do this?"

"Why don't you ask your husband? He sought me out."

"That's a lie."

"Ask Gary."

"He already told me you contacted him about designing your website."

"Me? Why would I need a website?"

"For your business—what is it? That New Age shit, right? Tarot, crystals, demonology?"

"All interests of mine, yes, but I'm hardly in one place long enough to set up a business. With all the lies he's told you, you can't accept one more?"

"Where are you?"

"So you are coming for him."

"I didn't say that. I just want to know where you are."

"1430 Wycombe Road. It's—"

"I know where it is."

"Very well."

"In fact, I'm guessing I can be there in about five minutes."

"Oh?"

"I wonder how long it'll take you to gather your shit and get out of there."

The line went dead. Lisa sprinted for the door, grabbing her handbag from the hall table on the way.

V

As her first day of driving drew to a close, in the parking lot of a Day's Inn on the outskirts of Watertown, Lisa's cell sounded. She didn't recognize the number. Sefira, calling to taunt her? She decided to let whoever it was say whatever they had to say to her voice mail. However, the phone kept up its song, which was strange, because she had emptied her mailbox, and even if she hadn't, by now the person on the other end of the line should have heard a message telling them to try again later. Was her phone crapping out on her? Given everything else that had occurred the past couple of days, it wouldn't be a surprise; if anything, it was perfectly in keeping with the flaming car wreck her life had become. She didn't bother removing the phone from its dash mount. She tapped the screen and said, "Hello?"

Gary said, "Hi. It's me."

Of all the possible responses to hearing her husband's voice, she would have ranked humor low if not at the absolute bottom of the list. Yet raw, hysterical laughter burst from her in a torrent. Through the laughs, she said, "You have got to be fucking kidding me."

There was no reply.

"What are you doing?" she said.

"I'm calling with information about Sefira."

The name stilled her hilarity. "What information is that? How to give a blowjob that'll leave your man begging for more? I read that issue of *Cosmo*, thanks."

"I have the next set of directions for you."

"No, you don't," she said. "Madame Sosostris is going to phone with those."

"What did she say?" Gary said. "She said she would ensure you received directions every day. She didn't say she would be the one delivering them. Because of . . . everything, I have a connection to Sefira. I know the route she's taking. Madame Sosostris says it's legit."

"This . . ." Lisa blew out a breath. "You can appreciate how fucked-up this is, right?"

"Yeah. I'm sorry."

"Whatever." She leaned over, dropped the glove compartment, found a pen and a form letter from some charity or another searching for cash. "Okay. Which way is the bitch headed?"

The route Gary detailed took her back over the Adirondacks, all the way south to Newburgh, and west across Pennsylvania, to Pittsburgh. When he said, "That's it. That's as far as I can see," Lisa said, "Are you sure about this? I just spent today driving up to this place, and now you're telling me to turn around and pretty much go back the way I came."

"I'm sure."

"How am I supposed to trust you? How am I supposed to know this isn't a plan you and Sefira came up with together?"

"You can trust my desire for self-preservation."

"Seems to me it's your desire that got us into this shit storm," Lisa said, and before Gary could reply, cut the connection.

He phoned the next day as she was speeding toward Pittsburgh. "I'm still driving," Lisa said. "Call me back in an hour."

"I can't," Gary said.

"What do you mean, you can't?"

"This link opens once a day," Gary said, "and then it's gone for another twenty-four hours. It's kind of a 'the-stars-are-in-alignment' deal. When the call breaks off, that's it."

"Seriously?"

"According to Madame Sosostris, this is how it works."

"Hang on." There was a rest area ahead. She steered off the highway into it, rolling to a stop in a parking slot near the toilets. She yanked the parking brake, but left the engine running. The day's directions were lying on the passenger's seat, along with the pen she'd used to record them. "Just a second." She reached above her to the dome light, switched it on, wincing as radiance filled the car. She picked up the envelope, leaned it on the steering wheel, and grabbed the pen. "Go ahead."

The roads Gary reeled off were local, a network of narrow routes that would take her over West Virginia's mountains to eastern Kentucky. "A lot of them are pretty windy," he said. "You'll need to be careful."

"Uh huh," Lisa said, writing down the last of his instructions.

There was a pause, then Gary said, "Do you have everything? Do you need me to repeat any of it?"

"I've got it."

"Good," he said, "good. Well . . . that's all, I guess."

"Yep." She replaced the envelope and pen on the passenger's seat, clicked off the dome light.

"Unless there's anything else."

"Like what?"

"I don't know. How are you holding up?"

"There's something wrong with my eyes."

"What do you mean?"

Irritation stabbed her. "Never mind," she said, and ended the call.

Gary asked about her eyes the following night. A not-insignificant part of her was gratified by his interest, was tempted to detail the changes occurring beneath her corneas. What a relief it would be, to talk to him. Only a few days ago, the two of them had been sitting at the kitchen table, the cartons from their preferred Chinese takeout standing open, discussing the latest adjustments in coverage by an insurance company she billed to. It was one of the things she liked best about marriage, the conversation with a person who knew you as well as anyone, informed by the people the two of you knew, the places you'd been together, the experiences you'd shared, all forming a kind of shorthand unique to your relationship. *And where does fucking Sefira fit into that?* She heard the question in her sister's voice. Whatever urge she felt to confide in Gary withered. Again, she ignored the question and disconnected.

For the next two calls after that, Gary was curt, listing the roads she was to take, then hanging up on Lisa before she could hang up on him. When she realized that he was upset with her, a blend of amusement and anger pulled her mouth into a smirk to which it returned throughout her drive up and down Illinois and across the Mississippi onto St. Louis's humid streets. Always, it had been one of Gary's talents to turn any situation in which he was to blame back on his accuser, employing a species of rhetorical jiu-jitsu he had developed as the middle child of five siblings in a large Irish Catholic household. Usually, he achieved this by going on the offensive, complaining about the way he was being treated, or finding an accusation to hurl in response to whatever complaint Lisa had against him. Sometimes, though, he chose silence, elaborate, extended silence, theatrical silence, maintaining it until Lisa broke down and half-apologized for accusing him of anything in the first place. It was maddening, but it happened infrequently enough not to concern her. Even if she were inclined to indulge him now, which she absolutely was not, she was far too tired to do so. Locating a motel in St. Louis seemed an impossibly complicated task. She found a McDonald's, drove to a dark corner of its parking lot, far from where clouds of insects swarmed the tall halogen lights, killed the engine, and reclined her seat as far as it would go.

Already, sleep was tugging at her. She closed her eyes. *You know Gary's going to call any minute, now,* she thought, but the certainty was not enough to halt her descent into the unconsciousness closing around her like black water. There was a moment of dissolution, of feeling everything, her fears, her anger, her hurt, the very self that threaded them together dissipate that was wonderful.

Distantly, she heard the phone warbling. She opened her eyes, saw the phone in its mount at one end of a black tunnel. She went to lift her right arm, but it was sluggish, leaden.

From the passenger's seat, a voice said, "Don't worry. I've got it." A hand with long fingers and nails slid into view and tapped the screen. Gary said, "I'm sorry it's so late; there's something weird—" and the voice cut him off. "It's me, Gary," it said. "Fuck off." The hand ticked the phone, ending the call.

Lisa tried to speak, but her tongue refused to move. *Sefira*, she thought.

"That's right," the voice said. "I came to have a look at you."

How . . . ?

"Gary has a connection to me. He also has a connection to you. Therefore, you and I are connected. It's simple math. Well, it's not that simple. Nor is it math, really. What it is, is exciting. Do you know what it means for him to have lain with you, after he had tasted the pleasures I had to offer? It's a sign either of great love, or of the most intense hatred."

Or overwhelming horniness.

A laugh that was as full and rich as honey being poured over warm bread. Despite herself, despite everything, Lisa found it one of the sexiest, the most erotic sounds she'd ever heard. "There's that, too. I'm pretty sure your hubby doesn't hate you, which leaves love as the explanation. Together with the urges of that lovely cock."

Lisa strained to turn her head, could not.

"Don't bother," Sefira said. "You are in my power and all that."

Why are you here?

"I told you: I popped in to see you. In the flesh, as it were."

Why?

"Because you are something new. You must understand, I have been doing this for a very, very long time. I won't bore you with the story of my origin; honestly, there's plenty of it I don't remember. I've seen the pyramids at Giza when they were new, encased in white limestone, brilliant in the sun. I've picked my way through waterlogged corpses on Crete, after the sea rose up and drowned them. I've heard the creak and splash of the oars when the Achaeans sailed for Troy.

"You get the idea: I've been around. In that time, most of the men who have come to me have stayed. And by most, I mean ninety-nine percent. More: I mean ninety-nine point nine nine nine ... Ninety-nine point a hundred nines, a thousand. Granted, given the number of years I've walked this plane, that still means a few dozen who have not succumbed to me immediately. Some killed themselves. Some tried to kill me, an ill-advised move on their part. Some fled to their wives or mistresses, and this fascinated me. Why go back to them, after having sought me out in the first place? Your joke aside, there is no lust I cannot sate. To know me is to know that I have no equal.

"All the same, they rose from the bed we'd shared and departed. This leaves hate and love for explanations. I understand hate, the urge not just to stick the knife in, but to turn the wrist, to drag the blade through the viscera, spill it steaming onto the dirt. Where I come from, it's the emotion underneath ... everything. Love, though, I am less certain of. Sometimes, I wonder if it's what I feel towards them, the men who seek me out. Not in the way you love Gary, but as the hunter loves the stag into whose heart she shoots her arrow. I know, you'll say it's not the same thing. Probably, you're right. You can understand, though, how it would intrigue me, this impulse, or habit, or whatever it is that allows even a small number of my partners to walk away from me. I should say, attempt to walk away from me, since I always reel them back in, in the end. The women for whom they thought they were forsaking me—none of them has survived long, after I have brought their men to me the second and final time. Some discover what I've left of their lovers and are driven to madness, suicide. Some never see their men again, and are soon consumed by what has been passed on to them. I've watched those women, revealed myself to a couple. After meeting me, one walked off a cliff. The other ran into a field and was gored to death by a bull.

"Of that tiny number, however, not one has threatened me with violence, let alone, undertaken to pursue me. In my experience, you are unprecedented. I doubt you can imagine how thrilling that is. This existence ... I would like to say it's a series of unending games of chess, but it tends to be more in the vein of checkers and occasionally, tic-tac-toe. No matter that every seduction were a chess match against an outstanding opponent, the game remains the same, the board the same number of squares stationed with the same distribution of pieces, each with its designated moves. You'll say that there are hundreds of thousands of possible combinations of moves, that the devil lives in the details (sorry), but however true such an argument might be, it loses its force after the first couple of millennia. You want to know what eternal torment looks like? It's repetition, doing the same thing over and over and over and over."

Gary might want to talk to you about that.

The laugh. "My dear, Gary's suffering hasn't begun, not truly. Once I'm home . . . Anyway, the point I'm trying to make is, you have disrupted what has become an exceedingly familiar routine, and that is marvelous. Whether you'll survive what's happening to you, I have no idea, though it would be a shame if you didn't. Should you catch up to me, which you very well may, you won't be so fortunate, but just the same, I hope it happens. You deserve it, as a reward for your hard work.

"And I'll admit, the prospect of the pain it will cause you, to die at the hand of the one you've chased this far, for this long, your quest unfulfilled, makes me tingle. That's a new kind of agony, and I cannot wait for it."

I'm going to kill you, Lisa thought, and for the first time since accepting the butcher knife from Madame Sosostris felt absolutely certain that she would, felt as if Sefira's words had uncovered something jagged within her, swept the soil away to reveal rock jagged and unforgiving.

"That's the spirit."

Lisa's right hand whipped out in a back-fist that slammed against the passenger's seat with sufficient force to make it shudder. From behind her, Sefira said, "Very impressive." Lisa's vision dilated. She twisted to face Sefira, but the back seat was empty.

"I'm going to kill you," Lisa said. Her voice was loud, hoarse. "I am going to fucking kill you."

There was no answer. Sefira, it appeared, had vanished. In the passenger's seat, the notepad on which Lisa had been recording Gary's directions since running out of room on the envelope was open to a fresh page, which was covered in her handwriting. She held it up to view, read a fresh sequence of roads. Another ploy by Sefira? If she could do whatever she'd just done, then surely it wouldn't be too hard for her to leave a false trail. Yet the route led west, into Kansas, and swung northwest, into Colorado, which seemed approximately right. *Therefore, you and I are connected.* "I think we are," Lisa said.

Despite his protestations that he couldn't, she half-expected Gary to phone a second time, especially since he'd heard Sefira's voice. He did not. When she answered the phone the following night, Gary was already talking, asking her if she was all right, apologizing for not being able to call back, reminding her that he could only communicate with her once a day, repeating how sorry he was for this, for all of it, asking again if she was okay. She waited for the torrent of questions and justifications to slow before saying, "I'm okay."

"Thank God," Gary said. "She was actually in the car with you?"

"Kind of."

"What do you mean?"

"It was weird. I heard her voice and I saw her hand, hanging up on you. You heard her, too."

"I did, yes."

"But when I took a swing at her, she wasn't there."

"You—what did she want?"

"To mess with my head. To tell me how old she is, how thrilled she is to have me chasing her, because it's such a change from her normal routine, but she's still going to win. Oh, and there's more suffering in store for you."

"Jesus. You said you tried to hit her?"

"I did."

"And you're sure you're okay?"

Briefly, Lisa weighed describing the day she had endured, her eyes feeling as if someone had dumped sand in them. Instead, she opted for, "I'm fine. I'm just tired. Tell me where I'm going tomorrow."

At the end of the latest set of roads, Gary said, "You're all right? Really?"

"You do realize the plan is for me to confront Sefira."

"It's—if anything were to happen to you—"

"Then you'd be fucked in an entirely new way, wouldn't you?" Annoyance surged in her and, before he could reply, she hung up.

His next call, Gary was subdued, contrite. Her mouth still smoldering from the inferno that had swept it, Lisa kept her responses to his questions about her day, how she was holding up, if she'd had any more contact with Sefira, to a minimum. Finally, he said, "What is it? Why won't you say anything?"

"Because it hurts," she said. "It hurts to talk. My teeth are a mess, you asshole. Now give me the Goddamn directions, so I can stop talking." Which, chastened, he did. Afterward, he said, "I'm sorry about before. I didn't realize . . . your mouth—" The concern lowering his voice made her eyes unexpectedly moist. "It's fine," she said, and broke the connection. Blood dripped from her lips; she wiped it with the back of her hand.

Never one for heights, Lisa was less than thrilled with the following day's route, which took her from Denver to Estes Park, and from there up into and through the Rockies. No highway, the road she drove was two lanes. As the altitude increased, it was bordered on the left first by blue spruce and fir and heavily overgrown meadows, then by short, steep slopes studded with boulders, then by carved rock face. On the right, fir and pine alternated with an ever-higher drop off, the stone guard wall from which appeared neither tall nor sturdy enough to prevent her car from tumbling into open space. Across from the mountain on whose side she was driving, she wasn't sure how far away, another mountain reclined, its long slope side grooved by the enormous rock slide at its base, its pointed peak like the comb of an enormous beast, its size, its mass, barely diminished by its distance, the sky seeming to gather over it like a mantle.

Making matters worse, Lisa was stuck in a line of slow-moving traffic, everyone's progress delayed by the fawn-colored RV rolling along eight cars ahead. No doubt, the surrounding view was impressive, but when the RV followed the road left around a curve, it opened a vista which made the route appear to lead straight into empty sky. An optical illusion, yes, but one convincing enough to make her palms slick. A couple of hundred feet before the bend, the nominal shoulder belled around an improbable rest area, its parking lot jammed with the cars of those standing photographing the scenery. She considered pulling off at the spot, decided against it. It wasn't as if she could turn back; what couldn't be cured must be endured; sooner war, sooner peace; pick your empty aphorism. She did her best to keep her eyes on the car directly in front of her, not to watch the sky as it wheeled overhead, its blue so deep she could almost see the black pressing behind it. She drove as close as possible to the center line, which placed her unnervingly near the traffic coming the opposite way. An oversized pickup rushed by, its slipstream jostling her car, and she fought the urge to swerve to the right, toward the minimal guard wall and the emptiness beyond, because she was momentarily certain she would oversteer, not lift her foot from the gas in time, and crash straight through the stone barrier into the high air. Why wasn't the CD player on? However slight, its distraction would have helped to ease the dread whose fingers were constricting her throat. If only she were in one of those cars with audio controls set on the steering wheel's arms, she wouldn't have to remove her right hand from the wheel to bring Dolly's voice into the car, a task at the moment impossible, a labor Hercules would have declined. On the far side of the guard wall, dense forest filled the bowl of the valley dizzyingly far below.

Now she was riding on top of a ridge, short spruce like Christmas trees hemming her in, flooding her with relief. Had she ever imagined she would, or could, be made so happy by the sight of trees? But any sense of shelter the evergreens provided was short-lived, as they came to a halt at treeless slopes, a Kelly green terrain falling off on the left, to another valley, beyond which stout mountains crowded. She passed a pull-off, this time on the left, its parking spaces full. Beyond it, a pair of metal gates, long inverted triangles, stood open to either side of the road. *For the snow*, she thought, *to close the road if it's too dangerous.* Emerald fields unfolded around her. An elk grazed in the distance. The road slanted down through successive notches in the rock, past a stone hut whose function she could not identify. To her left, the terrain plummeted to a bowl brimming with dark green forest. To her right, the ground dropped away, as well, leaving her driving along the spine of a mountain, a flea running along the back of a horse. Ahead, the road swept up and over the side of the next peak. A couple of cars in front of her opted to stop at the latest parking area, but the tan RV maintained its position at the head of the line, and would continue to do so for the remainder of Lisa's time on this road. Surely, there had to be a quicker way for its driver and passengers to reach their destination. If they had opted for this route to enjoy the scenery, then shouldn't they have taken advantage of one of the many rest areas they'd passed? Its reasons its own, the great box trundled on, keeping everyone behind it at a steady, slow speed, drawing out what already would have been a long drive into an exercise in endurance. When at long last the road descended from the high mountains and Lisa's turn appeared on the right, she raced onto it so fast her tires screamed on the curve. The road slid through steep canyons, paced fast-moving streams, ran across dense fields overseen by single mountains. Under other, better circumstances, she might have admired some of it, or even all. Not now: now, she wanted to hear the engine growling, to feel the wheels humming on the pavement, the gearshift vibrating under her palm, the dread that had enveloped her burning off, trailing behind her like a plume of heavy black smoke.

When the phone rang that night, Lisa was soaking in a bath as hot as she could stand it in a room at the Holiday Inn in Laramie. The cell was propped on the lid of the toilet, within easy reach; she leaned out of the tub and answered it. There was a pause, then Gary said, "It's me. Are you all right?"

If she spoke slowly and carefully, she could talk. "I'm okay."

"Oh thank God," he said, the words breaking. "I thought—I don't know what I thought, but it wasn't good. How's your mouth? You said there was something wrong with it."

"There is." She slid back into the hot water.

"What is it? What's happening?"

"My teeth, they're . . . I'm changing. There's something going on with my eyes, too."

"Changing? What do you mean? How? What's happening?"

"I think I'm becoming more like Sefira." She laughed without humor. "Worst STD ever."

"I didn't—I mean, I didn't know—I never meant—"

"Just . . . don't."

"I never intended to hurt you. Which sounds—I realize how it sounds. But I love you, Lise. You have to believe, I would never do anything to harm you."

For once, the first words to rise to her lips were neither sarcastic nor bitter. "I wish I could believe that. Which sucks."

"It's true."

"The thing is, I keep asking myself, 'If he didn't love you, then what have the two of you been doing for the last eight and a half years?' All of it can't have been a lie, can it? I mean, you hardly married me for my money. But if I'm right and you loved me, how do I explain Sefira? It's not as if she swept in and seduced you. You sought her out. So what's the answer, Gary? How can both of those things be true?"

"Because what I have with you is real. Sefira was a mistake."

"That's a hell of a mistake."

"I'm not arguing with you. I fucked up, big time."

"Why? What was it about us—about me—that made you look for someone else? And I hate having to ask that. I resent having to doubt myself, to doubt what I thought we had."

"I don't know," Gary said. "Didn't you—I mean, weren't you ever curious about what was out there? I'm not talking about online dating, I'm talking about . . ."

"Porn."

"Yes. And no. Not the professional stuff. Although maybe some of it. Among other things. Are you sure you want to hear this?"

All at once, she did. "Yeah."

"I wanted to see what there was to see. It was online; I figured it would be safe. I was looking, not touching. Every now and again, I would decide this was enough, I needed to stop, and I'd clear my browser history, stay away from those parts of the web for a couple of weeks, a month. Inevitably, though, I went right back to where I'd been. This was how I found Sefira's page. Actually, it was another site that led me to her. I'd searched for 'forbidden desires.' The results took me to a page called blackguide.com. It seemed to be for people interested in the occult. The design was weird, tiny red print on a black background, with gifs of laughing skulls and hissing snakes. Amateur, but kind of sinister, too. There was a link at the bottom of the page: 'Fulfill Your Wildest Fantasies with Sefira.' I clicked on it, and a window opened. It showed a white screen with a cursor blinking in the middle. Had it not been for the cursor, I would have assumed the link was dead. I was about to close the window when I decided to type, 'Hello' and see what happened.

"Right away, there was an answer: 'Hello.' Not the most original response, but it was enough to prompt me to continue. I wrote, 'Who is this?'

"'Sefira. Who is this?'

"'Gary,' I typed.

"'Why are you here?'

"'I'm looking around,' I wrote, which was bullshit, because I'd already seen what there was to see of the site.

"'What do you want?' the page asked.

"'What are you offering?' I typed. I was starting to suspect I was talking to some kind of chat-bot. When the question repeated, the suspicion intensified. I was annoyed, more than I should have been. It wasn't the first time I'd encountered this type of set-up. I wrote, 'Hot talk,' which I was pretty sure would cue the bot to take me to the next page. But no, it asked me a third time, 'What do you want?'

"So I told it. I typed in every sexual fantasy I could think of, from I want to watch myself having sex in a mirror to I want to do it dressed like Batman and Batgirl. All the search terms I had ever entered came pouring out of my fingers. I kept thinking I'd reach the character limit, but it let me keep going. I wasn't expecting a reply. Mostly, I was being a dick.

"Except it worked. After I hit enter, there was a pause, long enough for me to congratulate myself on having overwhelmed the bot, and then it said, 'My, that's an awful lot. Where would you like to begin?' Immediately, I understood that there was a person on the other end of the connection. If I was being truthful with myself when I said that I was only at these sites to see what there was to see, then this was the moment for me to close the screen. I didn't. It wasn't long before my cock was out and I was jerking off to her responses. I want to tell you I was plagued by guilt afterward, and I was aware of having crossed to a very dangerous place, but what I mostly felt was this kind of exhilaration. It was like, I had finally done it, I had experienced what was out there."

"You do realize," Lisa said, "plenty of people masturbate to online chat. It may be tacky, but it isn't especially high on the list of transgressive activities."

"I understand that," Gary said. "I guess it says something about how buttoned down I was. Remember, when we first started having sex, I used to shower once we were done?"

"Yeah," Lisa said, "I used to tease you about it."

"'Did I make you *dirty*?' you'd say."

"And you'd say, 'Not dirty enough.' I never believed you. Looks like I should have."

Gary paused. "Honestly, I should have believed what I was saying. Or taken it seriously, admitted it to myself, talked to you about it. In retrospect, it seems absurd that I didn't. I was just so embarrassed— embarrassed and ashamed by my own desires."

"I can't understand that," Lisa said. "I mean, it was sex. There was nothing to be self-conscious about. And it was me. You think there was anything you couldn't have told me?"

"Yes," Gary said, "I did. It's like, there was an image you had of me—or, an image of me I thought you had, I wanted you to have, and I was terrified to jeopardize it."

"Well, you didn't have to be."

"I guess so. At this point, it's all a bit academic, isn't it?"

"Finish your story."

"There isn't a lot more to it, not really. I communicated with Sefira for a couple of weeks. During that time, I kept waiting for her to ask for a credit card number, which I swore to myself would be the red line, the sign to break off contact. She didn't. Instead, she told me she was going to be passing through Huguenot in a few days, and asked if I wanted to meet for coffee. I said yes. I wish I could say I hesitated, but I didn't. Oh, had anyone asked, I would have said that coffee didn't mean sex, but I would have been lying, to them and to me. I was more anxious that our meeting wouldn't lead anywhere. There were moments I seemed to see myself from a distance and I'd panic, thinking, *What are you doing? Stop this.* But I'd continue with whatever activity I was in the middle of, say, withdrawing money from the ATM in case we needed a motel room. (I didn't want to use a credit card, leave a paper trail, and the places I figured we'd go to weren't very expensive.) A couple of times, I felt sick to my stomach at what I was contemplating. *How do you think this is going to turn out?* I asked myself. It wasn't that I didn't care. It was more a case of, I'd set something in motion, and I couldn't stop it. I'd been standing at a ledge, I'd taken a step off, and now my balance was gone, and my other foot was about to follow.

"And before you say it, I understand I was rationalizing, treating as fact what was choice.

"Anyway, I met Sefira at Pete's. She was waiting for me. My first thought when I slid into the booth across from her was, *She's hideous.* I'm not talking about an abstract, moralistic judgment. I mean a physical response, repulsion. It was as if I saw through her protective camouflage to her, to what she was. There was a second I could have left, and I almost did. By this point, though, I was committed to staying for at least a cup of coffee. My reaction, I chalked up to nerves.

"The true revulsion came later, after we'd left Pete's for four hours at a room in the Park motel on 9W. Five minutes of conversation with Sefira had transformed repugnance into desire. As repelled by her as I had been, now I wanted her more than I'd wanted any other woman, ever." Gary hesitated. "I'm sorry—"

"I get it. You wanted to fuck her, and you did. A lot."

"Yes," Gary said. "While I was . . . with Sefira, I felt fantastic, liberated. The minute I dropped her off in Huguenot and headed home, however, I was filled with such regret, such remorse, I nearly drove straight into the nearest tree. It was as if I'd spent the afternoon drunk and sobered up in an instant. I wanted to throw up. All I kept thinking was, *What have you done?* I tried to tell myself it was no different than that lap dance at the Cusp, only a matter of degrees, not kind, but however much I wanted that to be the case, I knew it was bullshit. I didn't know what I was going to do. I considered telling you right away, confessing everything the moment you stepped through the door, but I chickened out. I was certain what I'd done was written all over my face. At dinner, though, when you asked me about Sefira, I had no problem lying, and you accepted my explanation without a question."

"That's because I trusted you."

"I know—I knew this, and I was sure I was done with Sefira. I had made a terrible mistake, but if I didn't repeat it, maybe things could still be okay."

"Except that you did repeat it."

"The next morning, I panicked. It occurred to me that, were I to blow off Sefira, she might find a way to contact you and reveal what I intended to keep secret. We had agreed to meet at Starbucks. I thought

I could talk to her, explain that yesterday had been fun, but I wasn't up for anything more. If I'm being honest, even in the midst of my alarm, there was a small part of me that wanted to see Sefira again, that was hoping I'd overcome my anxiety so we could spend another afternoon together."

"I'll avoid the obvious joke about your small part."

Surprisingly, Gary laughed. "Yeah, I walked into that one."

"Ran full tilt, more like." Absurdly, she smiled. "Keep going. You and your small part met Sefira at Starbucks."

"She was waiting there for me. The place was crowded, which I was aware of today in a way I hadn't been yesterday. I guess because now I was trying to extricate myself from the situation I'd been only too happy to rush into. Sefira was pleasant, but reserved, almost formal. Considering our recent activities, there was something off about her manner, strange. It was hard to believe she could be having second thoughts, too, and yet this was exactly the impression she gave. I wasn't sure how to proceed. As we drank our coffee, she told me she had the sense I hadn't enjoyed our time together. Which was—I couldn't say where that idea had come from. As I recalled it, I had been very . . . appreciative. No, Sefira said, she had failed. Usually, her lovers stayed with her until it was time for her to depart. I had left her; therefore, something had been lacking. Nothing was lacking, I said, everything was terrific. I was confused. When I had paid for the motel room (the place had hourly rates), I'd asked for two hours. Sefira had said, 'Only two?' and I'd doubled the time, which had appeared to please her. Nothing she said while we were at or on our way back from the motel had led me to believe she expected us to spend the night together.

"Our conversation took us from Starbucks to Pete's. Over lunch, I reassured her that she was terrific, the sex had been amazing, we'd done things I had only dreamed of. The more I described the previous day, the more my regret and panic subsided, and were replaced by lust. Long story short, I talked myself into a return visit to the Park motel."

"Which was exactly what she wanted. She picked up on your doubt and adapted to it. She played you."

"I figured that one out myself, thanks."

"After a second debauched afternoon."

"It may have taken me a little longer."

"Seriously?"

"I've never been especially good at this stuff."

Lisa sighed. "Moving along. You fuck her, you come home, where I'm guessing you're assailed by remorse, which you assuage by fucking me later that night." Saying it out loud did not make the chain of events feel any better.

"More or less."

"Then the morning you ran out for a cup of coffee, a couple of donuts, and some wake-up sex with Sefira."

"I left—it was before sunrise. When I slotted the key in the ignition, I had every intention of driving to Dunkin Donuts and straight home again. For most of the car ride, I thought that's where I was headed. It was like, I was seeing the route I was taking, but it wasn't registering, you know? I was just distracted enough to steer out of town and north on 32. I made the right onto Wycombe—basically, only when I was turning into that house's driveway did I realize I was nowhere near where I wanted to be. I had the idea I should reverse out of here and head back into town. Instead, I put the car in park, leaned over, and opened the passenger door. Sefira emerged from the house and slid into the car. I drove her to town, we walked for a bit, I drove her back to the house, and . . . I want to say you can imagine the rest, which to a certain extent is true, but I'm not sure I can convey the way everything felt. All of it took place while I was in the same disconnected state. Somewhere in the back of my brain, there was a voice screaming that this was wrong. The same voice noticed a change in Sefira. The first day, she had been charming, the second, vulnerable. Today, she was aggressive, predatory. Looking at the curl of her lip, feeling her nails digging into my elbow as she chaperoned me around Huguenot, listening to the razor edge in her voice, I had no doubt something bad was on its way.

"I was right. But you know that. I swear, all this—it feels as if I stumbled into an especially heavy-handed cautionary tale, the kind of thing you'd find in a church pamphlet, the Perils of Internet Porn or something.

"The point, though, is that the reason Sefira put me through what she did on the third day was because I kept returning to you. You know what she is. She isn't used to anyone doing anything other than surrendering to her. According to Madame Sosostris, her keeping me subject to her will cost Sefira a lot in terms of energy. But since I'd wounded her pride by resisting her, it was worth it."

"You resisted, all right."

"Come on," Gary said. "You know what I mean."

There was an angry retort waiting for him, and one for his next reply, and another for whatever he said after that. There was a sea of fury heaving within her, like the magma ready to shatter the top of a volcano. There were words, sentences, to scar and shrivel and crisp him, and there was something else, as well, a sense that she could reach out through the same connection allowing their conversation and hurt Gary, punish him, turn her recriminations to fire and agony. She was aware of something shifting within her, down in her bones, which felt as if they were cracking, opening like the petals of a bizarre flower. She remembered yesterday, the sulfurous cloud she'd drawn within her. Now it was venting from her marrow, bubbling in her blood, pushing out of her pores. Her head swam. It was as if the cloud were solid, her body smoke. Her rage swelled, rose in a towering plume—

"Lisa?"

—and collapsed like a failed soufflé. It wasn't that she couldn't stay mad at Gary. The anger roiling within her would have a half-life of years, decades, maybe a lifetime. Nor was it that he was right. She couldn't accept his limping home after his motel romps with Sefira as a sign of his undying love for her. All the same, knowing what she did about Sefira, it was difficult for Lisa to dismiss Gary's interpretation of events entirely. Wasn't her anger an indication that her feelings toward him were not as simple as she wanted them to be? What was the saying? The opposite of love isn't hate, it's indifference. She certainly was not indifferent. Jesus: how fucked-up could things become between two people and you could still say they were in love?

Gary might not be right, but he wasn't wrong, either, not exactly, and the gap between the two was sufficient to cause the wrath boiling in her veins to subside to a simmer, retreat to its home in her marrow. Lisa swallowed and said, "Just tell me where I'm going."

On other occasions, Gary would have attempted to continue the conversation, forcing a prickly exchange into an outright argument, which might have led who could say where? This time, he said, "All right. You have a pen?" She did, with her notebook next to her phone. Gary reeled off the directions that would take her across Wyoming and into Montana. Once he was finished, he said, "Tomorrow."

"Tomorrow," Lisa said.

"Drive safely."

"I will." She had the sense he was building up to a declaration of love. Before he could, she leaned out of the tub and ended the call.

The bath had cooled. She stood, reaching for a towel. *Tomorrow.* A mix of eagerness and dread met the thought. She winced as the towel dragged over her knuckles, still raw and sore. Whatever the outcome, it would be a relief finally to face Sefira, and not another of her minions.

VI

Lisa had never been what anyone would have described as a fast driver, let alone, a reckless one. Janice, who had taught her to drive, had complained about her younger sister's timidity from their first lesson in the parking lot of the Newburgh Mall. "For God's sake," she'd said, "don't drive like you're afraid of it." In the intervening years, anytime Janice was in the car with her, she never missed the opportunity to confirm her initial assessment. "Jesus!" she'd half-shout, "It's the long skinny one to the right, Lise." Or, "I was hoping we'd get there sometime this week." Or, whenever Janice was especially frustrated with her, she'd quote George Carlin: "Christ almighty! You drive like old people fuck, you know that? Slow and sloppy." It hadn't taken Lisa long to learn that appeals to safety, the posted speed limit, or insurance rates counted for nothing with Janice. Nor was refusing to respond much use: her sister would continue her tirade until well after they had reached their destination. About the only reply she'd found effective was telling Janice to fuck off, which usually bought Lisa enough angry silence to guarantee a quiet remainder of the trip.

Now, though, Janice would have beamed with pride—assuming she recognized the woman behind the wheel of the Accord as her little sister. Lisa backed out of the driveway so fast the tires spat gravel at the garage door. She stomped the brakes, whipping her head against the headrest, jerked the gearshift into first, and literally put the pedal all the way to the metal. Engine roaring, the Honda leapt down her short street. At the intersection with Old Soldier's, she was already in fourth, spinning the wheel to the right, the stop sign little more than a red distraction. The rear end of the car wobbled as it made the turn. Lisa downshifted to third to bring it under a semblance of control, then up through fourth into fifth as she rushed past the stop signs marking the intersections of a half dozen other streets with this, the principal by-pass around Main Street and its assorted businesses. A pair of head-lights flashed by on her right. In the ten seconds it took her to reach the t-junction with 32, the speedometer's needle arced smoothly up to fifty and was closing on sixty. Almost at the larger road, she stood on the brake, put in the clutch, and pulled the steering wheel hard to the right. Tires shrieking, the Accord slid sideways onto 32. For an instant, an SUV reared in her windshield, horn blaring like a panicked beast. Lisa dropped the car into third, hit the gas, and swung to the right. The SUV banked to its right, into the parking lot of the cell phone store, fortunately empty at this late hour. She shifted up and sped north.

She was not thinking. She wasn't even thinking, *I'm not thinking*. She was not hearing Sefira's syrupy voice saying, "All day, and alllllllll night." She was not picturing Gary, naked, his cock half-raised and streaked with blood, his hands on the hips of a lithe naked woman, turning her around, bending her over. She was not smelling the rich funk of sex, the thick mix of sweat and semen. She was feeling the steering wheel thrumming against her palms. She was listening to the engine whine. She was watching the space the headlights cleared in front of her, trees, mailboxes, the ends of driveways flickering in and out of view at its margins.

Wycombe was two miles outside of town, on the right. She reached it in just over a minute. The reek of burning rubber filled the car as she braked hard and made the turn. The road rose alternating between slope and flat. She took them all at the same speed, the Honda lifting on its suspension as she crested each rise. A side street opened on the left. Two houses past it, the number 1430 glowed on a battered mailbox. She stomped clutch and brake, spinning the wheel left. There was an interval of time, some portion of a second, a half- or quarter-, during which the driver's side wheels raised from and threatened to leave altogether the unpaved driveway, to begin a sequence of events that would end with the Accord on its roof in the house's front yard. Then it passed, the car settled, and she was bringing it to a halt, yanking the parking brake, almost snapping the key off as she pulled it from the ignition. A glance at the house showed the silhouette of a split-level. From what she could see, it was unlit, so she left the car's headlights on. She flung open the door and was two running steps before she realized she'd left her handbag on the front passenger seat— her handbag in whose interior pocket was zipped the can of pepper spray she intended to empty into Sefira's face, and possibly Gary's, too. She doubled back to the car.

So much for the element of surprise. She ran up the front walk, left hand holding the handbag's strap against her chest, right hand inside the bag, tugging at the zipper to the pocket. Although—she hadn't seen Gary's Subaru or any other car in the driveway, or parked in the road. Her pace slowed. Her fingers had found the pepper spray, but she left it where it was. *Great. Wild goose chase, anyone?* What were the odds Sefira was speeding along the Thruway, on her merry way to another waiting husband?

Which begged the question, where was Gary? With Sefira? She had claimed she was done with him. Was she lying? If so, why? There hadn't been time for her to change her mind, had there? Or for Gary to convince Sefira to take him with her? Maybe he'd chased after her, or driven off in another direction.

You're here. You might as well check out the place. She was at the front door. She tried the doorknob. The door swung in with a creak straight out of the soundtrack of a classic horror film. She leaned forward, saw a bare landing. One short flight of stairs descended to the basement, another ascended to a large open space with a vaulted ceiling, the living room, from what she could see empty of furniture. Should she call out, announce herself? Was there any need to? Her arrival had probably woken half the neighborhood. It wouldn't be a surprise if someone called the cops. *Time's a-wasting.* She stepped onto the landing, pushing the door shut behind her. To the right, there was a light switch, but flipping it produced no result. She had left her cell, with its flashlight app, in the car; she would have to explore the house with the light admitted by the curtainless windows. Wincing as they sounded her passage, she climbed the stairs and walked to the center of the living room. A pair of dark rectangles on the wall opposite the front picture window marked the spots where photos or paintings had hung; otherwise, there was no sign the living room had been in use anytime in the recent past. The same was true of the dining room beyond it, and the kitchen past that, and the trio of bedrooms and bathroom off the short hallway on the house's other side. As she went, she worried less about the noise of her sneakers on the floor, opened each closed door with less hesitation, became less concerned about Sefira leaping out at her, a knife or other weapon in hand. In the months after their marriage, she and Gary had looked at a couple of places like this, before deciding to remain in their condo and save for a house more in line with what they wanted, some kind of farmhouse with a barn and a couple of acres. Had she seen a For Sale sign at the edge of the lawn? Not that she could remember; though she hadn't been on the lookout for one. Well and truly irritated, she returned to the front landing. Now that her eyes had adjusted to the gloom, she could see that the air appeared brighter by the slightest of degrees at the foot of the basement stairs. She pictured a single candle left burning beside a mocking note. The temptation to leave, to stride out of this place, get in car, and head home, where she would put on a pot of coffee and start researching divorce lawyers, was strong enough to put her hand on the front doorknob.

The next moment, she was descending the stairs, shaking her head at her compulsiveness. To the left, a pair of closed doors. Directly ahead and to the right, the basement was a large open space; a family room, she supposed. At the other end of the room, Gary lay with his back to her, in front of a pair of sliding glass doors. A trio of candles burned most of the way to wax puddles surrounded him. Except for his boxers, he was naked. At the sight of him, something inside Lisa twisted, and she had to fight to keep herself from running across the room and kicking him, all the while shouting, "You fucker! How could you?" Instead, she took a deep breath and started slowly toward him, as if she were in a museum, taking her time to admire the paintings crowding its walls. *Dignity*, she thought, *even in a situation like this, you can have dignity.* All the same, she slid her hand inside her bag, fingers searching for and finding the cylinder of pepper spray. *Dignity does not preclude revenge.*

Maybe halfway to Gary, who had not moved at the squeak of her soles on the linoleum, she noticed a faint, metallic odor that reminded her of raw steak. *Blood?* The nearer she drew to Gary's (still unmoving) form, the sharper the smell grew. *Blood.* Although her eyes saw only the candlelight flickering on Gary's bare flesh, throwing shadows across the floor, the walls, her nose told her the air was as full of blood as a slaughterhouse. It was as if each step were covering more ground than it appeared, plunging her deeper into the smell of gallons of blood, buckets of the stuff splashed everywhere around her, on the floor, the walls, up against the sliding glass doors, over Gary's prone form. Her pulse pounded at the base of her throat. Had Gary blundered into an encounter with a serial killer? The copper odor coated the insides of her nostrils, sat red on her tongue. Yet there was no blood visible, as if the wavering glow of the candles was obscuring it. Though she was practically standing over him, Gary remained motionless. Lisa extended her right foot and pushed the nearest candle out of her way.

With a groan, Gary sat up and turned to her, exposing the gaping ruin of his chest.

Lisa screamed, leaping back from him. "What the FUCK?" she shouted. "What the FUCK?" Her eyes bulged, her hands clutched her hair, the pose of a comedienne in a fifties sitcom.

Gary attempted to stand, couldn't. The center of his torso was split apart—not cleanly, but as if an animal, a bear perhaps, had cracked his breastbone and ribs and pried them apart haphazardly while it rooted for the delicacies underneath. Ribs whole and broken arced away from the ragged and bloody cavern from which his heart and other organs (his liver? Intestines?) had been excavated. (*That's a lung,* she thought, *I am looking at a fucking lung.*) Half-dried blood smeared the skin around his open mouth, under his nose; blood saturated his boxers. His eyes were rolled under his lids, which fluttered over the whites as if attempting to sweep some debris, a piece of dirt or an eyelash, from them. Ribs scraping and clicking against one another, he stretched his left hand toward Lisa, who retreated a half-dozen steps that would have been the start of her flight out of the house had Gary not immediately collapsed onto his back and lay there motionless.

Once, during her karate class, an opponent in what was supposed to have been a friendly sparring match had thrown a sidekick which struck her solar plexus dead on, dropping Lisa to the mat. Her lungs felt as if they had seized, and no matter what she did, she could not make them work again. A switch had been flipped off, one she did not know how to turn on again. Of course she panicked, but the emotion seemed to be happening at a remove, on the other side of the blow continuing to send shock waves through her. Eventually, the instructor had realized what had happened and rushed to her side, but in the ten seconds it took him to do so, she was reduced to a series of blown neurons, unable to transmit information and action back and forth. This was how she felt now, her vision full of the catastrophe of jagged bone and ravaged flesh that was Gary. Lips trembling, she forced her breath into a single word: "Gary?"

He did not answer. Was he dead? How could he be anything but? Yet he had sat up, had responded to her presence. If he was dead, how was that possible? Lisa had heard stories of corpses several hours or days old moving, the accumulated pressure of the gasses built up within their forms causing motions ranging from the minor to the dramatic. But the violence visited upon Gary was fresh; nor could she see any means for anything to remain trapped in him. A last impulse held onto until she appeared? That wasn't possible. His injuries were too much, devastating. Then what . . .?

As if a river of electricity were passing through him, Gary's spine arched, throwing his head back, lifting his hips and thighs. A chorus of cracks sounded from his chest. His arms hung limp to either side; his heels quivered and thudded on the floor. Lisa screamed, jammed her hand into her bag for the pepper spray. *Jesus! What now?* From his open mouth, Gary's voice emerged, high and faint, as if crossing a wide gulf. At first, Lisa couldn't pick out individual words in the babble pouring from him. Whatever he was saying might have been a recording played too fast. Then it found its proper speed, catching him mid-sentence: "dark, so very very dark, dark sky no stars, dark smoke, smoke from the fire, fires, all the fire, fire rivers, fire lakes, fire mountains, keep away from the fire, keep away from *them*, so hard, ground sharp, can't run, run from *them*, from the hives, run, can't run, run, can't, you must, you must run, don't let *them* catch you, take you into the hives, don't, run, run—" Whatever current was surging through him ceased, and he smashed against the floor.

This time, though, his face retained its animation. His head lolled in Lisa's direction. His eyes rolled from under the lids, found and focused on her. His tongue pushed between his lips, dragged over them. In a voice not all the way back from wherever it had been, but closer, much closer, a room or two away, he said, "Lisa?"

"Gary? Are you . . .?" She couldn't think of a way to complete the question. Are you okay? was ridiculous; are you alive? was nearer the mark but absurd to imagine asking.

"I'm fucked," Gary said, which Lisa supposed was as accurate a description of his situation as any. "I can't—how long have I been here?"

"I don't know," Lisa said. "Most of the day, maybe."

"A day?"

"Not even."

Tears mixed with blood streamed from his eyes. His mouth contracted in horror. "Not even? I was there for—it was months, at least. Maybe a year. When they took you into the hives, it was hard to keep track of time. Harder. But it was longer than a day, it had to be. Please tell me you're lying to me."

"I'm not," Lisa said, unable to believe that she was carrying on a conversation, however fragmented, with a man whose chest was a gory cavity.

"Oh God," Gary said, weeping, "oh God oh God oh God. I can't go back there. I can't."

"Where? Where were you?"

"Hell," Gary said. "I was in Hell." He sniffed. "Or . . . I don't know. Please, you have to help me. I know, I know I've done something terrible. I know I betrayed you. I'm sorry. I'm so . . . so sorry. But please help me. Please. Don't leave me here. Don't."

"I don't know what you're asking. What is it you want me to do? How am I supposed to help you?"

"While I was there," Gary swallowed. "While I was in Hell, I heard things. Secrets, rumors. There are people, people who know about where we were."

"What? Priests, ministers?"

"No," Gary said. "No. Other people."

"All right. One of them could help you?"

"Maybe. It's the only thing I can think of."

"Okay. Where's the nearest person? Can you tell me that?"

"In town," Gary said. "Madame Sosostris. It's what she calls herself. She tells fortunes. On Main Street. In the big purple house beside the plaza. The one with the deli and pharmacy."

"That place?" Lisa knew the location, a rambling, two-story farmhouse set back from the road between a pair of enormous poplars. The siding was purple, the trim violet. A flagstone walk led from the sidewalk to the front porch. The path was lined with slender metal rods, each of which was capped by a pinwheel in the shape of a different bird. When the wind blew, their wings spun. From the porch ceiling, blown glass globes hung on silver wires. A hand-painted sign on the front lawn advertised psychic readings from someone whose name Lisa had always been driving too fast to discern; Madame Sosostris, apparently. The house had seemed to her intended for the weekend tourist crowd, up from the City to indulge their appetites for the bucolic, as well as those locals for whom the New Age was a thing. Asked to pick the residence of someone with the kind of knowledge to which Gary was referring, she would have put the purple house near or at the bottom of her list, too blatantly obvious a choice to be believed.

Apparently, though, the obvious answer was the right one. Gary said, "Yes. Maybe."

"What if you're wrong?"

"I don't know. Please, Lise. I know. I fucked up. But this—" He nodded toward his opened chest, wincing.

It took her less time to reply than she would have predicted. "Yes," she said. "I'll take you to this Madame Sosostris."

"Oh thank you," Gary said, fresh bloody tears spilling over nose and cheeks. "Thank you thank you thank you. You have no idea what this means."

"We need to get you out of here."

"If you can move the other candles—it doesn't have to be much—you'll break the rest of the containment. I should be able to stand up and walk out of this place."

"Are you sure? You aren't going to . . ."

"I'll be fine. What Sefira did to me holds me together. Or so I heard."

"Let's hope you heard correctly."

With the side of her sneaker, Lisa shoved each of the remaining candles from its position. Gary shuddered, uttered a low moan. He appeared in control of his body, again. His voice had moved, not all the way back to his throat, but within the same room, somewhere close, an arm's length away. He turned on his left side, propped himself on his left elbow, attempted to push to his feet with that arm, which appeared to be stronger. He couldn't manage it. He looked to Lisa, who hesitated before holding out her hand for him. Though his grip was strong, his flesh was cold, dead.

VII

The first man came for her in the parking lot of a sprawling truck stop on the south side of Pittsburgh. She parked at one end of the enormous rectangle, next to a line of eighteen wheelers whose engines rumbled as if they were snoring. Tempted as she was to recline her seat and surrender to the fatigue pulling at her, dull hunger prompted Lisa to open the door and step into the night. Diesel fumes fogged the air. In the distance, the steady flow of traffic on the highway made a hollow, ghostly sound. For a moment, she leaned against the Honda and closed her eyes. She had been driving so long that, standing still, she continued to feel herself hurtling forward.

"Ma'am, are you all right? Ma'am?"

She glanced up and saw a big man standing in front of her, an expression of concern on his wide face. A foot taller than Lisa and at minimum a hundred pounds heavier, he was wearing a red plaid shirt, its buttons strained against the belly overlapping his jeans. A white captain's hat rode the waves of his curly blond hair.

"I'm fine, thanks," she said. "Just been on the road a while."

"I know how that feels," the man said. "Say, your name wouldn't happen to be Lisa, would it? Lisa . . . Murray?"

"Yes," Lisa said. "How—"

But the man's hands were already around her throat, so fast she was grabbing his wrists before she understood what was happening. His strength was terrifying. Immediately, she released his wrists and felt for the thumb of his right hand. His face had not lost its worried look. She pushed her fingers against his thumb, but his grip would not allow her to work under it. She needed a new plan, and quickly: blackness crowded the edges of her vision. The man's arms were too long for her to jab at his eyes. She let go of his hand and dropped to the ground, dead weight. Surprised, the man stepped forward, tilting over in an effort to maintain his hold on her. He could not. His fingers loosened, and Lisa swung her forearms up into his wrists, breaking the choke. The sensation of relief was instant, but there was no time to savor it: the man was reaching for her hair. She flattened against the pavement and kicked her right foot. With an audible crunch, her heel connected with the inside of her attacker's left knee, bowing his leg outward. He gave a high-pitched yelp and lost his balance, raising his arms too late to prevent his forehead from thumping off the side of the Accord. Lisa scrambled from the ground as he collapsed, stunned, the captain's hat rolling from his head under the car.

There was no way the man was returning to his feet, not after what she'd done to his knee, but she backed away from him all the same. Incredibly, her handbag had remained on her shoulder. She dug inside it, searching for the pepper spray. Her assailant did not stir from where he had fallen. In the deep shadows cast by the tall halogen lights stationed around the parking lot, she could not see whether or not the man's chest was moving. *So what?* she thought, rubbing her throat. *The guy tried to kill me.* If he wasn't breathing, too bad for him.

Except, he had said her name. This wasn't some random attack; it was a trap, one Sefira had laid for her. How she had known Lisa was going to pull off at this particular truck stop, she had no idea; though it was hardly the most remarkable event of the last couple of days. Her fingers had found the pepper spray. She withdrew it from her bag and, aiming the nozzle at her attacker's face, slid her feet closer to his prone bulk, ready for him to lunge at her. He remained motionless. She squinted, unable to decide whether his chest was rising and falling. A vision of him split the way Gary was, the buttons of his shirt concealing a bloody hollow, swam before her. She shook her head and prodded his left arm with the toe of her sneaker. No response. She pressed harder, saying, "Hey. Hey, you."

The man groaned, a sound of deep hurt. Relieved, Lisa retreated a couple of paces, depositing the pepper spray in her bag. For a moment, she considered running to the truck stop, summoning aid. A tractor trailer rolled past the front of her car. *And you're going to say what, exactly? This guy slipped and hit his head on your car? What about his knee?* Suppose the man regained consciousness, accused her of breaking his leg? Of course she would counter that she had acted in self-defense to an unprovoked attack, but there would be no way for the police not to be involved. She would have to provide a statement here, then likely at wherever the police station was. She would have to explain why she was so far from the home address she provided them. Even if the cops were as sympathetic and helpful as was possible, their attention would add hours to a timetable already precarious. She sighed.

Her phone was in the front pocket of her jeans. She retrieved it and searched for the local area code. When the 911 operator answered, she said, "You have to help—there's a man lying on the ground and he isn't moving—I think he might've had a heart attack—you have to send someone—he isn't moving," all in a breathless rush. As the woman on the other end of the line told her to calm down, asked her where she was, Lisa said, "In the parking lot of the truck stop off I-80, the big one, in one of the spaces between the trucks—please, he isn't moving—what if they don't see him, and he gets run over?" She broke the connection while the operator was asking, "You said a truck stop?"

She guesstimated she had at most a minute until a police cruiser put in an appearance, sweeping its searchlight over the rows of idling eighteen wheelers. Caution still the order of the moment, Lisa circled to the Accord's passenger door and let herself into the car on that side. She climbed into the driver's seat, started the engine, and lowered her window. Leaning her head out of the car to check her distance, she eased past her attacker. She heard a crack as a tire broke the plastic rim of his captain's hat. Once she was clear of him, she sped out of the truck stop. Accelerating onto the interstate, she checked the rearview mirror and saw a Pennsylvania State Trooper's gray SUV slowing down the off ramp into the parking area.

Although she intended to put an hour (minimum) between herself and the site of her attack, Lisa took the next exit because her hands started to shake with such intensity she could barely control the steering wheel. The honey-roasted peanuts which had served as a late afternoon snack hours earlier burned in her gut; the road in front of her wobbled. At the stop sign at the foot of the ramp, she turned left on to a road lined by vacant lots, its pavement punctuated by clumps of grass. A quarter mile along it, a small, single-story building, its windows boarded, stood in the midst of one of the lots. After making certain there was no one behind her, Lisa steered off the road and drove to the other side of what looked as if it had been a fast food restaurant, a regional answer to McDonald's or Burger King. She pulled in close to the place, parked, and slumped against her seat. The nausea had not yet subsided, and her arms and legs seemed rubbery. *Adrenaline crash*, she thought. She closed her eyes and concentrated on keeping the contents of her stomach in place. She soon fell into the sleep she had been resisting at the truck stop.

The following day was spent checking her eyes to monitor the blackness spreading over her irises, worrying about the pain that had started in her teeth, and navigating the twisting West Virginia roads onto which Gary's directions had set her. It wasn't that she didn't want to think about what had happened in the shadows between the tractor trailers; it was that the previous night's assault, her response to it, seemed unreal, dreamlike. Adding to the sense of unreality, the skin of her neck was unbruised, despite the terrible pressure the man's fingers had exerted on her throat. She sped through dense stretches of aspen, ash, and oak broken by occasional clearings in which stood a variety of houses: great log cabins whose sides were freshly stained; small saltbox cottages whose roofs were furred with moss; split levels whose yards were full of sandboxes, swing sets, and toys. A small girl wearing a pink tutu and green camouflage pants waved to her from the front stoop of a red brick house. Every now and again, a detail from the struggle in the parking lot barged to the front of her mind, the creamy smell of the soap with which her attacker had washed the hands he was using to strangle her, the shudder that had traveled her leg when her foot struck his knee, the momentary thrill that had swept her when he had fallen to the pavement. In the interest of fitness, she had been taking karate two or three times a week for the last three and a half years, and while the class was focused more on exercise than self-defense, every so often, the instructor would spend part or even all the fifty-minute session discussing and demonstrating what to do in the event someone laid hands on you. Lisa had followed the lessons with the rest of the students, but without any expectation of ever using the techniques they were learning. Although she knew the statistics when it came to violence against women, she felt self-conscious practicing to escape a choke, break an assailant's knee. The clients she worked with were generally in no condition to hurt anyone, and she hadn't been worried about Gary; indeed, he was the one who had purchased the pepper spray for her, filling out the paperwork necessary to do so in New York at the Gander Mountain in Wiltwyck. (Was that irony, or something else?) Yet when she had needed it, the knowledge was there for her. She hadn't expected the man in the captain's hat to grab her, but wasn't that the point? It was hardly a surprise to learn that Sefira's powers extended to the ability to bend a man to her will, but it was significant that she had placed him at the truck stop to ambush her. When she asked Madame Sosostris whether Sefira would know she was being pursued, the woman shrugged and said, "It's difficult to say for sure. I would operate under the assumption she will." *Guess we've settled that question.* Would Sefira know her pawn had failed? *Best to assume yes.* Best, too, to be prepared for another threat.

It came sooner than she would have predicted, the same evening, outside a gas station bathroom into which she'd gone for a round of vigorous brushing of her aching teeth. This man was smaller than the other, smaller than Lisa, dressed in khaki overalls and a white t-shirt. He was standing near the door, shuffling his feet in what she judged a grown-up version of a child's pee-pee dance. The bathroom was one-toilet-fits-all, so she didn't register anything unusual about his presence until he looked at her from under his heavy brows and said, "Mrs. Murray? Mrs. Lisa Murray?" Amazing the power of social conventions: while one part of her was noticing the man's right hand in his pocket, another, automated part of her was answering, "Yes?" Had the knife the man started to withdraw not snagged on the material of his overalls, she would have been in serious trouble. As it was, she leapt back into the bathroom, slammed the door shut, and shot the bolt. She had turned out the light over the sink on her way out; she left it off.

Shouting, "Mrs. Murray! Mrs. Lisa Murray!" the man hammered the door, rattling it in its frame. Lisa dug through her handbag, the darkness rendering its contents strange under her fingertips. The man's blows resounded in the bathroom's small space. Could he break down the door? It seemed sturdy enough, though its hinges screeched ominously with each of the man's strikes. If nothing else, he was going to attract additional attention any second now. The pepper spray was in her grip. Heart thudding, she positioned herself to one side of the entrance and reached over to unbolt the door. At the click of the lock releasing, the man ceased his pounding. "Mrs. Murray? Mrs. Lisa Murray?" He turned the doorknob and pushed the door open, admitting a bronze column of late day sunlight into the room. Standing flat against the wall, her right hand holding the metal cylinder at head level, she waited as the man called, "Mrs. Murray? Mrs. Lisa Murray?" She was hoping for him to lean his head over the threshold. Even better, he advanced two cautious steps into the bathroom, his clasp knife out before him like a flashlight. She allowed him one more step, then said, "Hey. Over here." He turned his head toward the sound of her voice, and she discharged the pepper spray into his face in a hissing jet. He jerked back, twisting away from the spray, but enough of the stuff spattered his eyes and nose for him to drop the knife and jam the heels of his palms against his face, bellowing as his eyes ignited with pain. Even standing on the opposite side of the pepper spray, Lisa felt her eyes flood with tears. There was no point attempting to inflict further injury on the man: the searing in his eyes would keep him out of commission long enough for her to escape. She slipped out of the bathroom, shutting the door behind her, and walked to her car at what she hoped was a normal pace. Once she was behind the wheel, she removed her sunglasses to dry her eyes; though they continued to tear for a little while thereafter.

This time, the shaking did not begin until she was over the Kentucky border and saw a yellow Motel 6 sign rising high in the distance, washed gold by the last of the sunset. She parked in front of the main office and sat there with her head against the headrest. *A knife*, she thought, *the guy had a fucking knife*. She saw it in his hand, a short, shining blade curved at the tip like a miniature scimitar. *A knife*. Yes, the first man had employed his hands to frightening effect, but a knife was something else, a dramatic escalation in threat. *What's next, a fucking gun?* And what was she going to do if someone aimed a pistol at her? She had used up the pepper spray, and to buy a new one, she would have to locate a store that sold guns (she assumed: that was how it worked in New York—maybe things were different in Kentucky?), which would consume more of the time of which she had so little. No matter that a firearms dealer appeared at the side of the road. She suspected she would have paperwork to complete, which no doubt would require ID to verify, and how was she planning to explain her New York State driver's license to the salesperson standing behind the display case? Driving this internal debate was the threat for whom the new pepper spray would be necessary, the as-yet blank silhouette of her inevitable next assailant. If Sefira's hope was to hurt or kill her, she was failing. If, however, her intent was to intimidate Lisa, make her doubt the path she had set out on, then mission accomplished.

Gee, Lise, way to overthink things. It was one of Gary's go-to expressions whenever she expressed anxiety about her job, the state of their savings, whether or not they should have kids. As often as not, she found his laid-back attitude frustrating and more than a little patronizing. All the same, she recognized in it a certain useful balance to the excesses of her own frantic tendencies. This was no less the case now, but the irritation it stirred in her was considerably sharper than usual.

Silly to sleep in the parking lot of a motel. Her legs were strong enough to carry her out of the car and through the office's glass doors. The front desk clerk, an older African-American woman whose hair was in braids, asked Lisa if she was all right. She had been watching her sitting in her car, she said, and had been getting ready to come see if she needed any help.

In the neutral tone of the woman's voice, Lisa heard more skepticism than concern. Was she, the clerk was asking, on drugs, or drunk? "I'm so sorry," Lisa said. "I'm diabetic, and I'm afraid I let my blood sugar drop a little too low." Her explanation appeared to satisfy the woman, who said there was a vending machine outside where she could buy a candy bar if she needed one. Lisa thanked her, and finished filling out the registration form the woman had slid across the counter.

In her room, Lisa switched on the TV and ran through its complement of channels. Nothing caught her interest long enough to still her thumb on the remote. Nor, despite the softness of its mattress, could she settle on the queen-sized bed. She contemplated calling her parents. She hadn't spoken with her mother for the better part of a

week, which was about the limit before one of them (Lisa) was supposed to pick up the phone. Her parents' thirty-fifth anniversary was
approaching in a few months, in December, and she was supposed to
be consulting with her mother about guests for the celebration Mom
insisted was unnecessary. (Janice was no help with this. "If she says she
doesn't want a party," she said, "then I'm going to take her at her
word." Which might be rational, but which willfully ignored everything
they knew about their mother.) The prospect of speaking with her,
though, was exhausting, as there was no way she could tell her what
was happening. Should she offer the merest hint of any trouble between her and Gary, Mom would spend the remainder of their conversation attempting to extract the details from her, which of course she
couldn't provide, so Lisa would have to invent another narrative, the
details of which would be simple enough for her to remember when
next she and her mother spoke, and the time after that, and so on, in-
definitely, and the idea of having to do now what she had done so often as a teenager was overwhelming and depressing. Better to wait until this mess was over, and accept her mother's reproaches for her
thoughtlessness.

That was assuming, of course, her quest succeeded. Should she
fail, she would not be speaking to anyone. Her most recent conversation with her mom, which had consisted principally of her mother re-
laying the story of the Alaskan cruise she and Lisa's father had taken in
anticipation of their anniversary, with a few remarks about prospective
guests for the party Lisa wasn't putting together, would be their last. At
the beginning of the call, her father had answered the phone and they
had exchanged their usual few sentences; those would be their final
words to one another. Sorrow unexpected and acute dried her mouth,
tightened her chest. They would have no idea what had happened to
her; all they would know was that their younger daughter had disappeared under mysterious circumstances. The same thing would be true
of Janice, with whom she'd last spoken a few weeks ago, a brief, frustrating exchange during which Janice had once again refused to help
plan their parents' anniversary party. Those terse exchanges would
have no sequel.

When Gary called, in addition to not answering his questions
about the changes affecting her eyes, Lisa did not mention either of

the men who had attacked her. In large part, this was due to her annoyance with him, sharpened by the realization about the possibility of not speaking to her family again, which manifested in a desire to punish Gary by withholding from him information he was not aware of. She refused to allow him the pleasure of worrying about her (any more than he already might be). As far as reasoning went, it was far from her proudest moment, but it was satisfying in a passive-aggressive way. Beyond that, she remained uncertain how much she could or should trust the man whose engagement and wedding rings she had yet to remove, despite having promised herself to do countless times. After what Sefira had done to him, the savagery she had visited upon him, it was difficult to believe Gary was in league with her. Yet consider the men Sefira had set on Lisa: clearly, she possessed the ability to control them. Who could say she wasn't exerting such power over Gary, Madame Sosostris's assurances to the contrary? If he was under Sefira's sway, possibly communicating with her through occult channels, then the less Lisa told him, the better. All of which exacerbated her annoyance.

The next morning, Lisa wiped her fingerprints from the empty pepper spray canister and deposited it in one of the green dumpsters behind the motel. She had no idea whether either man she had bested, or both, would have reported her to the police, but if the cops were on the lookout for her, she figured it would not do to be stopped with incriminating evidence. Her route took her through eastern Kentucky's dome-like mountains on local roads, through small towns wedged into narrow valleys, beside farms where fields had been plowed up steep slopes, past brick churches with signs advising, "Stop, Drop, & Roll Won't Work In Hell" and "Remember: Satan Was The First To Demand Equal Rights." She tried to recall what little she'd learned about confronting an opponent armed with a gun. If you are far enough away, run in a zig-zag pattern, because hitting a moving target is much harder than you would guess from TV and movies. If you are close, move closer, quickly, out of the line of fire. Attack and hurt the arm holding the weapon, but more importantly, incapacitate the person wielding it with an elbow to the face or throat. Considering her instructor had spent a single class on the technique, Lisa was amazed at how much of it she had retained; though recalling a slow-motion lesson in a dojo was different by several degrees of magnitude from using it against a man deliberately attempting to shoot you.

Eventually, the landscape relaxed into long, rolling hills as she approached Lexington, where she drove past the front entrance to Transylvania University, the name of which caused her to do a double-take. When she verified it, she muttered, "Seriously?" wondering if Sefira was mocking her. Throughout the day, stopped for lunch at a rest area, eating dinner at a Waffle House, and finally at the Day's Inn in Paducah where she took a room for the night, her eyes were watching for anyone approaching her, her ears listening for anyone calling her name. No one did, but she took scant comfort from it. Sefira, she assumed, was varying the tempo of her attacks, not allowing Lisa to grow comfortable anticipating them.

During the following day's drive up and down the length of Illinois, and across the Mississippi to St. Louis, she also went unassailed. That night, however, Sefira chose to visit Lisa in her car, and while it wasn't exactly a physical assault (although apparently Sefira could paralyze her, however briefly), it was a dramatic escalation of her psychological campaign. Lisa wondered if the irritation that plagued her eyes the succeeding day, slowing her process across Missouri to Kansas, and from Kansas to Colorado, was connected to Sefira's conversation with her. Certainly, the sensation of grit in her eyes distracted her from the men moving around her at the truck stop where she pulled in for a BLT and fries at Denny's and to gas up the Accord. Not until they were far too near did the men's presences register, too late to have avoided injury had they struck at her. She returned to the road with the feeling of having escaped a situation more precarious than she had fully appreciated. Despite the pledge she made to herself to maintain her vigilance, Lisa was caught off guard in the parking lot of the restaurant at which she ate lunch the following day. Her almost fatally delayed reaction she blamed on her teeth, whose deep constant hurt had outpaced the effectiveness of the Extra-Strength Tylenol she was taking to dull it. A former 1950s style gas station painted turquoise, the restaurant sat on the right side of the road Lisa had been driving for the last hour. A freestanding sign in front of the building gave its name as Vernon's, and advertised American, Italian, and Thai food. Hungry and curious, she turned into the narrow parking area and pulled up next to the only other vehicle in the lot, a sand-colored Ford Explorer.

The interior of the place was strung with multi-colored Christmas lights, its walls decorated with murals of green hills topped by Romanesque temples. Without looking up from her phone, the tall teenaged girl at the front register, her face draped by the long black hair hanging straight down either side of it, mumbled that Lisa could sit wherever she wanted.

A rudimentary idea of caution informing her choice, she opted to sit in the corner diagonally across the room from the entrance, a position which allowed her to keep an eye on the door to the kitchen, too, behind which she heard movement, clattering dishes. The tables were foldable. She had to scoot to the edge of the molded plastic chairs to eat her Pad Thai. The food was good enough to take her mind off the discomfort in her mouth. While she ate, she studied the girl, who had returned to her position at the register and who appeared oblivious to her attention. She was wearing faded jeans and a hooded sweatshirt washed from black to dark gray. Everything about her, from the nondescript clothes, to the way she wore her hair to obscure her face, to her mumbled speech, suggested someone trying desperately hard not to be noticed, which stirred memories in Lisa of her middle- and high-school years. Unlike the girl, she had dressed in whatever fashions were the latest uniform, been a member of the cheerleading squad, worked on her junior and senior prom committees. Yet her goal had been the same, to evade detection, only by hiding in plain sight, her camouflage so obvious it would never be noticed. At the heart of her behavior had been a deep loneliness the source of which she could not trace. Once, she had asked her sister if she ever felt that way, but Janice snorted and told her to get over herself. She hadn't bothered speaking to either of her parents about it. After she departed high school for college, and then college for a job and a marriage, the emotion gradually receded, leaving as mysteriously as it had arrived. She suspected a psychologist would identify the feeling as typical of adolescence, though such an explanation did nothing to diminish her almost visceral recollection of the emotion. As the girl removed her plate and offered her the desert menu, Lisa felt the urge to reassure her, tell her everything was going to be all right. She resisted the impulse, which was good, because she could imagine the sarcastic response it would evoke. Not to mention, sometimes things didn't turn out okay. There was disappointment, illness, accident, death. There was betrayal. There was finding your husband split open by the woman with whom he had been cheating on you, his chest a bloody space but his eyes still capable of seeing you, his lips still capable of uttering your name. Instead of saying any of that, she ordered a slice of the homemade apple pie, which was tart and cinnamony, and a cup of coffee that had been sitting in the pot too long. Once she was finished, she visited the restroom, left a generous tip on the table, paid at the register, and exited into the afternoon sunlight.

When she heard the girl's voice behind her calling, "Wait!" Lisa assumed it was because she had found the tip and thought the amount was a mistake. She slowed to allow her to catch up, a reassuring platitude at her lips. Her right hand at her side, the girl half-ran the remaining distance to where Lisa had paused at the trunk of her car. Hoping the exchange wouldn't take too long, as her teeth were really starting to hurt, now, Lisa said, "What is it?"

Instead of answering with some variety of, "You left this on the table," the girl said, "Is your name Lisa? Lisa Martinez?" So surprised was she to hear herself addressed by the name she hadn't used for seven years that Lisa failed to register the girl's right hand swinging up from where she had it pressed against her leg. The snub-nosed revolver in her grip was the kind of weapon you might keep under the counter of a restaurant too remote to expect a swift police response to your silent alarm. Flashing in the sun, the end of its abbreviated barrel swung toward her.

Almost as shocking as the gun, as someone pointing a gun at her, someone preparing to shoot her, to kill her, was the speed of Lisa's response. Moving toward the would-be murderer and to the right, she stepped past the pistol, circling the girl's right arm with her left, trapping it against her and forcing it to remain straight. The girl's eyebrows lifted, her mouth opened. Before she could react, Lisa threw her right elbow into the side of the girl's head. It struck with a thud that jarred the two of them. The girl's eyes widened, lost their focus. All the strength left her body and she sagged against Lisa heavily, the gun falling from her fingers.

Lisa eased her to the ground and retrieved the pistol. It was heavier than she expected. She fumbled with the cylinder until it opened, then held the gun barrel-up to allow the bullets to fall pinging on the gravel. The weapon empty, she snapped it closed and hurled it as far into the overgrown field bordering the parking lot as her muscles would allow.

Almost the instant the revolver left her hand and went spinning through the air, she realized it still had her fingerprints on it. But it hadn't been fired, was unloaded, and she didn't have the time to search for it in order to wipe it clean. And she was more concerned about the girl, who was slumped on her left side. Lisa squatted beside her. The girl's expression was blank, stunned. "Lisa," she murmured, "Lisa Martinez."

"I don't want to know how you know Sefira," she said, checking the girl's pulse, which was strong, her pupils, neither of which was dilated, and gingerly pressing the side of her skull, which elicited an "Ow!" from her but didn't reveal any obvious fracture. "All right," Lisa said. "Is your mom in the kitchen? Your dad?"

"Lisa," the girl said, "Lisa Martinez."

"Terrific," Lisa said. Gripping her under the armpits, she raised her to sitting. "Ow," the girl said. "Come on," Lisa said, helping her to her feet.

"Lisa," the girl said, "Lisa Martinez."

"If you say so," Lisa said. "I'm not so sure, myself." The girl leaning into her, Lisa walked them to the restaurant's front door and inside, where she deposited the girl on a plastic chair across from the register. She half-expected to find whoever was working the kitchen standing there, come in search of their hostess/server when they realized they hadn't heard from her in a while, but the place was empty. "Hey!" Lisa shouted, "Hey you! Hey, come here!" From the other side of the kitchen door, she heard someone call, "Hello?" "Hey!" she shouted again, "Hey, come here!" and ducked out of the building.

Disturbed as she was to have had a gun aimed at her, Lisa was equally troubled by someone the girl's age being involved with Sefira. Her own adolescence was fresh enough in her memory for her to know that, whatever they might tell their parents or guardians, most kids were sexually aware and interested far earlier than they let on, a knowledge and curiosity facilitated by the Internet, and given the opportunity to explore their interest with a willing partner, would do so. Sophomore year of high school, she had had a particularly intense make-out session with a cute junior she had noticed from a distance and with whom she found herself waiting for the late bus one afternoon. The situation had escalated quickly, the two of them progressing from kissing to sliding their hands under one another's shirts regardless of the fact that they were sitting on the school's front steps. (They had been wearing jackets, which afforded them a measure of concealment as she explored under his t-shirt and he popped the cups of her bra over her breasts.) The arrival of the late bus had startled them out of their activity, and although they took the same seat, their hearts pounding, their faces flushed, they had done no more than hold hands. Lisa had felt dizzy at how far she had been willing to go, and with what speed, with this boy she found attractive but didn't know especially well. From the stunned look on his face, his thoughts seemed to be running on parallel tracks. She had been afraid he might spread news of their encounter to his friends, brag about having felt a cheerleader's tits, but to the best of her knowledge, he told no one. On several occasions afterwards, they waited for the late bus together, but nothing else happened.

The point was, it was naive to think a girl old enough to be working couldn't have sexual feelings and experiences. Yet there was a difference—a profound difference between fooling around with the cute person you had your eye on and . . . she didn't know what to call it. A relationship with someone like Sefira? Technically, she supposed the word was accurate, but if it was a relationship, then it was of the same nature as the one between the fish and the lamprey suctioned to its flanks, chewing a hole in it to suck out its organs. Except, in this case, the fish had invited the lamprey to attach to it. All right, there were problems with her comparison, but the underlying meaning it aimed at was intact: Sefira was a parasite, using the desires of her hosts to allow her to fasten to and feed off them, in some cases, quite literally. That she had exploited the loneliness Lisa had recognized (and sympathized with) in the girl struck her as especially vile.

There was something else, too, mixed in with her continuing shock at having been threatened with a gun and her deepening disgust with Sefira, a memory of something which occurred in the quarter-second it had taken her to close the gap between herself and the girl and trap her arm. Within that sliver of time, she had seen the girl shrouded in darkness, as if wound in a sheet of black muslin. The darkness had been shot through with tiny points of light, or so she thought (she was less certain of this detail). Already, though, the pain in her teeth had worsened to the point it was making her head hurt. Concentrating on anything other than the road in front of her was difficult to nearly impossible. Maybe she could ask Gary to ask Madame Sosostris about it? Possibly. It would mean discussing the assailants Sefira had left waiting for her, their efforts to kill or at least harm her, but perhaps it would be worth hearing Gary exclaim for her safety, once again express his regret at involving her in all this, in the interest of further insight into what she had become part of. How would she respond were Gary to tell her to break off her pursuit, it was too dangerous, he would take the consequences heading his way? How would she respond were he not to?

Later that day, on the outskirts of Denver, came the conflagration that roared through her mouth, reshaping her teeth from the monument to her orthodontist's skills to a garden of yellowed fangs. All thought of anything else evaporated, burned away by the heat of the transformation that overtook her. Sitting in the enormous parking lot of the Wal-Mart to which she retreated to wait out the pain raging through her, Lisa was aware of how exposed she was, how vulnerable to yet another of Sefira's minions. Particularly if whoever it was held a firearm, it would be simple enough to approach the Honda, aim, and keep on squeezing the trigger until Lisa was a bloody mess. A similar feeling of vulnerability nagged at her as she drove across the Rockies the following afternoon. How difficult would it be for someone in Sefira's thrall to ram a car or truck into hers, shoving it through the safety barrier and down the mountain? If the low stone walls were sturdier than they looked, a simple head-on collision would serve the same purpose.

Yet she went unchallenged in the flat parking lot and in the high mountains. Not until she was gassing up the Accord at a rest area near Laramie did another of Sefira's puppets call her name. The confrontation was almost anticlimactic. Heavyset, wearing a white cowboy hat so large it might have been able to hold an actual ten gallons, jowls thick with stubble, the man was carrying a tire iron in his meaty right hand. As she was about to open her door, he walked toward her on cowboy boots whose worn heels made him rock from side to side. Huffing as he moved, he said, "Lisa?" Despite the gas station's brilliant lighting, the man appeared strangely dim—because, she realized, she was seeing him wound in the same glittering darkness which had wrapped the girl at the restaurant. "Lisa?" he said again.

"No," she said.

The man halted, confusion drawing his brows together. Lisa took advantage of the second this gained her to step in and bring her right fist up into his jaw. She was ready to follow with a straight left punch to his nose, but it wasn't necessary. His head wobbled, the tire iron clattered to the pavement, and the man sat down hard, his head forward. Lisa retreated to her car, slid into it, and exited the gas station, leaving her would-be attacker where he was. The darkness around him was no longer visible; though why that was, she wasn't sure. Later, as she was checking into the Holiday Inn, she glanced at the knuckles on her right hand and noticed that she had scraped them. The young Asian woman who was taking her information saw the raw flesh and said, "Ouch. How'd you do that?" In reply, Lisa invented a story about changing a tire on the highway and her grip on the tire iron slipping, sending her hand ricocheting off the road. "You have to be careful," the clerk said. "That's so true," Lisa said.

Early the following morning, her pulse already quickened by the prospect of the coming confrontation with Sefira, Lisa registered that her knuckles were healed. She drove out of the hotel parking lot under a sky washed in the crimson bleeding from the horizon. *Red sky at morning*, she thought. The day's drive was uncomplicated, north up I-25 through east central Wyoming. Sefira, it appeared, had been eager to return home. Lisa kept the gearshift in fifth, the speedometer anywhere from ten to fifteen miles an hour above 70, sliding out, around, and back in front of the tractor trailers hauling freight. Overhead, the sun was a bright ball in a blue bowl of sky which somehow appeared several orders of magnitude larger. From the corner of her eye, she was aware of flat expanses of earth stretching to either side of the highway, of distant mountains high and sharp, a landscape straight out of the middle of a Hollywood western, when the heroes are on their way to meet their destiny, but she maintained her focus on the road ahead of her. At least her teeth no longer hurt, and she had adjusted to their new configuration far more quickly than she had imagined she would. On three separate occasions, Wyoming state troopers loomed in her rearview mirror, only to speed past her when she eased into the travel lane. Near Buffalo, 25 merged with I-90, which brought her across the Montana state line.

With Montana came the final darkening of her eyes, and the opening of the other dimension to her vision, which revealed the grassy land glowing as if lit from within. She wondered if the black shrouds she had perceived around her last two attackers were related to this, early manifestations of the incipient expansion of her perception. It seemed likely. Now that she was at most another forty-five minutes from Sefira, nervousness knotted her stomach, diminished to almost nothing her appetite for the Big Mac and fries she ordered at the McDonald's off the second exit from 90. She forced herself to eat the meal and drink the large Coke that accompanied it. All the time, she was thinking about the butcher knife concealed under the Accord's spare tire, about the weight of it in her hand. She had assured Madame Sosostris—and Gary—she was up to the task of using the blade on Sefira; at the end of her conversation/confrontation with Sefira the other night, she had told herself she was going to drive it into her. Now, though, the prospect of actually stabbing her, of killing her, seemed as fantastical as any of the last nine days' events.

Gary's directions took her away from Wyola and its McDonald's, back under the interstate to the opposite side. After another five miles the road forked. She steered left and for the next half hour wound between low hills densely forested with Ponderosa pine and Douglas fir, until the terrain opened into a small, flat-bottomed valley. Ahead on the left, a rectangular sign atop a tall pole identified the Hide-Away Motel. *Holy shit*, Lisa thought, *this is it.* The sign was set at the roadside of a pocked and cratered parking lot, which spread in front of a long, single-story building punctuated at regular intervals by picture windows and doors. At the far end, the block of rooms connected to a box-like office. Parked before the office was a van whose aqua sides were painted with great, gaudy flowers, white daisies, pink carnations, yellow daffodils, all executed in a style that showed more enthusiasm than skill. *Sefira*, Lisa thought. *She's here. She's actually here.*

From the worn siding, the paint peeling from the doors, the dirt clouding the windows—not to mention the parking lot's lunar surface—it was clear no one had been renting rooms at the Hide-Away for years. Lisa braked and flipped on her turn signal, which was absurd. There was no one else on the road with her. That was habit for you. Looming behind the building was a dark mass she initially took for another of the surrounding hills, until she saw that, unlike those hills, which glowed with the same light her eyes had gained the ability to perceive, this one gave off no radiance. Despite the mid-afternoon sun, its features remained difficult to see clearly, its features obscure. The lopsided silhouette reminded her of the sand castles she and Janice used to build when they were kids on the family vacation to the Jersey shore. They would gather handfuls of wet sand and allow it to drip through their hands onto the beach, forming layered, tapering structures, like a cross between anthills and beehives. (Somewhere in her memory, Gary cried about the hives, about not wanting to be taken into the hives.)

Navigating potholes large and larger, Lisa rolled across the parking lot to Sefira's van, stopping crossways behind it, blocking Sefira from leaving. She set the parking brake and killed the engine, cutting off Dolly in the midst of her latest round of pleading with Jolene. She reached for the lever to release the trunk and, heart thudding with such force she felt it in her wrists, exited the car. The air was warm, humid. Keeping the door to the motel office in view, she walked to the back of the Accord and raised the trunk. A thick coat of dirt caught the sunlight, turning the office windows into bright rectangles. The entire time listening for the creak of the door's hinges, she ducked under the trunk, hoisted the trunk board, and unscrewed the nut securing the spare, fingers slipping in her haste. The tire loose, she lifted it with her left hand and reached under with her right for the rolled-up towel. Without replacing the nut, she lowered the board and spread the towel on it.

Through the words and symbols scratched onto its almost comically oversized blade, her reflection regarded her from the polished metal's depths. With her sunglasses on and her mouth closed, you wouldn't guess she had been through any of the past days' trials. She removed the Ray-Bans, folded them, and set them on the towel. Her lips peeled back, she snarled at the black-eyed woman in the knife, who showed her a mouth full of yellowed fangs in return. *That's more like it.* She picked up the knife with her right hand and closed the trunk with her left.

The door to the office, she saw, was open, a figure moving out of it toward her.

VIII

There was a zip-up sweat jacket in the back seat of the Accord. Lisa ran out of the house to fetch it. "You need to cover up . . . that," she said to Gary, gesturing at his opened chest, which she was struggling not to look at, because every time her eyes slid over his torn flesh and broken bone, the gory *space* in him, it was all she could do not to start screaming again. "I don't suppose you know where your clothes are?"

"No," Gary said. "I . . ." He glanced away and she realized that, amazingly, he was embarrassed.

"I think I have something in the car," she said. As she turned to go, Gary caught her arm in his cold hand. "What is it?"

"Don't leave me," he said, his shame replaced by fear.

She tugged out of his grip. "I'll be right back," she said, and headed for the stairs.

Leaving him would be easy enough, Lisa thought as she reached into the car for the jacket. Just get behind the wheel, put the key in the ignition, and don't look back. Where was he going to go in this condition? She could wait a day or two, then call the cops, tell them her husband hadn't been home or in touch for forty-eight hours and she was worried about him. Her friends, she would say, had reported seeing him with another woman; although he had reassured her she was a client for his web design business. Sefira: she didn't have the woman's last name; her husband hadn't mentioned it. The assumption would be that Gary had left her for this Sefira, run off with her to parts unknown. All she would have to do was forget about this house, 1430 Wycombe, and what she had found in it. Would that be so difficult? It required an enormous effort to accept the injury that had been done to Gary, although that dwindled in comparison to the Herculean effort necessary to deal with his continuing animation. (Was he alive? He was moving and speaking, which made the answer to the question seem to be yes; on the other hand, it simply wasn't possible to survive that degree of trauma. How was she supposed to think of him, then? A word from childhood monster movies bobbed to the surface of her thoughts: *undead.*) Sweat jacket in hand, Lisa hesitated. If she returned to the house, if she drove Gary to whomever it was he wanted to talk to, she would be committing herself to something whose ending she could not begin to conceive. Yet she was kidding herself if she imagined she could leave this place and never think of it again. She would do nothing but think about it; she would obsess over it. Better to exert what control she could over the situation.

When Gary saw her, he said, "I wasn't sure you were coming back."

"That makes two of us," Lisa said, holding out the jacket to him. "Do you need help with this?"

"I think I can manage," he said, which was true, or true enough. Lisa tried not to listen to the cracks and pops his bones made while he tugged the garment up his arms and zipped it over his chest. Several sizes too small for him, the jacket hugged Gary's torso, outlining the perimeter of his wound in baby blue fabric. At least the bloody cavity was hidden from view. "Ready?" Lisa said.

"Yeah."

This trip to the car took far longer. Gary walked slowly, hesitantly, as if concerned too sudden a motion might cause him to fall to pieces, literally. Lisa was reminded of some of her patients, adjusting to their bodies after a stroke or major injury, re-learning how to use it, how to be in it. (Was he serious about having been in Hell?) On the front step, Lisa pulled the door shut behind her and, on impulse, used the hem of her shirt to wipe her fingerprints from it. It occurred to her that she had opened several doors within the house, and if she was serious about removing evidence of her presence here, she should clean those doorknobs, too. "I'll be right back," she called to Gary, who was shuffling along the front walk.

As she rushed through dark halls, swiping the doorknobs with her shirt, she had a vision of emerging outside to find Gary collapsed, lifeless, a police car finally appearing to respond to the neighbors' complaints of someone driving like a lunatic on their usually quiet street. No one would believe anything other than that she had learned her husband was cheating on her and brutally murdered him. Based on what the cops found when they explored the house, they would assume she had killed Gary here and was in the process of moving his body someplace to dispose of it. At the trial, her effort to wipe her fingerprints would be taken as an indication not only of her guilt, but of her culpability, a clear sign she understood what she was doing and was attempting to evade capture for it. Her martial arts training would be invoked to present her as someone strong enough and aggressive enough for violence. Given the political climate, the prosecution would no doubt present her as an angry Latina, out for hot-blooded vengeance. All of which would be the final raised middle finger from a woman she had never met, but who seemed delighted to wreck her life.

So certain was Lisa of the scenario she had envisioned that, when she burst out the front door and found Gary still upright, standing next to the car, no police cruiser in sight, she almost lost her balance, made dizzy by the relief surging through her. For a second time, she shut the door and ran the bottom of her shirt over it. She hurried to the car, opening it and waiting while Gary lowered himself into the passenger's seat. He couldn't find the seatbelt. Impatient to leave, still half-expecting the cops to come rolling along the street, she yanked out the buckle and fastened him in, the hair on the back of her neck raising as she leaned close to his chest. "Thank you," he said, his voice somewhere to her right. She said, "You're welcome," the mutual courtesy ridiculous. In the depths of her mind, her father said, "There's always a place for good manners." *Even in a situation like this, Dad?*

She drove into Huguenot with the exaggerated care of someone who wasn't sure if she was all the way sober after a couple of drinks a couple of hours ago, keeping at or under the speed limit, watching for where it dropped from 55 to 40, then 40 to 30, a pair of changes the local cops exploited, signaling well in advance of her turns, coming to a full halt at the stop signs she encountered. All of which was potentially suspicious behavior at this time of night, but with any luck, a cop sitting at the side of the road would not deem it worth abandoning a hiding place for.

The sharp smell of blood hung in the car. The silence between her and Gary was great, made worse by the fact that, beneath the drone of the engine, she could not hear him breathing. *Of course not*, she thought, which did not remedy things. She glanced at Gary, who was staring straight ahead, his face shining with the crimson tears sliding down his cheeks. "What is it?" she said.

"This," he said, raising his hand to take in the trees, the darkened houses they were passing. "It's all so beautiful. It's too much."

"What happened to you?" she said.

"Sefira," he said, his lip trembling. "She isn't . . . She did this to me with her bare hands. Except, they weren't hands, anymore." He wiped his tears with his (her) sleeve.

"What are you talking about?"

"Sefira. She isn't human. She's a monster."

"Obviously."

"No," Gary said, his voice breaking. "I mean, an actual monster."

"You were fucking a monster."

"Yes. No. I mean, not when we were—she changed—"

"Forget it," Lisa said.

After another minute not listening to Gary's lungs not working, though, she said, "You were in Hell?"

He hesitated. "Yeah."

"What . . ."

"What was it like?"

"Yes."

"Dark," Gary said. "The ground was rocky, sharp. Every time you moved, it cut you. There was fire everywhere, rivers and lakes of it, like magma. In places, fire shot up out of the rock in geysers. The air was full of heavy smoke. You wanted to cry, or scream, but if you made too much noise, you would attract the demons."

"Demons?"

"Or devils. I heard them called both." Gary paused. Fresh tears leaked from his eyes. "They were terrifying. No two were the same. They were . . . all twisted. Some were tall, skinny, with an extra arm or two. Others moved closer to the ground, like spiders. There were a few who lived in the fire, in the pools of lava. Their skin was charred, covered in shards of cracked and broken armor that had melted into it. A few were on fire, in part or in whole. Their faces . . . you didn't want to be close enough to see their faces, because if you were, there was a good chance they were about to capture you, and once they had you, that was it. You were gone. But I saw one when I first arrived, and it was awful. Half its skull was caved in. The other half was taken up by this enormous round eye that had a half-dozen slivers of metal sticking out of it. Its mouth . . ." His voice trailed off.

Lisa turned left onto Old Soldier's. "And you just—went there?"

"You're asking me what it's like to die."

"I guess so, yeah."

"Horrible. Sefira, she—what she did to me—it took a long time. I was conscious for all of it. Which I wouldn't have thought possible." He swallowed. "I would have assumed that, after a certain point, your system would give out. Shock would stop your heart. I was wrong. Sefira did something to me—she paralyzed me. And then she . . . opened me. The pain—I don't know how to describe it. It went so far beyond anything I had ever felt before, I kept thinking, *This can't be real, there's no way this is real.* I want to say it was imaginary, which sounds like completely the wrong word, I know. But I was in a situation that could only have happened in my imagination, so the description kind of makes sense."

At the intersection with Golding, Lisa took a right.

"I always hoped—when I thought about dying—about how I would want to die—" Gary stopped.

"It's all right," Lisa said. "If you don't want to say any more, it's fine."

"I wanted to drift away," Gary said. "Like going to sleep at the end of a long day, when you're exhausted. As if sleep is a warm bed you're slipping into. I figured that was the best way to go. If not gently, then fast, so fast you wouldn't know what had happened to you. I dreaded suffering; although I was worried about cancer, not . . . evisceration." He shook his head.

"Beside where she had positioned me in the basement, Sefira had a red and white cooler. Not full-sized, maybe the next step down. Large enough for a picnic lunch. There were bags of ice stacked next to it, seven or eight of them. After she finished breaking my ribs apart . . . after . . . she stood. She had been straddling me. She stepped over to the cooler and emptied half the bags into it. The ice made a shushing sound as it fell. I was breathing so fast I was hyperventilating, but I couldn't pass out, which I was desperate to do. I could hear my heart beating. It sounded wet. I think I knew—I had put the pieces together, and I knew what was happening. I couldn't believe it, but I knew. Sefira was—she had changed. Transformed. Her hands, her forearms had become . . . sharp. Her face . . . She dropped the empty bag she was holding and sat back down on me. She said something—it might've been, 'Let's see.' I was trying to speak, to plead with her, but my jaw was paralyzed, too. All I was capable of were screams and moans. Sefira leaned forward and dug her right hand into me. I . . . The pain . . ." His tongue scraped across his lower lip. "It wasn't just the pain, it was the sensation of her fingers pushing around inside my chest. She murmured to herself, 'No, not this. Maybe this?' as if she were a butcher and me the animal on the slab. Finally, she found what she was looking for. She twisted her hand, corkscrewing those sharp fingers. When she removed it from me, it was full of meat. She stretched her hand over the cooler and let the bloody pieces drop onto the ice. Before she returned to working on me, Sefira raised her fingers to her mouth and licked the blood from them. Then she resumed butchering me."

The traffic light at the junction with Main Street was red. Lisa rolled to a stop, raising the turn signal for a right.

Gary said, "I was sure I was about to die. I couldn't understand how I hadn't already. I was certain I should have bled out. I wanted to die, more than I have ever wanted anything. The constant pain—the agony—I never appreciated how long the body can go on suffering, how, even when you're in pain, there can be room for additional pain, different pain. It wasn't just the physical agony: my mind felt as though it was on the verge of collapsing, my sanity disintegrating. I was desperate to escape the monster squatting on me, extracting my organs whole or in part and dumping them into her cooler."

Green light filled the car. Lisa turned right, immediately flipping the signal down for the left across Main into the driveway of the purple farmhouse.

"When I realized Sefira was reaching for my heart," Gary said, "I thought the end had finally arrived. I was almost relieved. But no. I watched her lift the heart from me, cradle it in her hands, and kiss it. I saw her place it in the cooler with exaggerated care, then stand so she could tear open the remaining bags of ice and pour them on top of what she had taken from me. She closed the lid, fastened it shut, and lifted the cooler. She carried it out of the basement—to her van, I assumed."

There was a small parking lot behind the house, its sole occupant an older model blue Volvo. Lisa drove in beside it, pulled the parking brake, and shut off the engine.

"Sefira came back once," Gary said, "to gather the empty bags and call you. She was—she had become human again. Though now that I had looked at her other face—her *true* face—it was impossible for me not to see it lying just beneath the surface of her features. I listened as she talked to you, taunted you. Strange as it sounds, I was waiting for her to say something to me, explain what had happened. You know, like the villain in a movie, revealing her evil plan. She didn't. She hung up on you and left the room without another word. I heard her exit the house, and after a minute, her car starting. I guess . . ."

"What?" Lisa pulled the key from the ignition and deposited it in her jeans pocket. Her phone was tilted in the cup holder; she removed it and slid it into her pocket.

"You asked me what dying was like, but what I've been describing isn't dying. Actually, while I was lying there, empty . . . I wondered if I hadn't died, already. Maybe you didn't go anywhere once your body ceased functioning; maybe you just . . . hung around. Except, I was still in pain—tremendous, unbearable pain—which seemed a pretty compelling argument for me remaining alive. I knew you were probably on your way, and the idea of you finding me like . . . this made the situation that much worse.

"I don't know how long it was, not very, but everything around me began to shimmer, the way a soap bubble does when it's on the verge of popping. *This is it*, I thought. The end had arrived. There was enough time for me to wonder if the torture Sefira had put me through was some kind of terminal hallucination—if Sefira had killed me immediately and what I had experienced had been a last fantasy my brain had conjured in its dying seconds—and then the room . . . burst.

"Darkness swallowed me. I thought, *So there's nothing, after all.* Which was a relief. I wouldn't have to face any kind of . . . anything. With the room, the pain went, too, which for a moment was paradise. I had avoided you showing up at the house, and that was a comfort, too." He stopped. "I know—that's a shitty thing to say."

Lisa did not reply.

"For a couple of minutes," Gary said, "I did nothing but lie where I was, savoring the absence of pain. I realized I could move. I ran my hands over my chest and found it whole, healed. Without warning, I burst into tears, into heaving sobs that went on and on. I cried for all of it, for the huge fucking mess I had made of my life, your life, our life. My tears came to an end as I became aware of the surface I was lying on, which was rocky, sharp. I sat up. The blackness around me was not uniform. Somewhere ahead was a dim, orange glow. I stood. Already, I understood the nowhere I had assumed I was was somewhere. I decided to investigate the light in the distance. Reaching it was slow going. The rocks were hard to walk on, painful, and for most of the journey, the terrain I was crossing was difficult to see clearly. I had this sinking feeling, this dread in the pit of my stomach, that I knew exactly where I was. As I drew nearer to it, the orange glow became an orange line winding across the horizon. After more time—a lot more time, the line widened, growing to a stream, and eventually a river, a vast river of lava, flames flickering on its molten surface. There were figures moving along its shores. If I had any doubt remaining as to my location, it vanished when one of the figures stalked by me. I was on the demon's blind side, which was the only way I escaped its notice."

Gary fell silent long enough for Lisa to assume he was done talking. She unfastened her seatbelt and opened the door. Before she could step out of the car, however, Gary said, "I was there for a year, Lise. It—I can't go back. I can't." She could hear his voice careening into hysteria. She released his seatbelt, which retracted into its slot, startling him out of his growing panic. "We're here," she said. "Let's go see if your Madame Whatever is awake."

After she helped Gary out of his seat, his chest popping, they walked to the house's back door. Due to the lateness of the hour, Lisa pressed on and held the doorbell for five seconds. "What do we do if she doesn't answer?" she said.

"She will," Gary said. His voice seemed to be coming from a couple of feet to his left.

"Suppose she can't help us," Lisa said. "Where do we go?"

"There's a guy who runs an antique shop near Albany," Gary said. "He might be able to help. If not, there's someone in . . . Gloucester, I think. In Massachusetts."

"Albany? Gloucester?" Lisa had a sudden vision of the two of them on a road trip that never ended, roaming farther and farther afield, continually searching for but failing to find someone who could aid them. She went to push the doorbell a second time, but the light perched next to the doorframe came on.

The woman who opened the door was wearing a fuzzy brown bathrobe over pink pajamas, her long brown hair a frizzy mess. She was younger than Lisa had anticipated, within a few years either side of her and Gary. "Can I help you?" she said, the tone of her question a reminder of how Lisa and especially Gary, in his blood-stained boxers and undersized sweat jacket, must look to anyone who wasn't party to their extended nightmare. "Hi," Lisa said. "I'm sorry to disturb you, but we heard you could help us."

"Help you?" the woman said. Her hand had stolen to the robe's right pocket, where, Lisa guessed, was concealed some means of defending herself, pepper spray or a Taser, even a pistol, should whoever had roused her in the middle of the night prove a danger.

"With this," Gary said, and drew down the jacket's zipper.

Lisa looked away. The woman inhaled sharply, said, "Holy shit." Her reaction was oddly reassuring, the mingled horror and wonder in her profanity an indication she found both Gary's emptied chest and his continuing animation as awful and incredible as did Lisa.

"The woman who did this is named Sefira," Gary said, leaving the jacket open. "Only, she's not a woman. She's not human. She looks like she is, but it's a disguise. She murdered me, and I went to Hell. That was where I heard your name. A guy named Aubrey Byrne gave it to me."

"Aubrey?" the woman said. "You spoke with Aubrey?"

"I did. He gave me a message for you, in case I ever escaped. Which he swore to me I wouldn't, but here I am. He said to tell you it wasn't your fault. You did everything you could for him. He chose the third path."

"You should come in," the woman said, removing her hand from whatever it had been clutching in her pocket. "If you would zip your jacket—"

"Of course," Gary said.

A short hallway led past a half-open bathroom door to a snug kitchen at whose round table the woman gestured for Lisa and Gary to seat themselves. Overhead, a line of track-and-rail lights glowed white. The faint odor of green apple dish liquid hung in the air. The red and white checked tablecloth was spread with an assortment of papers, which the woman gathered into a heap and moved to the counter behind her. "Taxes," she said. "Doing what I can to keep my receipts in order."

"It's a pain," Gary said. "We have our own businesses, and when tax time rolls around, our accountant has her work cut out for her."

Lisa caught herself nodding, and was startled at how quickly she had slipped from the stark madness of the current moment into a familiar routine, one in which Gary tried a little too hard to be friendly to a new acquaintance and she tried to reassure the person through her sympathetic expression that she knew her husband was overdoing things. She listened to the woman and Gary comparing their respective accountants, as if she and he were here for one of the psychic readings the sign on the front lawn promised. *What do you foresee for our marriage?* While she talked, the woman opened the cupboard above the counter and fetched a pair of short glasses, one of which she set before Lisa, the other at the spot she intended for herself. From the next cupboard over, she retrieved a mostly full bottle of Grey Goose, out of which she tipped a generous portion of silver liquid into Lisa's glass, a more modest serving into hers. Lisa reached for the glass and drank half of it without tasting the vodka. The alcohol flared in her stomach, sending a wave of heat rolling over her. She finished the remainder of the drink and held out her empty glass for a refill, which the woman poured before setting the bottle on the table and taking her seat. Already, the vodka was sanding the rough edges off her emotions, easing the tension that seemed to have gripped every last one of her muscles. Lisa considered speeding the process along, swallowing the second drink and adding a third and fourth to it. How long had it been since she had gotten good and drunk, head-swimming, falling-down shit-faced? As a rule, she avoided such excess, a part of the healthy lifestyle she did her best to maintain, but if ever there was a time for the rule to be excepted, surely, this was it.

Gary preempted any moves in that direction, however, by speaking. "Madame Sosostris—"

From the other pocket of her robe, Madame Sosostris produced a scrunchie, which she used to secure the mass of her hair into an approximate ponytail. "Tell me your names," she said, lifting her drink.

"I'm Gary," Gary said, "Gary Murray. This is my wife, Lisa."

"Is that how you would describe yourself?" Madame Sosostris said, looking at Lisa over the rim of her glass.

"Right now, I don't know how I would describe myself."

"You weren't aware of what your—what Gary was up to with this other woman."

"She isn't a woman," Gary said.

"No," Lisa said. "I mean, I heard from my friends that the two of them were hanging out, but when I asked him about her, he said she was his client."

"Then I'm sorry," Madame Sosostris said after tasting her drink. "Sometimes, in situations like this, both parties are full and willing participants. When one isn't, it's quite a shock to them."

"Yeah," Lisa said. "What do you mean, 'situations like this'?"

"I'm assuming Gary was involved with an inhabitant of the pneumasphere—a demon."

"A demon?" Lisa said.

"As a rule, demons appear to the people who summon them. The people who call them up tend to be after something: power, or money, or revenge—"

"Or sex," Lisa said.

"—or sex," Madame Sosostris said. She regarded Gary blankly. "Was that what it was? Sex?"

"Yes," he said.

"Once the demon has provided whatever it was brought for, it extracts its price. Someone who knows their way around this kind of thing will have negotiated that detail beforehand. Someone who doesn't . . ."

"Winds up like this," Gary said.

Madame Sosostris nodded.

"You were . . ." The rest of the question died in Lisa's mouth. Practicing sorcery? Raising a demon? Making a deal with it? She pictured Gary in black robes, standing in front of a pentagram chalked on the floor, a heavy book of spells open in his hands. Already, the situation had the feel of a horror movie, an extended blend of the supernatural and the gory, with plenty of sex thrown in; the image of Gary as a sinister magician threatened to tip the production into outright camp.

"I didn't know I was summoning a demon," Gary said, returning them to the realm of the horror movie. "I met Sefira online. It was on an adult website."

"A hookup site," Lisa said. The horror and awe twisting within her were joined by a third emotion: anger.

"Yes," Gary said.

"The kind of place where most of the women are bots," Lisa said, "or guys, getting off on pretending to be hot girls."

"Or demons, apparently," Gary said. "I messaged Sefira for a couple of weeks. She said she was on the road. She said she traveled a lot, for her work, and would be passing this way, if I wanted to meet. I did. And . . ."

"You fucked her," Lisa said.

"Yes. Then she did this to me." He nodded at his chest.

While they were talking, Madame Sosostris produced a deck of cards from Lisa didn't notice where. Larger than ordinary playing cards, their backs were white, unadorned. She placed the deck on her left and used her right hand to slide the top four cards onto the table-cloth in a line. Her hand drifted over the blank rectangles, pausing at the cards at either end, before turning over the second card from the right. The picture on the other side was in a style that reminded Lisa of stained glass, heavy black frames surrounding luminous colors. It showed a field of tall grass interspersed by an assortment of flowers. A bee hovered in the foreground, its course represented by a black line winding and looping from blossom to blossom. Madame Sosostris flipped the card to its left. Executed in the manner of a sketch done with colored pencils, this one featured a fiery rock crashing through a glass or crystal globe, shattering half of it. The decoration on the card at the left end appeared to be a photograph of an angular statue— based on the wear evident on its surface, an ancient one. Its subject was seated cross-legged, hands on knees, lap heaped with rounded objects, some of which had rolled onto the surrounding floor. Triangular shapes that reminded Lisa of shark's teeth ran up the statue's arms, while its head rose into a cone whose wavering lines suggested an elaborate arrangement of hair. The space its eyes and nose should have occupied was blank, its mouth weathered into a trio of vertical lines. A flat circle framed the figure's head. The rest of the piece had been carved from grainy, sand-colored rock, the disk was of black stone, its surface matte. Madame Sosostris lingered on the card, then revealed the last, which was empty, white as its other side. Lisa wondered if it was a mistake, if the woman would slip a replacement from the deck, but she left the white card where it was. She lifted her glass and drank from it. "She's a succubus," she said, "your demon."

"What does that mean?" Lisa said.

"It's a sex demon," Gary said.

"I think we knew that already."

"What's more," Madame Sosostris said, "she's one of the Shattered Company."

"I don't know what that is," Lisa said.

"It's a group of old powers. Very old—pre-human."

"I thought it all was pre-human," Gary said. "At least, that was what I learned in CCD. First there was God, and then He made the angels, and then some of them rebelled, and then they became the devils and demons. People don't enter the picture until after all that."

"The pneumasphere's a bit more complicated than that."

"That's the second time you've used that word," Lisa said, "pneumasphere. What is it?"

"The afterlife," Madame Sosostris said, "although I prefer not to use that word. 'Afterlife' makes the place sound separate from us. It isn't. It intersects this world in a multitude of ways. If it weren't so New-Age-y, I'd say it's the spirit world. Another dimension, or plane of existence. It has its own ecology, its flora and fauna, its inhabitants. This Sefira comes from an especially ancient chamber known as the Broken Land."

"Chamber?" Lisa said.

"Do you know what a rhizome is?"

"A potato?"

"For example. Something with no central organization, just a collection of connected nodes."

"All right."

"This is how the pneumasphere is arranged. Each of its chambers is vast, a universe in and of itself. There are links among the various nodes and major events here. You mentioned Aubrey Byrne," she said to Gary. "He and I thought it possible new chambers emerged in response to significant changes on this plane, to the ascent of new species to the top of our ecosystem. That's the other thing about the pneumasphere: it's reactive. Occurrences on Earth can effect conditions there. It takes something significant, something global, but a catastrophe for us has the potential to devastate the environment for them. This was the case with the Broken Land. There was a cataclysm—an asteroid struck the earth. The resulting firestorm killed off most life on the planet."

"You're talking about the dinosaurs, right?" Gary said, the eager student trying to impress the teacher.

Madame Sosostris shook her head. "Earlier. During the planet's lifespan, there have been half a dozen of these extinction-level events. When one occurs, it disrupts the pneumasphere. In this instance, the chamber most dramatically affected was connected to what was then the dominant form of life, the insects."

"Sefira's an insect?" Lisa said.

"Approximately," Madame Sosostris said. "She and her kind have the same relation to insects that an angel might have to a human."

"Except, she's not an angel," Gary said.

"No," Madame Sosostris said, "and yes. If you try to extend the comparison very far, it breaks down. I'd rather call her a power. When the asteroid smacks into the Earth, she and all the other inhabitants of her chamber are engulfed in fire. The air burns. The ground convulses, cracks. This goes on for—I should add, time doesn't work the same way in the pneumasphere."

"I can attest to that," Gary said.

For the first time, Lisa thought, *Good.*

"What lasts for decades, centuries here continues for eons there," Madame Sosostris said, "The inhabitants can't die, not really, but they can suffer. And they do, they endure agonies that last an eternity. Slowly, they change—adapt to what their home has become. At some point, after a long, long time, a few of them rediscover the routes from their space to our world. You can appreciate, this place seems like heaven to them. Not many can make the crossing, which requires a good deal of energy, and none can stay very long, likewise. Once humanity appears on the scene, however, all kinds of possibilities start to open up. We're the type of beings Sefira and her kind can make exchanges with, the kinds of transactions I mentioned previously. The principle purpose of those . . . trades is to permit members of the Shattered Company to prolong their stay here. The transactions tend to be pretty gruesome."

"Yes," Gary said.

"During the process, they hook your soul and fling it to their fellows in the Broken Land—as a kind of tithe, I think. I'm not sure if the creatures there draw nourishment from the souls who arrive there."

"If they catch you," Gary said, "they do."

"So what is Sefira planning for . . . what she took from Gary?" Lisa said.

"That's obvious," Gary said. "She's going to eat it. Or maybe she has already; I don't know."

"She hasn't," Madame Sosostris said. "If she had consumed your organs—your heart, really—you wouldn't be here."

"Why is she waiting?" Lisa said.

"For her feeding to have the optimum result, she has to do it in her nest."

"Which is where, exactly?" Lisa said.

"I don't know," Madame Sosostris said.

"Well, that's a bit of a problem," Lisa said.

"What are we supposed to do?" Gary said.

"Let me tell you what I do know," Madame Sosostris said. "Sefira is on her way home. Although by this point she has a head start of several hours, the route she is taking is not a straight line. It will be circuitous. This is part of her renewing her connection to this plane. Each day, she'll stop to rest, which will keep her from getting too far ahead. Once she reaches her nest, she'll remain there for a number of days—three, at least, possibly as long as a couple of weeks. At the end of that period, she will consume Gary's flesh. His soul will return to the Broken Land, and his body will be hers to do with as she pleases."

"Like a zombie?" Lisa said.

"Yes. The real question isn't where Sefira is now, or what address she's driving to: it's the use you intend to make of the knowledge I've given you."

"What use can we make of it?" Lisa said.

"We can stop her," Gary said, his de-centered voice full of a determination Lisa wasn't sure he felt. "We can go after her and take back what she stole from me."

"Hunt down a demon—a succubus—who tore you open—who

broke your bones with her bare hands and fight her: that's your solution?" As far as options went, it was no more ridiculous than the situation it addressed, but the apparent ease with which Gary's "we" committed her to it churned the anger already threatening to overwhelm her other emotions.

"I don't know—I mean, you won all those trophies for karate."

Lisa laughed without humor. "I'm going to defeat her with my roundhouse kick." She turned to Madame Sosostris. "Could you help us?"

"I can assist you," Madame Sosostris said. "I can provide information, and a certain amount of material support, but that's all."

"Could you put us in touch with someone who could handle Sefira?"

"There's one man I'm aware of," Madame Sosostris said. "He lives over in Highland. If you choose to seek his aid, you'd be as well leaving here, dropping Gary where you found him, returning to your house, and cutting your throat."

"So we don't have any options," Lisa said.

"Any *other* options," Gary said. "We find out where her nest is, drive there, and confront her." To Madame Sosostris, he said, "Is there a way to track Sefira? Is that something you can assist us with?"

"Yes."

"If we stay here, I'm headed back to Hell," Gary said. "I have nothing to lose by trying. If you don't want to be part of this," he said to Lisa, "I get it. I fucked up; it's on me to fix this."

"You can't," Lisa said. "How far do you think you can travel in this condition? You could clean yourself up, put on some decent clothes, but all it's going to take is for one person to catch a glimpse of what's under your shirt, and things go to shit. Even if you succeed in finding her nest, how are you supposed to fight a demon in this state? I hear what you're saying about not having any other options. It's just, I don't think this is one, either."

Madame Sosostris lifted the tarot card farthest to the left and returned it to the deck face-down. "What are you saying?" Lisa asked. Although she kept her eyes on the middle two cards, which she picked up and placed on the deck, Lisa had the sense the woman was utterly focused on her. She said, "Are you sure there's no one else we can turn to?"

"If there were, I would tell you."

Lisa hesitated. "Then it has to be me, doesn't it?"

"Does it?" Madame Sosostris asked. She left the blank card on the table.

"Lise—" Gary said.

"Which fucking sucks," Lisa said. Anger—rage as hot as any fire Gary had known in Hell incinerated her horror, her wonder, the surprising amount of pity she had felt for him. "You fuck up—Jesus, 'fuck up' doesn't begin to cover it—you wreck it all, our marriage, everything we worked so hard to build—you tear it down in an instant, all so you can fuck some other woman—*who isn't even a Goddamned woman*—and I have to clean up the fucking mess. I wish I could leave, drive away and let you deal with the disaster you've made. You're going to Hell? Oh well, actions have consequences, don't they?" Hand trembling with fury, she grabbed the glass of vodka and drank it. Fresh warmth bloomed in her stomach. Rather than dulling her anger, the alcohol stoked it.

"Lise," Gary said, "honey—"

"Shut up," Lisa said. "Let's fast-forward. Say I find Sefira, kick her ass, and recover Gary's . . . organs. What's next? Can you put him back together again, or is this a case of Humpty-Dumpty?"

"I don't know," Madame Sosostris said. "In these kinds of situations, destroying the demon may lead to the undoing of any magics it's performed."

"'May?' That's the best you can do?"

"At the moment, yes. But I'll research the matter."

"While I'm on the road, what happens to you?" Lisa said to Gary.

"I'll stay at the house."

"No," Lisa said. "You do not step foot in there. Never again."

"Where am I supposed to go?"

"He can stay here," Madame Sosostris said. "This house has a furnished basement. It's comfortable."

"What happens if I fail and he goes full Walking Dead?"

"I can handle that."

"Lisa," Gary said.

"I'm doing this because I am not a fucking monster," Lisa said. Set loose by the alcohol, her anger shaped the words that came next. "And because I don't have any other options, not really. I gave them up the instant I decided I was going to take Sefira's bait and drive to the address she gave me." It was true: the same calculus that had caused her not to abandon Gary at the house on Wycombe Street bound her in its equation. "You've already been seen around town with Sefira. Most of my friends called to report the two of you together to me. I have no doubt they've discussed it with one another. Why wouldn't they? As far as gossip goes, it's pretty juicy. 'Lisa's perfect husband is fooling around on her.' Yeah, I could say you disappeared with the woman, but then I still have to wait seven years to have you declared legally dead. If I want to hurry matters along, let you turn into a zombie, do whatever's necessary to put you down, and arrange for the authorities to find the corpse, that won't be any easier. They'll assume you were murdered, which I suppose will be close enough to the truth. Who do you think is going to be the number one suspect in the investigation into the death of her cheating husband? It doesn't matter that I'm innocent. It could take years for a trial to prove that. I still lose a portion of my life—not to mention, there's the possibility I could be found guilty, and I am not taking that chance. I don't feel like sacrificing any more, thanks.

"Here's what I intend to do. I will follow Sefira to this nest, I will send her skank ass back to insect hell, and I will hope that restores you. Prior to my departure, you are going to sign a simple divorce form giving me everything. Upon my return, we will take that form to a lawyer and I will not see you again. You will leave town and you will not return. You will make no effort to contact me. If anyone asks, I'll tell them you cheated on me with a woman you met online and that was that.

"I'm not going to ask if any of this is agreeable to you, because it's agreeable to me. Do you understand?"

"Yes," Gary said.

"All right," Lisa said. "How do we find out where Sefira is headed?"

Madame Sosostris pushed the empty card before her across the tablecloth to Gary. "Turn this over," she said.

He did. Done in heavy pen strokes and watercolors, the picture on the other side was of a fifties-era motel next to a wide stream and in front of low hills. Arcing across the top of the image, large yellow letters outlined in black invited whoever regarded the picture to ENJOY BEAUTIFUL MONTANA at the HIDE-AWAY MOTEL.

"Montana," Lisa said. It was farther than she'd anticipated, but at most forty-eight to seventy-two hours with the gas pedal to the floor. As if reading her thoughts, Madame Sosostris said, "It's going to be slightly more involved than hopping on I-90 and heading west."

"Of course it fucking is," Lisa said.

"I told you Sefira is taking the long way home. It's part of the process that began when she removed Gary's heart, and will conclude once she consumes it. In some ways, the route she's driving is the most important part of the ritual. As she goes, she's marking a pattern in space and time. In order for what you're planning to have the best chance of success, you have to follow the same design. Because of your connection to Gary, you're already a part of this larger process. Tracing Sefira's path will move you closer to its center, which should help your odds."

"How am I supposed to know which way she's going?"

"You have a smartphone?"

"Yes." Lisa withdrew it from her jeans.

"Place it on the table next to Gary." Lisa did. "Put your left hand on it," Madame Sosostris said to Gary. At the touch of his flesh, the phone chimed and its screen glowed. Startled, Gary pulled his hand away. To Lisa, Madame Sosostris said, "You can take it."

The phone's Google Maps App had been activated, a course plotted north from Huguenot past Albany, into the Adirondacks, then west via a series of local roads to Watertown. "That's convenient," Lisa said. She saved the information. "How about when Gary isn't around?"

"I'll ensure you receive updated directions."

"It occurs to me I should be asking you what this is going to cost us—me," Lisa said.

"What do you think is a fair price?"

"I'm no good at bargaining. I'll give you half of whatever I get from Gary. I'm not sure exactly how much that is. If I decide to sell the house, you could do all right."

Gary opened his mouth, shut it without saying anything.

"Of course," Lisa said, "if I fail, you get nothing. Maybe you'd rather have a check up front."

"I believe I'll wait," Madame Sosostris said. "While he's here, perhaps Gary can answer some questions I have about the Broken Lands. That kind of information is difficult to come by. It can serve as a down-payment."

"I'll tell you whatever I can," Gary said.

"There's one more thing you need," Madame Sosostris said, rising from her chair. She exited the kitchen through a door that led toward the front of the house.

"You're serious about—everything you said," Gary said.

"Yeah," Lisa said, "all of it." Anger sealed the plan she hadn't been fully aware of until she was speaking it.

"I'm not sure what to say."

"Try not saying anything."

Madame Sosostris returned carrying a large knife, which she set on the table. It was a butcher knife, of the type that came as part of a set of kitchen knives. The black plastic handle had been wrapped in rubber bands. The broad blade was covered in writing, incised with words and symbols. Some of them, Lisa knew: *Yahweh, Jehovah, Dios, Dieu, Deus, Gott.* Others were in characters she recognized but could not read: Greek, Cyrillic, Arabic, Korean, Japanese, Chinese. There was one in what she was pretty sure were Norse runes, another whose letters each resembled a small square drawing, which she thought was Mayan, and several more she couldn't place. Madame Sosostris crossed her arms and said, "I told you that the pneumasphere is reactive. To a certain extent, the same thing is true of its inhabitants. They're susceptible to our beliefs, particularly those strongly held. Every name on this blade was inscribed by someone for whom it's sacred. That should make it more effective against a demon."

"Like a +3 dagger," Gary said. "In *Dungeons & Dragons.*"

Lisa picked up the knife. It was solid, heavier than she expected. "Why the rubber bands?"

"For the grip," Madame Sosostris said.

"In case it gets bloody," Gary said.

"Until you arrive at Sefira's nest, I'd recommend keeping the knife hidden," Madame Sosostris said.

"Maybe in the glove compartment," Gary said.

Lisa shook her head. "In the trunk. I'll wrap it in a towel and put in under the spare."

"Whatever you think best," Madame Sosostris said.

"I assume I'm going to do more than threaten Sefira with this."

"You have to stab her in the heart with it."

Nodding, Lisa said, "Anything else?"

"Not really," Madame Sosostris said. "You must adhere to the path she is making. I know it's tempting to head directly to her nest, lie in wait for her, and were circumstances different, that might be the only option. It's not, though, so take advantage of the chance to improve your position."

"All right," Lisa said, "I will. What if I catch her before then?"

"You won't," Madame Sosostris said. "She has a head start, and you still have to go home and pack a bag. If you could close your eyes for a couple of hours, that would be good, too."

"Suppose something happens and I do end up at the same rest stop as Sefira, though? I don't want to miss her."

Madame Sosostris frowned. "Check your phone's pictures."

At the head of her photos, there was a new image. It showed an older minivan, of the rounded design that reminded Lisa of a giant jelly-bean. The vehicle was aqua, its sides pained with huge flowers. "Huh," Lisa said. "I thought she would be driving something less . . . tacky. Shouldn't be too hard to spot." She pocketed the phone. "If you don't have any more information for me, then I'm just about ready to leave."

"I can't think of anything else. I wish I knew more."

"Lise," Gary said.

"What?"

"I'm sorry. And thank you." He smiled weakly.

"Do you have a computer?" Lisa said to Madame Sosostris, "With a printer?"

"Yes. Why?"

"Before I go, I want to print a divorce form and have the two of us sign it. If you could keep it somewhere safe until I get back, I'd be grateful."

"Of course."

Amazing, Lisa thought as she wrote *Lisa Murray* on the line designated for the plaintiff, how so simple an act as signing your name could have such momentous consequences. All of the planning that had gone into their wedding, the dramas large and small they'd been through in the years since, from buying their house to Gary stepping on a rusty nail and requiring a tetanus shot last summer, from taking ballroom dancing lessons at the dance studio in Wiltwyck to binge-watching all the *Harry Potter* movies one long weekend—all undone in the length of time it took for the pen Madame Sosostris had given her to finish its course across the paper. It seemed as remarkable as anything else she had been part of the past few hours. She half-expected Gary to refuse to add his name to the document, to plead with her to forgive him, grant him a second chance, but he took the pen from her and signed the form without comment. She wanted to say something, to deliver a remark fitting to the sudden and disastrous end of their marriage, but could think of none. Sadness bitter as lemon rind mixed with her anger, soured it, and she left soon thereafter.

IX

And here she was, eight days and thirty-three hundred miles later, in the parking lot of a motel in Montana, watching first one man, then another, and then a third emerge through the door to the Hide-Away's office. Each was enveloped in the same cloud of shining darkness Lisa had glimpsed around her last two attackers, now clearly visible. The first man was shirtless, his gut an empty cavity, dried and darkened blood in patches and streaks on his tan slacks and spotted on his brown loafers. Although his eyes were unfocused, his skin gray, he moved toward Lisa with the confident stride of a veteran salesman approaching a new customer. The man behind him appeared younger, his long hair floating around his head, the tatters of his black Slayer concert t-shirt embedded in the hole punched in the center of his chest. He held a long-handled ax in both hands, advancing with it held high and to the left, the position of a batter waiting for a pitch. From the look of him, the third man had been dead a long time. His skin had withered, shrunk to his bones; his eyes were sunken, his lips drawn back from his yellowed teeth. His left arm appeared to have been tied to his shoulder with several loops of rusted barbed wire. Except for a

belt hanging from his desiccated hips, he was naked, the space between
his legs a ragged wound. He staggered more than walked, as if his
joints had lost the trick of moving.

Here was Gary's fate, should she fail, illustrated. Horror churned
her stomach, brought her Big Mac and fries to the top of her throat.
Fighting the urge to run, to leap into her car and burn rubber out of
there, she swallowed, inhaled deeply. The first man was circling to her
left, the second to the right. The third was trailing behind the first.
Their feet scraped on the pavement. She should have asked Madame
Sosostris what the precise method was for dealing with the husk of
one of Sefira's victims. Was it a case of destroying the brain? Wasn't
that zombie-killing 101? Were these men covered by those rules? The
question was academic: she wasn't in possession of a handgun, and she
didn't like her chances of driving the butcher knife through each of
their skulls. She slipped the weapon into the back of her jeans as the
first man reached her, his hands out in a flurry of sloppy punches.

She ducked them easily. She could hear the shadow wrapping him,
a metallic, shimmering sound like the song of a cicada, which she had
the sense was being produced by the points of brightness floating
within the darkness. *Swarm*, she thought, but had no idea what the
word signified.

There was no time to dwell on it. From the corner of her eye, she
saw the second man almost to her, the blade of his ax shining in the
afternoon sun. She stepped in close to the first man and hammer-
fisted his right collar bone twice. The second strike broke bone with a
sharp crack, and the man's right arm dropped to his side. His left fist
grazed the side of her head. Before he could swing it back towards her,
she moved with unexpected speed, catching his arm at the wrist and
elbow and twisting to her left. As far as take-downs went, it wasn't the
most graceful, but it did the trick. The man lost his balance and toppled, his skull rebounding from the pavement with a *crack*. She pivoted
into a retreat from the second man, who had broken into a slow run
that culminated in a clumsy swing of the ax, which missed Lisa and
struck the driver's window of the Accord, caving it in. *My car!* While he
was attempting to withdraw the ax from the car, she lunged forward
and grabbed the handle with both hands. The same clashing song surrounded him. The man tried to yank the weapon from her grip; rather

than fighting it, she went with his pull, unbalancing him into the Honda. He thudded against it, the impact loosening his grasp on the ax. She tore it from his fingers and snapped the end of the handle into the side of his face, crushing his cheek.

A hand seized her ankle: the first man, who had turned onto his ruined abdomen to grab at her. She swept the blade of the ax down and struck his forearm. The edge took a generous bite of the limb, the handle shuddering as it met bone. Lisa tugged her foot free of the man's hold, but the ax proved more difficult to remove. It had lodged in his arm, and as she attempted to work it loose, the second man caught her in a tackle, wrenching her hands from the handle and carrying her to the ground.

She landed on her side, and though she kept her head from striking the pavement, the impact knocked the wind from her. The second man was clambering on top of her, his cold hands clutching at her throat. She drove her elbow into his damaged face one, two, three times, then lifted her hips, dumping him off her. Although his features were a jumble worthy of Picasso, he continued to reach for her. She scrambled away and to her feet.

A glance in his direction showed the third man maintaining his slow advance, but still a safe distance from her. The second man was pushing himself up on his hands and knees. Using his one functioning arm, the first man struggled to do the same thing, but his injured forearm would not support his weight and the bones snapped, spilling him onto his face. Freed of its bony trap, the ax clattered on the ground. Lisa ran at the second man and kicked his head as hard as she could, as if it were a soccer ball and she intent on sending it to the opposite end of the field. With a crunch she felt through her sneaker, the man's head leapt up and back on his neck, farther than anatomy intended. Lisa went around him to where the first man, still struggling to his feet, had dragged himself backward onto his knees. She leaned down, grabbed the ax, and swung it, smashing the blunt side of the head into his skull, the force of the blow knocking him over.

Turning, she saw the second man, his head hanging at an angle which would not have been survivable had he been alive, renew his effort to stand. She looked at the first man. Despite the considerable depression in his head, he had not stopped moving, either. *So much for zombie-killing 101*, she thought. The third man's shuffles had brought him almost to her. He grasped his left wrist with his right hand and pulled, tearing the arm and its barbed-wire ligament from his shoulder. Swaying as he approached, he brandished the limb at her, a grotesque parody of an old man shaking his cane at the kids on his lawn.

"Oh come on," Lisa said.

The third man whipped his arm like a flail. A step back took her out of its range. Darting in and to the right, she struck his left hip with the ax. The joint splintered, the leg tilting into the pelvis, and with a lurch, the third man fell, still waving his arm as he went. Behind her, she heard sneakers scrape the pavement. His head lolling, the second man had risen to his feet. She smashed his left knee with the blunt side of the ax head, returning him to the ground. She might not be able to kill these men outright, but she could render them incapable of endangering her. She walked to where the first man lay writhing like an enormous grub and hammered his left leg with the ax until the knee popped. Leaving her opponents twisting on the parking lot, she headed for the door to the motel's office, ax in hand.

Her heart was pounding, adrenaline racing through her in a flaming rush. Looming behind the motel, the lopsided hill appeared more distinct, its bare surface the texture of dried mud, perforated at random intervals by oblong holes. This was her destination, she assumed. The question was, how was she supposed to access it?

The interior of the Hide-Away's office was dim, the ceiling low, the air still swirling with the dust stirred by the three men exiting. From the look of things, the trio had been here for some time, two of them seated in the wooden chairs backed to the front window, the other leaning with his back to them on the counter which bisected the room. To the right on the countertop, a green ceramic flowerpot held the remains of a plant dried to an anonymous stalk. On the wall opposite her, next to an open doorway, the hands of a lacquered wooden clock in the shape of Montana held at two forty-three. A saloon-style door hanging on the counter's left, whose hinges screamed their protest at being used, admitted passage behind the barrier, where faded pamphlets advertising the wonders of Montana lay sprayed across the floor. Ready for a fourth assailant concealed next to the doorway, Lisa ducked her head into the room beyond.

It was empty. She entered what must have been the living quarters for whoever was working the counter. A single bed whose sheetless mattress bore a large, dark stain had been pushed against the wall to the right. At the foot of the bed, an end table supported a modest TV whose glass eye was fuzzed with dust. An open, empty mini-fridge held a hotplate and a coffee maker with a cracked carafe. Facing the fridge was a low bookcase stacked with Reader's Digest volumes. To her left, a door set in the wall stood ajar. Lisa walked to it, peered through the gap, and saw a motel room. She nudged the door wider with her foot. The doorway connected the front office to the adjacent motel room, as the door open across that space led to the room beyond, and the door she could see in its far wall linked to the third room, and so on, all the way to the last room, transforming the Hide-Away into a single space with a dozen chambers. With a look back to check that no one was approaching behind her, she crossed the threshold.

The first room's heavy yellow curtains were drawn, glowing gold with the afternoon sun, as were the curtains in each room she walked into. The rooms were arranged in the same fashion, a pair of double beds or a single queen-size positioned parallel to the front door, a dresser mounted with a big TV across from them, the bathroom door, the walls, carpet, and bedspreads in earth tones. Every last bed was unmade, the rumpled sheets strewn with articles of clothing: blouses, men's dress shirts, t-shirts that might have been worn by anyone; skirts long and short, slacks, trousers, jeans; formal dresses and three piece suits; panties and bras plain and fancy; boxers and briefs; stockings, knee-highs, dress and athletic socks. The floors around the beds were littered with footwear, high heels, flats, sandals, men's dress shoes, loafers, boots, sneakers. The styles were those of the last several decades, wide collars and bell bottoms tangled with shoulder pads and skinny jeans, ankle-length skirts wrapped around parachute pants. It was as if she were watching whoever had worn the clothes engaged in activities erotic and obscene, as if the motel had been the site of a decades-long orgy, a carnival of the flesh presided over by Sefira. At the bottom limit of her hearing, Lisa fancied she could hear the mingled gasps and groans, the cries and calls, of the people who had embraced on top of their discarded clothing. The ghosts of perfumes and colognes, Chanel No. 5, Shalimar, Opium, and Axe body spray mixed with stale sweat and another, spoiled meat odor, which made her nose wrinkle and which grew stronger as she advanced through the motel. By the time she reached the fifth room, her eyes were watering. In the sixth room, Lisa had to breathe through her mouth, and that was barely enough to keep her from retching at the smell of decay clouding the air. As with the house on Wycombe, so strong was the stench that she was certain she should have been seeing the sheets and clothes stiff with blood, the beds and carpets spread with rotting viscera. Even with the extra dimension open to her sight, though, there was nothing visible beyond what lay in front of her. Her pulse had subsided from the height to which it had climbed during her confrontation in the Hide-Away's parking lot, the aggression that had powered her replaced by unease bordering on dread.

Beside the bathroom door in the sixth room, a jagged hole had been torn in the wall, as if someone had taken a sledgehammer to it. Tall and wide enough to allow a big man entry, it opened into a dim space, like a cave. Shifting the ax in her hands, Lisa approached the improvised doorway. Its dimensions not much larger than the entrance to it, the chamber extended back toward the lopsided hill (*Sefira's nest*) an indefinite distance, its shadowy length lit by the naked bulbs of electric lamps hung on its sides every fifteen to twenty feet. Careful to avoid the edges of the hole, some of which appeared sharp enough to draw blood, she stepped out of the motel room and into the passageway. While its floor was smooth underfoot—earth trod flat—its walls were a collage of wooden boards, tree limbs, and sundry other objects: a wooden sign from which the paint had worn off, a piece of a door, a shutter, nailed and plastered together. At least the spoiled meat smell was not as bad, here.

As she proceeded, though, she was aware of faint sounds audible through the walls, a steady rustling, as if the layered wreckage were crawling with insects, home to a vast colony of termites or wasps, audience to the last stage of her quest.

Ahead, the passage widened, the floor cut by long, deep trenches to either side. Each channel was heaped with debris, rounded objects the size of her hand whose surfaces shone black and green. Too flat to be spheres, they were decorated on one side by raised lines, on the other by elaborate designs which suggested faces caught in extremes of pain—or pleasure, she supposed. As she passed between them, the things shifted, as if something underneath them was moving, roused by her presence. They rang against one another, filling the passage with a tinny, off-key chorus, which gained in volume as Lisa hastened to the other side of the trenches. Once past them, she turned, watching their contents wobble and rock. Each channel, she assumed, held another of Sefira's husks, concealed under the saucer-sized objects. The question was, did she wait until they emerged from their hiding places and deal with them, or did she run, hope she could leave them behind? Phrased this way, it wasn't difficult to answer. Better not to have anything sneaking up on her.

One of the rounded things rolled onto the passage floor. Two from the opposite trench joined it, then another handful from both sides. Where they came to a halt, the black and green objects see-sawed, their motion increasing rather than diminishing. The raised lines curled against their undersides lifted, spread, and Lisa saw that they were legs, eight segmented limbs, and a single sharp proboscis. Those of the things on their backs flipped onto their bellies and began crawling across the dirt. Lisa was reminded of ticks, grown obscenely large. The faces inscribed on them shifted, their features twisting from agony to agony. She retreated a step, the hairs on the back of her neck, her arms, raising. Legs chiming, a tick crept toward her. Pulse pounding at the base of her throat, she continued backing up the tunnel.

When the first tick drew too close, she struck it with the ax. The blow cut the creature in half, its body crumpling as if made of foil. Greenish gas vented from the wound, along with a woman's scream—which, Lisa understood, was the same as the swirling cloud (though how she knew, she couldn't say). There was no time to dwell on the matter; the remaining ticks were hastening toward her. She split the next, heel-stomped the third, releasing more of the green shrieking. Ticks scurried around her. She chopped at another, severing one set of limbs. Something tickled her left ankle: a tick raised on its back legs, attempting to scale her jeans. She kicked and flung it into the wall, where it was speared by a wood splinter. Two more ticks grabbed at her right leg. She swept them onto their backs with the ax, then burst them under her sneaker. Screaming clouded the air, vibrated the passage. Lisa hacked at a tick, missed. A tick lunged at her, driving its proboscis through her jeans, into her left calf. Pain flared in her leg, the white hot intensity of it dropping her to her knees. She smashed the tick with the ax handle, its snout pulling loose as its body caved in. Taking advantage of her lowered position, one of the surviving ticks stabbed her right thigh. Lisa shouted, her voice lost in the shrieking green. She released the ax, hammering the tick with her fist, the blow tearing it from her leg and crushing it. Green vapor writhed around her knuckles. There was one tick left. It went to spear her hand, but foundered on the remains of a comrade. Lisa drew her arm away, caught hold of the ax, and added its screams to the rest. The wounds in her legs burning, she stood, prepared for the ticks still shifting in the trenches to come streaming out at her.

For the moment, however, none did. Despite the blood dampening her jeans, a thrill of triumph swept her as she surveyed the broken and crushed forms of her attackers. She was tempted to carry the fight to the rest of the ticks, to leap in amongst their surprisingly fragile bodies and trample them. Instead, she resumed her trek along the passageway, albeit with frequent glances over her shoulders. Were it not for the shrieking, which had yet to subside, and which would conceal the ring of their approach, she would not have been concerned. The ticks were ineffectual as guards. She had been in more jeopardy from the trio of husks in the parking lot.

Around her, the tunnel went from wood patched with plaster to plaster smeared and layered on bare rock. Cemented into the walls in a seemingly random arrangement, human skulls with varying degrees of flesh and hair hanging from them stared open-jawed at her. In the jaundiced glow of the lamp hung amidst them, the skulls appeared to shift expressions as Lisa walked past them, shock and horror bleeding into outrage and anger, which in turn slid toward malevolent humor. The continuing screams, she could almost fancy, were pouring out of their bony mouths. Although the blood seemed to be flowing more slowly from her calf and thigh, the injuries throbbed, keeping weird time with the shrieking, in whose hoarse depths she thought she could discern a rhythm, an ebb and flow of agony. She was suddenly warmer than she had ever been before, sweat rushing from her pores, saturating her shirt and jeans. As quickly, she was freezing, shivering with such ferocity, she dropped the ax, stumbling on and half-tripping over it. *The ticks*, she thought. *Infection.*

The screaming was louder, or her ears more sensitive, or both. Easier to hear, the rhythm wrapped in it approached familiarity, sense, until she recognized in its rises and falls words, sentences, rendered nigh-indecipherable by being shrieked. Having realized this, she further understood that she was hearing sentences on top of sentences, sentences layered on and braided around one another, six, eight, ten of them. As many as there had been ticks—which weren't ticks at all, but soul cages. Two of the tortured chains of words were almost decipherable; if she concentrated, she could just about make them out—

—she lay naked and spread-eagled on a queen-size bed in one of the Hide-Away's rooms, unable to move beyond the trembling that shook her as a grotesquely thin woman straddled her, drawing bloody loops of intestine out of the gaping wound below Lisa's navel and heaping them on the mattress. In the background, the room's TV was on and the theme from Hogan's Heroes *was playing—*

—she lay naked on the carpet at the foot of a double bed in another of the hotel's rooms, paralyzed, her arms at her sides, her legs together, while the same rail-thin woman knelt at her side, her hair tickling Lisa's chin and shoulders as she bent her head to Lisa's neck, which she was chewing through. Lisa could hear the breath whistling out of the hole the woman had bitten in her windpipe, could feel blood trickling into her lungs, filling them, suffocating her. In the distance, a motorcycle rumbled past the motel—

—she lay dead on the bed—

—she lay dead on the carpet—

—her heart had tightened, knotted, stopped—

—but she was still aware, still in pain, her nerves a net of fire, binding her consciousness to her—

—the agony threaded with other emotions, regret deep enough that all the tears in the world would never fill it, fear so profound it was worse than the pain, it made her want to hide the way she had hidden from the dark as a child—

—she was running down a rocky hillside, its surface slicing the soles of her feet, the sky low black clouds reflecting an orange glow. She was trying not to lose her balance, not to fall, because they were right behind her, they were so close—

—she was screaming, pleading for mercy, as several sets of thin arms pushed her head-first into a narrow tube in a rock wall, within which a blindingly white flame roared—

—her blood boiled—her brains steamed in her skull—

—she was inside an impossibly small space, bound within a prison whose surface admitted no communication with any of the others she could see in similar chambers, confined with the hurt whose memory was identical with its occasion, with the remorse and dread and rage that amplified her suffering, a black cocktail which might be less bitter if she could share its taste with someone else, could force it into them—

Lisa vomited, doubling over, her stomach's convulsion squeezing a flood of tears from her eyes. Directly in front of her, a little more than an arm's length distant, a figure halted its approach toward her. Vision wavering with her tears, Lisa had the impression of a person horribly thin, wearing a tall hat or a crown, their arms hung with bracelets studded with spikes and blades. Wiping her eyes, Lisa retreated. Arms out to either side, long fingers spread, the figure advanced. Lisa spat. Already, she had identified the spindled form as the one she had seen in the memories the soul cages had driven into her, which meant that this was Sefira, she had finally found her.

She was horrifying. Beyond skeletal, she moved with the strange, mechanical grace of an insect, a mantis grown hideously large. (Which one of her friends had called Sefira a stick insect? Whoever it was, the description was truer than they had known.) Fungous-white, Sefira's flesh was embedded with a mosaic of what appeared to be cracked and broken glass, which winked and flashed in the corridor's light, as if she had been coated in the stuff and then it had shattered. Her skull rose in a corona of glass and bone. Her face was an approximation of the human, the dark eyes large, the nose a pair of slots, the mouth lined with bone and glass needles. Sefira's eyes glittered, and Lisa saw that they were dusted with particles of glass. Malice animated her features, the expression of a predator stalking prey whose death would satisfy urges beyond hunger. She brought her hands up in a guard, displaying the glass shards protruding from her forearms, making of each a serrated blade.

Fear purer than any she'd known during the last eight days (which was to say, ever) carried Lisa backwards, out of range of those glass weapons. For an instant, the impulse to run, to flee out of the tunnel, out of the motel, to climb into her car with its broken window and drive as far away from all this as fast as she could almost overcame her. Her assurances to Madame Sosostris (and Gary), her angry vow to herself, echoed hollowly in her memory. The green shrieking had subsided, but that allowed her to hear the fragments of glass embedded in Sefira dragging against one another as she advanced, surrounding her in a screeching fugue. Had her stomach not emptied itself already, the terror Lisa felt would have precipitated that event now. Could she outrun Sefira? She couldn't say, but she found the prospect of showing her back to this monster absolutely unappealing. Incredible as it seemed, the only reasonable course of action appeared to be confrontation. Lisa reached behind her back with her right hand and slipped the butcher knife from the waistband of her jeans.

The weapon's effect on Sefira was immediate. Eyes wide, she halted where she was. The knife's appearance startled Lisa, as well. The names and symbols scratched on its blade were shining, glowing with white light, weird constellations in a metal sky. The glow reflected off Sefira's glass armor, making of its shards a kaleidoscope. Her fear tempered if not extinguished, Lisa held the knife ready to stab straight out, her left hand in front to deflect whatever attack Sefira might attempt. (Though she didn't like her fingers' odds against the shards jutting from Sefira's flesh.) Lisa spat again. Voice wavering, she said, "Can we talk?"

No answer. All of Sefira's attention appeared focused on the butcher knife.

"I'm here for what you took from Gary," Lisa said. "I followed your trail. I dealt with the people you left for me—your traps. I handled the men from the front office. I came through the ticks—the soul cages. I'm prepared for you if I have to be. I don't know if I can kill you, but I'm pretty sure I can hurt you; pretty badly, I think. I'm wondering if there's a way it doesn't have to come to that, if you can give me what I want, I can leave, and that's it."

The skin around Sefira's mouth shifted, puffing into a pair of lips, while the needles in her gums retracted, leaving a set of squared teeth in their wake. When she spoke, it was in the same honeyed tones Lisa had heard in her car, on her phone. "Come to make a deal with the Devil?" she said.

"You're hardly the Devil," Lisa said.

"I'm as close as you're going to get."

"That may be. You're half right: I'm here to deal."

"Is that what you call it?" Sefira said. "I give you what is rightfully mine, and you give me . . . what was that? Oh yes, nothing."

"You weren't listening to me. You return Gary's heart to me, and in return, I don't kill you."

"Try to kill me," Sefira said, "which is hardly much to bargain with."

"All right then," Lisa said, "what do you want?"

"I have what I want," Sefira said. "You seem to believe you can threaten me with pain—that pain is something I'm afraid of. It's almost charming. Where I'm from, pain is a fact of life. It's like sunlight or air for you, part of the surroundings, taken for granted. And it's been that way for—as long as I can remember. I know there was a before-time, but honestly, it was so long ago, it might as well never have been. What I'm trying to say is, you're going to have to do better than that."

"I intend to," Lisa said, and lunged with the knife.

She was hoping to catch Sefira by surprise, plant the blade in her chest before she knew what was happening. Fast as she was, though (and she was fast, faster than she ever had been), Sefira still succeeded in moving her right arm to deflect the attack; although the edge of the blade found the space between two of the glass shards jutting from her skin and cut a deep slice there. Thank God for the rubber bands wound around the knife handle, which allowed her to maintain her grip on the weapon as Sefira jerked her arm away, hissing.

"I'm sure you didn't feel that," Lisa said, resuming her guard position.

"Bitch," Sefira said. She pressed her arm to her chest. Clear fluid oozed from the wound.

"I'm trying."

Sefira snapped a back-fist with her left arm, but Lisa anticipated the blow and swayed out of its reach. She was less prepared for the right kick Sefira followed with, a roundhouse that fell short of its target, the nerve cluster in Lisa's left thigh, but still dragged the glass razors capping her toes across Lisa's leg, ripping her jeans and the skin beneath. With a, "Fuck!" Lisa shuffled back, her heel striking the handle of the fire ax where she had dropped it. Eyes on Sefira, she knelt, feeling for the ax with her lead hand. Her fingers closed on the haft as Sefira leapt at her. She flung the ax across the floor, putting what spin on it she could. Sefira attempted to hop over it, but she mistimed the jump and landed with her left foot on the handle, throwing her into a stumble that she barely arrested in time to keep herself from running onto the out-held knife. While Sefira was off balance, Lisa attacked, stabbing and slashing, pressing her advantage. Sefira met her blows with her good arm and then her injured arm, metal and glass ringing against one another. Lisa drew blood a couple more times. Neither wound was as deep as her initial strike, though Sefira exhaled sharply at each. She aimed a sweep at Lisa's left leg, but with a speed of which she would not have believed herself capable, Lisa pulled her leg out of reach while reversing the knife, which she drove into Sefira's thigh with such force it pierced through to the other side. Shrieking, Sefira pulled back. This time, the rubber bands wrapping the knife handle were not sufficient to allow Lisa to maintain her grip on it. Eyes full of shock and panic, Sefira staggered and went down on the knee of her injured leg, grabbing the knife's hilt and attempting to work the blade free. Lisa moved toward her.

During her karate classes, the portion Lisa had found most challenging was free sparring. Not because she was too timid: in fact, just the opposite. She had been an enthusiastic combatant, her punches and kicks fueled by the anger toward her opponent she summoned as soon as she crossed the sparring ring's blue tape boundary. At the tournaments at which she had competed as a white and yellow belt, her forcefulness had led to a string of victories. Once she was promoted to her green belt, however, and began facing more experienced fighters both at her dojo and at those same competitions she formerly had dominated, the effectiveness of her strategy decreased, as her opponents were less likely to be overwhelmed by her onslaught, and more likely to find and exploit the openings it provided them. Discouraged, she skipped one tournament, which became two, which became the entire fall season. To the instructors at her school who asked if anything was wrong, she claimed a desire to focus on other aspects of her training, her hand techniques, forms, and self-defense combinations, which she did, but with a falling off in the enthusiasm she had previously brought to them.

Finally, after a sparring class at which she lost every match, including one against a beginning student she should have defeated easily, a senior student, a brown belt named Jess, had taken her out to Pete's

Corner Pub for a postmortem of her performance. Her assessment of Lisa's losses was simple: "Your problem is, you're fighting angry." "Isn't that how you're supposed to fight?" Lisa said. Jess shook her head, sipped her hard cider. "You're confusing anger and aggression," she said, "which is normal. Most people think that if you're going to fight, even if it's free sparring, you need to get mad. That's because for normal people, it's actually kind of hard to engage another person physically. They have to work themselves up to it. The problem is, anger's unreliable. It makes you frontload your attacks, so by the end of the fight, you're gassed out. It makes you sloppy, reckless, gives your opponents all kinds of opportunities they never should have had. Sound familiar?" Lisa nodded, color rising in her cheeks. "If you want to continue sparring," Jess said, "you have to transition from anger to aggression. Aggression is forceful, but it's calmer. It's smarter. It combines technique and training. Your emotions may still run high, but you channel them into helping you fight a better fight." Jess drank more of her cider. "If you work on developing your aggression, you could kick my ass, easy." While perhaps overselling the approach, the certainty with which Jess had delivered this prediction had encouraged Lisa to resume sparring. It was a cliché out of every sports movie she had ever watched, the seasoned veteran giving the promising but frustrated rookie the advice that would allow them to advance to the next level of performance, but Jess's reframing of how to approach fighting worked for Lisa, and while Jess had left the karate school shortly thereafter—headed to Alaska for reasons of which Lisa hadn't been clear—Lisa suspected that, had her senior stuck around, her prediction might have come true.

Now that the contest with Sefira was well and truly under way, this was the mode into which Lisa had entered, funneling her dread and horror into watching Sefira's every motion, looking for the hint of her next attack. She was angry, too, the accumulated shocks and travails of the last eight days having heaped fuel on an emotion hot enough to liquefy steel, a fury venting from deep within her bones. She could feel the sulfurous cloud she had drawn within herself outside Denver, when her teeth had changed, and which had threatened to erupt from her during her most recent conversation with Gary, loose in her blood, rolling through her, its tumult making her move faster, strike harder.

Somewhere in the depths of her mind, a voice murmured something about consequences, but she ignored it.

Clenching teeth returned to fangs, Sefira drew the butcher knife from her leg, clear fluid spilling from the wound to spatter on the floor. With the weapon in her left hand, she pushed to her feet. Lisa circled to Sefira's right, considering a grab for the ax lying behind her. Sefira anticipated her plan and shoved the ax away with her injured leg, grimacing at the effort. Keeping her distance, Lisa continued to circle, arms up and in close. Sefira feinted with her right arm, stabbed with her left, but Lisa shuffled out of range. Sefira retreated, moving, Lisa realized, toward the motel and the prospect of escape. Attempting to bait her into continuing the fight, Lisa moved closer than she would have liked, in danger of the knife's blade, its characters still glowing through the transparent film of Sefira's blood. Sefira slashed at her; Lisa twisted out of the way and aimed a hammer-fist at her hand that would have taken the knife out of it had she connected. Sefira swept the blade back in the opposite direction, dragging its tip across the top of Lisa's forearm. Lisa threw a roundhouse kick at Sefira's right knee, but she missed, and Sefira came close to repeating her move and stabbing the knife through Lisa's thigh.

To either side of them, the soul cages trembled in their gutters, filling the passageway with their metal shivering. Sefira snapped a front kick at Lisa that she blocked by turning to her right and lifting her leg, which put her in a position to throw a side kick into Sefira's midsection, the force of which staggered Sefira backward. Her wounded leg gave out, and she tripped into the trench full of soul cages behind her. The force of her fall crushed a host of the objects, releasing their mingled screams in a heavy green fog. Sefira struggled to right herself, but the remaining soul cages took advantage of her proximity to unfold their legs and proboscises and grasp at her limbs. She swatted away some, but there were too many for her to deal with them all, and they stabbed her arms and legs, her sides and her neck. Shouting with rage, Sefira climbed out of the channel, hung with the soul cages. She sliced them from her with the butcher knife, tore them loose with her other hand, green shrieking swirling about her.

Lisa positioned herself between Sefira and the route to the motel. Clear blood leaking from a score of punctures, Sefira snarled, brandishing the knife. Lisa readied for her attack, but before Sefira could strike, she convulsed, her back arching, her arms flailing, as the pain the soul cages had injected slammed into her. Even with the screams dyeing the air, Sefira's were audible. Based on her experience with only two sets of memories, Lisa would have estimated ten times that amount fatal, or, at the very least, incapacitating. Although she swayed drunkenly, however, Sefira kept both her footing and her hold on the butcher knife, swinging the weapon from side to side. She shook her head, trying to dislodge the memories cramming her mind. Lisa didn't think Sefira was seeing her, but wasn't sure enough to draw any nearer. Instead, she followed Sefira as she limped out of the screaming cloud along the passageway, brandishing the knife. Accompanied by the soul cages' shrieks, they moved past the skulls cemented to the walls, Lisa stooping to retrieve the ax, through a stretch of tunnel whose white plaster was covered in streaks of charcoal, arcs and spirals and twists that almost appeared to be writing, characters in an alphabet strangely familiar. A few of the swirls seemed to cohere into words she could read: "altar," "cell," and "meat."

Ahead, the passage opened into a larger space, a cave the size of a small house. Its walls were hung with a tapestry of drapes, some bright and new, others faded and worn. As Lisa entered it, the chorus of screaming diminished almost to nothing, as if she had traveled a great distance from it. Sefira made a beeline towards a trio of long metal tables positioned at the chamber's center, a phalanx of floor lamps, their electric cords cemented into the floor, glowing around them. Atop one of the tables sat a large red cooler, its white lid open, Sefira's goal. The sight of the plain plastic container was somehow as shocking as anything Lisa had encountered, its pebbled surface a reminder of the violence that had set her on this course, brought her to this destination. She ran at Sefira, holding the ax out in both hands crosswise. Already facing the tables, Sefira couldn't turn in time to meet Lisa's charge. The ax handle pinned her right arm against her body as Lisa's momentum pushed her into the rows of lamps, tipping them into one another and over like so many skinny, clanging dominoes, their bulbs popping against the floor, their shades rolling loose. Astonishingly, Sefira did not release the knife, even as the lamps fell on and across her, forming a makeshift cage. Stepping back, Lisa shifted her grip on the ax, raised it, and swung it at Sefira's head. With her free hand, Sefira grabbed a lamp and levered it in front of her, deflecting the ax head in a shower of sparks. She whipped the lamp at Lisa, its shade crumpling, its bulb smashing against the side of her head with sufficient force to make her vision flare white, cause her to stumble. Lamps clashing off one another, Sefira pushed free of them. Lisa went to raise the ax, but Sefira seized the handle, pulling it out of Lisa's hands and casting it away. In one fluid motion, she stepped forward and caught Lisa in a headlock, hugging her face against the jagged arch of her side. The headlock wasn't perfect—Lisa was able to wedge her chin and mouth under Sefira's forearm—but she was still reeling from the blow Sefira had dealt her, and it was sufficient to hold her.

"I'm going to tell you something," Sefira said. She aimed the tip of the butcher knife at Lisa's left eye. "You lost."

Lisa opened her mouth as wide as she could and bit into Sefira's arm, her razored teeth slicing into glass-studded flesh. Blood the taste of burnt metal flooded her mouth. Sefira screamed, her hold slacking. Teeth sunk in stringy muscle, Lisa caught Sefira's left hand in both of hers and broke the wrist. The knife dropped. At the same time, Lisa tugged her head back, tearing away a ragged mouthful of Sefira's forearm. Sefira shouted, releasing Lisa and shoving her away. Lisa spat the chunk of bitter meat onto the floor and picked up the knife. Cradling her right arm, an expression on her face that might have been incredulity, Sefira watched as Lisa closed the distance separating them.

"But you lost," she said, in the instant before Lisa drove the knife through the glass shards layering her chest and into her heart. Blood fountained out of the wound. Sefira started to raise her left hand toward her chest, as it to verify the blade piercing it. Through the handle, Lisa felt the organ shudder to a halt. Sefira's arm went limp. As the realization of what had just happened overtook her, Sefira's features tightened with fear, as if she could see the hell she had fled so long coalescing in the surrounding shadows. Then her eyes lost focus and she collapsed, her glass armor tinkling. Lisa left the knife in her.

For a moment, there was something standing where Sefira had been, a collection of smoky lines like a sketch of her. The figure drew in on itself, as if it was being drawn through a seam in the air, and was gone. The curtains hanging on the walls shifted. Sefira's corpse rustled;

Lisa watched it shrivel, the flesh drying to dust, the glass fragments clouding and cracking. In a matter of seconds, all that remained of her was a heap of dust and broken glass surrounding the butcher knife, all in the midst of a pool of viscous, colorless blood, which was beginning to soak into the floor.

A profound exhaustion descended on Lisa, the prolonged adrenaline high that had carried her through the fight with Sefira deflating, leaving her dizzy and weak. The punctures in her calf and thigh, the slices to her leg, the trailing cut to her arm burned. The copper flavor of her own blood mixed with the acrid residue of Sefira's. She hawked, spat, wiped her chin with the back of her hand. Her lips trembled. Unconsciousness threatened to take her whole, and it was all she could do not to succumb to it. She closed her eyes, concentrated on slowing her heart's thunderous gallop to a canter, then a trot, then a pace approaching a walk.

When she opened her eyes, she saw the cooler waiting for her, the object of her nightmarish quest. Knees unsteady, she picked her way through the ranks of lamps to the metal table on which it rested. Obscured by the container's red bulk, the table was spread with what appeared to be a dozen pieces of rock candy, their fragmented surfaces the color of honey. Below the amber clusters, Gary floated within the table's polished surface, naked, his chest open, his face blank. Lisa looked inside the cooler. It was empty. Dread tightening her throat, she lifted one of the lumps of candy and saw encased in it a curl of meat. She checked another, a third, all of them, but the results were the same. The conclusion was inescapable: here were Gary's heart, the other pieces of him Sefira had extracted, prepared and ready for consumption.

Sefira was right: she had lost.

X

While Lisa was concealing the butcher knife under the spare, Madame Sosostris came hurrying out of the purple house after her. "What is it?" Lisa said, lowering the trunk.

"Listen," Madame Sosostris said, "there's something you should know. When I did the drawing, the blank card . . ."

"You mean the white one? What about it? What does it mean?"

"That's just it: it doesn't mean anything. Or it means everything. I know, I'm not making any sense. I'm sorry. Let me try again. The cards I drew for you function not only on their own, but in relation to one another. Think of it as the way the words in a sentence can affect one another's meaning, and you'll have the basic idea. The blank card destabilizes the reading the other cards construct, usually because there's some element at play the deck can't accommodate."

"Are you saying the information you gave me is wrong?"

"No." Madame Sosostris shook her head. "It's more a case of, it's incomplete, which, given the gravity of the circumstances, can't be a good thing."

"Is there anything we can do about it?"

"Not that I know of. But the last person I drew a white card for was Aubrey Byrne."

"Your friend," Lisa said, "the one Gary met in Hell."

"Him."

Lisa shut the trunk. "Thank you for telling me this," she said, "but I better get going."

Overhead, a meteor streaked to its fiery end. What kind of omen it was, if any, Lisa could not guess, nor did she ask Madame Sosostris. For her part, the medium said nothing.

XI

Hands pressed flat on the metal table, Lisa regarded the candied slices of Gary's organs. Beneath them, Gary lay inside the reflection, unmoving. Lisa still could not bear to look at the open cavern of his chest, which, considering all she had seen, was odd, but there you had it. The nerves in her legs, her arm, were aflame, a foul taste on her tongue. She stared at what had been Gary's heart, now an assortment of blocky shapes. A vast, nameless emotion, something like grief, surrounded her.

Had Madame Sosostris known—had she foreseen this would be the endpoint of Lisa's journey? How was that possible? She had said that killing Sefira would undo any magic she'd performed, hadn't she? Yes, although Lisa hadn't asked her to clarify the statement, to describe exactly what would happen; instead, she had imagined that once Sefira was no more, Gary would be magically restored to wholeness, the same way, in vampire movies, the destruction of the principle vampire cured everyone in the process of becoming a vampire. (And as her eyes and teeth had steadily changed, she had added her own condition to the list of things Sefira's death would reverse—yet she was as yet untransformed.) *Different monster, different rules* (apparently). Was that the significance of Madame Sosostris's last, cryptic warning, an attempt to prepare her for this moment? If that was the case, if she had known this was coming, then why send Lisa on the road? Why subject her to the last eight days?

She reached for the nearest chunk of candy, picked it up. Its rough surface was warm, as if it had been produced only a short time ago. She raised it to her nose. The smell was incredible, overpowering, a sweet, creamy odor that caused her mouth to fill with saliva, roused her stomach, still aching, to hunger. She quickly replaced the block on the table. As she did, Gary's image flinched. "Hello?" she said. "Gary? Can you hear me?"

He did not respond. She could feel his presence within the mirrored space, even as she was simultaneously aware of him lying on a cot in the basement of Madame Sosostris's house in Huguenot, the sensation of a piece with her ability to read the graffiti outside the entrance to this room, her knowledge that the metallic ticks were called soul cages. She slid another chunk of candy across the table, and saw Gary wince.

Maybe "undo" wasn't the correct word to describe the effect Sefira's death would have on her actions. Maybe the kinds of things she'd done couldn't be undone. If they couldn't be reversed, though, maybe they could be loosened from the intention that had prompted them, unknotted from the plans they were part of and . . . what? Repurposed? Discarded, abandoned? She wasn't sure exactly what she was contemplating. Did she want to release Gary into death, into whatever might be awaiting him aside from a return trip to the Broken Land? Or did she want to keep him here, make of him a servitor? *My own personal zombie.* Apparently, resuming the life she had been living a little more than a week ago was not in the cards. Did that mean she would have to assume Sefira's role, prey on the faithless, the lonely, and the weak? The prospect was revolting. Should she remove herself from this place, seek more infernal surroundings? Assuming she could figure out how to travel there, she couldn't believe she'd be welcome in the Broken Land. Was there another hell to receive her? During their exchange in the car, Sefira had called her something new, not unlike Madame Sosostris's blank card. Was she to found a new inferno, rule as a queen over a populace of the damned, hand-selected, Gary enslaved beside her? The image was equal parts absurd and repugnant.

If nothing else, she could leave the sugared remnants of Gary's heart on the table and walk away, exit the chamber without a backward glance. She could withdraw what remained in her bank account, use it to help her establish a new life, leave Madame Sosostris to worry about Gary. Except, with her eyes and especially her teeth in the condition they were, how was she supposed to accomplish the first part of her plan? Nor did the second half sit well with her. Not because she owed anything to Gary: she had saved him from the worst of Sefira's plans for him, and at a far higher cost than she had anticipated paying. If things between them weren't exactly balanced, though, she was prepared to let that be. No, what bothered her about the idea of leaving matters unresolved had more to do with her, with her desire to see what she had started through to a conclusion, however imperfect.

Doubtless, there were other possibilities she was not thinking of, but at the moment, only one avenue appeared open. Before she could change her mind, she selected the nearest piece of candy and bit it in half.

Its flavor was like nothing she had tasted, a rush of milky sweetness that did not clash with, but rather accentuated, the rich iron redness of the meat. She swallowed the bite and popped the rest of the candy in her mouth, reaching for another. The flavor expanded on her tongue, gaining in depth and complexity as she chewed. She should be horrified at herself, disgusted, which she supposed she was, but those emotions diminished to insignificance beside the pleasure overflowing her mouth. The rush of sensation reached out to and encompassed the sulfurous turbulence still subsiding in her veins. Within the table's silver space, something was happening to Gary, he was thrashing from side to side, his eyes squeezed shut, his teeth gritted. But though she noticed him writhing below her, she continued to devour the candied chunks, whose taste assumed hints of fruits, peaches, pears, and apples. Contained within its subtleties was a world of knowledge, as if to experience this delight was to enter the consciousness that had devised it. She understood what was written on the threshold to this room, the precise non-location of the place and how to reach the Broken Land from it, the nature of the swarms and how to summon and employ them. And there was more, much more, waiting for her attention.

The candied meat was done, nothing left of it but a sweet residue Lisa sucked from her fingertips, nicking them on her teeth. It didn't matter; the copper tang added to the flavor. She looked at the table, saw her reflection gazing back at her, her black eyes glassy, a bit of candy stuck to her bottom lip. Of Gary, there was no trace. That was all right. She knew—or, she knew that she knew what had happened to him. He was in her power, hokey as the words sounded. She would have to decide what to do with him.

She realized how easy it would be to conceal her appearance, not restore so much as disguise it. No longer caged within her marrow, the yellow cloud and the force it embodied was hers to use as she saw fit. Her image rippled, and she was once more Lisa Martinez. Her wounds complained; she concentrated and closed them.

There was no reason for her to remain here. She could occupy Sefira's nest, but to what end? There was another of her kind, she now knew, a member of the Shattered Company, roaming the western edge of the continent, and the moment she became aware of Sefira's de-struction, she would be on her way to challenge Lisa for the Hide-Away Motel. Having defeated one succubus, she felt reasonably confi-dent of her ability to repeat the act, but why should she? She was not interested in adopting the job of demon slayer. What she most wanted was to return to her house and her bed, haunted by bitter memories as they were.

Leaving the cooler where it was, she picked her way through the mass of lamps. As she did, she licked the last fragment of candy from her lower lip, savoring the brief burst on her tongue. It was going to be difficult not to taste that sweetness again, especially now that she knew how to prepare it. On her way out of the chamber, she took the butch-er knife.

In Paris, in the Mouth of Kronos

I

"You know how much they want for a Coke?"

"How much?" Vasquez said.

"Five euros. Can you believe that?"

Vasquez shrugged. She knew the gesture would irritate Buchanan, who took an almost pathological delight in complaining about everything in Paris, from the lack of air conditioning on the train ride in from De Gaulle to their narrow hotel rooms; but they had an expense account, after all, and however modest it was, she was sure a five-euro Coke would not deplete it. She didn't imagine the professionals sat around fretting over the cost of their sodas.

To her left, the broad Avenue de la Bourdonnais was surprisingly quiet; to her right, the interior of the restaurant was a din of languages: English mainly, with German, Spanish, Italian, and even a little French mixed in. In front of and behind her, the rest of the sidewalk tables were occupied by an almost even balance of old men reading newspapers and youngish couples wearing sunglasses. Late afternoon sunlight washed over her surroundings like a spill of white paint, lightening everything several shades, reducing the low buildings across the Avenue to hazy rectangles. When their snack was done, she would have to return to one of the souvenir shops they had passed on the walk here and buy a pair of sunglasses. Another expense for Buchanan to complain about.

"*M'sieu? Madame?*" Their waiter, surprisingly middle-aged, had returned. "*Vous êtes—*"

"You speak English," Buchanan said.

"But of course," the waiter said. "You are ready with your order?"

"I'll have a cheeseburger," Buchanan said. "Medium-rare. And a Coke," he added with a grimace.

"Very good," the waiter said. "And for Madame?"

"Je voudrais un crêpe de chocolat," Vasquez said, *"et un café au lait."*

The waiter's expression did not change. *"Très bien, Madame. Merci,"* he said as Vasquez passed him their menus.

"A cheeseburger?" she said once he had returned inside the restaurant.

"What?" Buchanan said.

"Never mind."

"I like cheeseburgers. What's wrong with that?"

"Nothing. It's fine."

"Just because I don't want to eat some kind of French food—ooh, *un crêpe, s'il vous-plait.*"

"All this," Vasquez nodded at their surroundings, "it's lost on you, isn't it?"

"We aren't here for 'all this,'" Buchanan said. "We're here for Mr. White."

Despite herself, Vasquez flinched. "Why don't you speak a little louder? I'm not sure everyone inside the café heard."

"You think they know what we're talking about?"

"That's not the point."

"Oh? What is?"

"Operational integrity."

"Wow. You pick that up from the *Bourne* movies?"

"One person overhears something they don't like, opens their cellphone and calls the cops—"

"And it's all a big misunderstanding officers, we were talking about movies, ha-ha."

"—and the time we lose smoothing things over with them completely fucks up Plowman's schedule."

"Stop worrying," Buchanan said, but Vasquez was pleased to see his face blanch at the prospect of Plowman's displeasure.

For a few moments Vasquez leaned back in her chair and closed her eyes, the sun lighting the inside of her lids crimson. *I'm here,* she thought, the city's presence a pressure at the base of her skull, not unlike what she'd felt patrolling the streets of Bagram, but less unpleasant. Buchanan said, "So you've been here before."

"What?" Brightness overwhelmed her vision, simplified Buchanan to a dark silhouette in a baseball cap.

"You *parlez* the *français* pretty well. I figure you must've spent some time—what? In college? Some kind of study abroad deal?"

"Nope," Vasquez said.

"'Nope' what?"

"I've never been to Paris. Hell, before I enlisted, the farthest I'd ever been from home was the class trip to Washington senior year."

"You're shittin' me."

"Uh-uh. Don't get me wrong: I wanted to see Paris, London— everything. But the money—the money wasn't there. The closest I came to all this were the movies in Madame Antosca's French 4 class. It was one of the reasons I joined up: I figured I'd see the world and let the Army pay for it."

"How'd that work out for you?"

"We're here, aren't we?"

"Not because of the Army."

"No, precisely because of the Army. Well," she said, "them and the spooks."

"You still think Mr.—oh, sorry—*You-Know-Who* was CIA?"

Frowning, Vasquez lowered her voice. "Who knows? I'm not even sure he was one of ours. That accent . . . he could've been working for the Brits or the Aussies. He could've been Russian, back in town to settle a few scores. Wherever he picked up his pronunciation, dude was not regular military."

"Be funny if *he* was on Stillwater's payroll."

"Hysterical," Vasquez said. "What about you?"

"What about me?"

"I assume this is your first trip to Paris."

"And there's where you would be wrong."

"Now you're shittin' me."

"Why, because I ordered a cheeseburger and a Coke?"

"Among other things, yeah."

"My senior class trip was a week in Paris and Amsterdam. In college, the end of my sophomore year, my parents took me to France for a month." At what she knew must be the look on her face, Buchanan added, "It was an attempt at breaking up the relationship I was in at the time."

"It's not that. I'm trying to process the thought of you in college."

"Wow, anyone ever tell you what a laugh riot you are?"

"Did it work—your parents' plan?"

Buchanan shook his head. "The second I was back in the US, I knocked her up. We were married by the end of the summer."

"How romantic."

"Hey." Buchanan shrugged.

"That why you enlisted—support your new family?"

"More or less. Heidi's dad owned a bunch of McDonald's; for the first six months of our marriage, I tried to assistant manage one of them."

"With your people skills, that must have been a match made in heaven."

The retort forming on Buchanan's lips was cut short by the reappearance of their waiter, encumbered with their drinks and their food. He set their plates before them with a *"Madame"* and *"M'sieu,"* then, as he was distributing their drinks, said, "Everything is okay? *Ça va?"*

"Oui," Vasquez said. *"C'est bon. Merçi."*

With the slightest of bows, the waiter left them to their food.

While Buchanan worked his hands around his cheeseburger, Vasquez said, "I don't think I realized you were married."

"Were," Buchanan said. "She wasn't happy about my deploying in the first place, and when the shit hit the fan . . ." He bit into the burger. Through a mouthful of bun and meat he said, "The court-martial was the excuse she needed. Couldn't handle the shame, she said. The humiliation of being married to one of the guards who'd tortured an innocent man to death. What kind of role model would I be for our son?

"I tried—I tried to tell her it wasn't like that. It wasn't that—you know what I'm talking about."

Vasquez studied her neatly folded crêpe. "Yeah." Mr. White had favored a flint knife for what he called *the delicate work.*

"If that's what she wants, fine, fuck her. But she made it so I can't see my son. The second she decided we were splitting up, there was her dad with money for a lawyer. I get a call from this asshole—this is right in the middle of the court-martial—and he tells me Heidi's filing for divorce—no surprise—and they're going to make it easy for me: no alimony, no child support, nothing. The only catch is, I have to sign away all my rights to Sam. If I don't, they're fully prepared to go to court, and how do I like my chances in front of a judge? What choice did I have?"

Vasquez tasted her coffee. She saw her mother, holding open the front door for her, unable to meet her eyes.

"Bad enough about that poor bastard who died—what was his name? If there's one thing you'd think I'd know . . ."

"Mahbub Ali," Vasquez said. *What kind of a person are you?* her father had shouted. *What kind of person is part of such things?*

"Mahbub Ali," Buchanan said. "Bad enough what happened to him; I just wish I'd know what was happening to the rest of us, as well."

They ate the rest of their meal in silence. When the waiter returned to ask if they wanted dessert, they declined.

II

Vasquez had compiled a list of reasons for crossing the Avenue and walking to the Eiffel Tower, from *It's an open, crowded space: it's a better place to review the plan's details* to *I want to see the fucking Eiffel Tower once before I die, okay?* But Buchanan agreed to her proposal without argument; nor did he complain about the fifteen euros she spent on a pair of sunglasses on the walk there. Did she need to ask to know he was back in the concrete room they'd called the Closet, its air full of the stink of fear and piss?

Herself, she was doing her best not to think about the chamber under the prison's sub-basement Just-Call-Me-Bill had taken her to. This was maybe a week after the tall, portly man she knew for a fact was CIA had started spending every waking moment with Mr. White. Vasquez had followed Bill down poured concrete stairs that led from the labyrinth of the basement and its handful of high-value captives in their scattered cells (not to mention the Closet, whose precise location she'd been unable to fix), to the sub-basement, where he had clicked on the large yellow flashlight he was carrying. Its beam had ranged over brick walls, an assortment of junk (some of it Soviet-era aircraft parts, some of it tools to repair those parts, some of it more recent: stacks of toilet paper, boxes of plastic cutlery, a pair of hospital gurneys). They had made their way through that place to a low doorway

that opened on carved stone steps whose curved surfaces testified to
the passage of generations of feet. All the time, Just-Call-Me-Bill had
been talking, lecturing, detailing the history of the prison, from its time
as a repair center for the aircraft the Soviets flew in and out of here,
until some KGB officer decided the building was perfect for housing
prisoners, a change everyone who subsequently held possession of it
had maintained. Vasquez had struggled to pay attention, especially as
they had descended the last set of stairs and the air grew warm, moist,
the rock to either side of her damp. *Before,* the CIA operative was saying, *oh, before. Did you know a detachment of Alexander the Great's army
stopped here? One man returned.*

The stairs had ended in a wide, circular area. The roof was flat and
low, the walls no more than shadowy suggestions. Just-Call-Me-Bill's
flashlight had roamed the floor, picked out a symbol incised in the
rock at their feet: a rough circle, the diameter of a manhole cover, broken at about eight o'clock. Its circumference was stained black, its interior a map of dark brown splotches. *Hold this,* he had said, passing her
the flashlight, which had occupied her for the two or three seconds it
took him to remove a plastic baggie from one of the pockets of his sa-
fari vest. When Vasquez had directed the light at him, he was dumping
the bag's contents in his right hand, tugging at the plastic with his left
to pull it away from the dull red wad. The stink of blood and meat on
the turn had made her step back. *Steady, specialist.* The bag's contents
had landed inside the broken circle with a heavy, wet smack. Vasquez
had done her best not to study it too closely.

A sound, the scrape of bare flesh dragging over stone, from behind and to her left, had spun Vasquez around, the flashlight held out
to blind, her sidearm freed and following the light's path. This section
of the curving wall opened in a black arch like the top of an enormous
throat. For a moment, that space had been full of a great, pale figure.
Vasquez had had a confused impression of hands large as tires grasping either side of the arch, a boulder of a head, its mouth gaping
amidst a frenzy of beard, its eyes vast, idiot. It was scrambling towards
her; she didn't know where to aim—

And then Mr. White had been standing in the archway, dressed in
the white linen suit that somehow always seemed stained, even though
no discoloration was visible on any of it. He had not blinked at the

flashlight beam stabbing his face; nor had he appeared to judge Vasquez's gun pointing at him of much concern. Muttering an apology, Vasquez had lowered gun and light immediately. Mr. White had ignored her, strolling across the round chamber to the foot of the stairs, which he had climbed quickly. Just-Call-Me-Bill had hurried after, a look on his bland face that Vasquez took for amusement. She had brought up the rear, sweeping the flashlight over the floor as she reached the lowest step. The broken circle had been empty, except for a red smear that shone in the light.

That she had momentarily hallucinated, Vasquez had not once doubted. Things with Mr. White already had raced past what even Just-Call-Me-Bill had shown them, and however effective his methods, Vasquez was afraid that she—that they all had finally gone too far, crossed over into truly bad territory. Combined with a mild claustrophobia, that had caused her to fill the dark space with a nightmare. However reasonable that explanation, the shape with which her mind had replaced Mr. White had plagued her. Had she seen the Devil stepping forward on his goat's feet, one red hand using his pitchfork to balance himself, it would have made more sense than that giant form. It was as if her subconscious was telling her more about Mr. White than she understood. Prior to that trip, Vasquez had not been at ease around the man who never seemed to speak so much as to have spoken, so that you knew what he'd said even though you couldn't remember hearing him saying it. Afterward, she gave him a still wider berth.

Ahead, the Eiffel Tower swept up into the sky. Vasquez had seen it from a distance, at different points along hers and Buchanan's journey from their hotel toward the Seine, but the closer she drew to it, the less real it seemed. It was as if the very solidity of the beams and girders weaving together were evidence of their falseness. *I am seeing the Eiffel Tower,* she told herself. *I am actually looking at the goddamn Eiffel Tower.*

"Here you are," Buchanan said. "Happy?"

"Something like that."

The great square under the Tower was full of tourists, from the sound of it, the majority of them groups of Americans and Italians. Nervous men wearing untucked shirts over their jeans flitted from group to group—street vendors, Vasquez realized, each one carrying an oversized ring strung with metal replicas of the Tower. A pair of gendarmes, their hands draped over the machine guns slung high on their chests, let their eyes roam the crowd while they carried on a conversation. In front of each of the Tower's legs, lines of people waiting for the chance to ascend it doubled and redoubled back on themselves, enormous fans misting water over them. Taking Buchanan's arm, Vasquez steered them toward the nearest fan. Eyebrows raised, he tilted his head toward her.

"Ambient noise," she said.

"Whatever."

Once they were close enough to the fan's propeller drone, Vasquez leaned into Buchanan. "Go with this," she said.

"You're the boss." Buchanan gazed up, a man debating whether he wanted to climb *that* high.

"I've been thinking," Vasquez said. "Plowman's plan's shit."

"Oh?" He pointed at the Tower's first level, three hundred feet above.

Nodding, Vasquez said, "We approach Mr. White, and he's just going to agree to come with us to the elevator."

Buchanan dropped his hand. "Well, we do have our . . . persuaders. How do you like that? Was it cryptic enough? Or should I have said 'guns'?"

Vasquez smiled as if Buchanan had uttered an endearing remark. "You really think Mr. White is going to be impressed by a pair of .22s?"

"A bullet's a bullet. Besides," Buchanan returned her smile, "isn't the plan for us not to have to use the guns? Aren't we relying on him remembering us?"

"It's not like we were BFFs. If it were me, and I wanted the guy, and I had access to Stillwater's resources, I wouldn't be wasting my time on a couple of convicted criminals. I'd put together a team and go get him. Besides, twenty grand a piece for catching up to someone outside his hotel room, passing a couple of words with him, then escorting him to an elevator: tell me that doesn't sound too good to be true."

"You know the way these big companies work: they're all about throwing money around. Your problem is, you're still thinking like a soldier."

"Even so, why spend it on us?"

"Maybe Plowman feels bad about everything. Maybe this is his way of making it up to us."

"Plowman? Seriously?"

Buchanan shook his head. "This isn't that complicated."

Vasquez closed her eyes. "Humor me." She leaned her head against Buchanan's chest.

"What have I been doing?"

"We're a feint. While we're distracting Mr. White, Plowman's up to something else."

"Like?"

"Maybe Mr. White has something in his room; maybe we're occupying him while Plowman's retrieving it."

"You know there are easier ways for Plowman to steal something."

"Maybe we're keeping Mr. White in place so Plowman can pull a hit on him."

"Again, there are simpler ways to do that that would have nothing to do with us. You knock on the guy's door, he opens it, pow."

"What if we're supposed to get caught in the crossfire?"

"You bring us all the way here just to kill us?"

"Didn't you say big companies like to spend money?"

"But why take us out in the first place?"

Vasquez raised her head and opened her eyes. "How many of the people who knew Mr. White are still in circulation?"

"There's Just-Call-Me-Bill—"

"You think. He's CIA. We don't know what happened to him."

"Okay. There's you, me, Plowman—"

"Go on."

Buchanan paused, reviewing, Vasquez knew, the fates of the three other guards who'd assisted Mr. White with his work in the Closet. Long before news had broken about Mahbub Ali's death, Lavalle had sat on the edge of his bunk, placed his gun in his mouth, and squeezed the trigger. Then, when the shitstorm had started, Maxwell, on patrol, had been stabbed in the neck by an insurgent who'd targeted only him. Finally, in the holding cell awaiting his court-martial, Ruiz had taken advantage of a lapse in his jailers' attention to strip off his pants, twist them into a rope, and hang himself from the top bunk of his cell's bunkbed. His guards had cut him down in time to save his life, but

Ruiz had deprived his brain of oxygen for sufficient time to leave him a vegetable. When Buchanan spoke, he said, "Coincidence."

"Or conspiracy."

"Goddammit." Buchanan pulled free of Vasquez and headed for the long, rectangular park that stretched behind the Tower, speedwalking. His legs were sufficiently long that she had to jog to catch up to him. Buchanan did not slacken his pace, continuing his straight line up the middle of the park, through the midst of bemused picnickers. "Jesus Christ," Vasquez called, "will you slow down?"

He would not. Heedless of oncoming traffic, Buchanan led her across a pair of roads that traversed the park. Horns blaring, tires screaming, cars swerved around them. *At this rate,* Vasquez thought, *Plowman's motives won't matter.* Once they were safely on the grass again, she sped up until she was beside him, then reached high on the underside of Buchanan's right arm, not far from the armpit, and pinched as hard as she could.

"Ow! Shit!" Yanking his arm up and away, Buchanan stopped. Rubbing his skin, he said, "What the hell, Vasquez?"

"What the hell are you doing?"

"Walking. What did it look like?"

"Running away."

"Fuck you."

"Fuck you, you candy-ass pussy."

Buchanan's eyes flared.

"I'm trying to work this shit out so we can stay alive. You're so concerned about seeing your son, maybe you'd want to help me."

"Why are you doing this?" Buchanan said. "Why are you fucking with my head? Why are you trying to fuck this up?"

"I'm—"

"There's nothing to work out. We've got a job to do; we do it; we get the rest of our money. We do the job well, there's a chance Stillwater'll add us to their payroll. That happens—I'm making that kind of money—I hire myself a pit-bull of a lawyer and sic him on fucking Heidi. You want to live in goddamn Paris, you can eat a croissant for breakfast every morning."

"You honestly believe that."

"Yes I do."

Vasquez held his gaze, but who was she kidding? She could count on one finger the number of stare-downs she'd won. Her arms, legs, everything felt suddenly, incredibly heavy. She looked at her watch. "Come on," she said, starting in the direction of the Avenue de la Bourdonnais. "We can catch a cab."

III

Plowman had insisted they meet him at an airport café before they set foot outside de Gaulle. At the end of those ten minutes, which had consisted of Plowman asking details of their flight and instructing them how to take the RUR to the Metro to the stop nearest their hotel, he had passed Vasquez a card for a restaurant, where, he had said, the three of them would reconvene at 3:00 P.M. local time to review the evening's plans. Vasquez had been relieved to see Plowman seated at a table outside the café. Despite the ten thousand dollars gathering interest in her checking account, the plane ticket that had been fedexed to her apartment, followed by the receipt for four nights' stay at the Hôtel Resnais, she had been unable to shake the sense that none of this was as it appeared, that it was the set-up to an elaborate joke whose punchline would come at her expense. Plowman's solid form, dressed in a black suit whose tailored lines announced the upward shift in his pay grade, had confirmed that everything he had told her the afternoon he had sought her out at Andersen's farm had been true.

Or true enough to quiet momentarily the misgivings that had whispered ever louder in her ears the last two weeks, to the point that she had held her cell open in her left hand and the piece of paper with Plowman's number on it in her right, ready to call him and say she was out, he could have his money back, she hadn't spent any of it. During the long, hot train ride from the airport to the Metro station, when Buchanan had complained about Plowman not letting them out of his sight, treating them like goddamn kids, Vasquez had found an explanation on her lips. *It's probably the first time he's run an operation like this,* she had said. *He wants to be sure he dots all his i's and crosses all his t's.* Buchanan had harrumphed, but it was true: Plowman obsessed over the minutiae; it was one of the reasons he'd been in charge of their detail at the prison. Until the shit had buried the fan, that attentiveness had seemed to forecast his steady climb up the chain of command. At his court-martial, however, his enthusiasm for exact strikes on prisoner nerve clusters, his precision in placing arm restraints so that a prisoner's shoulders would not dislocate when he was hoisted off the floor by his bonds, his speed in obtaining the various surgical and dental instruments Just-Call-Me-Bill requested, had been counted liabilities rather than assets, and he had been the only one of their group to serve substantial time at Leavenworth—ten months.

Still, the Walther Vasquez had requested had been waiting where Plowman had promised it would be, wrapped with an extra clip in a waterproof bag secured inside the tank of her hotel room's toilet. A thorough inspection had reassured her that all was in order with the gun, its ammunition. If he were setting her up, would Plowman have wanted to arm her? Her proficiency at the target range had been well known, and while she hadn't touched a gun since her discharge, she had no doubts of her ability. Tucked within the back of her jeans, draped by her blouse, the pistol was easily accessible.

That's assuming, of course, that Plowman's even there tonight. But the caution was a formality. Plowman being Plowman, there was no way he was not going to be at Mr. White's hotel. Was there any need for him to have made the trip to West Virginia, to have tracked her to Anderson's farm, to have sought her out in the far barns, where she'd been using a high-pressure hose to sluice pigshit into gutters? An email, a phone call would have sufficed. Such methods, however, would have left too much outside Plowman's immediate control, and since he appeared able to dunk his bucket into a well of cash deeper than any she'd known, he had decided to find Vasquez and speak to her directly. (He'd done the same with Buchanan, she'd learned on the flight over, tracking him to the suburb of Chicago where he'd been shift manager at a Hardee's.) If the man had gone to such lengths to persuade them to take the job, if he had been there to meet them at Charles de Gaulle and was waiting for them even now, as their taxi crossed the Seine and headed toward the Champs Elysées, was there any chance he wouldn't be present later on?

Of course, he wouldn't be alone. Plowman would have the reassurance of God-only-knew-how-many Stillwater employees, which was to say, mercenaries (no doubt heavily armed and armored) backing him up. Vasquez hadn't had much to do with the company's personnel; they tended to roost closer to the center of Kabul, where the high-value targets they guarded huddled. Iraq: that was where Stillwater's bootprint was the deepest; from what Vasquez had heard, the former soldiers riding the reinforced Lincoln Navigators through Baghdad not only made about five times what they had in the military, they followed rules of engagement that were, to put it mildly, less robust. While Paris was as far east as she was willing to travel, she had to admit, the prospect of that kind of money made Baghdad, if not appealing, at least less unappealing.

And what would Dad have to say to that? No matter that his eyes were failing, the center of his vision consumed by macular degeneration, her father had lost none of his passion for the news, employing a standing magnifier to aid him as he pored over the day's *New York Times* and *Washington Post,* sitting in his favorite chair listening to *All Things Considered* on WVPN, even venturing online to the BBC using the computer whose monitor settings she had adjusted for him before she'd deployed. Her father would not have missed the reports of Stillwater's involvement in several incidents in Iraq that were less shootouts than turkey-shoots, not to mention the ongoing Congressional inquiry into their policing of certain districts of post-Katrina and Rita New Orleans, as well as an event in upstate New York last summer when one of their employees had taken a camping trip that had left two of his three companions dead under what could best be described as suspicious circumstances. She could hear his words, heavy with the accent that had accreted as he'd aged: *Was this why I suffered in the Villa Grimaldi? So my daughter could join the* Caravana de la Muerte? The same question he'd asked her the first night she'd returned home.

All the same, it wasn't as if his opinion of her was going to drop any further. *If I'm damned,* she thought, *I might as well get paid for it.*

That said, she was in no hurry to certify her ultimate destination, which returned her to the problem of Plowman and his plan. You would have expected the press of the .22 against the small of her back to have been reassuring, but instead, it only emphasized her sense of powerlessness, as if Plowman were so confident, so secure, he could allow her whatever firearm she wanted.

The cab turned onto the Champs Elysées. Ahead, the Arc de Triomphe squatted in the distance. Another monument to cross off the list.

IV

The restaurant whose card Plowman had handed her was located on one of the side streets about halfway to the Arc; Vasquez and Buchanan departed their cab at the street's corner and walked the hundred yards to a door flanked by man-sized plaster Chinese dragons. Buchanan brushed past the black-suited host and his welcome. Smiling and murmuring, *"Pardonnez, nous avons un rendezvous içi,"* Vasquez pursued him into the dim interior. Up a short flight of stairs, Buchanan strode across a floor that glowed with pale light—glass, Vasquez saw, thick squares suspended over shimmering aquamarine. A carp the size of her forearm darted underneath her, and she realized that she was standing on top of an enormous, shallow fish tank, brown and white and orange carp racing one another across its bottom, jostling the occasional slower turtle. With one exception, the tables supported by the glass were empty. Too late, Vasquez supposed, for lunch, and too early for dinner. Or maybe the food here wasn't that good.

His back to the far wall, Plowman was seated at a table directly in front of her. Already, Buchanan was lowering himself into a chair opposite him. *Stupid,* Vasquez thought at the expanse of his unguarded back. Her boots clacked on the glass. She moved around the table to sit beside Plowman, who had exchanged the dark suit in which he'd greeted them at de Gaulle for a tan jacket over a cream shirt and slacks. His outfit caught the light filtering from below them and held it in as a dull sheen. A metal bowl filled with dumplings was centered on the tablemat before him; to its right, a slice of lemon floated at the top of a glass of clear liquid. Plowman's eyebrow raised as she settled beside him, but he did not comment on her choice; instead, he said, "You're here."

Vasquez's "Yes" was overridden by Buchanan's "We are, and there are some things we need cleared up."

Vasquez stared at him. Plowman said, "Oh?"

"That's right," Buchanan said. "We've been thinking, and this plan of yours doesn't add up."

"Really." The tone of Plowman's voice did not change.

"Really," Buchanan nodded.

"Would you care to explain to me exactly how it doesn't add up?"

"You expect Vasquez and me to believe you spent all this money so the two of us can have a five-minute conversation with Mr. White?"

Vasquez flinched.

"There's a little bit more to it than that."

"We're supposed to persuade him to walk twenty feet with us to an elevator."

"Actually, it's seventy-four feet three inches."

"Whatever." Buchanan glanced at Vasquez. She looked away. To the wall to her right, water chuckled down a series of small rock terraces through an opening in the floor into the fish tank.

"No, not 'whatever,' Buchanan. Seventy-four feet, three inches," Plowman said. "This is why the biggest responsibility you confront each day is lifting the fry basket out of the hot oil when the buzzer tells you to. You don't pay attention to the little things."

The host was standing at Buchanan's elbow, his hands clasped over a pair of long menus. Plowman nodded at him and he passed the menus to Vasquez and Buchanan. Inclining toward them, the host said, "May I bring you drinks while you decide your order?"

His eyes on the menu, Buchanan said, "Water."

"Moi aussi," Vasquez said. *"Merci."*

"Nice accent," Plowman said when the host had left.

"Thanks."

"I don't think I realized you speak French."

Vasquez shrugged. "Wasn't any call for it, was there?"

"Anything else?" Plowman said. "Spanish?"

"I understand more than I can speak."

"You folks were from—where, again?"

"Chile," Vasquez said. "My dad. My mom's American, but her parents were from Argentina."

"That's useful to know."

"For when Stillwater hires her," Buchanan said.

"Yes," Plowman answered. "The company has projects under way in a number of places where fluency in French and Spanish would be an asset."

"Such as?"

"One thing at a time," Plowman said. "Let's get through tonight first, and then you can worry about your next assignment."

"And what's that going to be," Buchanan said, "another twenty K to walk someone to an elevator?"

"I doubt it'll be anything so mundane," Plowman said. "I also doubt it'll pay as little as twenty thousand."

"Look," Vasquez started to say, but the host had returned with their water. Once he deposited their glasses on the table, he withdrew a pad and pen from his jacket pocket and took Buchanan's order of crispy duck and Vasquez's of steamed dumplings. After he had retrieved the menus and gone, Plowman turned to Vasquez and said, "You were saying?"

"It's just—what Buchanan's trying to say is, it's a lot, you know? If you'd offered us, I don't know, say five hundred bucks apiece to come here and play escort, that still would've been a lot, but it wouldn't—I mean, *twenty thousand dollars,* plus the air fare, the hotel, the expense account. It seems too much for what you're asking us to do. Can you understand that?"

Plowman shook his head yes. "I can. I can understand how strange it might appear to offer this kind of money for this length of service, but . . ." He raised his drink to his lips. When he lowered his arm, the glass was half drained. "Mr. White is . . . to say he's high-value doesn't begin to cover it. The guy's been around—he's been around. Talk about a font of information: the stuff this guy's forgotten would be enough for a dozen careers. What he remembers will give whoever can get him to share it with them permanent tactical advantage."

"No such thing," Buchanan said. "No matter how much the guy says he knows—"

"Yes, yes," Plowman held up his hand like a traffic cop. "Trust me. He's high-value."

"But won't the spooks—What does Just-Call-Me-Bill have to say about this?" Vasquez said.

"Bill's dead."

Simultaneously Buchanan said, "Huh," and Vasquez, "What? How?"

"I don't know. When my bosses greenlighted me for this, Bill was the first person I thought of. I wasn't sure if he was still with the Agency, so I did some checking around. I couldn't find out much— goddamn spooks keep their mouths shut—but I was able to determine that Bill was dead. It sounded like it might've been that chopper crash in Helmand, but that's a guess. To answer your question, Vasquez, Bill didn't have a whole lot to say."

"Shit," Buchanan said.

"Okay," Vasquez exhaled. "Okay. Was he the only one who knew about Mr. White?"

"I find it hard to believe he was," Plowman said, "but thus far, no one's nibbled at any of the bait I've left out. I'm surprised: I'll admit it. But it makes our job that much simpler, so I'm not complaining."

"All right," Vasquez said, "but the money—"

His eyes alight, Plowman leaned forward. "To get my hands on Mr. White, I would have paid each of you ten times as much. That's how important this operation is. Whatever we have to shell out now is nothing compared to what we're going to gain from this guy."

"Now you tell us," Buchanan said.

Plowman smiled and relaxed back. "Well, the bean counters do appreciate it when you can control costs." He turned to Vasquez. "Well? Have your concerns been addressed?"

"Hey," Buchanan said, "I was the one asking the questions."

"Please," Plowman said. "I was in charge of you, remember? Whatever your virtues, Buchanan, original thought is not among them."

"What about Mr. White?" Vasquez said. "Suppose he doesn't want to come with you?"

"I don't imagine he will," Plowman said. "Nor do I expect him to be terribly interested in assisting us once he is in our custody. That's okay." Plowman picked up one of the chopsticks alongside his plate, turned it in his hand, and jabbed it into a dumpling. He lifted the dumpling to his mouth; momentarily, Vasquez pictured a giant bringing its teeth together on a human head. While he chewed, Plowman said, "To be honest, I hope the son of a bitch is feeling especially stubborn. Because of him, I lost everything that was good in my life. Because of that fucker, I did time in prison—fucking *prison*." Plowman swallowed, speared another dumpling. "Believe me when I say Mr. White and I have a lot of quality time coming."

Beneath them, a half-dozen carp that had been floating lazily, scattered.

V

Buchanan was all for finding Mr. White's hotel and parking themselves in its lobby. "What?" Vasquez said. "Behind a couple of newspapers?" Stuck in traffic on what should have been its short way to the Concorde Opera, where Mr. White had the junior suite, their cab was full of the reek of exhaust, the low rumble of the cars surrounding them.

"Sure, yeah, that'd work."

"Jesus—and I'm the one who's seen too many movies?"

"What?" Buchanan said.

"Number one, at this rate, it'll be at least six before we get there. How many people sit around reading the day's paper at night? The whole point of the news is, it's new."

"Maybe we're on vacation."

"Doesn't matter. We'll still stick out. And number two, even if the lobby's full of tourists holding newspapers up in front of their faces, Plowman's plan doesn't kick in until eleven. You telling me no one's going to notice the same two people sitting there, doing the same thing, for five hours? For all we know, Mr. White'll see us on his way out and coming back."

"Once again, Vasquez, you're overthinking this. People don't see what they don't expect to see. Mr. White isn't expecting us in the lobby of his plush hotel, ergo, he won't notice us there."

"Are you kidding? This isn't 'people': this is Mr. White."

"Get a grip. He eats, shits, and sleeps same as you and me."

For the briefest of instants, the window over Buchanan's shoulder was full of the enormous face Vasquez had glimpsed (hallucinated) in the caves under the prison. Not for the first time, she was struck by the crudeness of the features, as if a sculptor had hurriedly struck out the approximation of a human visage on a piece of rock already formed to suggest it.

Taking her silence as further disagreement, Buchanan sighed and said, "All right. Tell you what: a big, tony hotel, there's gotta be all kinds of stores around it, right? Long as we don't go too far, we'll do some shopping."

"Fine," Vasquez said. When Buchanan had settled back in his seat, she said, "So. You satisfied with Plowman's answers?"

"Aw, no, not this again . . ."

"I'm just asking a question."

"No, what you're asking is called a leading question, as in, leading me to think that Plowman didn't really say anything to us, and we don't know anything more now than we did before our meeting."

"You learned something from that?"

Buchanan nodded. "You bet I did. I learned that Plowman has a hard-on for Mr. White the size of your fucking Eiffel Tower, from which I deduce that anyone who helps him satisfy himself stands to benefit enormously." As the cab lurched forward, Buchanan said, "Am I wrong?"

"No," Vasquez said. "It's—"

"What? What is it now?"

"I don't know." She looked out her window at the cars creeping along beside them.

"Well, that's helpful."

"Forget it."

For once Buchanan chose not to pursue the argument. Beyond the car to their right, Vasquez watched men and women walking past the windows of ground-level businesses, tech stores and clothing stores and a bookstore and an office whose purpose she could not identify. Over their wrought-iron balconies, the windows of the apartments above showed the late afternoon sky, its blue deeper, as if hardened by a day of the sun's baking. *Because of him, I lost everything that was good in my life. Because of that fucker, I did time in prison—fucking prison.* Plowman's declaration sounded in her ears. Insofar as the passion on his face authenticated his words, and hence the purpose of their mission, his brief monologue should have been reassuring. And yet, and yet . . .

In the moment before he drove his fist into a prisoner's solar plexus, Plowman's features, distorted and red from the last hour's interrogation, would relax. The effect was startling, as if a layer of heavy makeup had melted off his skin. In the subsequent stillness of his face, Vasquez initially had read Plowman's actual emotion, a clinical detachment from the pain he was preparing to inflict that was based in his utter contempt for the man standing in front of him. While his mouth would stretch with his screams to the prisoner to *Get up! Get the fuck up!* in the second after his blow had dropped the man to the concrete floor, and while his mouth and eyes would continue to express the violence his fists and boots were concentrating on the prisoner's back, his balls, his throat, there would be other moments, impossible to predict, when, as he was shuffle-stepping away from a kick to the prisoner's kidney, Plowman's face would slip into that non-expression and Vasquez would think that she had seen through to the real man.

Then, the week after Plowman had brought Vasquez on board what he had named the White Detail, she'd found herself sitting through a Steven Seagal double-feature—not her first or even tenth choice for a way to pass three hours, but it beat lying on her bunk thinking, *Why are you so shocked? You knew what Plowman was up to—everyone knows.* An hour into *The Patriot,* the vague sensation that had been nagging at her from Seagal's first scene crystallized into recognition: that the blank look with which the actor met every ebb and flow in the drama was the same as the one that Vasquez had caught on Plowman's face, was, she understood, its original. For the remainder of that film and the duration of the next (*Belly of the Beast*), Vasquez had stared at the undersized screen in a kind of horrified fascination, unable to decide which was worse: to be serving under a man whose affect suggested a sociopath, or to be serving under a man who was playing the lead role in a private movie.

How many days after that had Just-Call-Me-Bill arrived? No more than two, she was reasonably sure. He had come, he told the White Detail, because their efforts with particularly *recalcitrant* prisoners had not gone unnoticed, and his superiors judged it would be beneficial for him to share his knowledge of enhanced interrogation techniques with them—and no doubt, they had some things to teach him. His back ramrod straight, his face alight, Plowman had barked his enthusiasm for their collaboration.

After that, it had been learning the restraints that would cause the prisoner maximum discomfort, expose him (or occasionally, her) to optimum harm. It was hoisting the prisoner off the ground first without dislocating his shoulders, then with. Waterboarding, yes, together with the repurposing of all manner of daily objects, from nail files to pliers to dental floss. Each case was different. Of course you couldn't believe any of the things the prisoners said when they were turned over to you, their protestations of innocence. But even after it appeared you'd broken them, you couldn't be sure they weren't engaged in a more subtle deception, acting as if you'd succeeded in order to preserve the truly valuable information. For this reason, it was necessary to keep the interrogation open, to continue to revisit those prisoners who swore they'd told you everything they knew. *These people are not like you and me,* Just-Call-Me-Bill had said, confirming the impression that had dogged Vasquez when she'd walked patrol, past women draped in white or slate *burqas,* men whose *pokool* proclaimed their loyalty to the *mujahideen. These are not a reasonable people. You cannot sit down and talk to them,* Bill went on, *come to an understanding with them. They would rather fly an airplane into a building full of innocent women and men. They would rather strap a bomb to their daughter and send her to give you a hug. They get their hands on a nuke, and there'll be a mushroom cloud where Manhattan used to be. What they understand is pain. Enough suffering, and their tongues will loosen.*

Vasquez could not pin down the exact moment Mr. White had joined their group. When he had shouldered his way past Lavalle and Maxwell, his left hand up to stop Plowman from tilting the prisoner backwards, Just-Call-Me-Bill from pouring the water onto the man's hooded face, she had thought, *Who the hell?* And, as quickly, *Oh—Mr. White.* He must have been with them for some time for Plowman to upright the prisoner, Bill to lower the bucket and step back. The flint knife in his right hand, its edge so fine you could feel it pressing against your bare skin, had not been unexpected. Nor had what had followed.

It was Mr. White who had suggested they transfer their operations to the Closet, a recommendation Just-Call-Me-Bill had been happy to embrace. Plowman, at first, had been noncommittal. Mr. White's . . . call it his taking a more active hand in their interrogations, had led to him and Bill spending increased time together. Ruiz had asked the CIA man what he was doing with the man whose suit, while seemingly filthy, was never touched by any of the blood that slicked his knife, his hands. *Education,* Just-Call-Me-Bill had answered. *Our friend is teaching me all manner of things.*

As he was instructing the rest of them, albeit in more indirect fashion. Vasquez had learned that her father's stories of the Villa Grimaldi—which he had withheld from her until she was fifteen, when over the course of the evening after her birthday she had been first incredulous, then horrified, then filled with righteous fury on his behalf—had little bearing on her duties in the Closet. Her father had been an innocent man, a poet, for God's sake, picked up by Pinochet's *Caravana de la Muerte* because they were engaged in a program of terrorizing their own populace. The men (and occasional women) at whose interrogations she assisted were terrorists themselves, spiritual kin to the officers who had scarred her father's arms, his chest, his back, his thighs, who had scored his mind with nightmares from which he still woke screaming, decades later. They were not like you and me, and that difference authorized and legitimized whatever was required to start them talking.

By the time Mahbub Ali was hauled into the Closet, Vasquez had learned other things, too. She had learned that it was possible to concentrate pain on a single part of the body, to the point that the prisoner grew to hate that part of himself for the agony focused there. She had learned that it was preferable to work slowly, methodically—religiously was how she thought of it, though this was no religion to which she'd ever been exposed. This was a faith rooted in the most fundamental truth Mr. White taught her, taught them all, namely, that the flesh yearns for the knife, aches for the cut that will open it, relieve it of its quivering anticipation of harm. As junior member of the Detail, she had not yet progressed to being allowed to work on the prisoners directly, but it didn't matter. While she and Buchanan sliced away a prisoner's clothes, exposed bare skin, what she saw there—a fragility, a vulnerability whose thick, salty taste filled her mouth—confirmed all Mr. White's lessons, every last one.

Nor was she his best student. That had been Plowman, the only one of them to whom Mr. White had entrusted his flint knife. With Just-Call-Me-Bill, Mr. White had maintained the air of a senior colleague; with the rest of them, he acted as if they were mannequins, placeholders. With Plowman, though, Mr. White was the mentor, the last practitioner of an otherwise dead art passing his knowledge on to his chosen successor. It might have been the plot of a Steven Seagal film. And no Hollywood star could have played the eager apprentice with more enthusiasm than Plowman. While the official cause of Mahbub Ali's death was sepsis resulting from improperly tended wounds, those missing pieces of the man had been parted from him on the edge of Mr. White's stone blade, gripped in Plowman's steady hand.

VI

Even with the clotted traffic, the cab drew up in front of the Concorde Opera's three sets of polished wooden doors with close to five hours to spare. While Vasquez settled with the driver, Buchanan stepped out of the cab, crossed the sidewalk, strode up three stairs, and passed through the center doors. The act distracted her enough that she forgot to ask for a receipt; by the time she remembered, the cab had accepted a trio of middle-aged women, their arms crowded with shopping bags, and pulled away. She considered chasing after it, before deciding that she could absorb the ten euros. She turned to the hotel to see the center doors open again, Buchanan standing in them next to a young man with a shaved head who was wearing navy pants and a cream tunic on whose upper left side a name tag flashed. The young man pointed across the street in front of the hotel and waved his hand back and forth, all the while talking to Buchanan, who nodded attentively. When the young man lowered his arm, Buchanan clapped him on the back, thanked him, and descended to Vasquez.

She said, "What was that about?"

"Shopping," Buchanan said. "Come on."

The next fifteen minutes consisted of them walking a route Vasquez wasn't sure she could retrace, through clouds of slow-moving tourists stopping to admire some building or piece of public statuary; alongside briskly moving men and women whose ignoring those same sights marked them as locals as much as their chic haircuts and the rapid-fire French they delivered to their cellphones; past upscale boutiques and the gated entrances to equally upscale apartments. Buchanan's route brought the two of them to a large, corner building whose long windows displayed teddy bears, model planes, dollhouses. Vasquez said, "A toy store?"

"Not just 'a' toy store," Buchanan said. "This is *the* toy store. Supposed to have all kinds of stuff in it."

"For your son."

"Duh."

Inside, a crowd of weary adults and overexcited children moved up and down the store's aisles, past a mix of toys Vasquez recognized (Playmobil, groups of army vehicles, a typical assortment of stuffed animals) and others she'd never seen before (animal-headed figures she realized were Egyptian gods, replicas of round-faced cartoon characters she didn't know, a box of a dozen figurines arranged around a cardboard mountain). Buchanan wandered up to her as she was considering this set, the box propped on her hip. "Cool," he said, leaning forward. "What is it, like, the Greek gods?"

Vasquez resisted a sarcastic remark about the breadth of his knowledge; instead, she said, "Yeah. That's Zeus and his crew at the top of the mountain. I'm not sure who those guys are climbing it . . ."

"Titans," Buchanan said. "They were monsters who came before the gods, these kind of primal forces. Zeus defeated them, imprisoned them in the underworld. I used to know all their names: when I was a kid, I was really into myths and legends, heroes, all that shit." He studied the toys positioned up the mountain's sides. They were larger than the figures at its crown, over-muscled, one with an extra pair of arms, another with a snake's head, a third with a single, glaring eye. Buchanan shook his head. "I can't remember any of their names now. Except for this guy," he pointed at a figurine near the summit. "I'm pretty sure he's Kronos."

"Kronos?" The figure was approximately that of a man, although its arms and legs were slightly too long, its hands and feet oversized. Its head was surrounded by a corona of gray hair that descended into a jagged beard. The toy's mouth had been sculpted with its mouth gaping, its eyes round, idiot. Vasquez smelled spoiled meat, felt the cardboard slipping from her grasp.

"Whoa." Buchanan caught the box, replaced it on the shelf.

"Sorry," Vasquez said. *Mr. White had ignored her, strolling across the round chamber to the foot of the stairs, which he had climbed quickly.*

"I don't think that's really Sam's speed, anyway. Come on," Buchanan said, moving down the aisle.

When they had stopped in front of a stack of remote-controlled cars, Vasquez said, "So who was Kronos?" Her voice was steady.

"What?" Buchanan said. "Oh—Kronos? He was Zeus's father. Ate all his kids because he'd heard that one of them was going to replace him."

"Jesus."

"Yeah. Somehow, Zeus avoided becoming dinner and overthrew the old man."

"Did he—did Zeus kill him?"

"I don't think so. I'm pretty sure Kronos wound up with the rest of the Titans, underground."

"Underground? I thought you said they were in the underworld."

"Same diff," Buchanan said. "That's where those guys thought the underworld was, someplace deep underground. You got to it through caves."

"Oh."

In the end, Buchanan decided on a large wooden castle that came with a host of knights, some on horseback, some on foot, a trio of princesses, a unicorn, and a dragon. The entire set cost two hundred and sixty euros, which struck Vasquez as wildly overpriced but which Buchanan paid without a murmur of protest—the extravagance of the present, she understood, being the point. Buchanan refused the cashier's offer to gift-wrap the box, and they left the store with him carrying it under his arm.

Once on the sidewalk, Vasquez said, "Not to be a bitch, but what are you planning to do with that?"

Buchanan shrugged. "I'll think of something. Maybe the front desk'll hold it."

Vasquez said nothing. Although the sky still glowed blue, the light had begun to drain out of the spaces among the buildings, replaced by a darkness that was almost granular. The air was warm, soupy. As they stopped at the corner, Vasquez said, "You know, we never asked Plowman about Lavalle or Maxwell."

"Yeah, so?"

"Just—I wish we had. He had an answer for everything else, I wouldn't have minded hearing him explain that."

"There's nothing to explain," Buchanan said.

"We're the last ones alive—"

"Plowman's living. So's Mr. White."

"Whatever—you know what I mean. Christ, even Just-Call-Me-Bill is dead. What the fuck's up with that?"

In front of them, traffic stopped. The walk signal lighted its green man. They joined the surge across the street. "It's a war, Vasquez," Buchanan said. "People die in them."

"Is that what you really believe?"

"It is."

"What about your freak-out before, at the Tower?"

"That's exactly what it was—me freaking out."

"Okay," Vasquez said after a moment, "okay. Maybe Bill's death was an accident; maybe Maxwell, too. What about Lavalle? What about Ruiz? You telling me it's normal two guys from the same detail try to off themselves?"

"I don't know." Buchanan shook his head. "You know the Army isn't big on mental health care. And let's face it, that was some pretty fucked-up shit went on in the Closet. Not much of a surprise if Lavalle and Ruiz couldn't handle it, is it?"

Vasquez waited another block before asking, "How do you deal with it, the Closet?"

Buchanan took one more block after that to answer: "I don't think about it."

"You don't?"

"I'm not saying the thought of what we did over there never crosses my mind, but as a rule I focus on the here and now."

"What about the times the thought does cross your mind?"

"I tell myself it was a different place with different rules. You know what I'm talking about. You had to be there; if you weren't, then shut the fuck up. Maybe what we did went over the line, but that's for us to say, not some panel of officers don't know their ass from a hole in the ground, and damn sure not some reporter never been closer to war than a goddamn showing of *Platoon*." Buchanan glared. "You hear me?"

"Yeah." How many times had she used the same arguments, or close enough, with her father? He had remained unconvinced. *So only the criminals are fit to judge the crime?* he had said. *What a novel approach to justice.* She said, "You know what I hate, though? It isn't that people look at me funny—*Oh, it's her*—it isn't even the few who run up to me in the supermarket and tell me what a disgrace I am. It's like you said, they weren't there, so fuck 'em. What gets me are the ones who come up to you and tell you, 'Good job, you fixed them Ay-rabs right,' the crackers who wouldn't have anything to do with someone like me, otherwise."

"Even crackers can be right sometimes," Buchanan said.

VII

Mr. White's room was on the sixth floor, at the end of a short corridor that lay around a sharp left turn. The door to the junior suite appeared unremarkable, but it was difficult to be sure, since both the bulbs in the wall-sconces on either side of the corridor were out. Vasquez searched for a light switch and, when she could not find one, said, "Either they're blown, or the switch is inside his room."

Buchanan, who had been unsuccessful convincing the woman at the front desk to watch his son's present, was busy fitting it beneath one of the chairs to the right of the elevator door.

"Did you hear me?" Vasquez asked.

"Yeah."

"Well?"

"Well what?"

"I don't like it. Our visibility's fucked. He opens the door, the light's behind him, in our faces. He turns on the hall lights, and we're blind."

"For, like, a second."

"That's more than enough time for Mr. White to do something."

"Will you listen to yourself?"

"You saw what he could do with that knife."

"All right," Buchanan said, "how do you propose we deal with this?"

Vasquez paused. "You knock on the door. I'll stand a couple of feet back with my gun in my pocket. If things go pear-shaped, I'll be in a position to take him out."

"How come I have to knock on the door?"

"Because he liked you better."

"Bullshit."

"He did. He treated me like I wasn't there."

"That was the way Mr. White was with everyone."

"Not you."

Holding his hands up, Buchanan said, "Fine. Dude creeps you out so much, it's probably better I'm the one talking to him." He checked his watch. "Five minutes till show time. Or should I say, 'T-minus five and counting,' something like that?"

"Of all the things I'm going to miss about working with you, your sense of humor's going to be at the top of the list."

"No sign of Plowman yet." Buchanan checked the panel next to the elevator, which showed it on the third floor.

"He'll be here at precisely eleven ten."

"No doubt."

"Well . . ." Vasquez turned away from Buchanan.

"Wait—where are you going? There's still four minutes on the clock."

"Good: it'll give our eyes time to adjust."

"I am so glad this is almost over," Buchanan said, but he accompanied Vasquez to the near end of the corridor to Mr. White's room. She could feel him vibrating with a surplus of smart-ass remarks, but he had enough sense to keep his mouth shut. The air was cool, floral-scented with whatever they'd used to clean the carpet. Vasquez expected the minutes to drag by, for there to be ample opportunity for her to fit the various fragments of information in her possession into something like a coherent picture; however, it seemed practically the next second after her eyes had adapted to the shadows leading up to Mr. White's door, Buchanan was moving past her. There was time for her to slide the pistol out from under her blouse and slip in into the right front pocket of her slacks, and then Buchanan's knuckles were rapping the door.

It opened so quickly, Vasquez almost believed Mr. White had been positioned there, waiting for them. The glow that framed him was soft, orange, an adjustable light dialed down to its lowest setting, or a candle. From what she could see of him, Mr. White was the same as ever, from his unruly hair, more gray than white, to his dirty white suit. Vasquez could not tell whether his hands were empty. In her pocket, her palm was slick on the pistol's grip.

At the sight of Buchanan, Mr. White's expression did not change. He stood in the doorway regarding the man, and Vasquez three feet behind him, until Buchanan cleared his throat and said, "Evening, Mr. White. Maybe you remember me from Bagram. I'm Buchanan; my associate is Vasquez. We were part of Sergeant Plowman's crew; we assisted you with your work interrogating prisoners."

Mr. White continued to stare at Buchanan. Vasquez felt panic gathering in the pit of her stomach. Buchanan went on, "We were hoping you would accompany us on a short walk. There are matters we'd like to discuss with you, and we've come a long way."

Without speaking, Mr. White stepped into the corridor. The fear, the urge to sprint away from here as fast as her legs would take her, which had been churning in Vasquez's gut, leapt up like a geyser. Buchanan said, "Thank you. This won't take five minutes—ten, tops."

Behind her, the floor creaked. She looked back, saw Plowman standing there, and in her confusion did not register what he was holding in his hand. Someone coughed, and Buchanan collapsed. They coughed again, and it was as if a snowball packed with ice struck Vasquez's back low and to the left.

All the strength left her legs. She sat down where she was, listing to her right until the wall stopped her. Plowman stepped over her. The gun in his right hand was lowered; in his left he held a small box. He raised the box, pressed it, and the wall sconces erupted in deep purple—black light, by whose illumination Vasquez saw the walls, the ceiling, the carpet of the short corridor covered in symbols drawn in a medium that shone pale white. She couldn't identify most of them: she thought she saw a scattering of Greek characters, but the rest were unfamiliar, circles bisected by straight lines traversed by short, wavy lines, a long, gradual curve like a smile, more intersecting lines. The only figure she knew for sure was a circle whose thick circumference was broken at about the eight o'clock point, inside which Mr. White was standing and Buchanan lying. Whatever Plowman had used to draw them made the symbols appear to float in front of the surfaces on which he'd marked them, strange constellations crammed into an undersized sky.

Plowman was speaking, the words he was uttering unlike any Vasquez had heard, thick ropes of sound that started deep in his throat and spilled into the air squirming, writhing over her eardrums. Now Mr. White's face showed emotion: surprise mixed with what might have been dismay, even anger. Plowman halted next to the broken circle and used his right foot to roll Buchanan onto his back. Buchanan's eyes were open, unblinking, his lips parted. The exit wound in his throat shone darkly. His voice rising, Plowman completed what he was saying, gestured with both hands at the body, and retreated to Vasquez.

For an interval of time that lasted much too long, the space where Mr. White and Buchanan were was full of something too big, which had to double over to cram itself into the corridor. Eyes the size of dinner plates stared at Plowman, at Vasquez, with a lunacy that pressed on her like an animal scenting her with its sharp snout. Amidst a beard caked and clotted with offal, a mouth full of teeth cracked and stained black formed sounds Vasquez could not distinguish. Great pale hands large as tires roamed the floor beneath the figure—Vasquez was reminded of a blind man investigating an unfamiliar surface. When the hands found Buchanan, they scooped him up like a doll and raised him to that enormous mouth.

Groaning, Vasquez tried to roll away from the sight of Buchanan's head surrounded by teeth like broken flagstones. It wasn't easy. For one thing, her right hand was still in her pants pocket, its fingers tight around the Walther, her wrist and arm bent in at awkward angles. (She supposed she should be grateful she hadn't shot herself.) For another thing, the cold that had struck her back was gone, replaced by heat, by a sharp pain that grew sharper still as she twisted away from the snap and crunch of those teeth biting through Buchanan's skull. *God.* She managed to move onto her back, exhaling sharply. To her right, the sounds of Buchanan's consumption continued, bones snapping, flesh tearing, cloth ripping. Mr. White—what had been Mr. White—or what he truly was—that vast figure was grunting with pleasure, smacking its lips together like someone starved for food given a gourmet meal.

"For what it's worth," Plowman said, "I wasn't completely dishonest with you." One leg to either side of hers, he squatted over her, resting his elbows on his knees. "I do intend to bring Mr. White into my service; it's just the methods necessary for me to do so are a little extreme."

Vasquez tried to speak. "What . . . is he?"

"It doesn't matter," Plowman said. "He's old—I mean, if I told you how old he is, you'd think . . ." He looked to his left, to the giant sucking the gore from its fingers. "Well, maybe not. He's been around for a long time, and he knows a lot of things. We—what we were doing at Bagram, the interrogations, they woke him. I guess that's the best way to put it; although you could say they called him forth. It took me a while to figure out everything, even after he revealed himself to me. But there's nothing like prison to give you time for reflection. And research.

"That research says the best way to bind someone like Mr. White is—actually, it's pretty complicated." Plowman waved his pistol at the symbols shining around them. "The part that will be of most immediate interest to you is the sacrifice of a man and woman who are in my command. I apologize. I intended to put the two of you down before you knew what was happening; I mean, there's no need to be cruel about this. With you, however, I'm afraid my aim was off. Don't worry. I'll finish what I started before I turn you over to Mr. White."

Vasquez tilted her right hand up and squeezed the trigger of her gun. Four pops rushed one after the other, blowing open her pocket. Plowman leapt back, stumbled against the opposite wall. Blood bloomed across the inner thigh of his trousers, the belly of his shirt. Wiped clean by surprise, his face was blank. He swung his gun toward Vazquez, who angled her right hand down and squeezed the trigger again. The top of Plowman's shirt puffed out; his right eye burst. His arm relaxed, his pistol thumped on the floor, and, a second later, he joined it.

The burn of suddenly hot metal through her pocket sent Vasquez scrambling up the wall behind her before the pain lodged in her back could catch her. In the process, she yanked out the Walther and pointed it at the door to the junior suite—

—in front of which Mr. White was standing, hands in his jacket pockets. A dark smear in front of him was all that was left of Buchanan. *Jesus God . . .* The air reeked of black powder and copper. Across from her, Plowman stared at nothing through his remaining eye. Mr. White regarded her with something like interest. *If he moves, I'll shoot,* Vasquez thought, but Mr. White did not move, not the length of time it took her to back out of the corridor and retreat to the elevator, the muzzle of the pistol centered on Mr. White, then on where Mr. White would be if he rounded the corner. Her back was a knot of fire. When she reached the elevator, she slapped the call button with her left hand while maintaining her aim with her right. Out of the corner of her eye she saw Buchanan's gift for his son, all two hundred and sixty euros worth, wedged under its chair. She left it where it was. A faint glow shone from the near end of the corridor: Plowman's black-lighted symbols. Was the glow changing, obscured by an enormous form crawling toward her? When the elevator dinged behind her, she stepped into it, the gun up in front of her until the doors had closed and the elevator had commenced its descent.

The back of her blouse was stuck to her skin; a trickle of blood tickled the small of her back. The interior of the elevator dimmed to the point of disappearing entirely. The Walther weighed a thousand pounds. Her legs wobbled madly. Vasquez lowered the gun, reached her left hand out to steady herself. When it touched, not metal, but cool stone, she was not as surprised as she should have been. As her vision returned, she saw that she was in a wide, circular area, the roof flat, low, the walls no more than shadowy suggestions. The space was lit by a symbol incised on the rock at her feet: a rough circle, the diameter of a manhole cover, broken at about eight o'clock, whose perimeter was shining with cold light. Behind and to her left, the scrape of bare flesh dragging over stone turned her around. This section of the curving wall opened in a black arch like the top of an enormous throat. Deep in the darkness, she could detect movement, but was not yet able to distinguish it.

As she raised the pistol one more time, Vasquez was not amazed to find herself here, under the ground with things whose idiot hunger eclipsed the span of the oldest human civilizations, things she had helped summon. She was astounded to have thought she'd ever left.

The Third Always Beside You

I

That there had been another woman in their parents' marriage was an inference that for Weber and Gertrude Schenker had taken on all the trappings of fact. During the most recent of the late-night conversations that had become a Christmas Eve tradition for them, Weber had christened the existence of this figure "The Keystone," for *her* and her intersection with their mother and father's marriage were what supported the shape into which that union had bent itself.

Over large-bowled glasses of white wine at the kitchen table, his back against the corner where the two window seats converged, Web met his eleven-months-younger sister's contention that, after all this time, the evidence in favor of *her* remained largely circumstantial by shaking his head vigorously and employing the image of the stone carved to brace an arch. Flailing his hands with the vigor of a conductor urging his orchestra to reach higher, which sent his wine climbing the sides of its glass, Web called to his aid a movie's worth of scenes that had led to their decision—during another Christmas Eve confab a decade earlier—that only the presence of another woman explained the prolonged silences that descended on the household without warning, the iciness that infused their mother's comments about their father's travels, the half-apologetic, half-resentful air that clung to their father after his trips like a faint, unpleasant smell. The other woman—*her,* the name custom had bestowed—was the stone that placed a quarryful of cryptic comments and half-sentences into recognizable arrangement.

As for why, ten years on, the two of them were no closer to learning *her* real name, much less any additional details concerning *her* appearance or the history of *her* involvement with their father, when you thought about it, that wasn't so surprising. While both their parents had insisted that there was nothing their children could not tell them, a

declaration borne out over thirty-one and thirty years' discussion of
topics including Web's fear that his college girlfriend was pregnant
(which, as it turned out, she wasn't) and Gert's first inkling that she
might be gay (which, as it turned out, she was), neither their mother
nor their father had asked the same openness of their children. Just the
opposite: their parents scrupulously refrained from discussing anything
of significance to their interior lives. Met with a direct question, their
father became vague, evasive, from which Web and Gert had arrived at
their secret nickname for him, the Prince, as in the Prince of Evasion.
Their mother's response to the same question was simple blankness,
from which her nickname, the Wall, as in the Wall of Silence. With the
Prince and the Wall for parents, was it any wonder the two of them
knew as little as they did?

Web built his case deliberately, forcefully—not for the first time,
Gert thought that he would have made a better attorney than docu-
mentary filmmaker. (They could have gone into practice together:
Schenker and Schenker, Siblings in Law.) Or perhaps it was that he
was right, from the necessity of the other woman's existence to their
parents' closed-mouthed-ness. Yet if the other woman was the Keystone, her presence raised at least as many questions as it answered,
chief among them, why were their mother and father still together? A
majority of their parents' friends—hell, of their parents' siblings—were
on their second, third, and in one case fourth marriages. If their mother and father were concerned about standing out in the crowd, their
continued union brought them more sustained attention than a divorce, however rancorous, could have. Both their parents were traversed by deep veins of self-righteousness that lent some weight to the
idea of them remaining married to prove a point—especially to that
assortment of siblings moving into the next of their serial monoga-
mies. However, each parent's self-righteousness was alloyed by another
tendency—self-consciousness in their mother's case, inconstancy in
their father's—that, upon reflection, rendered it insufficient as an explanation. Indeed, it seemed far more likely that their mother's almost
pathological concern for how she was perceived, combined with their
father's proven inability to follow through on most of his grandilo-
quent pledges, had congealed into a torpor that caught them fast as
flies in amber.

It was a sobering and even depressing note on which to conclude their annual conversation, but the clock's hands were nearing 3 A.M., the second bottle of wine was empty, and while there was no compulsion for them to rise with the crack of dawn to inspect Santa's bounty, neither of them judged it fair to leave their significant others alone with their parents for very long. They rinsed out their glasses and the emptied bottles, dried the glasses and returned them to the cupboard, left the bottles upended in the dishrack, and, before switching off the lights, went through their old ritual of checking all the locks on the downstairs windows and doors. Something of a joke between them when their family first had moved from Westchester to Ellenville, the process had assumed increased seriousness with an increase of home invasions over the last several years. When they were done, Web turned to Gert and, his face a mask of terror, repeated the line that concluded the process, cadged from some horror movie of his youth: "But what if they're already inside?" Gert, who had yet to arrive at a satisfactory response, this year chose, "Well, I guess it's too late then."

The fatalism of her answer appeared to please Web; he bent to kiss her cheek, then wound his way across the darkened living room to the hallway at whose end lay the guest room for which he and Sharon had opted—the location, Gert had reflected, the farthest possible distance from their parents' room but still in the house. This had left her and Dana the upstairs room, her old one, separated from her mother and father's bedroom by the upstairs bathroom. Gert could not decide whether Web's choice owed itself to a desire to maintain the maximum remove from their parents for his new wife and himself, or was due to an urge to force the closest proximity between her and Dana and her parents, who, seven years after Gert's coming out and three years since she'd moved in with Dana, were still not as reconciled to their daughter's sexuality as they claimed to be. Of course, Web being Web, both explanations might have been true. Since sometime in his mid-to-late teens, the closeness with which he had showered their mother and father, the hugs and kisses, had been replaced with an almost compulsive need for distance—if either parent drew too near for too long, tried to prolong an embrace, he practically vibrated with tension. At the same time, he had inherited their parents' self-righteousness and, given an opportunity to confront them with what he viewed as their shortcomings, was only too happy to do so. If Gert was uncomfortable, it wasn't in the plastic pleasantness that her mother and father put on whenever she and Dana visited, to which she'd more or less resigned herself as the lesser of many evils; it was in being fixed to the point of the spear with which Web wanted to jab their parents.

As she mounted the stairs to the second floor, she wondered if Web was anxious about his marriage going the way of their mother and father's, if his need for the downstairs room was rooted in anxiety about him and Sharon being contaminated by whatever had stricken their parents. It wasn't only their behavior that displayed the souring of their union. Physically, each appeared to be carrying an extra decade's weight. Their father's hair had fallen back to the tops of his ears, the back of his head, while their mother's had been a snow-white that she refused to dye for as long as either of their memories stretched. Their parents' faces had been scored across the forehead, to either side of the mouth, and though they kept in reasonable shape, their mother with jogging, their father racquetball, the flesh hung from their arms and legs in that loose way that comes with old age, the skin and muscle easing their grip on the bones that have supported them for so long, as if rehearsing their final relaxation. The formality with which their parents treated hers and Web's friends buttressed the impression that she and her brother were a pair of last-minute miracles or accidents. Without exception, Gert's friends had been shocked to learn that her mother and father were, if not the same age as their parents, then younger. She thought Web had received the same response from his classmates and girlfriends.

Although she swung it open gently, the hinges of the door to her and Dana's room shrieked. *No sneaking around here.* In the pale wash of streetlight over the window, she saw Dana fast asleep on her side of the bed, cocooned in the quilt that had covered it. Leaving the door open behind her, Gert crossed to the hope chest at the foot of the bed and unlatched it. The odor of freshly laundered cotton rose to meet her, and along with it came the groan of the floorboards outside the door.

"Mom?" She stood. "Dad?" The hall sounded with whichever of them it was hurrying to their room. Gert waited for the hinges on their door to scream, wondering why they hadn't when whoever it was had opened it. After ten years of promising to do so, had her father finally oiled them? She listened for the softer snick of their door unlatching. She could feel someone standing there, one hand over the doorknob, their eyes watching her doorway for movement. "For God's sake . . ." Five steps carried her out into the hall, her face composed in an expression of mock-exasperation.

The space in front of the door to her parents' bedroom was empty, as was the rest of the hallway. For a moment Gert had the sensation that she was *not* seeing something, some figure in the darkness—the feeling was kin to what she had experienced looking directly at the keys for which she was tearing up the apartment and not registering them—and then the impression ceased. The skin along her arms, her neck, stood. *Don't be ridiculous,* she told herself; nonetheless, she made certain that the door to her room was shut tight. Later on, she did not hear footsteps passing up and down the hallway.

II

Gert's decision to pursue the question of the other woman, to ascertain her identity, was prompted not so much by that most recent Christmas Eve conversation as it was by a chance meeting with an old family friend in the din of Grand Central the week after New Year's. While waiting in line to purchase a round-trip ticket to Rye (where lived an obscenely wealthy client of her firm who insisted on conducting all her legal affairs in the comfort of her tennis-court of a living room), she felt a hand touch her elbow and a voice say, "Gertie?" Before she turned, she recognized the intonations of her Aunt Victoria— not one of her parents' sisters or their brothers' wives, but an old friend, perhaps their oldest, at a dinner party at whose house their father first had met their mother. With something of the air of its presiding genius, Aunt Vicky, Auntie V, had floated in and out of their household, always happy to credit herself for its existence and therefore, by extension, for hers and Web's. During Gert's teenage years, Victoria had been a lifesaver, rescuing her from her parents' seemingly deliberate lack of understanding of everything to do with her life and treating her to shopping trips in Manhattan, weekends at the south Jersey shore, even a five-day vacation on Block Island her senior year of high school. In recent years Victoria's presence in their lives had receded, the consequence of her promotion to vice president of the advertising company for which she worked, but she was still liable to put in an appearance at the odd holiday.

Victoria's standing in the line was due to a speaking engagement with a sorority at Penrose College, in Poughkeepsie, to which she had decided it would be pleasant to ride the train up the east shore of the Hudson. She was dressed with typical elegance, in a black suit whose short skirt showed her legs fit as ever; and although her cheeks and jaw had lost some of their firmness of definition, her personality blazed forth, and Gert once more found herself talking with her as she would have one of her girlfriends. The result of their brief exchange was a decision to meet for lunch, which consultation with their respective Blackberries determined would occur a week from that Saturday; there was, Victoria said, a new place in NoHo she was dying to try, and this would provide the perfect opportunity. Gert left their meeting feeling as she always did after any time with Victoria: refreshed, recharged.

Not until the other side of her visit with Miss Bruce (ten minutes of business wrapped inside two hours of formalities), as she was watching the rough cut of Web's latest film on her laptop, did the thought bob to the surface of her mind: *Maybe Aunt Vicky was the other woman.*

The idea was beyond absurd: it was perverse; it was obscene. Victoria Godfrey had been a de facto member of their family, closer to the four of them than a few of their blood relations. She had been present during the proverbial thick, and she had been there through the proverbial thin. To suggest that she and Gert's father had carried on, were carrying on, an affair was too much, was over the top.

Try as she might, though, Gert could not banish the possibility from her thoughts. The same talents for analysis and narration that had placed her near the top of her class at NYU seized on the prospect of Auntie V being *her* and found that it made a good deal of sense. While both her parents had known Victoria, her father's friendship with her predated her mother's by several years. In fact, Victoria and her father had spoken freely of the marathon phone conversations with which they'd used to pass the nights, the restaurants they'd sought out together, the bands they'd seen in concert. Certainly, the connection between them had endured the decades. And during those years, her father's consulting job had required him to travel frequently and far, as had Aunt Vicky's work, first in journalism and then in advertising. That Victoria, despite her declarations that all she wanted was a good man to settle down with, continued to live alone seemed one more piece of evidence thrown on top of what had suddenly become a sizable pile.

But her mother . . . Gert closed her laptop. In the abstract, at least, Gert long had admitted to herself the probability that her father had been unfaithful to her mother, perhaps for years. Restricting her consideration to her father and Aunt Vicky, she supposed she could appreciate how, given the right combination of circumstances, their friendship could have led to something else. (Wasn't that what had brought her and Dana together?) Factor her mother into the equation, however, and the sides failed to balance. Her father's relationship with Victoria might be longer, but her mother's was deeper; all you had to do was sit there quietly as they spoke to know that, while their conversation's focus might be narrow, it was anchored in each woman's core. Gert had no trouble believing her aunt might be involved with a married man if the situation suited her, but she could not credit Auntie V betraying one of her dearest friends.

Nonetheless, the possibility would not quit her mind; after all, how many divorces had she assisted or managed in which the immediate cause of the marriage's disintegration was a friend or even in-law who had gone from close to too-close? That the same story might have repeated itself in her parents' marriage nauseated her; without changing its appearance in the slightest, everything surrounding her looked wrong, as if it were all manifesting the same fundamental flaw. She shook her head. *All right,* she told herself, *if this is the truth, I won't run from it. I'll meet it head-on.* False bravado, perhaps, but what was her alternative?

A week and a half later, pulling open the heavy glass door to Lettuce Eat and stepping into its low roar of voices, Gert repeated to herself the advice that she gave the new lawyers: *Act as if you're in control, and you will be.* She had not been this nervous arguing her first case: her heart was thwacking against her chest; her palms were wet; her legs were trembling. In moments scattered across the last ten days, she had auditioned dozens of opening lines, from the innocuous (*Hi, Aunt Vic*) to the confrontational (*What do you say we talk about you and my father?*); and although she hadn't settled on one (she was leaning toward *I'm so glad you came: there's something I'd like to talk to you about*), she was less concerned about the exact manner in which they would begin than she was with the substance of their talk. What she would do should Auntie V confirm the narrative whose principal points Gert had posited on a legal pad she hadn't shown anyone, she could not predict. Nor did it help matters any that Victoria, in addition to a black turtleneck and jeans, was wearing a pair of dark sunglasses, the necessity of which, she explained as she stood to kiss Gert, arose from an office party that had not ended until 5 A.M. "I'm not dead yet, by God," Victoria said as she resumed her seat and Gert took hers. "I can still give you kids a run for your money."

Gert answered her aunt's assertion with a polite smile that she maintained for the waitress who appeared at her side proffering a menu. In reply to the girl's offer to bring her something to drink, Gert requested a Long Island iced tea and focused her attention on the menu, whose lettuce leaf shape was printed with the names of eight lunch salads. After the waitress had left for her drink, Victoria said, "That's kind of heavy-duty for Saturday brunch, don't you think?"

"Oh?" Gert nodded at Victoria's Bloody Mary.

"Darling, this is practically medicinal. Really, if I thought my HMO would cover it, I'd have my doctor write a prescription."

Despite herself, Gert laughed.

"Now," Victoria continued, "you don't look as if you were sampling new cocktails till dawn, so that drink is for something else, isn't it? Everything okay with Dana? Work?"

"Fine," Gert said, "they're both fine. Couldn't be better."

"All right, then, how about your brother? Or—his wife, what's her name, again? Sharon?"

"Sharon's fine, too. Web is Web. He's working on a new film; it's about this painter, Belvedere, Thomas Belvedere. Actually," Gert continued, "there is something—in fact, it's something I need to talk to you about."

"Sweetie, of course. What is it?"

"It has to do with my parents."

"What is it? Is everything okay? Nobody's sick, are they?"

"Here you go," the waitress said, placing Gert's drink before her. "Do you know what you'd like to order?"

Gert chose the Vietnamese salad, which, Victoria said, sounded much more interesting than what she'd been thinking of, so she ordered one as well, dressing on the side. Once the waitress had departed, Victoria said, "The last time I saw your mother, I told her she was too skinny."

"Nobody's sick," Gert said.

"You're sure?"

"Reasonably."

"Oh, well, thank God for that." Victoria sipped her Bloody Mary. "Okay, everybody's healthy, everybody's happy: what do you want to discuss?"

The Long Island iced tea bit her tongue; Gert coughed, lowered her glass, then raised it for a second, longer drink. The alcohol poured through her in a warm flood, floating the words up to her lips: "It's my dad. I need to talk to you about the other woman—the one he had the affair with."

At NYU, the professor who had taught Gert and her classmates the finer points of cross-examination had employed a lexicon drawn from fencing to describe the interaction between attorney and witness. Of the dozen or so terms she had elaborated, Gert's favorite had been the *coup droit,* the direct attack. As she had seen and continued to see it, a witness under cross-examination was expecting you to attempt to trick them, trip them up on some minor inconsistency. If the opposing counsel were conscious, they would have prepped the witness for exactly such an effort; thus, in Gert's eyes, it was more effective (unexpected, even) to get right to the point. The strategy didn't always succeed—none did—but the times it worked, a certain look would come over the witness's face, the muscles around their eyes, their mouths responding to the words their higher faculties were not yet done processing, which Gert fancied was the same as the one you would have witnessed on the person whose chest your blade had just slid into. It was a look that mixed surprise, fear, and regret; when she saw it, Gert knew the witness, and probably the case, were hers.

It was this expression that had overcome Victoria's face. For an instant, she seemed as if she might try to force her way past it, pretend that Gert's question hadn't struck her as deeply as it had, but as quickly as it appeared to arise, the impulse faded. Her hands steady, she reached up to her sunglasses and removed them, uncovering eyes that were sunken, red-rimmed with the last night's extravagances. Trading her eyeglasses for her drink, Victoria drained the Bloody Mary and held up the empty glass to their waitress, passing near, who nodded to the gesture and veered toward the bar. With a sigh, Victoria replaced the glass on the table and considered Gert, who was helping herself to more of her drink, her mind reeling with triumph and horror. The thrill that sped through her whenever her *coup droit* succeeded carried with it a cargo of anguish so intense that she considered bolting from her chair and running out of the restaurant before the conversation could proceed any further. The next time she and Aunt Vicky saw each other, they could pretend this exchange had never happened.

But of course, it was already too late for that. Victoria was speaking: "How did you find out? Your father didn't tell you, did he? I can't imagine—was it your mother? Did she say something to you?"

"No one said anything," Gert said. "Web and I put it together one night—I guess it was ten years ago. We were up late talking, and the subject turned to Mom and Dad, the way it always does, and all their little . . . quirks. I said something along the lines of, *It's as if there's another woman involved,* and Web took that idea and ran with it. It was one of those things you wouldn't have dreamed could be true—well, I wouldn't have—but the more we discussed it, the more sense it made, the more questions it answered. Since then, it's something we've pretty much come to take for granted."

"Jesus," Victoria said. "Ten years?"

Gert nodded.

"And this is—why haven't you asked me about this before?"

"For a while, we were happy to let sleeping dogs lie. Web still is, actually; he doesn't know I'm talking to you. Recently I've—I guess I'm at a point where I want to know for sure, one way or the other. At least, I think I do."

"No, no," Victoria said, "you're right. You should know. I should've spoken to you—not ten years ago, maybe, but it's past time. You have to understand—"

Whatever was necessary for Gert's understanding was pre-empted by the return of their waitress with Victoria's drink and their salads. Gert stared at the pile of bean sprouts, mango, banana, rice noodles, and peanut in front of her and thought that never had she felt less like eating. With each breath she took, her internal weather shifted sharply, raw fury falling into deep sadness, from which arose bitter disappointment. That she managed an "I'm fine, thanks" to the waitress's "Can I bring you anything else?" was more reflex than actual response.

Before the waitress left, Victoria was sampling her next Bloody Mary. She did not appear any more interested in her salad than Gert was in hers. "All right," Victoria said once she had lowered her glass. "I want—you need to remember that your father loves your mother. She loves him, too—despite everything, they love each other as much as any couple I've ever known. Promise me you'll do that."

"I know they love each other," Gert said, although she could think of few facts in which she currently had less confidence.

"They do, honey; I swear they do. But your dad . . ." As if she might find what she wanted to say written there, Victoria's eyes searched the ceiling. "Oh, your father."

"Yes," Gert said.

"Let me— When you were, you must have been two, your father spent about three days calling everyone he knew. Anyone he couldn't reach by phone, he wrote to. All those calls, those letters, said the same thing: for the past seven years I have been having an affair. He had decided to end it, and the only way he was going to be able to follow through on that choice was if he came clean with all his family, all his friends, starting with your mother."

Gert tried to imagine her father being that decisive about anything. "How did you feel about this?"

"In a word, shocked. It's one of those times I can remember exactly where I was, what I was doing. I was in this sleazy motel outside D.C., prepping an interview with a guy who claimed he had dirt on the junior senator from New York. There was a single, coin-operated bed in the room that had the most hideous green and orange spread on it. The walls were covered in cheap paneling and were too thin: for about an hour, I'd been listening to a couple on one side of me having drunken sex, and a baby on the other side of me wailing. Very nice. It was a little after nine o'clock; I had the TV on in an attempt to drown out the circle of life around me, and the theme from *Dallas* was playing. When the phone rang, I thought it was my editor, calling with yet another last-minute question. The senator already had a reputation as a vengeful son of a bitch, and my editor was nervous about any story that wasn't ironclad.

"Anyway, I heard your father's voice, and at first all I could think was, *How did he get this number?* Then I caught up to what he was saying and—" Victoria shook her head. "If you'd had a feather, you could have knocked me to the floor with it. I consider myself pretty perceptive. There isn't much that happens with my friends that I didn't see coming a mile away. But this . . ."

"What was it that surprised you?" Gert said.

"Are you kidding? Your father was cheating on your mother. He had been all through their relationship, their engagement, their marriage. Who does that? Okay, plenty of people, I know, but your father, he was—I guess you could say, he played the part of the devoted husband so convincingly . . . that isn't fair. He was devoted; it's just, he'd gotten himself into such a mess. I screamed at him: *What the fuck have you done, you asshole?* I mean, there was your mother with two little kids. What was she supposed to do?"

Was the alcohol slowing her comprehension? Gert said, "What about the other woman?"

"*Her.*" Victoria spat out the word as if it were a piece of spoiled meat. "I know," she said, holding up her hand to forestall the objection Gert wasn't about to make, "that isn't fair. It takes two and all, but . . ." Victoria slapped the table, drawing glances from the diners to either side of them. "She was already married, for Christ's sake! She had been for years."

"Did—did you know her?"

"No, which is funny, because she lived three doors down from me. This is back when I had the place on West Seventy-first. Over the years, I must have seen her God knows how many times, but I'd never paid any attention to her. Why should I have? Little did I know she was—well, little did I know.

"That changed. Although it was after eleven when I finally hung up with your father, I was back on the phone right away. There was this guy, Phil DiMarco, a private investigator we used at the paper. He specialized in the cheating spouses of the rich and powerful; we turned to him whenever the rumor mill whispered that this politician or that movie star wasn't living up to their marriage vows. He was expensive as all hell, but he and I had this kind of thing, so he said he'd have a look around and get back to me."

"Why?" Gert said. "Why did you call a p.i.?"

"One of my oldest friends had just admitted that he'd been lying to me for years: not exactly a statement to inspire you with trust. Who knew if this was him coming clean, or some other lie? I was pissed off. I was afraid, the way you are for your friends when they're sliding down into something very bad. I felt sick. I kept thinking about your mom and you and your brother. This was when you were living in the house on Oat Street; I don't know if you remember it, but the front door was this gigantic thing you'd expect on a castle, not a modified Cape. It was ridiculous. Whenever I hauled it open, Web would shout, *Aunt Wicky!* and run at me on those chubby legs of his. You were much more reserved: you'd hide behind your mom with that bear, Custard, clutched to your chest like a shield, until she stepped aside and urged you forward. And now . . . your father had fucked up your lives royally. The whole situation was so unfair. I figured I could at least find out if he was telling the truth; it seemed like one thing I could do for your mother, for you."

"What did this Phil guy find out?" Gert asked. "Was my father telling the truth?"

"As far as Phil DiMarco was able to determine—he did a more thorough job than I'd expected, although he said he could take things further if I wanted him to, which I decided I didn't—anyway, yes, your dad had been honest with me, with us.

"Which was good," Victoria said. "I mean, it beat the alternative. But there was still the matter of what he'd been so honest about. There's no way you and Web could remember any of what followed the next year. Not to sound melodramatic, but there are large portions of it I'd like to forget. There wasn't—it's difficult to see, to hear people you love in pain. And I did love both of them. Furious as I was with your father, he was still my friend who'd made a terrible mistake he was trying to set right. Your mother was—she'd been very happy with your father, with you and Web, with all you as a family, and then it was like . . ." Victoria waved her hand, a gesture for chaos, unraveling.

"How is everything?" Their waitress stood beside the table, nodding at their untouched salads.

"Wonderful," Victoria said.

"Are you sure?" the girl asked. "Because—"

"Wonderful," Victoria said. "Thank you."

While Victoria had been speaking, Gert had been aware of restraining her emotions; in the pause created by the waitress's interruption, a flood of feeling rushed through her. Gert could distinguish three currents in it: relief, regret, and dread. The relief, sweet and milky as chai, was that her Auntie V could remain her Auntie V, that Gert would not have to hate her for an error she had made decades prior. The regret, sour as a rotten lime, was that her father had in fact betrayed her mother, that her and Web's elegant theory had been incarnated into sordid fact. The dread, blank as water, was that she had not yet heard the worst of Victoria's story, a groundless anxiety that, the instant she recognized it, she knew was true.

Some of what she was feeling must have been visible on her face, set loose by the alcohol she'd dropped into her empty stomach; it prompted Victoria to say, "Oh, honey, I'm so sorry. This is too much, isn't it? Maybe we should change the subject, talk about the rest later."

Gert shook her head. "It's all right. I mean, it is a lot, but—go on, keep going. Tell me about the woman, the one my dad was with. What was her name?"

"Elsie Durant. Did I mention she was married? I did, didn't I? She was a few years older than he was; I can't remember exactly how much, six or seven, something like that. Coming and going from my apartment, I kept an eye out for her and managed to walk past her a couple of times. She was nothing special to look at: pointy nose, freckles, mousy hair that she wore up. About my height, big in the hips, not much of a chest. When I saw her, she was dressed for work, dark pantsuits that looked as if she'd bought them off the rack at Macy's."

"How did they meet?"

"At a convention out west, in Phoenix, I'm pretty sure. Your dad was looking to drum up clients for his business, which was only a thing on the side back then. She was a sales rep for one of the companies he was hoping to snag. When they met, it was as professionals, and the fact that they both came from the same town was a coincidence to be exploited so he could continue his sales pitch. Their conversation led to drinks, which led to dinner, which led to more drinks, which led to her hotel room." Victoria shrugged. "You've attended these kinds of things, haven't you?"

Gert nodded.

"You know: a certain percentage of the attendees treat the event as an opportunity to hook up. It's like, while the cat's away, she's gonna play. If I were a sociologist, I'd do a study of it, try to work out the exact numbers.

"So your dad and Elsie started out as one more tacky statistic. They could've stayed that way if he hadn't called her the week after they returned from the convention—to follow up on the matters they'd discussed. Fair enough. He had a legitimate interest in securing this contract. It was just about enough to allow him to ditch his day job, and it was the kind of high-profile association that would put him on the map. Obviously, though . . ."

"His motives were ulterior."

Victoria smirked. "You might say that. I'm not sure if he knew that she was married, at first, but if he didn't, then he found out pretty soon. Her husband was a doctor, an endocrinologist at Mount Sinai. He was Polish, had immigrated when he was eighteen. In another instance of six degrees of separation, one of my friends was under his care for her thyroid. She said he was a great physician, but had all the personality of a pizza box."

"Did he know? About them?"

"I don't know. Your father insisted he must have, and it's hard to believe he didn't suspect something. Although apparently he was a workaholic, out early in the morning, home late at night, busy weekends, so maybe he wasn't paying attention. Or could be, he was carrying on his own affair.

"To be honest," Victoria said, "there's a lot of this part of the story I have only the faintest idea of. The night your father called me, I wasn't especially interested in hearing the detailed history of his relationship with this other woman. Later on—when, I admit it, I was curious—encouraging him to revisit the details of his and Elsie's affair seemed less than a good idea. I have the impression that things were pretty intense at first, but aren't they always? If you're in the situation, it's—its own thing, fresh, new; if you're outside looking in, it's a movie you've seen one too many times. He wanted her to leave her husband.

She promised she would, then changed her mind. He threatened to go to her husband. She swore she'd never speak to him again if he did. Eventually they settled into an unhappy routine. A couple of pleasant weeks would be followed by one or the other of them promising to break things off because of her marriage.

"After your father met your mother, he and Elsie didn't see each other for a while. Apparently she was pretty pissed at him for becoming involved with somebody else. Hypocritical, yes, but what's that line about contradicting yourself? I don't know why he returned to her, and I cannot understand how he continued the affair once he was engaged, and then married, to your mother. I gather their encounters had slipped from regular to occasional, but even so . . ."

"You must have asked him about it," Gert said.

"Oh, I did. He told me he'd been in love with two women. He had been, but he'd decided to make a choice, and that was your mother."

"Do you—?"

"Do I what? Think he was still in love with Elsie?"

"Yes."

"Your mother asked the same question," Victoria said. "She was obsessed with it. Of course your father had told her that she was the only woman he loved, but really, what else was he going to say and have any chance of her not leaving him? This left it to me to hash out with her whether he was telling the truth."

"You told her he was."

"What else was I going to do? I knew that he loved your mother— that he loved you and your brother. If he and your mom could hang in there, gain some distance from what he'd done, I was sure they would work things out. Which they did," Victoria said, "more or less."

"You still haven't answered the question."

"You noticed that. Sweetie, I don't know what to tell you. I thought he was fixated on her, mostly because he'd been unable to have her . . . completely, I guess you could say. Because she'd remained with her husband. I tend to think that isn't love—it certainly isn't the same as what he felt toward your mother."

"But it could be as strong."

"It could."

"Obviously, Mom decided to stay with him," Gert said.

"She told me your father had chosen her, and that was enough. Maybe she believed it, too—maybe it would have been, if—"

"What? If what?"

Victoria answered by draining the remainder of her Bloody Mary. Her heart suddenly jumping in her throat, Gert brought her own glass to her lips. The alcohol eased her heart back into her chest, allowing her to repeat her, "What?"

"That first year was bad," Victoria said. "Your father spent months alternating between the couch—until your mom couldn't stand having him around and ordered him out of the house—and a motel room—until your mom freaked out at the prospect of him there by himself and ordered him back to the house. There wasn't much I could do for him: when I phoned, your mom wanted to speak with me, and it wouldn't have worked for me to take him out somewhere. He had done wrong; it was his duty to suffer. Once in a while I would stop over and find your mother out; then I would have a chance to talk to him. Not that there was much to say. Mostly, I asked him how he was doing and told him to hang in there, your mom still loved him.

"Which was the same thing I said to your mom: *He loves you; he loves you so much; he's made a terrible mistake, but he loves you.* Nights your dad was home to watch you guys, I'd take her out. There was a little bar down the road from the house you were living in, Kennedy's—we'd go there and order girly drinks and she could say whatever she needed to. What didn't help matters any was that your father hadn't stopped traveling. In fact, he was gone more. He'd won that contract with Elsie's company, and their association had had exactly the effect he'd expected. By the time he met your mom, he was worth a couple of million; by the time you arrived, that amount had tripled. But whatever the money his firm brought in, it wasn't enough. (I swear, how he found the *time* to carry on an affair, I'll never know.) For about a month after he came clean on Elsie Durant, your dad put that part of his life on hold, turned the day-to-day running of the firm over to his number two guy. During that month, though, Number Two was on the phone to him at least three or four times a day, and in the end he made the decision to return. I wanted him to sell the business, take the money and invest it, live off that, but that was a non-starter."

Their waitress passing near, Victoria held up her glass.

182 SEFIRA AND OTHER BETRAYALS

"So . . . what?" Gert asked. "Was my father meeting this woman on his trips?"

"Not as far as Phil DiMarco could tell. Your dad went where he was supposed to, met with whom he was supposed to, and otherwise kept to himself. No clandestine meetings, phone calls, or postcards. His one indulgence was presents, mainly toys for you and your brother, although he brought back things for your mom sometimes. Most of it was jewelry, expensive but generic. Your dad's never had much taste when it comes to stuff like that; all your mom's nice jewelry is stuff I told him to buy for her. There was one thing he brought back for her, a little figure he found on a trip to, I think it was Utah of all places, that was kind of interesting. It was a copy of that statue, the Venus of Willendorf. It's this incredibly old carving of a woman, a goddess or fertility figure, or both, all boobs and hips. The copy had been done in this grainy stone, not sandstone but like it, coarser. It was just the right size to sit in your hand."

"Okay," Gert said, "I'm lost."

"Here you are." Their waitress placed a fresh Bloody Mary beside Victoria and removed the empty glass. "How is everything?"

"Wonderful," Victoria said. This time, the waitress did not pursue the matter, but smiled and departed. Looking over the rim of her drink, Victoria said, "By your third birthday, your parents were—I wouldn't say they were back to normal, but they were on the mend. Finally. And then, one afternoon, the phone rings. Your mom picks it up, and there's a woman on the other end. Not just any woman: her, Elsie Durant."

"No."

"Yes. She said, *My name is Elsie Durant. I know you know who I am. I'm sorry to call you, but I need to speak to your husband.*"

"What did Mom say?"

"What do you think? *What the fuck are you doing calling here, you fucking bitch? Haven't you done enough?* She was so angry, she couldn't relax her grip on the phone enough to slam it down—which gave Elsie the time to say, *Please. I'm dying.*"

"No."

"Yes."

"What kind of . . . ?"

"I know," Victoria said. "Your mother said the same thing, *How stupid do you think I am?* But the woman was ready for her. She told your mother she'd sent a copy of her latest medical report to your parents' house, along with her most recent X-ray. Your mother would have it tomorrow, after which she could decide what she wanted to do."

"Which was?"

"To start with, she called me and asked me what I thought. I said she should forget she'd ever spoken to the woman and find out what she'd have to do to have her blocked from phoning them. What about the report, the X-ray? *Don't even open that envelope,* I said. *Take it out back to the barbecue and burn it.*"

"She didn't."

"She didn't. As I'm pretty sure Elsie Durant must have known, the lure of that plain brown envelope was too much. She tore it open and learned that the woman who had been the source of so much pain in her marriage was suffering from *glioblastoma multiforme*. It's the most common type of brain cancer. It's aggressive, and there were fewer options for treating it then than I imagine there are now. The patient history included with the report revealed that Elsie hadn't sought out treatment for her headaches until the tumor was significantly advanced. As of this moment, she was down to somewhere between six weeks and three months; although three months was an extremely optimistic prognosis. When your mother held up the X-ray to the light, she could see the thing, a dark tree sending its branches throughout the brain."

Gert said, "She told him."

"She did. How could she not? That was what she said to me. *How could I keep this from him? She's dying.* It was too much for her to keep to herself. I would lay money that bitch knew that was exactly how she'd feel."

"What happened? Did my father see her?"

"He spoke with her. Your mother told him everything, and when she was finished, he went to the phone and called her."

"What did he say?"

"I don't know. Your mom walked away—"

"She what?"

"She couldn't be there—that was how she put it to me."

Gert found her drink at her lips. There was less left in it than she'd realized. When the glass was empty, she said, "You must have asked Dad what they talked about."

"He wouldn't tell me."

"Why not?"

Victoria shook her head. "He wouldn't say anything. He just looked away and kept silent until I changed the subject. At first I thought it might be too soon for him to discuss it, but no matter how much time elapsed he wouldn't speak about it."

"What about Mom? Did he ever tell her?"

"She refused to ask him. She said if he wanted her to know he'd tell her. I may be wrong, but I think he was waiting for her to ask him, which he would have taken as a sign that she had truly forgiven him."

"While Mom was waiting for him to come to her as a sign that he had truly repented."

"Exactly."

"Jesus." Gert searched for the waitress, couldn't find her. "How long—after she and Dad spoke, how long did Elsie Durant last?"

"Two weeks."

"Not long at all."

"No."

"How did they find out?"

"The obituary page in the *Times*," Victoria said. "I saw it, too, and let me tell you, I breathed a sigh of relief. As long as Elsie Durant was alive—not to mention, local—she was . . . I wouldn't call her a threat exactly, but she was certainly a distraction. They could have moved, someplace out of state, but your father traveled as much as he ever had. With Elsie permanently out of the picture, I assumed your parents would be able to go forward in a way they couldn't have before—free, I guess you might say, of her presence. I had half a mind to drop in her funeral, just to make sure she was gone.

"As it turned out, I got my wish."

"You were there?" As soon as the question had left her mouth, its answer was evident: "For my father: you went to find out if he went."

"Your mother was convinced he would attend. To be honest, so was I, especially after his silence about his and Elsie's final conversation. Of course, I didn't say this to your mom; to her I said there was no way he'd be at the funeral. I mean, if nothing else, the woman's husband would be there, and wouldn't that be awkward? She didn't buy it. It was all I could do to convince her not to go herself. *For God's sake,* I said, *stay home. Hasn't this woman had enough of your life already? Why give her anything more?* That had more of an effect on her, but in the end I had to promise her that I would attend. If anybody asked, I figured I could pass myself off as a sympathetic neighbor."

"Did my dad—"

"Yes. Elsie Durant's funeral was held upstate, at St. Tristan's, this tiny church about ten minutes from the Connecticut state line. It was a pretty place, all rolling hills and broad plains. I don't know what her connection to it was. The church itself was small, much taller than it was deep, so that it seemed as if you were sitting at the bottom of a well. The windows—some of the stained-glass windows were old, original to the church, but others were more recent—replacements, I guess. The newer ones had been done in an angular, almost abstract style, so that it was if they were less saints and more these strange assemblies of shapes.

"Your father and I sat on opposite sides at the back of the church, which still wasn't that far from the altar. The funeral was a much smaller affair than I'd expected: counting the priest and the altar boys, there were maybe ten or eleven people there. The rest of the mourners sat in the front pews. There was an older man with a broad back who appeared to be the husband, a cluster of skinny women who were either sisters or cousins of the deceased, and a couple of nondescript types who might have been family friends. Honestly, I was shocked at how empty the church was. I—it sounds silly, but Elsie Durant had been such a—she had loomed over your parents' lives, their marriage, over my life, too—she had been such a presence that I had imagined her at the center of all sorts of lives. I had pictured a church packed with mourners—maybe half of them her illicit lovers, but full, nonetheless. I was unprepared for the stillness of— You know how churches catch and amplify each sob, each cough, each creak of the pew as you shift to make yourself more comfortable. That was what her funeral was to me, an assortment of random sounds echoing in an almost-empty church.

"After the service was over, before they'd wheeled the coffin out, I snuck out and waited in my car. Not only did your dad shake Elsie's husband's hand—and say I can't imagine what to him—he accompanied the rest of the mourners as they followed the hearse on foot across the parking lot and into the cemetery. He stayed through the graveside ceremony, and after that was over, the coffin lowered into the ground, everybody leaving, he remained in place. He watched the workmen use a backhoe to maneuver the lid of the vault into place. He watched them shovel the mound of earth that had been draped with a green cover into the hole. Once the grave was filled and the workers had heaped the floral arrangements on top of it, he held his position. Finally I had to go: I hadn't been to the bathroom in hours, not to mention I was starving. I left with him still standing there."

"He'd seen you—I mean, in the church."

"Oh, yes," Victoria said. "We'd made eye contact as soon as I sat down, glanced around, and realized he was directly across from me. I blushed, as if he were the one catching me doing something wrong, which irritated me no end. I kept my eyes forward for the rest of my time there—when I left, I stared at the floor."

"What did he say to you about it?"

"Nothing. We never discussed it."

"What? Why not?"

"I assumed he would call me; it was what he'd done before. And I was—frankly, I was too pissed off to pick up the phone myself."

"Because he'd done what you thought he would."

"Yes. But—"

"You were afraid of what he might say if you did talk."

"All things considered, wouldn't you have been?"

"What did you tell Mom?"

"Pretty much what I said to you: that he'd been at the back of the church and I'd left before he did."

"Did you mention him standing at the grave?"

"She didn't need to hear that."

"I assume they never talked about it."

Victoria shook her head. "No. She knew, and he knew she knew, but neither wanted to make the first move. Your mother discussed it with me—for years. I would come over and we would sit at the dining-room table—this was when you were in the house on Trevor Lane, the one with the tiny living room. However our conversation started, it always ended with her asking me what your father attending Elsie Durant's funeral meant. Needless to say, she was certain she knew what his presence in that back pew had implied. Well, that's not it, exactly: she was afraid she knew its significance. Who am I kidding? So was I. Not that I ever let on to your mom. To her I said that your father hadn't been doing anything more than paying his respects. If he'd loved Elsie Durant that much, he never would have ended things with her; he wouldn't have elected to stay with your mom. All the while I was thinking, *What, are you kidding me? Maybe he changed his mind after he called things off. Maybe he wasn't the one who ended the affair: maybe she did, and in a fit of pique he made his confessions. Maybe—God help me—he was in love with two women at once.* The possibilities were—it would be an exaggeration to say that they were endless, or even that they were all that many, but they were enough.

"We would make our way through a bottle of red, repeating what had become a very familiar argument. Your mom would have the little statue—the souvenir your dad had brought her, the Venus of Willendorf—in one hand. While we talked, she'd turn it over in her palm—by the end of the night, her skin would be raw from the stone scraping it. On more than one occasion, that statue's pores were dotted with blood.

"After one of those conversations, I had a nightmare—years later, and I can recite it as clearly as if I'd sat up in my bed this very minute. Your mom and dad were standing in a dim space. It was your house—it was all the houses you'd lived in—but it was also a cave, or a kind of cave. The walls were ribbed, the gray of beef past its sell-by date. Your parents were dressed casually, the way they were sitting around the house on a Sunday. They looked—the expressions on their faces were—I want to say they were expectant. As I watched, each held out an arm and raked the nails of their other hand down the skin with such force they tore it open. Blood spilled over their arms, streaming down onto the floor. When enough of it had puddled there, they knelt and mixed their blood with the material of the floor, which was this gray dirt. Once they had a thick mud, they started pressing it into a figure. It was the statue, the Venus, and the sight of it sopping with their blood shot me out of sleep.

"You don't need to be much of a psychiatrist to figure out what my dream was about; although, given how your parents have been looking these past few years, I sometimes wonder if it wasn't just a little bit predictive. But I think about them—I have thought about them; I imagine I'll keep thinking about them—alone in that big house with that space between them, that gap they've had all these years to fill with their resentments and recriminations. Visiting them, there have been times I've been sure I could feel . . . I don't know what. A something there in the house with us. Not a presence—a ghost, no, I don't think they're being haunted by the spirit of Elsie Durant, but something else."

Gert thought of standing in the hallway looking at the door to her parents' room and not seeing anything there. She said, "What? What do you mean?"

Victoria said, "I don't know."

Returned at last, the waitress took Gert's empty glass and her request for another with an "Of course." Once she had left, Gert sat back in her chair. "So that's it," she said. "The outline, anyway. Jesus Christ. If anyone had bothered to talk to anyone else . . . Jesus."

Victoria remained silent until after the waitress had deposited Gert's second drink on the table and Gert had sampled it. Then she said, "I understand, Gertie. When I arrange everything into a story, it seems as if it would have been so easy for the situation to have been settled with a couple of well-timed, honest conversations. But when I remember how it felt at the time—it was like having been dumped in the middle of the ocean. You were trying to keep treading water, to keep your head above the swells. If we had all been different people, maybe we could have avoided this . . . It's quite the clusterfuck, isn't it?"

"It's my life," Gert said, "mine and Web's. This . . . what happened . . . what's still happening . . ."

"I understand," Victoria said. "I'm sorry; I'm so, so sorry. I don't know what else to say. I tried—we all tried. But—"

"Sometimes that isn't enough," Gert said. "It's just—why? Why did they stay together?"

"I told you, sweetie: your mom and dad love each other. That's . . . I used to think the worst thing in the world was falling out of love with someone. Now, though, I think I was wrong. Sometimes you can stay in love with them."

III

One week after her lunch with Aunt Veronica, well before she had come to terms with much if any of what they'd discussed—well before she'd shared the details of Elsie Durant with Dana—Gert found herself opening the front door to her parents' house. She had spent the day a few miles up the road, surrounded by the luxury of the Mohonk Mountain House, at which she'd been attending a symposium on estate law that seemed principally a tax-cover for passing the weekend at Mohonk. While Gert could have stayed at the hotel—which would have allowed her to continue talking to the attractive young law student with whom she'd shared dinner and then an extensive conversation at the hotel bar—she had arranged to stay at her parents', whom she'd felt a need to see in the flesh since Aunt Vicky's revelations. That need, together with a sudden spasm of guilt over having spent so long in the company of another woman so clearly available when Dana was at home working, sped her to the hotel's front portico, where a valet fetched her Prius without remarking the lateness of the hour. Her reactions slowed by the pair of martinis she'd consumed, Gert had navigated the winding road down from the mountain with her palms sweaty on the wheel. With the exception of a pair of headlights that had followed her for several miles, while she worried that they were attached to a police car, the drive to her parents' had been less exciting.

Now she was pushing the door shut behind her, gently, with the tips of her fingers, as she had when she was a teenager sneaking home well after her curfew's expiration. She half expected to find her mother sitting on the living-room couch, her legs curled under her, the TV remote in one hand as she roamed the wasteland of late-night programming. Of course, the couch was empty, but the memory caused Gert to wonder if her mother hadn't been holding something in her other hand, that weird little statue that seemed to follow her around the house. She wasn't sure: at the time, she had been more concerned with avoiding her mother's wrath, either through copious apologizing or the occasional protest at the unfairness of her having to adhere to a curfew hours earlier than any of her friends'. Had her mother been rolling that small figure in her palm, or was this an image edited in as a consequence of Auntie V's disclosures?

The air inside the house was cool, evidence of her father's continuing obsession with saving money. His micro-management of the heating had been a continuing source of contention, albeit of a humorous stripe, between him and the rest of the family. Shivering around the kitchen table, Web and she would say, *You know how much you're worth, right?* which would prompt their father to answer, *And how do you suppose that happened?* to which Web would reply, *You took all those pennies you saved on heating oil and used them to call the bank for a loan?* at which he, Gert, and Mom would snort with laughter, Dad shake his head. Gert decided she would keep her coat and gloves on until she was upstairs.

Halfway across the living room, she paused. The last time she had stood in this space, the Christmas tree had filled the far right corner, its branches raising three decades' worth of ornaments, its base bricked with presents. Together, she and Dana, Web and Sharon, Mom and Dad had spent a late morning that had turned into early afternoon opening presents, exchanging Christmas anecdotes, and consuming generous amounts of Macallan-enhanced eggnog. It had been a deeply pleasant day, dominated by no single event, but suffused with contentment. *Except,* Gert thought, *that all the time, she was here with us. Elsie Durant. She watched Dana tear the wrapping from the easel Mom and Dad bought her. She sat next to me as I held up the new Scott Turow Web had given me. She hovered behind Sharon at the eggnog.*

Nor was that all. Elsie Durant had been present at the breakfast table while she, Web, and their mother had teased their father about his stinginess. During the family trips they had taken, she had accompanied them, walking the streets of Rome, climbing the Eiffel Tower, staring up at the Great Pyramid of Giza. As Gert had walked down the aisle at her high school graduation, Elsie Durant had craned her neck for a better look; when Web's first film had played over at Upstate Films, she had stood at the front of the line, one of the special guests. Every house in which they had lived was a house in which Elsie Durant had resided, too, as if all their houses had possessed an extra room, a secret chamber for their family's secret member.

A sound broke Gert's reverie, a voice, raised in a moan. She crossed to the foot of the stairs, at which she heard a second, louder moan, this one in a different voice from the first—a man's, her father's. Her foot was on the first stair before she understood what she was listening to: the noises of her parents, making love. It was not a chorus to which she ever had been privy; although Web claimed to have eavesdropped on their mother and father's intimacy on numerous occasions, Gert had missed the performances (and not-so-secretly, thought Web had, as well). Apparently freed of the inhibitions that had stifled them while their children were under their roof, her parents were uttering a series of groans that were almost scandalously expressive; as they continued, Gert felt her cheeks redden.

The situation was almost comic: she could not imagine remaining in place for the length of her mom and dad's session, which might take who knew how long (was her father using Viagra?), but neither could she see creeping up the stairs as a workable option, since at some point a stray creak would betray her presence, and then how would she explain that? After a moment's reflection, Gert decided her best course would be to play slightly drunker than she was, parade up the stairs and along the hall to her room as if she'd this minute breezed in and hadn't heard a thing. Whether her parents would accept her pretense was anyone's guess, but at least the act would offer them a way out of an otherwise embarrassing scenario.

To Gert's surprise and consternation, however, the clump of her boots on the stairs did not affect the moans emanating from the second floor in the slightest. Unsure if she were being loud enough, Gert stomped harder as she approached the upstairs landing, only to hear the groans joined by sharp cries. *Oh, come on,* she thought as she tromped toward her room. Was this some odd prank her parents were playing on her? They couldn't possibly be this deaf, could they?

She supposed she should be grateful to learn that her mother and father had remained intimate with each other, despite everything, despite Elsie Durant. Yet a flurry of annoyance drove her feet past the door to her bedroom, past the door to the bathroom, to the door to her parents' room, open wide. She had raised her hands, ready to clap, when what she saw on the big bed made her pause, then drop her hands, then turn and run for the front door as fast as her legs would carry her. Later, after a frantic drive home, the fact that she had not tripped down the stairs and broken her neck would strike her as some species of miracle.

Of course, Dana would awaken and ask Gert what she was doing home, wasn't she supposed to be staying at her parents'? The smile with which Gert greeted her, the explanation that she had missed her lover so much she had opted to return that night, were triumphs of acting that brought a sleepy smile to Dana's lips and sent her back to bed, satisfied. *I am my father's daughter.* On top of the tall bookcase in her office, dust clung to a bottle of tequila that had been a gift from a client whose divorce Gert's management had made an extremely profitable decision. She retrieved it, wiped the dust from it, and carried it through to the kitchen, where she poured a generous portion of its contents into a juice glass. She had no illusions about the alcohol's ability to cleanse her memory of what she'd seen: the image was seared into her mind in all its impossibility; however, if she were lucky, its potency would numb the horror that had crouched on her all the drive back. At her first taste of the liquor, she coughed, almost gagged, but the second sip went down more smoothly.

IV

The streetlight that poured through the tall windows in her parents' room reduced its contents to black and white. The king-size bed at its center was a granite slab, the figures on it statues whose marble limbs enacted a position worthy of the *Kama Sutra.* Startled as Gert was by her mother and father's athletics, she was more shocked by their skin taut against their joints, their ribs, their spines, as if, in the few weeks since last she had seen them, each had shed even more weight. In the pale light, their eyes were blank as those of Greek sculptures.

There seemed to be too many arms and legs for the couple writhing on the bed. Her father stroked her mother's cheek with the back of his hand, and another hand lingered there, brushing her hair behind her ear. Her mother tilted her head to the right, and another head moved to the left. Her parents arched their backs, and in the space between them a third figure slid out of her father and into her mother with the motion of a swimmer pushing through the water. While her mother braced her hands on the mattress, the figure leaned forward from her and drew its hands down her father's chest, then turned back and cupped her mother's breasts. Her parents responded to the figure's caresses with a quickening of the hips, with louder moans and cries that might have been mistaken for complaints. In the space between her mother and father, Elsie Durant drew herself out of their conjoined flesh, the wedge that braced their marriage, the stone at its heart.

The Unbearable Proximity of
Mr. Dunn's Balloons

I

"Come, now," Dunn said. His voice sounded as reasonable as it had at any point these last seven days. "Surely you must have expected something like this."

On reflection, Coleman supposed the man had a point. That did not stop him from thrusting his rapier into the nearest of the balloons.

II

"I'm sorry?" Coleman said, turning from the train's window. Under the pretense of watching the Hudson slide past, he had been studying his reflection, renewing his debate with himself over shaving the beard he had worn since his mid-twenties, the white hairs of which he feared added a full decade to his appearance, advancing (distinguished) middle age to premature old age.

"I asked if you are planning to interview Mr. Dunn," the young man seated across the compartment said. "You had said you write, so it occurred to me that you might be at work on an article about him."

"I am not," Coleman said. "I no longer write as much for the magazines as I used to. Of late, I've been concentrating my efforts on my fiction."

"Oh," said the young man, who had introduced himself at Grand Central as Cal Earnshaw. While the suit in which he traveled appeared of reasonable quality, there was a leanness to Cal's face that suggested those of beggars Coleman had passed along the Venetian canals. The even younger woman seated beside Cal, his wife, Isabelle, said, "If I may be forward, Mr. Coleman, why are you on your way to Mr. Dunn's? From what I've read of your novels, it doesn't seem as though the . . . extravagances of Mr. Dunn and his followers would hold much of interest for you."

Despite himself, a little thrill raced up Coleman's spine at Mrs. Earnshaw's admission of familiarity with his work; a similar confession, he felt certain, would not trouble her husband's lips. He said, "You underestimate me, Madame. My father was a Swedenborgian, albeit an idiosyncratic one."

"You don't say," Cal said.

"I do."

"Do you imply that you have inherited your father's beliefs?" Isabelle said.

"I imply nothing of the kind," Coleman said. "My father found Swedenborg sufficient to his needs; my interest, however, has tended toward the manner in which we make our way through this life, rather than any other."

"Yet surely," Isabelle said, "the nature of our beliefs about the life to come may exert a profound influence upon our conduct in the life that is."

"Undoubtedly," Coleman said. "Although, from my observations, that influence is frequently more occult than direct."

"Then why have you joined us?" Cal said. "Not that we regret the company."

"I am on this train," Coleman said, "in hopes of seeing Mr. Dunn's balloons, about which so much has been written."

"You have read Mrs. Barchester's report of them?" Isabelle said.

"It was that which brought them to my attention," Coleman said. "A friend passing through London made me a gift of her book. My thoughts of late have tended in the direction of the place of my birth. I would not call any point along the Hudson my home, but so much of my childhood was spent traveling up and down the shores of what we used to call the North River that something of the word's glamor attaches to the region, as a whole. When my friend's generosity presented me with Mrs. Barchester's record of her tour up the Hudson, I took it as practically an omen that I should revisit the scenes of my boyhood. Her description of Mr. Dunn's rather remarkable paper balloons iced the cake, so to speak. Even before I had turned the last page, I had booked my trip and written to another friend to ask if it were in

his powers to arrange a visit to Summerland for me. It was, and"—
Coleman spread his hands—"I have the pleasure of your company. I
take it your motivations are of a more spiritual character."

"We are going to prepare for my crossing," Cal said.

"I beg your pardon?"

"My husband is ill, Mr. Coleman." Isabelle laid a gloved hand on
her husband's. "We have exhausted all his inheritance and most of
mine in search of a cure. There is none. The last physician we consulted—Sir Luke Strett: perhaps you have heard of him? He is very well
known on the Continent."

Coleman was unsure. "The name is familiar, yes."

"He advised us that Cal's time is short, and that there are better
ways to spend it than chasing false hope."

"I've long had an interest in the writings of Mr. Dunn and his set,"
Cal said. "Mr. Davis, the Fox sisters . . . the picture of the next life they
have advanced seems so much more *reasonable* than that of the tradi-
tional faiths. Upon our return to Brooklyn, I threw myself into a study
of their work. I read their books; I sat in on their séances; I heard their
lectures. Had my health been firmer, I would have attended one of
their conventions, although there was no real need of that. What I had
learned was enough to justify my previous interest."

Isabelle said, "During one of Mr. Dunn's lectures, he mentioned
that, upon occasion, he had aided those approaching this life's end in
readying themselves for the next. Afterwards, Cal and I succeeded in
speaking to the man, and once he knew our story, he volunteered his
services upon the spot."

"Is that so?"

"Yes." Cal nodded. "Not only did Mr. Dunn refuse what little payment we could offer, he provided for our travel from our home to his."

"How very generous of him."

"It was—it is," Isabelle said.

"Perhaps you had rather I defer my visit to Summerland," Coleman said. "Compared to yours, my reasons for this trip are trivial. I
would not wish to interfere with Mr. Dunn's plans for you."

"Nonsense," Cal said. "You won't be interfering a bit."

"According to Mr. Dunn's letter to us," Isabelle said, "he will require some time alone with my husband. Although he assures us his

house's library is thoroughly stocked, I should be grateful for a companion to help me pass the hours."

"You may consider me at your disposal," Coleman said.

III

Summerland, Poughkeepsie
June 16, 1888

Strange to meet Parrish Dunn today. I wouldn't say I've been brooding on the man, but he has engaged my thoughts for much of the last several months. The successful arms merchant who washes his hands of the blood in which he's steeped them for nigh on twenty years to devote himself to the promulgation of his new Spiritualist beliefs—not to mention, to fashioning his elaborate balloons—how could such a figure not be of interest? I've spent enough time—enough pages in this notebook—supplementing the scant description of him in Mrs. Barchester's North Along the Hudson *that to meet the original to whom my speculations owe their existence gave me a jolt.*

He looks like an arms merchant—strike that, he looks like an arms maker, one of those powers charged by the other gods with forging their spears and shields deep in the bowels of a smoking volcano. Until this point in my life, I have considered my five foot ten inches a more than adequate height, but Dunn must stand somewhere in the vicinity of six foot seven, six foot eight. He rises up to that measurement like a mountain; I've never done well at estimating anyone's weight, so it may be more useful to write that he appears almost as wide as he is tall. Every item he was wearing— black suit, white shirt, black shoes—must have been specially made for him.

Because of his size, Dunn's face, which would otherwise fall somewhere in the broad middle of the human spectrum, has something of the grotesque to it. He is bald, and the expanse of his great skull somehow contributes to this impression. His heavy lips frame a mouth whose thick teeth seem formed for tearing the meat from a leg of venison. His nose is flat, wide, crossed by a white scar that continues across the right cheek. His eyes protrude from their sockets, so that he appears to watch you intensely.

His appearance aside, Dunn has been the model host. His carriage was waiting for us at the train station, and he was waiting for us at the front gate to Summerland. (Note: Must check details of house. I'm fairly sure it's the style known as Second Empire—tall and narrow, like a collection of rectangles stood on their short ends. Roof—Mansard roof?—like a cap. White with black trim, freshly painted, the white blinding in the afternoon, the black shining. Extensive gardens in the

English fashion. Situated on a hilltop overlooking the Hudson and the steep hills on the other shore.) The room in which I have been housed is easily four times as large as the cabin in which I crossed the Atlantic, and extravagantly furnished.

The single most interesting feature of my room, though, is the balloon floating in the center of it, at the foot of the bed. I've read Mrs. Barchester's description of Dunn's balloons over and over again; it's one of the few passages in her book in which my fascination with the subject matter blinds me to the dreadfulness of her prose. Not surprisingly, she has not done the things justice. The size, for example: no doubt she's measured the diameter correctly as three feet, but she has failed utterly in conveying a sense of the balloon's volume, of the manner in which it fills the space in which it hangs like a globe set loose from its moorings. The things are apparently composed of brown paper, which appears heavy, coarse-grained, and which still bears the folds and creases necessary to achieve the balloon's shape. Its seams are dark with whatever Dunn used to seal them. Perhaps the most serious defect in Mrs. Barchester's account of the balloons, however, lies in her remarks upon the designs that cover their surfaces. She writes of the "quaint Oriental patterns with which Mr. Dunn has decorated his inventions." Yet the arrangement of the figures in latitudinal lines, their irregular repetition, give more the impression of communication than ornamentation. The script is none I can read or even recognize: its characters appear drawn from the loops and twists woven into the room's Turkish carpet; nor am I certain of the medium in which Dunn has applied them, which shines as if fresh, and in whose depths I catch traces of crimson, viridian, and purple.

And there is more to note. A distinct odor clouds the air around the balloon. It mixes the wood-pulp smell of the paper with another, faintly medicinal scent, possibly that of ether. (Is this due to the manner in which Dunn suspends his creations?) Underneath the combined smells, I perceive a third, damp, earthy. The balloon's surface produces a low and constant crackling as it shifts in the currents of air wafting into the room through its windows. I went to touch the thing, to add its texture to my catalogue of impressions, only to hesitate with the tips of my fingers a hairsbreadth from its paper. I was seized by the most overpowering repugnance, such that the hairs from the back of my hand right up my forearm stood rigid. I swear, my flesh actually shrank from the thing. For the briefest of instants, I wanted nothing more than to see the balloon destroyed—torn apart, set alight. It was the kind and intensity of response I would have expected confronting an especially loathsome insect, not an eccentric's amusement. I dropped my hand and decided my investigations had proceeded far enough for the moment.

Such a curious reaction—a consequence of the day's travel?

IV

Given his response to the balloon in his chamber, Coleman did not expect that he would be able to sleep in its presence, and he intended to ask Dunn to have it removed after dinner. At the conclusion of the meal, however, Dunn retreated to the library with Cal, whose preparations for their imminent work together the man declared must be seen to posthaste. Not to mention, removed from close quarters with the thing, Coleman's initial antipathy toward it seemed vague, ridiculous. He could wait, he decided, for morning.

Outside the door to his room, though, the self-assurance of minutes before felt cavalier, reckless. So he was relieved when he found the balloon had drifted to the window, where its presence was, if not pleasant, not as repellent.

V

"Do you believe Mr. Dunn?" Isabelle asked.

"Heavens, no," Coleman laughed. "A meeting with old Ahasuerus, the Wandering Jew himself, on the eve of the battle at Gettysburg? Tutelage in the secret arts of Simon Magus? A saving intercession in his later life by the spirits of his mother, Paracelsus, and Swedenborg? It's like a distillation of every melodrama produced these last fifty years. No, I suspect Mr. Dunn's narrative is no more than a way for him to align his past acts with his present practices."

Isabelle frowned, but did not reply. She inclined toward a bush whose name Coleman didn't know but on whose branches a large orange-and-black butterfly moved its wings.

"I am much more interested," Coleman said, "in our host's reluctance to describe the means by which he fashions his balloons."

VI

"You are preoccupied today," Isabelle said.

"Am I?" Coleman turned his gaze from the blue sheet of the Hudson.

She nodded. "Since Mr. Dunn's recitation of his years as an arms merchant last night, your thoughts have been elsewhere, I believe."

Coleman smiled. "I fear I am not as cryptic as I would like."

"Or I am becoming more adept at deciphering you."

One of Dunn's balloons had drifted near. Coleman raised his hand to push it away, only to find himself once more hesitating before his fingers touched its papery surface, his skin literally crawling at the thing's proximity. Instead, he stood from the bench upon which he and Mrs. Earnshaw had admired the view from Dunn's garden and set off at a slow pace along its paths. Isabelle hurried after him. He preempted her question about his response to the balloon by saying, "You are correct. I have been distracted, and our host's words were the cause of it, specifically, his account of the bargain he struck for the rifles taken from the so-called Paris Commune. I was in Paris during the Commune. I'd come in with the second or third shipment of food Great Britain sent after the Prussians lifted their siege of the city. I'd thought I might write a series of articles about the state of the capital, which during the siege had become a focus of international attention and sympathy. It was a project for which I was well suited. Not only was I fluent in the language, but I had visited Paris several times during my youth, and I had maintained my correspondence with several of the friends I had made during those trips. One of these friends helped me secure lodgings in the Vaugirard district, and I settled down to work.

"I was staying at the edge of the city, so each morning I set out to walk into it. While I was cautious at first, I soon became more confident and was ranging far and wide. Some parts of the city seemed hardly to have been affected at all; others—I can recall my shock at seeing the Ministry of Finance, which had been pounded almost entirely into rubble by the Prussian guns, so that what remained resembled an antique ruin. Toward the end of the day I would return home and record my experiences. Once a week I would write a short essay detailing my impressions, which I sent off to Rupert Cook at *Howell's*. He liked the pieces well enough, although he paid the bare minimum for them. To be frank, I did not expect Cook would continue to purchase my essays for very long, once their novelty wore off. For the moment, however, I was in Paris, gathering details for my next novel, which (I hoped) would meet with more success than either of my previous attempts had. If I husbanded my resources, I judged I might be able to extend my stay by as much as another year.

"In the wake of the French defeat, the city—the country—was in tumult. Indeed, the new government chose to convene in Versailles, for fear of the Parisian crowds. One of President Thiers's first moves was to pass the Law of Maturities, whose ostensible purpose was to refill the coffers depleted by the war, but whose not-so-secret intent was to bring Paris, which was to provide an undue share of the revenue, to heel. The Commune arose as an attempt by the residents of the city to administer their own affairs more justly. For the two months of the Commune's rule, Paris was—it was no less turbulent, but the daily chaos was shot through with optimism, with excitement. There was a significant population of foreigners living in the city, exiles, many of them, from more repressive states, and perhaps because of this, what was taking place felt as if its implications went far beyond the city's borders. I filled one notebook and most of a second.

"There had been some skirmishes between the forces defending Paris and those loyal to the national government, but nothing of consequence, or so I judged. How naïve do I sound if I say that I did not believe the dispute between the city and the country would be settled through force of arms? Yet the morning of May twenty-first, I awakened to the sound of the first of the national government's forces marching through the streets. I had not appreciated the unhappiness the residents of the city's western districts felt toward the Commune. This included one of my oldest correspondents, a former professor of classics who I later learned had been passing information along to the president's agents. In fact, he was among those to suggest the route by which the French army might gain access to the city, and to offer reassurance that the soldiers would receive a warm welcome when they arrived.

"Which they did: the avenue outside my window was lined with men, women, children, there to greet the troops as liberators. I stared down at the ranks of men in their blue jackets and red trousers, their kepi caps perched on their heads, their rifles shouldered, and it was as if I were witnessing a performance, some new variety of theater performed in the open air. I could not accept its reality. I kept thinking, *Surely not, surely not.*

"The seven days that followed have come to be known as *La Semaine Sanglante,* the Bloody Week. In short order, Thiers's forces took the western districts; the east, however, was the seat of the Commune, and the fighting there was fierce. Travel through the streets was difficult, sometimes impossible, but it wasn't necessary to go very far to know what was happening. All you had to do was walk to your window to hear the crack of the rifles, the boom of the cannons. The sharp smells of gunpowder and burning wood stained the air. Later I read that, at the president's request, the Prussians had expedited the release of thousands of the French soldiers they had captured, in order to swell the ranks of the national army. The Commune had no centralized plan for defense; rather, each district was charged with its own security. This allowed the army to divide and conquer the Commune. I, who had missed the civil war in the land of my birth, found myself at the heart of another.

"Nor was the Bloody Week the worst of it. Following the army's conquest of the city, the members of the Commune were subject to extended reprisals. Having been associated with the city's government to the slightest degree might lead to trial and execution. The cemetery at Père Lachaise, the Luxembourg Gardens, were taken over by firing squads. I might have fallen under suspicion myself, were it not for my old friend the professor of classics, who testified to my character.

"I could have stayed, I suppose, but the prospect of remaining in the ruin of the Commune was too bleak. Rupert Cook had lost interest in my reports, so I judged the time right to depart Paris. I stopped at Geneva for a few months, spent the winter in Florence, and settled in Venice. There I remained for the next fifteen years, for the first five of which Paris remained under martial law. Needless to say, the novel I had hoped would emerge from my time in the city remained unwritten. It has only been the past few years that I have been able to return to Paris. I had thought I might live there again, but it was impossible. The ghosts of seventeen years past would not allow it.

"So to hear that Mr. Dunn had built his early fortune by trading in the Commune's weapons was . . . unsettling. To say the least." His smile was humorless.

Another balloon had drawn close to them. "I believe your husband's afternoon session should be drawing to a close," Coleman said. He walked away from the balloon, toward the house.

VII

"Were you of age during the War Between the States?" Dunn asked.

"I was," Coleman said without turning his gaze from the swords racked between two of the library's considerable bookcases. He touched the pommel of a rapier. "May I?"

"Of course."

The sword was heavier than Coleman anticipated. It took him a moment to find its balance, after which he slashed right to left, left to right, theatrically.

"You were an officer," Dunn said.

"I was not," Coleman said, replacing the sword. "I suffered an . . . injury a few years before the outbreak of hostilities. I was visiting family friends, and there was a fire in their barn, which I joined the effort to extinguish. I was standing too close to one of the walls when it collapsed and showered me with debris. The quick response of my fellows saved me, but I was left unfit for service. Both my older brothers, Will and Bob, distinguished themselves in the war; in fact, Bob became one of Grant's aides." He spared a glance at Dunn, who was studying him intently. Coleman went on, "Since moving to London I've taken up fencing as a way to hold the effects of aging at bay."

"The effects of your injury have lessened with the years," Dunn said.

"They have not hindered my exercise, no."

"Perhaps they would have allowed you to join your brothers."

"Perhaps," Coleman said. "I was in England when Sumter was shelled, and my father insisted I remain there."

"Due to your wound."

Coleman felt his face redden. "If there is an inference you would like to make clear—"

"Nothing of the kind," Dunn said, waving one of his massive hands. "You should be grateful—you should fall on your knees and give thanks to whatever God you venerate for that injury. Whatever discomfort, whatever pain it has brought to you has preserved you from an experience vastly more terrible, from wading knee-deep in a tide of blood and gore. It was something of a witticism among my fellow soldiers that should any of us fall in battle, he need have no fear of the Christian hell, because next to the sights we had witnessed, its famous torments would count as naught." Dunn paused. "I beg your pardon: I don't mean to bore you with an old soldier's platitudes. Lunch should be ready on the patio."

Coleman followed Dunn out of the library with the enormous oak table at its center, the handful of balloons floating amidst its bookcases. He was thinking that Dunn had uttered his description of the war in a tone not of horror, but nostalgia.

VIII

"I wonder, sir, what you regret," Cal Earnshaw said.

"I beg your pardon?" Coleman looked up from his book.

Cal pushed himself slightly higher in his Adirondack chair. "You may imagine," he said, panting from the effort, "a man in my position finds a great deal he wishes he could do, or undo. Some of it is fairly obvious: Isabelle and I will never have a family. Some of it is more idiosyncratic: I will not see the pyramids, which has been an ambition of mine since I read about them as a boy. I've tried to reconcile myself to these facts, for really, what else can I do? Yet I am so far unable to rise above my frustration—my anger, if I am to speak candidly—at everything I am to lose. I keep hoping that the peace which is supposed to descend on those nearing death's precincts will find me, but it has not.

"All of which," he continued, "is preamble to my asking what regrets a man like you might harbor. You have lived longer than have I; you have traveled far, resided in places that are only names on a map to me. You have authored several novels, many more stories; you have written extensively for an assortment of periodicals. In short, you have had a life whose fullness, if not its exact details, I should have liked for mine. I know that you must have had your disappointments, but weighed against that fullness, I find it difficult to believe that any mistake or missed opportunity could matter that much."

Coleman set his book on the arm of his chair. A quartet of balloons hovered in the near distance; he fought the urge to depart the porch with all due speed. He had promised Isabelle that he would sit with her husband while he recovered from his morning session with Dunn (which appeared to be hastening the end they were supposed to be preparing him for: in the last five days, Cal had gone from gaunt to skeletal, his skin stretched taut over his bones—his skin had become gray, papery, and a sour odor clung to him). Doing his best not to listen to the balloons' soft, incessant rustling, Coleman let his gaze drift to the Hudson, full of craft large and small this sunny day.

"When I was a young man," he began, "not very much older than you . . ." His voice trailed off.

After a moment, Cal said, "Mr. Coleman?"

With a shake of his head, Coleman said, "Forgive me, Mr. Earnshaw. In many ways you're right: my life has been much as I wished it to be. What part of it I could control, at least. And what has lain outside my control, I have tried to cultivate a philosophical attitude toward. Often I've been able to console myself with the thought that whatever reversal of fortune I was experiencing would serve as the germ of a future story. In fact, what I'm about to tell you made it to a rather lengthy opening.

"That scene was from the point of view of a young Venetian gondolier. I can't remember the name I gave him. What was important was that he was a poet whose verses had not found success—thus his employment in the gondola—and his youth. This was contrasted with that of his passenger, whose middle age seemed to the gondolier just this side of the grave." Coleman caught himself. "I apologize—"

Cal waved his words away. "Go on. Please."

"Very well. The young man stares at his passenger openly, but the older man is too preoccupied either to notice or to mind. He is dressed for mourning, which may explain his distraction. Heaped on the passenger's lap are a dozen dresses—well made, as far as the gondolier can tell, though a bit threadbare.

"It is early morning. The sky is light, but the sun has yet to rise into it. In his heavily accented Italian, the passenger has requested that he be rowed out of the city and into the lagoon that borders it. The deepest point in the lagoon, he has said—he has insisted. The gondolier is not certain where the water is deepest. He waits until they are a suitable distance from the city, slows the gondola, and announces to the man that they have reached their destination.

"The passenger does not question him. Instead, he shifts to his right, raises the dress on top of the pile, and places it into the dark water. He does the same with the next dress, and the dress below that, laying each in the water with remarkable tenderness, so that the gondolier is reminded of a groom bringing his new bride to the wedding bed.

"However, when the man only has a handful of dresses in his lap, something happens that causes him to start back from the water. The dresses he has submerged have returned, buoyed to the surface by the air trapped in their folds. On his knees, the passenger rushes to the side of the gondola with such violence that the gondolier has to shift his stance to keep the craft from tilting into the lagoon. Without removing his jacket, the passenger thrusts his arms into the water up to the elbow, pushing down on the risen dresses. It does no good. Pressing one part of the dress causes the rest of it to rise even higher. The man shoves the dresses down frantically, as if he is trying to drown them. He is soaked, but he doesn't care. The gondolier thinks that he should speak to his passenger, but he cannot decide what to say.

"At last the man slumps against the side of the gondola, exhausted, drenched, his face a mask of sorrow. That was where the scene ended, with him contracted in grief, the gondola surrounded by floating dresses, each moving slightly in the green water, the gondolier watching everything and contemplating a new poem he might write."

"The man," Cal said, "the passenger—"

"Yes," Coleman said.

"But the dresses—"

"Belonged to a woman named Philippa Irving Ventner. She was a writer, an American—in fact, she was born in Phoenicia, up in the Catskills. I met her in Geneva. She was touring the Continent along with her younger sister, Grace. She was supposed to be educating Grace in the finer points of European civilization, but her knowledge of the subject was less than complete. Not that this stopped her: if there was one thing she had perfected, it was in moving ahead, regardless of the circumstances. To be fair, it had led to her producing a novel, *The Naturalist's Lament*, which had done extremely well. If I'm to be completely frank with you, none of my books has sold anywhere close to what hers did. The profits had funded her trip with Grace, which in turn led to another novel, *Joanna's Secret*, which allowed her to remain abroad after she had returned her sister home.

"No picture does her justice. There are many of them. She was happy to sit for any artist who cared to paint her, and she loved to be photographed. Look at the better portraits in either medium, and you will see her high cheekbones, her pointed nose, her brown hair. You will not see the watchfulness, the attentiveness that was her habitual expression. You will not see the wit that animated her eyes, her lips—the tilt of her head ever so slightly forward—when she was engaged in conversation. She had a keen sense of humor, though her response to most humorous stories and remarks was to hide her laughter behind her hands."

"You were—were you—"

"I met her several times over the next half a dozen years," Coleman said, "most often in Venice after I had settled there. She tried life in London, then Berlin, then Vienna, before finally taking up my suggestion that Venice might prove more agreeable to her. For a time it was. We saw a great deal of one another, and the circles each of us frequented soon grew used to the pair of us attending their functions together. We had our routines, our rituals, our walks to St. Mark's, our meals at Café Florian, our trips to the opera. She was the most agreeable person I have ever known; in her company, time ran more quickly, so that our excursions were over much too soon.

"When she approached me about renting rooms in a palace together, the idea struck me as inspired." At the expression of shock on Cal's face, Coleman hurried on: "The palace was the property of Constance Aspern, a very old woman who in her youth was supposed to have been one of Lord Byron's lovers. The fortune that had sustained her decades in Venice was drying up, the consequence of a series of bad investments, and she thought that by taking in lodgers she might at least slow its loss. She offered a suite of rooms on the top floor and another on the ground floor, but really, whichever floor you chose, you had the run of it, since Miss Aspern did not stray often or far from her rooms on the middle floor. The entire palace had seen better days, but there was a kind of shabby glory to it—not to mention, the rent was ridiculously low. I took the top floor, Philippa the ground floor, and we settled into what seemed a particularly fortuitous arrangement.

"For one winter and part of the following spring, it was. Philippa and I passed our mornings working, then joined Miss Aspern for lunch, then ventured out into Venice. So might we have continued to this very day, I daresay."

"What happened?" Cal asked.

"Our friendship changed," Coleman said after a moment. "It . . . deepened. I was—Philippa was a good ten years my junior. Children were . . . I . . . a long time ago, I had decided that, in order for me to achieve the art it was my ambition to produce, I would have to lead a certain kind of life. Until this point, I had remained true to my original plan. I suppose my resolve had borne fruit, albeit in books that were more praised than read. At private moments over the years I had wondered whether the course I'd chosen was the best one, but I'd never had so clear an alternative presented to me. For a week in early spring, I—we . . .

"The end of that time found me on a train to Paris. I was not—I had been contacted by an editor about the possibility of writing a piece for his magazine about the French capital ten years after its emergence from martial law. I decided that the ten days such a trip would require would allow me to evaluate the path onto which my life had swerved. I feared—I knew how my departure would appear to Philippa, and I did my best to reassure her that I was not fleeing her. She wasn't pleased, but neither was she overwrought. I would be back soon, and we would talk when I was.

"That was the last I saw of her. The night I left, the railing on which she was leaning as she stood at the window gave way, plummeting her to the courtyard thirty feet below. She was not killed instantly; she survived another three days in the hospital. No one knew how to reach me. Philippa departed this life without regaining consciousness, with only Miss Aspern for company. By the time I returned, a day later than I'd planned, she had been buried for several days."

"You had decided . . ."

"Does it matter?" Coleman said.

Cal did not answer.

"I left Venice not long after," Coleman said. "Miss Aspern had no objection to my maintaining my rooms; I believe she had some notion of congruence between us. I had neither the inclination nor the desire to figure in her tableau. I did see Grace—Philippa's younger sister, now married with four children. I met her at her sister's grave. I hadn't remembered Grace as especially remarkable, and in the years since I had seen her last she had grown into one of those Americans who

make you embarrassed for the country: vain, provincial, willfully igno-
rant. I had expected, had steeled myself for, an outpouring of sorrow
at the sudden extinguishing of so bright a light. Instead, I was subject-
ed to a torrent of scorn for such an 'odd duck.' I did my best to defend
Philippa, but I was so astonished, I fumbled the effort. I grew angry,
furious, so much so that I had no choice but to leave the cemetery
immediately or risk doing violence to the woman."

Coleman slumped back in his chair. The quartet of balloons had
settled into close orbit around him and Cal. He picked up his book and
said, "In no way do I wish to minimize what you face losing. But there
are times I have thought that, the longer I've lived, the more elaborate
have grown the disasters in which I have enmeshed myself."

IX

"And how is your work proceeding, Mr. Coleman?" Dunn asked. Isa-
belle and Cal had retired to their room for an hour before a late dinner.
Coleman was seated in the lounge, his notebook open in his lap, when
Dunn walked into the room. Closing the notebook, Coleman said,
"My latest is still in the early stages."

"Would I be presumptuous," Dunn said, seating himself on the
chair next to Coleman's, "if I asked its plot?"

"I don't suppose so," Coleman said, "although I should warn you
that most of the interest in my fiction arises from its execution rather
than its conception."

"You do yourself a disservice. You must forgive me—I have a terrible memory for the titles of these sorts of things—but your story
about the man who is haunted by the ghosts of the family he did not
have struck me as very original."

"'The Undiscovered Country,'" Coleman said, "and thank you.
The piece I am working on now is in a similar vein. It concerns a man
who, as a result of an injury received in battle, has lost the ability to
feel. He is a scientist, and he devotes his efforts to understanding the
nature or source of human feeling. This leads to his performing a series of ghastly experiments upon a pair of innocents who seek his aid."

"Fascinating," Dunn said. "You intend the scientist as a villain."

"Not a villain so much as a . . . monomaniac, I would say. Of course, his inability to feel complicates the matter. Can he be held responsible for his actions if he is deficient in so fundamental a way?"

"Yes," Dunn said. "I thought you were going to say that it is the knowledge he pursues that muddies the waters."

"Oh?"

"Surely a great deal may be forgiven if the objective is the advancement of human understanding."

"I'm not sure," Coleman said. "It seems to me more the case that a great number of sins have sought to hide themselves under the fig leaf of knowledge."

"Sin? I am surprised to hear you employ such a useless word. What the world calls sin, Mr. Coleman, is little more than the courage of the uncowed intellect to follow its inclinations."

"A sentiment worthy of Goethe's Faust."

"A character, I remind you, who is rewarded for his ceaseless striving."

"What a consolation to poor Gretchen," Coleman said.

Dunn laughed. "You have an answer to everything, sir."

"So my brothers always complained."

X

"It will not be long, now, will it?" Isabelle said.

Coleman opened his mouth to offer a comforting platitude, but none would come. The sour smell that emanated from Cal had spread throughout the house. He said, "Your husband is in a great deal of pain."

"He is," Isabelle said. "I cannot understand how he bears it. But I might wish he were bearing it with me rather than with Mr. Dunn. I will lose my husband soon enough, Mr. Coleman; I would like to spend what time I have left with him in his company."

"Didn't Dunn inform you—?"

"That he would be taking my husband from me for sessions morning, afternoon, and evening? That those sessions would continue for a week, with no end in sight save Cal's? No, Mr. Coleman, he did not. I assumed our stay would last a few days, no more. And I assumed that Mr. Dunn would require a few hours at most to prepare my husband for what is to come. I had read about Mr. Dunn's house—the beauty of its location, its garden—and I fancied that coming here with Cal would be a kind of farewell occasion for us. Instead, it has been a rehearsal for the solitude I am too soon to know."

"Has your husband told you what the sessions consist of?"

"He has. Apparently, Mr. Dunn has him lie on the table in the library. Then he positions several of his balloons around the room."

"The balloons?"

"They are supposed to aid Cal in the process."

"Which consists in what?" Coleman said. "Does Dunn fill his head with pictures of the life to come?"

"No," Isabelle said, "just the opposite. He tells Cal to allow his mind to fill with the agony that afflicts him."

"Whatever for?"

"Mr. Dunn says that since Cal's pain is the route that will lead him out of this world and into the next, it is necessary for him to immerse himself in it, in order for his transition to be a smooth one."

Coleman frowned. "Does your husband at least feel that Dunn's ministrations are helping him?"

"He insists they are when I ask him, but if you could see the look in his eyes . . . I think he cannot stand for his sessions with Mr. Dunn to be anything other than helpful."

XI

Summerland, Poughkeepsie
June 22, 1888

According to Dunn, not just the Hudson, but the stretch of the river next to Poughkeepsie is the site of a doorway from this world to the next. Of course, it would be, wouldn't it? But (supposedly) all manner of phenomena were visible on the surface of the water during the late 1850s, reported in local papers. Must research.

Strange how tired I am—not from any exertion, obviously, but from the stress of Cal Earnshaw's rapidly worsening condition, and its effect on his wife. Tonight she made her most direct plea yet for Dunn to allow her to take Cal and depart for home. Dunn would have none of it, insisting that he and Cal still have a great deal of preparation to do. He tried to draw me in on his side, but I refused. Perhaps I should have spoken more forcefully, insisted that Dunn send the Earnshaws on their way.

Would that I could climb into bed and sink into slumber—but the combination of the memories the last few days have stirred and the balloon that floats near my window keeps me awake.

XII

"I intend to take my husband and depart this house immediately," Isabelle said. "Will you help me?"

"Yes," Coleman said.

XIII

There was a moment's resistance, then the tip of the rapier broke the balloon's skin. Coleman couldn't say what he had expected—for the paper sphere to burst, or deflate, or shoot across the library on its suddenly released contents—but assuredly, it was not the gout of thick, black fluid over the blade of the sword, across the floor. He drove the rapier in to the hilt, through the balloon's other side, and withdrew it as his tutor had instructed him, ready for a second thrust.

He need not have bothered. Listing to the right, the balloon was sinking, dark liquid dripping from the cuts Coleman had made to it. The stuff was thick as treacle and struck the marble tiles with a wet splat. With a strangled cry, Dunn ran for the sword rack. Coleman stabbed the next balloon, stepped forward, and slashed the balloon after that. By the time he heard Dunn's shoes slapping the floor behind him, Coleman had opened a vent in the fourth of the man's inventions. His sword was coated in whatever filled the balloons, which oozed across the floor in growing puddles that stank of rot. It seemed impossible that such a substance could cause the balloons to rise, and yet—

Coleman turned, sweeping his sword in a wide arc that caught Dunn's stab and flung his blade to the side. The man recovered quickly, cutting an X in front of him. Rather than parry, Coleman retreated several paces. Dunn was considerably stronger than he and had selected a heavy cavalry saber for his weapon; Coleman did not rank his chances of defeating the man especially high. If he could distract him from Isabelle, who had assisted Cal up from the table and was supporting him as he limped toward the library door, then Coleman would consider his performance a success.

Truth to tell, he was surprised by the fury with which Dunn now attacked him. Without a doubt, the balloons had cost him no small amount of time and effort. But Dunn's face was scarlet, his large eyes protruding with fury. Coleman had little doubt that, were he to allow Dunn the opportunity, his host would put his saber to deadly use. The man's moves were exaggerated, almost parodic, those of someone whose notions of handling a sword were drawn from the stage; should any of his swipes connect, however, its effects would be real enough.

Dunn had backed him to the foot of the table. A pair of balloons floated to Coleman's right, closer to the broad oak expanse (which, he had time to notice, was incised with row after row of the same figures written on the balloons' paper surface). There was no need for him to slash the two of them, yet there was no denying the deep rush of pleasure that accompanied the act. At this latest insult to his inventions, Dunn roared and charged. Coleman ducked the swing at his head and jabbed Dunn's right arm high, near the shoulder. Dunn yelped and retreated a step.

The library door slammed shut behind Isabelle and Cal Earnshaw. Coleman doubted Cal would last out the next hour, let alone the remainder of the night, but at least he would do so in the company of his wife and not splayed on a table surrounded by a charlatan and his paper toys. Coleman lowered the tip of his sword. His breath coming fast, he said, "There. Mrs. Earnshaw's wishes have been fulfilled. Now perhaps you and I can settle matters between us in a more civilized fashion. I apologize for the destruction of your creations. I would be willing to recompense you a fair amount—"

"You fucking idiot," Dunn said. He had pressed his left hand over the wound Coleman had given him; his fingers were scarlet. He had not dropped his saber, which he pointed at the first balloons Coleman had vandalized. "You think these are works of *art*? They are cages."

"More metaphors?" Coleman looked to the other end of the room. The balloons he had stabbed were in a state of half-collapse on the floor, surrounded by ever-widening pools of brackish ichor. Those he had sliced open were sagging downwards, raining their contents as they descended. Through the vents he had cut in them he could distinguish something, a mottled surface his blade had torn and which was the source of the viscous liquid. That layer was pierced by additional holes, lozenge shaped and anywhere in size from that of a small coin to a handbreadth. Each of the holes was moving, opening and closing with a motion that was repellently familiar. Coleman stared at them blankly, before understanding rushed in and he recognized the apertures as mouths. For a moment he felt the room around him tilt crazily. He reached his left hand to his forehead. "My God . . ."

With a sudden burst of speed, Dunn lunged forward and stabbed Coleman in the chest. The blade was a white shock. For a moment Coleman was propelled out of his body to a lightless place. When he returned, he had fallen to his knees and Dunn was holding forth. "—true," he said. "The veil between the worlds is thinner here. With the proper preparations, the inhabitants of the other realm may be lured across, captured, and put to work. Their physical capabilities are limited, but what they offer in terms of knowledge . . . Their appetites, however, are considerable, and they require a rather specialized diet. Human sensation sustains them—the more intense, the better the meal. Pain they find particularly satisfying. The agonies of the dying will keep them happy and compliant for days."

"Your . . . services . . ." Coleman panted. With each breath, his chest filled with white fire.

"No doubt some of my clients have taken comfort from their time with me," Dunn said. "They've certainly been more use here than at any other time in their lives. It's a pity," he continued. "I had hoped that you—an artist—might understand the work in which I am engaged here. It was not my intention for your stay to end this way. But since it has, and since you have deprived my friends of their meal . . ." Dunn surveyed the balloons at the head of the table, the pair at its foot. The injuries of the nearer balloons did not appear as grave; indeed, while Dunn had been speaking, they had drifted closer to him. Through the rents in their paper cages, Coleman could see their excess of mouths gulping with a motion that reminded him of hungry fish at the surface of a pool. Dunn said, "Your attempt at gallantry has cost me more than you can conceive."

Coleman's shirt and trousers were warm, sticky, heavy with the blood emptying him. The library paled almost to blank, then returned. "As," he said to Dunn, "as . . . a gentle—gentleman . . . I wonder if . . . if you . . ."

"You must be joking," Dunn said; nonetheless, his bulk inclined toward Coleman.

Gripping its hilt as tightly as he could, Coleman slashed the rapier across Dunn's face. As he did so, something broke loose inside him and a tide of blood poured from the wound in his chest. He let go of the sword and fell beside it.

A thin, high-pitched scream rose from Dunn's throat. Coleman's sword had raked his eyes, and his cheeks were wet with blood and fluid. He had dropped the saber and held his hands up on either side of him, as if imploring some supernatural agency to his aid. Still screaming, Dunn crashed into the table with such force that it jolted across the floor. He staggered back from the collision, lost his footing, and tumbled down.

The balloons were waiting for him. Their prisons ruptured, the creatures they had contained surged out of them and over Dunn. His vision was failing, but Coleman had the impression of something more liquid than solid, enough like a jellyfish to warrant the comparison. Dunn's voice climbed higher, then failed. He clawed at the things on his chest, but that only allowed them to attach to his hands. With what must have been herculean effort, Dunn sat up. His lips were forming words Coleman could not hear. Before he had uttered more than a few of them, one of the creatures spread itself over his face. His body shook as if with a seizure, then sagged backwards. In the quiet that followed, Coleman heard the noises of eating. Apparently the balloons' prisoners were capable of taking their nourishment more directly.

The library faded a second time. When it returned, it was less distinct. Coleman guessed more of his blood was outside his body than remained in it. How odd to die so quickly. How odd to die in a library. In some ways it was as appropriate a location as any. He hoped that Isabelle had managed to get Cal out of the house. He had waited too long to take her concerns seriously and try to aid her; he hoped it wouldn't be held against him. He wasn't much of a believer in an afterlife, hadn't been for decades. He supposed he'd been mistaken. He wondered what he should expect. Whatever it was, he hoped it wouldn't be hungry.

XIV

From *Benét's Reader's Encyclopedia* (third edition):

Coleman, Mark Stephen (1842–1888). American novelist and short story writer. Born in Kingston, New York, Coleman left for study at Cambridge at the age of eighteen and spent almost the entire rest of his life abroad, living successively in London, Paris, Venice, and then London again before returning to the Hudson Valley in his final months. Like Henry James, with whom he is often compared, Coleman took as his subject the experiences of Americans in Europe; however, Coleman's Americans are plagued by remorse of past sins personal and familial, a preoccupation that links his work to that of Nathaniel Hawthorne. His most famous novel is *Belgrave's Garden* (1879), an account of a wealthy American's attempt to cultivate the land on which his ancestor ordered a brutal massacre during the second Jacobite rebellion in 1745. Coleman's death was notorious: he died as a result of an apparent duel with the spiritualist Parrish Dunn, who also was slain.

Bloom

I

"Is that—do you see—"

Already Rick was braking, reaching for the hazards. Connie turned from the passenger-side window at whose streaky surface she had spent the last half-hour staring. Eyes on something ahead, her husband was easing the steering wheel left, toward the meridian. Following the line of his gaze, she saw, next to the guardrail about ten yards in front of them, a smallish red and white container. "What?" she said. "The cooler?"

"It's not a cooler," Rick said, bringing the Forrester to a stop. His voice was still sharp with the edge of their argument.

"What do you—" She understood before she could complete her question. "Jesus—is that a—"

"A cooler," Rick said, "albeit of a different sort."

The car was in neutral, the parking brake on, Rick's door open in the time it took her to arrive at her next sentence. "What's it doing here?"

"I have no idea," he said, and stepped out of the car. She leaned forward, watching him trot to the red and white plastic box with the red cross on it. It resembled nothing so much as the undersized cooler in which she and her roommates had stored their wine coolers during undergrad: the same peaked top that would slide back when you pressed the buttons on either side of it. Rick circled around it once clockwise, once counter-clockwise, and squatted on his haunches beside it. He was wearing denim shorts and the faded green Mickey Mouse T-shirt that he refused to allow Connie to claim for the rag drawer, even though it had been washed so many times it was practically translucent. (It was the outfit he chose whenever they went to visit his father.) He appeared to be reading something on the lid. He stood, turned his head to squint up and down this stretch of the Thruway, empty in both directions. He blew out his breath and ran his hand through his hair—the way he did when he was pretending to debate a question he'd already decided—then bent, put his hands on the cooler, and picked it up. Apparently, it was lighter than he'd anticipated, because it practically leapt into the air. Almost race-walking, he carried the container toward the car.

Connie half expected him to hand it to her. Instead, he continued past her to the trunk. She tilted the rearview mirror to see him balancing the cooler against his hip and unlocking the trunk. When he thunked the lid down, his hands were empty.

The answer was so obvious she didn't want to ask the question; nonetheless, once Rick was back behind the wheel, drawing his seatbelt across, she said, "What exactly are you doing?"

Without looking at her, he said, "We can't just leave it there."

"If the cellphone were charged, we could call 911."

"Connie—"

"I'm just saying. You wanted to know why that kind of stuff was so important, well, here you are."

"You—" He glanced over his shoulder to make sure the highway was clear. As he accelerated onto it, he said, "You know what? You're right. If I'd charged the cellphone last night as you asked me to, we could dial 911 and have a State Trooper take this off our hands. That's absolutely true. Since the phone is dead, however, we need another plan. We're about forty, forty-five minutes from the house. I say we get home as quickly as we can and start calling around the local hospitals. Maybe this is for someone in one of them. In any event, I'm sure they'll know who to call to find out where this is supposed to go."

"Do they even do transplants in Wiltwyck?"

"I don't know. Maybe. I think Penrose might."

"We could stop at the next State Trooper barracks."

"The nearest one is our exit, up 209. We're as quick going to the house."

"You're sure there's something in there?"

"I didn't look, but when I lifted it, I heard ice moving inside."

"It didn't look that heavy."

"It wasn't. But I don't know how much a heart, or a kidney, would weigh. Not too much, I think."

"I don't know, I just—" She glanced over her shoulder. "I mean, Jesus, how does something like that wind up in the middle of the Thruway? How does that happen?"

Rick shrugged. "They don't always hire the most professional guys to transport these things. Maybe someone's tail flap was down, or they swerved to avoid a deer in the road and the cooler went tumbling out."

"Surely not."

"Well, if you knew the answer to the question—"

For a second their argument threatened to tighten its coils around them again. Connie said, "What about the lid? I thought you were reading something on it."

"There's a sticker on top that looks as if it had some kind of information, but the writing's all blurred. Must have been that storm a little while ago."

"So it's been sitting here at least that long."

"Seems likely. Maybe that was what happened: maybe the truck skidded and that caused the cooler to come loose."

"Wouldn't you stop and go back for something like that? Someone's life could be on the line."

"Could be the driver never noticed, was too busy trying to keep himself from crashing into the guardrail."

The scenario sounded plausible enough—assuming, that was, you accepted Rick's assertion about underqualified drivers employed to convey freshly harvested organs from donor to recipient. Which was, now that Connie thought about it, sufficiently venal and depressing to likely be the truth. "What if it's supposed to be heading north, to Albany?"

"There's probably still enough time, even if whoever it is has to drive back the way we came."

"Maybe they could fly it wherever it needs to go. Doesn't Penrose do that?"

"I think so."

Already she was buying into Rick's plan. Would it make that much difference to call the hospitals from their house instead of the police station? Equipped with a fully charged cellphone, they could have been rushing whatever was packed in the cooler's ice to the surgical team that at this moment must be in the midst of preparations to receive it.

Connie could picture herself and Rick striding into the Emergency
Room at Wiltwyck, the cooler under Rick's arm, a green-garbed sur-
geon waiting with gloves outstretched. With the cell inert, though,
home might be their next best option. Based on her experiences with
them at an embarrassing number of stops for speeding, the Wiltwyck
Troopers would require more time than whoever was waiting for this
cooler's contents could spare for her and Rick to make clear to them
the gravity of the situation.

That's not true, she thought. You know that isn't true. You're just
pissed because that guy wouldn't agree to plead down to ten miles an
hour over the speed limit. She was justifying Rick's plan, shoring up
his ambition to be part of the story—an important part, the random,
passing stranger who turns out to be crucial to yanking someone at
death's very doorway back from that black rectangle. Because ... because it was exciting to feel yourself caught up in a narrative like this,
one that offered you the opportunity to be part of something bigger
than yourself.

Rick had the speedometer to the other side of eighty-five. Connie
reached her left hand across and squeezed his leg lightly. He did not
remove his hands from the wheel.

II

Four hours later, they were staring at the cooler sitting on the kitchen
table. Its surface was pebbled plastic; Connie wondered if that contributed in any way to keeping its contents chilled. The red cross stenciled
on its lid was faded, a shade lighter than the bottom half of the cooler,
and beginning to flake off. The symbol didn't look like your typical red
cross. This design was narrow at the join, the sides of each arm curving
outwards on their way to its end—the four of which were rounded,
like the edges of a quartet of axes. Connie had seen this style of cross,
or one close to it, before: Alexa, the first girl with whom she'd shared
an apartment, and who had been more Catholic than the Pope, had
counted a cross in this style among her religious jewelry. A Maltese
cross? Cross of Malta? Something like that, although Connie remembered her old roommate's cross ornamented with additional designs—
little pictures, she thought; of what, she couldn't recall. To be honest,

this version of the cross seemed less a religious icon and more the image of something else—an abstract flower, perhaps, or an elaborate keyhole. For a moment, the four red lines opening out resembled nothing so much as the pupil of some oversized, alien eye, but that was ridiculous.

What it meant that the cooler resting on the blond wood of their kitchen table bore this emblem, she could not say. Did the Red Cross have subdivisions, local branches, and might this be one of their symbols? She'd never heard of such a thing, but she was a manager at Target; this was hardly her area of expertise.

Rick said, "Maybe it's a Mob thing."

"What?" Connie looked across the table at him, slouched back in his chair, arms folded over his chest.

"I said, maybe it's a Mob thing."

"What do you mean?"

He straightened. "Maybe it's part of someone who, you know, messed with the Mob. Or someone they had a contract on."

"Like what—a finger?"

"Finger, hand—proof that the job was done."

"Seriously?"

He shrugged. "It's a possibility."

"I don't know."

"You don't know what?"

"I don't know—I mean, the Mob? Transporting—what? Severed body parts in medical coolers? Wasn't that a movie?"

"Was it?"

"Yes—we saw it together. It was on TNT or TBS or something. Joe Pesci was in it. Remember: he's a hit man and he's got these heads in a duffle bag—"

"Eight Heads in a Duffel Bag."

"That's it!"

"So there was a movie. What does that prove?"

"It's just—"

"Or maybe it's some kind of black market thing, a kidney for sale to the highest bidder, no questions asked."

"Isn't that an urban legend?"

"Where do you think these things come from?"

"I—"

"Look—all I'm saying is, we've exhausted the legitimate avenues, so it makes sense to consider other possibilities."

Connie took a breath. "Granted. But we don't even know what's inside the cooler—if there's anything in it."

"You're the one who said we shouldn't open it."

"I know. It's—if there's something in it, then we need to be careful about not contaminating it."

"Are you listening to yourself? We don't know if there's anything in the cooler, so we shouldn't be too concerned about it, but we shouldn't open it, in case there is something in there. What are we supposed to do?"

Before she could answer, Rick pushed himself up from his chair and stalked to the refrigerator, the bottles in whose door rattled as he yanked it open. Connie bit the remark ready to leap off her tongue. Instead, she stood and leaned over to have another look at the square sticker on the cooler's lid. There were no identifying names on the label, no hospital or transport service logos, no barcode even, which, in the age of global computer tracking, struck her as stranger than the absence of a corporate ID. There were only four or five lines of smeared black ink, unintelligible except for one word that she and Rick had agreed read "Howard" and another that he guessed was "orchid" but of which Connie could identify no more than the initial "o." Now, as her gaze roamed over the ink blurred into swirls and loops, she had the impression that the words that had been written on this sticker hadn't been English, the letters hadn't been any she would have recognized. Some quality of the patterns into which the writing had been distorted suggested an alphabet utterly unfamiliar, which might smear into a configuration resembling "Howard" or "orchid" by the merest coincidence.

God, you're worse than Rick. She resumed her seat as he returned from the fridge, an open bottle of Magic Hat in hand. Not that she wanted a drink, exactly, but his failure to ask her if she did sent Connie on her own mission to the fridge. They were out of hard cider, dammit. She had intended to stop at Hannaford for a quick shop on the way home, then the cooler had appeared and obscured all other concerns. They were almost out of milk, too, and butter. She selected a Magic Hat for herself and swung the door shut.

Rick had set his beer on the table and was standing with his back to her, bent forward slightly, his arms out, his hands on the cooler. "Rick?" Connie said. "What are you doing?"

"Is that a trick question?"

"Very funny," she said, crossing the kitchen to him. He was staring at the cooler as if he could will its contents visible. He said, "We have to open it."

"But if there's something inside it—"

"I know, I know. I can't see any other choice. We called Wiltwyck, and they didn't know anything about it. Neither did Penrose or Albany Med or Westchester Med. The transport services they gave us the numbers for weren't missing any shipments—the one said they aren't even using coolers like this anymore. The cops were useless. Hell, that guy at the sheriff's thought it was probably just someone's cooler. Maybe there'll be some kind of information inside that'll tell us where this is supposed to go."

"What if it's a Mob thing?"

"Do you really believe that?"

"No, but I could be wrong, in which case, what would we do?"

"Get rid of it as quickly as possible. Burn it. I don't think there's any way it could be traced to us."

To her surprise, Connie said, "All right. Go ahead."

Rick didn't ask if she were sure. He pressed in the catches on the lid and slid it back. As Connie inclined toward it, he drew the cooler toward them. It scraped against the table; its contents shifted with a sound like gravel rasping. Connie had been anticipating a strong odor washing out of the cooler's interior, raw meat full of blood; instead, there was the faintest blue hint of air long chilled and another, even fainter trace of iodine. Rick's arm was blocking her view; she nudged him. "What is it?"

"I don't know."

"Let me see."

He shifted to the right. The cooler was full of ice, chips of it heaped in shining piles around, around—

She registered the color first, the dark purple of a ripe eggplant, shot through with veins of lighter purple—blue, she thought, some shade of blue. It was maybe as wide as a small dinner plate, thicker at the center than at its scalloped circumference. At five—no, six spots around its margin, the surface puckered, the color around each spot shading into a rich rose. The texture of the thing was striated, almost coarse.

"What the fuck?"

"I know—right?"

"Rick—what is this?"

"A placenta?"

"That is not a placenta."

"As if you've seen one."

"As a matter of fact, I have. There was a show on Lifetime—I can't remember what it was called, but it was about women giving birth, in living color, no detail spared. I saw plenty of placentas, and trust me, that is not a placenta."

"Okay, it's not a placenta. So what is it?"

"I—is it even human?"

"You're saying what? that it's an animal?"

"I don't know—some kind of jellyfish?"

"Looks too solid, doesn't it? Besides, wouldn't you store a jellyfish in water?"

"I guess."

Rick started to reach into the cooler. Connie grabbed his wrist. "Jesus! What are you doing?"

"I thought I'd take it out so we could have a better look at it." He tugged his hand free.

"You don't know what it is."

"I'm pretty sure it isn't someone's kidney."

"Granted, but you can't just—it could be dangerous, toxic."

"Really."

"There are animals whose skin is poisonous. Haven't you heard of Poison Dart Frogs?"

"Oh." He lowered his hand. "Fair enough." He stepped away from the cooler. "Sweetie—what is this?"

"Well, I'm pretty sure we can say what it isn't. I doubt there's anyone whose life depends on receiving this, and I'm pretty sure it wasn't attached to any Mob informer. Nor was it feeding a fetus nutrients for nine months. That leaves us with—I don't have the faintest idea. Some kind of animal."

"I don't know."

Connie shrugged. "The world's a big place. There are all kinds of crazy things living at the bottom of the ocean. Or it could be from someplace else—deep underground. Maybe it's a new discovery that was being transported to a museum."

Rick grunted. "Okay. Let's assume this was on its way to an eager research scientist. What's our next move?"

"Another round of phone calls, I guess."

"You want to start on that, and I'll get dinner going?"

She wasn't hungry, but she said, "Sure."

Rick reached for the cooler. "Relax," he said as she tensed, ready to seize his arms. Steadying the cooler with his left hand, he closed it with the right. The lid snicked shut.

III

No surprise: she dreamed about the thing in the cooler. She was in Rick's father's room at the nursing home (even asleep, she was unable to think of him as "Gary" or "Mr. Wilson," let alone "Dad"). Rick's father was in the green vinyl recliner by the window, his face tilted up to the sunlight pouring over him in a way that reminded Connie of a large plant feeding on light. The green Jets sweatsuit he was wearing underscored the resemblance. His eyes were closed, his lips moving in the constant murmur that had marked the Alzheimer's overwhelming the last of his personality. In the flood of brightness, he looked younger than fifty-eight, as if he might be Rick's young uncle, and not the father not old enough for the disease that had consumed him with the relentless patience of a python easing itself around its prey.

Connie was standing with her back to the room's hefty dresser, the top of which was heaped with orchids, their petals eggplant and rose. The air was full of the briny smell of seaweed baking on the beach, which she knew was the flowers' scent.

Although she hadn't noticed him enter the room, Rick was kneeling in front of his father, his hands held up and out as if offering the man a gift. His palms cupped the thing from the cooler. Its edges overflowed his hands. In the dense sunlight, the thing was even darker, more rather than less visible. If the scene in front of her were a photograph, the thing was a dab of black paint rising off its surface.

"Here," Rick said to his father. "I brought it for you." When his father did not respond, Rick said, "Dad."

The man opened his eyes and tilted his head in his son's direction. Connie didn't think he saw what Rick was offering him. He croaked, "Bloom."

"Beautiful," Rick said.

His father's eyes narrowed, and his face swung toward Connie. He was weeping, tears coursing down his cheeks like lines of fire in the sunlight. "Bloom," he said.

Almost before she knew she was awake, she was sitting up in bed. Although she was certain it must be far into the night, one of those hours you only saw when the phone rang to announce some family tragedy, the digital clock insisted it was two minutes after midnight. She had been asleep for an hour. She turned to Rick and found his side of the bed empty.

There was no reason for her heart to start pounding. Rick stayed up late all the time, watching *Nightline* or Charlie Rose. For the seven years Connie had known him, he had been a light sleeper, prone to insomnia, a tendency that had worsened with his father's unexpected and sudden decline. She had sought him out enough times in the beginning of their relationship to be sure that there was no cause for her to leave the bed. She would find him on the couch, bathed in the TV's glow, a bag of microwave popcorn open on his lap. So prepared was she for him to be there that, when she reached the bottom of the stairs and discovered the living room dark, something like panic straightened her spine. "Rick?" she said. "Honey?"

Of course he was in the kitchen. She glimpsed him out of the corner of her eye the same instant he said, "I'm in here." By the streetlight filtering through the window she saw him seated at the kitchen table, wearing a white t-shirt and boxers, his arms on the table, his hands on the keyboard of his father's laptop, which was open and on. The cooler, which he had pushed back to make room for the computer, appeared to be closed. (She wasn't sure why that detail made her heart slow.) She walked down the hallway to him, saying, "Couldn't sleep, huh?"

"Nah." His eyes did not leave the computer screen.

"You're like this every time we visit your dad."

"Am I? I guess so."

She rubbed his back. "You're doing all you can for him. It's a good place."

"Yeah."

On the laptop's screen, a reddish sphere hung against a backdrop of stars. Connie recognized the painting from the NASA website, and the next picture Rick brought up, of a rough plane spread out under a starry sky, at the center of which a cluster of cartoonishly fat arrows identified a handful of the dots of light as the sun and planets of the solar system. A third image showed eight green circles arranged concentrically around a bright point, all within one end of an enormous red ellipse.

The screen after that was a photo of a massive stone monument, a rectangular block stood on its short end, another block laid across its top to form a T-shape. The front of the tall stone was carved with a thick line that descended from high on the right to almost the bottom of the left, where it curved back right again; in the curve, a representation of a four-legged animal Connie could not identify crouched. The image that followed was another painting, this one of a trio of circular structures set in the lee of a broad hill, the diameter of each defined by a thick wall, the interior stood with T-shaped monoliths like the one on the previous screen.

Rick sped through the next dozen screens, long rows of equations more complex than any Connie had encountered in her college math class, half of each line composed of symbols she thought were Greek but wasn't sure. When he came to what appeared to be a list of questions, Rick stopped. Connie could read the first line: 12,000-year orbit coincides with construction of Gobekli Tepe: built in advance of, or in response to, seeding?

Oh God, Connie thought. She said, "You want to come to bed?"

"I will. You go ahead."

"I don't want you sitting up half the night feeling guilty."

He paused, then said, "It isn't guilt."

"Oh? What is it?"

He shook his head. "I had a dream."

Her mouth went dry. "Oh?"

He nodded. "I was sitting here with my dad. We were both wearing tuxedoes, and the table had been set for some kind of elaborate meal: white linen tablecloth, candelabra, china plates, the works. It was early in the morning—at least, I think it was, because the windows were pouring light into the room. The plates, the cutlery, the glasses— everything was shining, it was so bright. For a long time, it felt like, we sat there—here—and then I noticed Dad was holding his fork and knife and was using them to cut something on his plate. It was this," he nodded at the cooler, "this thing. He was having a rough time. He couldn't grip the cutlery right; it was as if he'd forgotten how to hold them. His knife kept slipping, scraping on the plate. The thing was tough; he really had to saw at it. It was making this noise, this high-pitched sound that was kind of like a violin. It was bleeding, or leaking, black syrupy stuff that was all over the plate, the knife, splattering the tablecloth, Dad's shirt. Finally he got a piece of the thing loose and raised it to his mouth. Only, his lips were still trembling, you know, doing that silent mumble, and he couldn't maneuver the fork past them. The piece flopped on the table. He frowned, speared it with his fork again, and made another try. No luck. The third time, the piece hit the edge of the table and bounced off. That was it. He dropped the cutlery, grabbed the thing on his plate with both hands, and brought it up. His face was so eager. He licked his lips and took a huge bite. He had to clamp down hard, pull the rest away. There was a ripping noise. The thing's blood was all over his lips, his teeth, his tongue; his mouth looked like a black hole."

Connie waited for him to continue; when he didn't, she said, "And?"

"That was it. I woke up and came down here. There was nothing on TV, so I thought I'd get out Dad's laptop and . . . It's like a connection to him, to how he used to be, you know? I mean, I know he was already pretty bad when he was working on this stuff, but at least he was there."

"Huh." Connie considered relating her own dream, decided instead to ask, "What do you think your dream means?"

"I don't know. I dream about my Dad a lot, but this . . ."

"Do you—"

"What if it's from another planet?"

"What?"

"Maybe the dream's a message."

"I don't—"

"That would explain why there's no record of it, anywhere, why none of the museums knows anything about it."

"That doesn't make any sense," Connie said. "If this thing were some kind of alien, you'd expect it'd be all over the news."

"Maybe it's dangerous—or they aren't sure if it's dangerous."

"So they pack it into a cooler?"

"They're trying to fly under the radar."

"I don't know—that's so low, it's underground."

"Or—what if a couple of guys found it—somewhere, they were out hunting or fishing or something—and they decided to take it with them in the cooler they'd brought for their beers?"

"Then why the red cross on the cooler? What about the sticker?"

"Coincidence—they just happened to take that cooler."

"I could— Look, even if that is the case, if a couple of hunters came upon this thing, I don't know, fresh from its meteorite, and emptied out their oddly decorated cooler so they could be famous as the first guys to encounter E.T., how does that help us know what to do?"

"We could call NASA."

"Who what? Would send out the Men in Black?"

"I'm serious!" Rick almost shouted. "This is serious! Jesus! We could be—we have—why can't you take this seriously?" He turned to glare at her as he spoke.

"Rick—"

"Don't 'Rick' me."

Connie inhaled. "Honey—it's late. We're tired. Let's not do this, okay? Not now. I'm sorry if I'm not taking this seriously. It's been a long day. Whatever it is, the thing in the cooler'll keep until we get some sleep. If you want, we can call NASA first thing in the morning. Really—I swear."

"I—" She readied herself for the next phase of his outburst, then, "You're right," Rick said. "You're right. It has been a long day, hasn't it?"

"Very. I can't believe you aren't exhausted."

"I am—believe me, I'm dead on my feet. It's just, this thing—"

"I understand—honest, I do. Why don't you come up to bed? Maybe once you lie down—"

"All right. You go up. I just need a minute more."

"For what?" she wanted to ask but didn't, opting instead to drape her arms over his shoulders and press her cheek against his neck. "Love you," she said into his skin.

"Love you, too."

Her heart, settled after its earlier gallop, broke into a trot again as she padded down the hall to the stairs. The sight of Rick, once more staring at the computer screen, did nothing to calm it, nor did her lowering herself onto the bed, drawing the covers up. If anything, the thoroughbred under her ribs charged faster. She gazed at the bedroom ceiling, feeling the mattress resound with her pulse. Was she having a panic attack? *Don't think about it,* she told herself. *Concentrate on something else.*

Rick. What else was there besides him at the table, his fingers resting on the keyboard's sides, sifting through his father's last, bizarre project? Not the most reassuring behavior; although it was true: each monthly pilgrimage to his father left him unsettled for the rest of that day, sometimes the next. No matter how many times she told him that his dad was in the best place, that the home provided him a quality of care they couldn't have (not to mention, his father's insurance covered it in full), and no matter how many times Rick answered, "You're right; you're absolutely right," she knew that he didn't accept her reasoning, her reassurance. In the past, thinking that anger might help him to articulate his obvious guilt, she had tried to pick a fight with him, stir him to argument, but he had headed in the opposite direction, descended into himself for the remainder of the weekend. She had suggested they visit his dad more often, offered to rearrange her work schedule so that they could go up twice a month, even three times. What good was being store manager, she'd said, if you couldn't use it to your advantage? Albany wasn't that far, and there were supposed to be good restaurants there; they could make a day of it, spend time with his father and have some time for themselves, too.

No, no, Rick had said. It wasn't fair for her to have to rework the schedule (arriving at which she'd compared to the circus act where the clown spins the plates on the ends of all the poles he's holding while balancing his unicycle on the high wire). It wasn't as if his dad would know the difference anyway.

He might not, Connie had said, but you will.

It was no good, though; Rick's mind had been made up before their conversation had started. He had never admitted it, but Connie was sure he was still traumatized by his father's last months of—you couldn't call it lucidity exactly, since what he would call to yell at Rick about was pretty insane. Gary Wilson had been an astronomer, his most recent work an intensive study of the dwarf planets discovered beyond Neptune in the first decade of the 2000s: Eris, Sedna, and Orcus were the names she remembered. From what she understood, his research on the surface conditions on these bodies was cutting-edge stuff; he had been involved in the planning for a probe to explore some of them. Plenty of times she and Rick had arrived at his apartment to take him to dinner, only to find him seated at his desk, staring at his computer monitor, at a painting of one or the other of the dwarf planets. At those moments he had seemed a million miles away, further, as far as one of the spheres he studied. Hindsight's clarity made it obvious he was experiencing the early effects of Alzheimer's, but the spells had always broken the moment Rick shook him and said, "Dad, it's us," and it had been easier to accept her father-in-law's assurance that he had merely been daydreaming.

Not until his behavior became more erratic did it dawn on them that Rick's father might not be well. His attention had been focused on one dwarf planet, Sedna, for months. Connie had sat beside him at the Plaza diner as he flipped over his mat and drew an asterisk in the center of it, which he surrounded with a swirl of concentric circles, all at one end of a great oval. "This is Sedna's orbit," he had said, jabbing his pen at the oval. "Twelve thousand years, give or take a few hundred. Over the next couple of centuries it will be as close to us as it's been during the whole of recorded history. The last time it was this near, well . . ."

"What?" Rick had said.

"You'll see," his father had declared.

They hadn't, though, not directly. One of Rick's father's friends at the State University had phoned after a presentation during which the extent of Gary Wilson's breakdown had become manifest. Connie had heard the lecture herself, in person, on the phone, and in a long, rambling voicemail. She considered herself reasonably well educated in a hold-your-own-at-Trivial-Pursuit kind of way, but Rick's father's discussion strained her comprehension. Almost thirteen thousand years ago, a comet had burst over the Great Lakes—yes, that was a controversial claim, but how else to explain the high levels of iridium, the nano-diamonds? The glaciers were already in retreat, you see; it was the right time, if you could measure time in centuries—millennia. This was when the Clovis disappeared—wiped out, or assimilated in some way, it was hard to say. You wouldn't think a stone point much of a threat, but you'd be surprised. The drawings at Lascaux—well, never mind them. It's what happens at Gobekli Tepe that's important. Those curves on the stones—has anyone thought of mapping them onto Sedna's orbit? The results—as for the shape of the monuments, those giant T's, why, they're perches, for the messengers.

And so on. The thing was, while Rick's father was propounding this lunatic hodgepodge of invention, he sounded as reasonable, as kindly, as he ever had. Perhaps that was because she hadn't challenged him in the way that Rick did, tell him that his ideas were crazy, he was flushing his career down the toilet. Confronted by his son's strenuous disbelief, Gary flushed with anger, was overtaken by storms of rage more intense than any she had witnessed in the seven years she had known him. He would stalk from their house and demand that Connie drive him home, then, once home, he would call and harangue Rick for another hour, sometimes two, until Rick reached his boiling point and hung up on him.

The end, when it came, had done so quickly: she had been amazed at the speed with which Rick's father had been convinced to accept early retirement and a place in an assisted living facility. There had been a brief period of days, not even a full week, during which he had returned to something like his old self. He had signed all the papers necessary to effect his departure from the college and his relocation to Morrison Hills. He had spoken to Rick and Connie calmly, with barely a mention of Sedna's impending return. Two days after he settled into his new, undersized room, Gary had suffered a catastrophic event somewhere in his brain that the doctors refused to call a stroke, saying the MRI results were all wrong for that. (Frankly, they seemed mystified by what had happened to him during the night.) Whatever its name, the occurrence had left him a few steps up from catatonic, intermittently responsive and usually in ways that made no sense. There was talk of further study, of sub-specialists being brought in, possible trips to hospitals in other states, but nothing, as yet, had come to pass. Connie doubted any of it would. There were more than enough residents of the facility who could and did vocalize their complaints, and less than enough staff to spare on a man whose tongue was so much dead weight.

Harrowing as Rick's father's decline had been, she supposed she should be grateful that it had not stretched out longer than it had. From talking with staff at Morrison, she knew it could take years for a parent's worsened condition to convince them/their family that something had to be done. At the same time, though, Rick had been ambivalent about his father entering assisted living. There was enough room in the house for him: he could have stayed in the downstairs bedroom and had his own bathroom. But neither of them was available for—or, to be honest, up for—the task of caring for him. Rick's consent to his father's move had been conditional; he had insisted and Connie had agreed that they would re-evaluate the situation in six months. Their contract had been rendered null and void by Gary's collapse, which had left him in need of a level of care far beyond that for which either of them was equipped. However irrational the sentiment might be, Connie knew that Rick took his father's crash as a rebuke from the universe for having agreed to send him away in the first place.

Connie didn't realize she had crossed over into sleep again until she noticed that the bedroom's ceiling and walls had vanished, replaced by a night sky brimming with stars. Her bed was sitting on a vast plane, dimly lit by the stars' collective radiance. Its dark red expanse was stippled and ridged, riven by channels; she had the impression of dense mud. That and cold: although she could not feel it on her skin, she sensed that wherever this was was so cold it should have frozen her in place, her blood crystallized, her organs chunks of ice.

To her left, a figure was progressing slowly across the plane. It was difficult to be sure, but it looked like a man, dressed in black. Every few steps, he would pause and study the ground in front of him, occasionally crouching and poking it with one hand. Connie watched him for what might have been a long time. Her bed, she noticed, was strewn with orchids, their petals eggplant and rose. At last she drew back the blanket, lowered herself onto the red mud, and set out toward him.

She had expected the mud to be ice-brittle, but while it was firm under her feet, it was also the slightest bit spongy. She wasn't sure how this could be. A glance over her shoulder showed the bed and its cargo of flowers unmoved. While she was still far away from him, she saw that the man ahead of her was wearing a tuxedo, and that he was Rick's father. She was not surprised by either of these facts.

In contrast to her previous dream of him, Gary Wilson stood tall, alert. He was following a series of depressions in the plane's surface, each a concave dip of about a foot, maybe six feet from the one behind it. At the bottom of the depressions, something dark shone through the red mud. When he bent to prod one, he licked his finger clean afterwards. Connie could feel his awareness of her long before she drew near, but he waited until she was standing beside him to say, "Well?"

"Where is this?"

"Oh, come now," he said, disappointment bending his voice. "You know the answer to that already."

She did. "Sedna."

He nodded. "The nursery."

"For those?" She pointed at the depression before him.

"Of course."

"What are they?"

"Embryos." The surface of his cheek shifted.

"I don't understand."

"Over here." He turned to his left and crossed to another row of depressions. Beside the closest was a small, red and white container—a cooler, its top slid open. To either side, the depressions were attended by thermoses, lunchboxes, larger coolers, even a small refrigerator. Rick's father knelt at a dip and reached his hand down into the mud, working his fingers in a circle around whatever lay half-buried in it. Once it was freed, he raised it, using his free hand to brush the worst of the mud from it. "This," he said, holding out to Connie a copy of the thing she and Rick had found on the Thruway. Its surface was darker than the spaces between the stars overhead.

"That's an embryo?" she said.

"Closest word." Bending to the open cooler, he gently deposited the thing inside it. His hands free, he clicked the cooler's lid shut. "Someone will be by for this shortly," he said, raising his fingers to his tongue.

"I don't," Connie started, and there was an explosion of wings, or what might have been wings, a fury of black flapping. She put up her hands to defend herself, and the wings were gone, the cooler with them. "What . . . ?"

"You have to prepare the ground, first," Rick's father said, "fertilize it, you could say. A little more time would have been nice, but Tunguska was long enough ago. To tell the truth, if we'd had to proceed earlier, it wouldn't have mattered." He stepped to the next hole and its attendant thermos and repeated his excavation. As he was jiggling the thing into the thermos, Connie said, "But—why?"

"Oh, that's . . ." Rick's father gestured at the thermos's side, where the strange cross with the slender join and rounded arms was stenciled. "You know."

"No, I don't."

Gary Wilson shrugged. His face slid with the movement, up, then down, the flesh riding on the bone. The hairs on Connie's neck, her arms, stood rigid. She did not want to accompany him as he turned left again and headed for a deep slice in the mud, but she could not think what else to do. Behind her there was a chaos of flapping, and silence.

The fissure in the mud ran in both directions as far as she could see. It was probably narrow enough for her to jump across. She was less sure of its depth, rendered uncertain by dimness. At or near the bottom something rose, not high enough for her to distinguish it, but sufficiently near for her to register a great mass. "Too cold out here," Rick's father said. "Makes them sluggish. Inhibits their"—he waved his hands—"development. Confines it."

There were more of whatever-it-was down there. Some quality of their movement made Connie grateful she couldn't see any more of them.

"Funny," Rick's father said. "They need this place for infancy, your place for maturity. Never known another breed with such extreme requirements."

"What are they?"

"I guess you would call them . . . gods? Is that right? *Orchidaceae deus*? They bloom."

"What?"

"Bloom."

IV

There was a small deck at the back of the house, little more than a half-dozen planks of unfinished wood raised on as many thick posts, bordered by an unsteady railing, at the top of a flight of uneven stairs. A door led from the deck into the house's laundry room, whose location on the second floor had impressed Connie as one of the reasons to rent the place two years ago, when her promotion to manager had allowed sufficient money to leave their basement apartment and its buffet of molds behind. Mornings she didn't have to open the store, and Rick hadn't worked too late the night before, they would carry their mugs of coffee out here. She liked to stand straight, her mug cradled in her hands, while Rick preferred to take his chances leaning on the rail. Sometimes they spoke, but mostly they were quiet, listening to the birds performing their various morning songs, watching the squirrels chase one another across the high branches of the trees whose roots knitted together the small rise behind the house.

A freak early frost had whited the deck and stairs. Once the sun was streaming through the trunks of the oaks and maples stationed on the rise, the frost would steam off, but at the moment dawn was a red hint amidst the dark trees. Red sky at morning, Connie thought.

She was seated at the top of the deck stairs, wrapped in the green and white knitted blanket she'd grabbed when she'd left the laundry room hours ago. The bottle of Stolichnaya cradled in her arms was almost empty, despite which, she felt as sober as she ever had. More than sober—her senses were operating past peak capacity. The grooves in the bark of the oaks on the rise were deep gullies flanked by vertical ridges. The air eddying over her skin was dense with moisture. The odor of the soil in which the trees clutched their roots was the brittle-paper smell of dead leaves crumbling mixed with the damp thickness of dirt. It was as if she were under a brilliant white light, one that allowed her no refuge, but that also permitted her to view her surroundings with unprecedented clarity.

She had emerged from her dream of Rick's father to silence, to a stillness so profound the sound of her breathing thundered in her ears. Rick's side of the bed was still cold. Except for a second strange dream on the same night, there had been no reason for Connie to do anything other than return to sleep. Her dream, however, had seemed sufficient cause for her to rouse herself and (once more) set out downstairs in search of Rick. In the quiet that had draped the house, the creaks of the stairs under her feet had been horror-movie loud.

She had not been sure what she would find downstairs, and had walked past the front parlor before her brain caught up to what it had noticed from the corner of her eye and sent her several steps back. The small room they called the front parlor, whose bay window overlooked the front porch, had been dark. Not just nighttime dark (which, with the streetlight outside, wasn't really that dark), but complete and utter blackness. This hadn't been the lack of light so much as the overwhelming presence of its opposite, a dense inkiness that had filled the room like water in a tank. Connie had reached out her hand to touch it, only to stop with her fingers a hairsbreadth away from it, when the prospect of touching it had struck her as a less than good idea. Lowering her hand, she had retreated along the hall to the dining room.

Before the dining room, though, she had paused at the basement door, open wide and allowing a thick, briny stench up from its depths. The smell of seaweed and assorted sea-life baking on the beach, the odor had been oddly familiar, despite her inability to place it. She had reached around the doorway for the light switch, flipped it on, and poked her head through the doorway. Around the foot of the stairs, she had seen something she could not immediately identify. There had been no way she was venturing all the way into the basement; already, the night had taken too strange a turn for her to want to put herself into so ominous, if clichéd, a location. But she had been curious enough to descend the first couple of stairs and crouch to look through the railings.

When she had, Connie had seen a profusion of flowers, orchids, their petals eggplant and rose. They had covered the concrete floor so completely she could not see it. A few feet closer to them, the tidal smell was stronger, almost a taste. The orchids were motionless, yet she had had the impression that she had caught them on the verge of movement. She had wanted to think, *I'm dreaming; this is part of that last dream,* but the reek of salt and rot had been too real. She had stood and backed upstairs.

Mercifully, the dining room had been unchanged, its table, chairs,

and china cabinet highlighted by the streetlight's orange glow. Unchanged, that was, except for the absence of the cooler from the table,
and why had she been so certain that, wherever the container was, its
lid was open, its contents gone? Rick's father's laptop had remained
where her husband had set it up, its screen dark. Connie had pressed
the power button, and the rectangle had brightened with the image of
one of the T-shaped stone monuments, its transverse section carved
with what appeared to be three birds processing down from upper left
to lower right, their path taking them over the prone form of what
might have been a man—though if it was, the head was missing. The
upright block was carved with a boar, its tusks disproportionately large.

Thinking Rick might have decided to sleep in the guest room, she
had crossed to the doorway to the long room along the back of the
house, the large space for which they had yet to arrive at a use. To the
right the room had wavered, as if she had been looking at it through
running water. One moment it had bulged toward her; the next, it had
telescoped away. In the midst of that uncertainty, she had seen . . . she
couldn't say what. It was as if that part of the house had been a screen
against which something enormous had been pushing and pulling, its
form visible only through the distortions it caused in the screen. The
sight had hurt her eyes, her brain, to behold; she had been not so
much frightened as sickened, nauseated. No doubt she should have
fled the house, taken the car keys from the hook at the front door and
driven as far from here as the gas in the tank would take her.

Rick, though: she couldn't leave him here with all this. Dropping
her gaze to her feet, she had stepped into the back room, flattening
herself against the wall to her left. A glance had showed nothing between her and the door to the guest room, and she had slid along the
wall to it as quickly as her legs would carry her. A heavy lump of dread,
for Rick, alone down here as whatever this was had happened, had
weighed deep below her stomach. At the threshold to the guest room
she had tried to speak, found her voice caught in her throat. She had
coughed, said, "Rick? Honey?" the words striking the silence in the air
like a mallet clanging off a gong; she had flinched at their loudness.

Connie had not been expecting Rick to step out of the guest room
as if he had been waiting there for her. With a shriek, she had leapt
back. He had raised his hands, no doubt to reassure her, but even in

the dim light she could see they were discolored, streaked with what looked like tar, as was his mouth, his jaw. He had stepped toward her, and Connie had retreated another step. "Honey," he had said, but the endearment had sounded wrong, warped, as if his tongue had forgotten how to shape his words.

"Rick," she had said, "what—what happened?"

His lips had peeled back, but whatever he had wanted to say, it would not come out.

"The house—you're—"

"It's . . . okay. He showed me . . . Dad."

"Your father? What did he show you?"

Rick had not lowered his hands; he gestured with them to his mouth.

"Oh, Christ. You—you didn't."

Yes he did, Rick had nodded.

"Are you insane? Do you have any idea what—you don't know what that thing was! You probably poisoned yourself . . ."

"Fine," Rick had said. "I'm . . . fine. Better. More."

"What?"

"Dad showed me."

Whatever the cooler's content, she had been afraid the effects of consuming it were already in full swing, the damage already done. Yet despite the compromise in his speech, Rick's eyes had burned with intelligence. Sweeping his hands around him, he had said, "All . . . the same. Part of—" He had uttered a guttural sound she could not decipher, but that had hurt her ears to hear.

"Rick," she had said, "we have to leave—we have to get you to a doctor. Come on." She had started toward the doorway to the dining room, wondering whether Wiltwyck would be equipped for whatever toxin he had ingested. The other stuff, the darkness, the orchids, the corner, could wait until Rick had been seen by a doctor.

"No." The force of his refusal had halted Connie where she was. "See."

"What—" She had turned to him, and seen . . . she could not say what. Hours later, her nerves calmed if not soothed by the vodka that had washed down her throat, she could not make sense of the sight that had greeted her. When she tried to replay it, she saw Rick, then saw his face, his chest, burst open, pushed aside by the orchids thrust-ing their eggplant and rose petals out of him. The orchids, Rick, wa-vered, as if she were looking at them through a waterfall, and then erupted into a cloud of darkness that coalesced into Rick's outline. Connie had the sense that that was only an approximation of what she actually had witnessed, and not an especially accurate one at that. As well say she had seen all four things simultaneously, like a photograph overexposed multiple times, or that she had seen the cross from the top of the cooler, hanging in the air.

She had responded with a headlong flight that had carried her up-stairs to the laundry room. Of course, it had been a stupid destination, one she was not sure why she had chosen, except perhaps that the side and front doors had lain too close to one of the zones of weirdness that had overtaken the house. The bottle of Stolichnaya had been wait-ing next to the door to the deck, no doubt a refugee from their most recent party. She could not think of a reason not to open it and gulp a fiery mouthful of its contents; although she couldn't think of much of anything. She had been, call it aware of the quiet, the silence pervading the house, which had settled against her skin and become intolerable, until she had grabbed a blanket from the cupboard and let herself out onto the deck. There, she had wrapped herself in the blanket and seat-ed herself at the top of the deck stairs.

Tempting to say she had been in shock, but shock wasn't close: shock was a small town she had left in the rearview mirror a thousand miles ago. This was the big city, metropolis of a sensation like awe or ecstasy, a wrenching of the self that rendered such questions as how she was going to help Rick, how they were going to escape from this, immaterial. From where she was sitting, she could look down on their Subaru, parked maybe fifteen feet from the foot of the stairs. There was an emergency key under an overturned flowerpot in the garage. These facts were neighborhoods separated by hundreds of blocks, connected by a route too byzantine for her understanding to take. She had stayed where she was as the constellations wheeled above her, the sky lightened from blue-bordering-on-black to dark blue. Her breath plumed from her lips; she pulled the blanket tighter and nursed the vodka as, through a process too subtle for her to observe, frost spread over the deck, the stairs.

When the eastern sky was a blue so pale it was almost white, she had noticed a figure standing at the bottom of the stairs. For a moment she had mistaken it for Rick, had half stood at the prospect, and then she had recognized Rick's father. He had been dressed in the same tuxedo he'd worn in her second dream of him, the knees of his trousers and the cuffs of his shirt and jacket crusted with red mud. His presence prompted her to speech. "You," she had said, resuming her seat. "Are you Rick's dad, or what?"

"Yes."

"Great. Can you tell me what's happened to my husband?"

"He's taken the seed into himself."

"The thing from the cooler."

"He blooms."

"I don't—" She'd shaken her head. "Why . . . why? Why him? Why this?"

Rick's father had shrugged, and she had done her best not to notice if his face had shifted with the movement.

She had sighed. "What now?"

"He will want a consort."

"He what?"

"His consort."

She would not have judged herself capable of the laughter that had burst from her. "You have got to be fucking kidding me."

"The process is under way."

"I don't think so."

"Look at your bottle."

"This?" She had held up the vodka. "It's alcohol."

"Yes. He thought that might help."

"What do you—" Something, some glint of streetlight refracting on the bottle's glass, had caused her to bring it to her eyes, tilting it so that the liquor sloshed up one side. In the orange light shimmering in it, Connie had seen tiny black flakes floating, dozens, hundreds of them. "Oh, no. No way. No."

"It will take longer this way, but he thought you would need the time."

"He? You mean Rick? Rick did this?"

"To bring you to him, to what he is."

"Bring me—"

"To bloom."

"This is—no. No." She had wanted to hurl the bottle at Rick's father, but had been unable to release her grip on it. "Not Rick. No."

He had not argued the point; instead, before the last denial had left her mouth, the space where he'd stood had been empty.

That had been . . . not that long ago, she thought. Time enough for the horizon to flush, for her to feel herself departing the city of awe to which the night's sights had brought her for somewhere else, a great gray ocean swelling with storm. She had squinted at the bottle of Stolichnaya, at the black dots drifting in what remained of its contents. Rick had done this? So she could be his consort? Given what she'd witnessed this night, it seemed silly to declare one detail of it more outrageous than the rest, but this . . . She could understand, well, imagine how an appearance by his father might have convinced her husband that eating the thing in the cooler was a good idea. But to leap from that to thinking that he needed to bring Connie along for the ride, that was something else.

The thing was, it was entirely typical of the way Rick acted, had acted, the length of their relationship. He plunged into decisions like a bungee-jumper abandoning the trestle of a bridge, confident that the cord to which he'd tethered himself, i.e. her, would pull him back from the rocks jagged below. He dropped out of grad school even though it meant he would lose the deferment for the sixty thousand dollars in student loans he had no job to help him repay. He registered for expensive training courses for professions in which he lost interest halfway through the class. He overdrew their joint account for take-out dinners when there was a refrigerator's worth of food waiting at home. And now, the same tendencies that had led to them having so much difficulty securing a mortgage—that had left the fucking cellphone's battery depleted—had caused him to . . . she wasn't even sure she knew the word for it.

The sky between the trees on the rise was filling with color, pale rose deepening to rich crimson, the trunks and branches against it an extravagant calligraphy she could not read. The light ruddied her skin, shone redly on the bottle, glowed hellishly on the frosted steps, deck. She stared through the trees at it, let it saturate her vision.

The photons cascaded against her leaves, stirring them to life.

(What?)

She convoluted, moving at right angles to herself, the sunlight fracturing.

(Oh)

Blackness.

(God.)

She lurched to her feet.

Roots tingled, blackness, unfolding, frost underfoot. Connie gripped the liquor bottle by the neck and swung it against the porch railing. Smashing it took three tries. The last of the vodka splashed onto the deck planks. She pictured hundreds of tiny black—what had Rick's father called them?—embryos shrieking, realized she was seeing them, hearing them.

Blackness her stalk in-turning glass on skin. Connie inspected the bottle's jagged top. As improvised weapons went, she supposed it wasn't bad, but she had the feeling she was bringing a rock to a nuclear war.

The dawn air was full of the sound of flapping, of leathery wings snapping. She could almost see the things that were swirling around the house, could feel the spaces they were twisting. She released the blanket, let it slide to the deck. She crossed to the door to the laundry room, still unlocked. Had she thought it wouldn't be? Connie adjusted her grip on her glass knife, opened the door, and stepped into the house.

Renfrew's Course

"So this is the wizard," Neil said.

"Supposedly," Jim said.

Six feet tall, the statue had been carved from wood that retained most of its whiteness, even though the date cut into its base read 2005, seven years ago. Jim thought the color might be due to its not having been finished—splinters stood from the wood's uneven surface—but didn't know enough about carpentry to be certain.

"Looks kind of Gandalf," Neil said.

He was right. The wide-brimmed hat, long beard, staff, and robe all suggested Tolkien's character, an impression the squirrel at the figure's left foot, fox behind its right, owl on its shoulder did little to argue.

"I know," Jim said. "It's like that statue of William Wallace—did I tell you about that? They wanted to put up a new statue of Wallace—somewhere out near Stirling, I think—so what did the artist come up with? Mel Gibson in *Braveheart*."

"No wonder there're so few Jews in Scotland."

"Apparently, the real guy was much stranger."

"Gibson? I know," Neil said, starting up the hill toward the dirt path that would take them into the nature preserve.

"No, the wizard." Once he had caught up to Neil and they were walking under the tall pine and oak, Jim continued, "In one story, the king of France was causing some kind of difficulty for the local merchants—an embargo, I think. Michael Renfrew mounted his iron horse and in a single bound crossed the distance from Kirkcaldy to Paris. When he showed up at the French palace, its doors flew open for him. The king's guards found their swords red hot in their hands. Needless to say, Louis-the-whatever changed his mind, and quickly at that."

"An iron horse, huh?"

"Legend says you can still see its hoof print on the cliff it leapt off."

245

To their right, separated from them by dense rows of pine, a stone tower raised its crenellated head above the tree line. "See?" Jim said, pointing to it. "Over there—that's Renfrew's keep."

"Which has seen better days."

"It's like seven hundred years old."

"So's Edinburgh Castle, isn't it?"

"Anyhoo," Jim said, "Renfrew only stayed there part of the time. He was the court astrologer for the Holy Roman Emperor."

Neil grunted. No longer angry about the Rose incident, neither was he all the way over it. Had he been familiar with Scotland, he might have gone off for a few days on his own and left Jim to worry about what he was up to, whom he was having long, heartfelt conversations with over steaming mugs of chai. The trip, however, had been Jim's baby, a chance to share with Neil the place in which he'd passed the summers of his childhood while also promoting his surprisingly successful book. Neil could not make sense of the timetables for the trains or buses, and as for driving on the other side of the road, forget it. He had no choice but to remain with Jim and his revelation about his *affaire de coeur* with Rose Carlton, which he had dealt with from inside a roiling cloud first of anger, then pique. Jim met this change in their personal weather the way he always did, the way he always had, by talking too much, filling the charged air with endless facts, opinion, speculation.

Not for the first time, the irony of his book's title, *The Still Warrior,* struck him. How often had he urged his students at the dojo not to be afraid of their own quiet, of remaining in place, controlling their sparring bouts by forcing their opponents into committing to action first? It was a perspective he'd spent one hundred and forty-eight pages applying to a wide range of activities and situations, and based on the early sales figures, it was a viewpoint in which a significant portion of the reading public was interested. Look at his life off the dojo's polished hardwood, though, and he might as well have been writing fiction, fantasy rooted in the deepest wish-fulfillment. Especially when it came to Neil, he was almost pathologically unable to leave things be, let the kinks and snarls in their relationship work themselves out, as the vast majority of them likely would. Instead, he had to plan excursions like this one, a walk along a nature path that was supposed to bring them . . . what? Closer? "You can't make a scar heal any faster," Neil had said, which Jim wasn't sure he believed but which Neil certainly did.

Ahead, the path was intersected by a secondary trail slanting up from the right. The new trail was little more than a disturbance in the forest's carpet of needles, but Neil turned onto it. "Hey," Jim said.

"I want to see where this goes."

Neil knew he wouldn't argue. *Prick.* Jim followed him off the main path and was seized by a vertigo so extreme he might have been standing at the edge of a sheer cliff, rather than a not especially steep trail. He leaned forward, and it was as if he were on the verge of a great abyss, an emptiness that was coaxing him forward, just one more step . . .

A hand gripped his arm. "Hey—you all right?" The voice was high, familiar.

Vision swimming, Jim said, "I don't," and heard the words uttered in a different—in what sounded like the voice on his and Neil's videos of their old vacations, his voice of ten years ago.

The hand steadying him belonged to a young man—to Neil, he saw, Neil as he had been when Jim had met him at a mutual friend's Y2K party. His hair was down to his shoulders and, as was the case when he let it grow, both more curly and a shade closer to strawberry blond. The lines on his face were not cut as deep, and his skin was pale from a life lived in front of the computer. Mouth tucked into the smirk that had first caught Jim's notice, he said, "Steady," and released Jim's arm.

Jim raised his right hand and brushed the half-dozen earrings that climbed his ear. He could feel his own hair ponytailed along the back of his neck. "Oh my God," he said.

"What is it?" Neil said.

"I—don't you—"

"Maybe the mushrooms weren't such a good idea."

"Mushrooms?" Jim said, even as he was thinking, *Yes, mushrooms, because that's the kind of shit you do now, at twenty-five, psilocybin and pot and occasionally hash and once in a great while a little E, because you're still five years away from the ambush of turning thirty, when you'll throw away all this stuff and more besides—soda, fast food, desserts—in favor of Shotokan karate seven days a week, fifty-two weeks a year. That's the future: right now, you're pursuing your private version of the systematic derangement of the senses.*

"Man," Neil said, "I guess those things were strong. I've never seen you like this before. Wish they would do something for me." He waved his hand in front of his eyes. "Nada."

"We—how did we get here?"

"We walked."

"No, I mean Kirkcaldy—Scotland."

"Wow."

"How did we get here?"

"Easy, there, easy," Neil said. "Work exchange, remember? I'm over here six weeks, that guy—Doug Moore, right?—is enjoying life in NYC. You tagged along because—well, because you're cute and I like you. Okay?"

Of course that was the case. The moment Jim heard Neil's explanation, he realized he already knew it. Cheeks burning, he said, "Okay. I'm sorry, it's just—those were some strong mushrooms."

"Yeah?"

"Yeah. I was having this whole fantasy that you and I were here, only in the future."

"The future, huh? What were we like?"

"I had written this really popular book. We were here promoting it. You were . . . still programming, I think."

"Oh, so you're the famous writer and I'm just some computer nerd. Very nice."

"Hey, you were my computer nerd."

"Flattery."

"It's gotten me everywhere."

"You're feeling better."

"I guess."

"Good." The expression on Neil's face looked as if it might portend sex, a quickie amidst the trees, but he turned and continued down the secondary path. As Jim followed, he said, "Before you went all freaky, you were talking about the wizard, old Michael Renfrew."

"I was? Yeah, I suppose I was. Look to your right, ahead and you'll see Renfrew's keep."

"Where? Oh, yeah. What part is that?"

"Must be near the base. That's—I think that's a doorway. Hard to tell through the trees."

"So what about Renfrew?"

"Did I tell you about the iron horse?"

"And the king of France, yeah."

"There's a story about him and the Devil."

"Oh?"

"Or a devil: I can't remember which. At some point, he summoned a devil. I'm not sure why. Maybe for knowledge, or maybe to prove his power. It's one of those things magicians do all the time in old stories. Anyway, dealing with this guy was more dangerous than your run-of-the-mill evil spirit. If Renfrew could name a single task the devil could not perform, then he could make whatever use of him he wished for a year and a day. If not, the devil would pull him down to hell."

"And?"

"Renfrew took him to the beach and commanded him to weave a rope out of sand."

"Not bad. What did he have the devil do for him?"

"The story doesn't say. It's more concerned with him outsmarting the devil than with Renfrew using him for his personal gain."

"Maybe that was how he got the iron horse."

"Could be."

"Anything else?"

"Not really. He's supposed to have had something to do with this book, *Les Mystères du ver,* but I'm not sure what."

"*Les*—what?"

"*Les Mystères du ver. The Mysteries of the Worm.* It's some kind of evil book, Satanic Bible, witch's spell list, that sort of thing."

"*The Mysteries of the Worm,* huh? No wonder you're interested in this guy."

"Worm? Try snake."

"Somebody's overcompensating."

"Merely stating the facts."

Neil did not answer, and Jim could not think of a way to extend their banter that did not sound forced, banal. *It's all right,* he told himself. *Silence is all right. You don't always have to be talking.* Wasn't that one of the things that had attracted him to Neil in the first place, his ability to be comfortable in his own quiet? Even in the length of time they'd been together, hadn't he learned that Neil's sometimes prolonged periods of silence rarely had anything to do with them, that he was usually turning over some work-related problem? He didn't feel the need to fill the air with words, and if that made Jim anxious, that wasn't Neil's fault, was it?

Plus, the sex is fantastic.

Maybe fifteen feet in front of Neil, the path leveled off and was met by another, slanting down from the right to join theirs at an acute angle. When Neil turned at the junction and started up it, Jim said, "Hey."

"Come on," Neil said. "This should take us back to the main trail."

No arguing with that. This track appeared clearer than the one they'd just descended, more sharply defined. He followed onto it—and it was as if he'd tried to walk up a wall. The path rose above him, impossibly high; he staggered backwards, dropped onto his ass. The path loomed overhead, a dark strip of ground about to fall on him, and—

A silhouette leaned in front of him. "What happened?" The voice was flat, familiar.

Struggling against the urge to throw his hands in front of his face, protect himself from the collapse of dirt and rock, Jim said, "I don't," and was shocked to hear the fragment delivered in a voice whose underlying tones were his but which had been roughened, broadened.

The outline before him resolved into Neil, but a different Neil, a Neil whose face might have received the attentions of a makeup artist instructed to advance his age by twenty, twenty-five years. His hair was crewcut short. His skin was grooved across the forehead, beneath the eyes, to either side of the mouth. Under the open collar of his shirt, a faded line of green ink scaled the left side of his neck, the edge of a tattoo, Jim knew—remembered. Were he to look into a mirror, he would see its twin on the left side of his neck, a memento of the aftermath of the Rose Carlton incident, when he and Neil had sought a way to reaffirm their bond. The eclipse had been Jim's idea, a symbol that, whatever events might darken their relationship, they would pass.

(Except that he'd developed a staph infection, which the tattooist, a mutual acquaintance, had spent days insisting could not be happening, he ran a clean shop, until Jim had wound up in the hospital, tethered to an IV antibiotic drip for a week. Nor had Neil moved past Rose, not really: every time an argument escalated to a certain pitch, he reached for her like a favorite weapon.)

"You all right?" Neil asked, the words tinted with something resembling concern.

He's worried about my heart, Jim thought. *The infection affected my heart, weakened it. (What the hell is happening to me?)* "Fine," he said, climbing to his feet. "I'm fine, just . . . a little lightheaded." *(Is this some kind of long-term after-effect of being sick? Did it mess with my head?)* He gestured at the path. "Go on."

"You're sure?"

"Go."

"Take it easy," Neil said. "This isn't a race." Nonetheless, he hurried to keep in front. "Okay?" he called over his shoulder.

"Great."

After a minute of trudging up the thick, rocky earth, Neil said, "Do you feel like continuing the story?"

"Story?"

"Story, chapter, whatever you want to call it. 'Renfrew and the Giant.'"

Almost before he knew he was speaking them, Jim found the words at his lips. "Having endured Renfrew's displays of power, the Giant was less than impressed by his offer of an alliance between them. He said, 'Little man, you have already shown me that I have nothing to fear from you. Why should I cast my lot in with yours?'

"Although obviously exhausted, Renfrew stood straighter and answered, 'Because you have everything to benefit if you do, and everything to lose if you do not.'

"At this, the Giant laughed, and it was the sound of an avalanche, of boulders crashing into one another. 'Little man,' he said, 'your boldness does you credit. I will eat you quickly.' He reached one enormous hand toward the wizard.

"Renfrew did not flinch. He said, 'I know your name—your true name.'

"The Giant's hand halted, inches from Renfrew. His vast brow lowered. 'Impossible,' he said. 'I hid that where no man—no one might find it, ever.'

"'Yes,' Renfrew said, 'in a cavern under a lake watched over by three mountains, locked inside a brass casket guarded by a basilisk. I have been there.'

"The Giant's hand retreated. He said, 'You read of this in one of your wizard's books.'

"Renfrew said, "The sole means to open the casket is the tooth of a hydra, which is in the basilisk's stomach. The casket contains a pale blue egg resting on a white pillow. To touch the egg is like touching a furnace; to hear its shell crack is like hearing your own death. Within the egg there is a stone into which has been carved a single word.'

"The Giant's hand had retreated all the way to his great mouth.

"Renfrew said, 'That word is *Mise*.'"

Neil said, "Meesh?"

"I think that's how it's pronounced. It's Gaelic, means 'I am.'"

"I am?"

"Yeah. The original story doesn't say what the Giant's true name was, only that Renfrew had discovered it and used it against him. I thought about making it something like 'stone' or 'mountain,' but that seemed too obvious."

"Why?"

"Well, giants are big, you know; if you were going to associate them with anything, it would be a mountain."

"I guess."

"Anyway, it made sense to me that the Giant's name would be his life, so, 'I am.'"

"If you say so. Just as long as this one brings another big advance."

Jim said, "Karen's pretty optimistic. Post–Harry Potter, wizards and magic are big business in kids' publishing," even as he was thinking, *Karen Lowatchee, your agent, who repped you on* The Still Warrior *and, when the heart thing made you scale back karate, suggested you try fiction. She'd liked the chapters on karate for kids, said they showed a real grasp of tween psychology. She was the one who came up with the* Jenny Ninja *series title and got you the big advances for the last two. Neil calls her Glenda the Good Bitch; she calls him Microsoft.*

"What happens next?" Neil said.

"In the chapter? Renfrew turns the Giant into his keep."

"That's it?"

"That's what happens in the original legend."

"Yeah, but—couldn't he have used the Giant first?"

"Invaded England with him?" Jim said.

"Something."

"I don't know. I kind of like the idea of Renfrew living inside the

Giant, wandering around him, listening to the echo of his thoughts, his dreams."

"Sounds pretty creepy, if you ask me."

"And what's wrong with that?"

"Isn't this book supposed to be for kids?"

"It's YA," Jim said, "Young Adult. Older kids."

Over the tops of the pines to their right, Renfrew's keep raised its ragged crown. "See," Jim said, pointing at it, "the windows look like eyes."

"What has eyes like that?"

"It's supposed to be a monster."

"Aren't giants big people?"

"Not all them. The ancient Greeks described giants with a hundred arms."

"Where do you get this stuff?"

"Depends. The ancient Greek stuff's available all over the place. Information on Renfrew is harder to come by. Mostly I use that website, Blackguide.com."

"The one that crashed the computer?"

"I told you, it wasn't that: it was all the porn you'd been looking at."

"Very funny."

Neil's pace slowed. In front of him, their path intersected another sloping steeply down from the right. As he stepped onto it, Jim said, "Hey."

"I'm pretty sure this'll lead back to the beginning of the trail," Neil said.

This place isn't that big. I'm sure if I kept on a straight line, I'd come out on a side street eventually. However discouraging the prospect of an even more strenuous climb was, though, the inevitable spat that would result from him not following Neil, not to mention the two or three days after that before the situation returned to normal, prompted him up the new path. As he did so, his vision went dark. He had the impression of something huge in front of him, something vast hanging over him, like a wave, only solid, ready to crash down on him. He wanted to cry out, but his tongue was dead in his mouth; his heart lurched like a racehorse stumbling mid-stride.

Somewhere close by an old man's voice said, "What is it? What's the matter with you?" The words vibrated with rage, barely controlled.

What's Neil's father doing here? Jim thought. He tried to speak. "Mr. Marshall—"

"Don't Mr. Marshall me. I know who I am. I'm still lucid."

The host of the questions the outburst raised were silenced by the clearing of Jim's sight, which revealed Neil's face inches from his. Its angry expression was almost parodic: eyes wide and staring under lowered brows, top lip arched, teeth visible, chin jutting forward. It was also the face of a man in his mid-seventies. Neil's hair was white, as were his eyebrows; both hair and brows were thick, bushy. The lines across his forehead, to either side of his mouth, appeared cut right down to the bone, while his skin looked loose, its grip on his skull slipping. His gaze was fierce yet unfocused, as if he were unable to pinpoint the source of his rage; already, his lips were retreating from their snarl into the tremors that shook them incessantly.

The Alzheimer's, Jim thought. *That was the first symptom: before the memory loss, the mood swings, that spasm was telling us what was on the way.*

"What happened to you?" Neil said. "Is it your heart? Are you having another heart attack?" The emotion under his words was sliding into panic.

"I'm fine," Jim said. "Just caught up in . . ." *What? What do I call whatever's happening to me? (And, by the way, what the hell is happening to me? Is this some kind of stroke?)* "In a rather vivid daydream, I suppose—a memory, really, of one of our past visits here."

"Oh? Was that before or after you fucked Rose?"

"I didn't—"

"Yes, yes, that's what you always say; what you've always said."

"But you've never believed me, have you?"

"I don't know what I believe. I'm the one whose brain is disintegrating, remember?"

"It isn't," Jim started, then stopped. Technically speaking, Neil's brain wasn't disintegrating, but there were worse ways to describe what was happening to his personality, to the aggregate of memories and attitudes that composed Neil. Anyway, Neil already had turned his back on him and was striding up the path. The disease might be wrecking his mind, but so far his vitality was undiminished. Jim labored not to fall too far behind.

Neil said, "Do you remember the end of Renfrew's story?"

"Do you mean my book or the legend?"

"Which was which?"

"My book ends with Renfrew entering the cave at Wemyss in search of the path to the Graveyard of the Old Gods. He leaves Thomas, his apprentice, in charge until his return, which doesn't take place during Thomas's very long life, or that of his apprentice, or that of any of the men and women who have come since. However, the book says, that doesn't mean that one day the old wizard won't emerge from the mouth of the cave, squinting at the light, and begin the long walk back to his old home."

"That wasn't it."

"You want the legend, then. That ends with a group of the Covenanters coming armed to Renfrew's keep in order to arrest him on charges of sorcery. When they arrived, though, they found the place deserted, as if no one had lived there for decades, or longer."

"That isn't it, either."

"I don't—there's a tradition, a kind of afterword to the legend proper, that if you follow a certain course through the woods around Renfrew's keep—and if certain conditions are right: the stars are in alignment, that sort of thing; I think an eclipse is supposed to figure into the equation somehow—then Renfrew himself will appear to you and offer to teach you what he knows. Is that what you were thinking of?"

"Yes," Neil said.

Jim waited for Neil to add something more; when he did not, he said, "What makes you ask?"

"Ask what?"

"About Renfrew's course?"

"What about it?"

"You just asked me to tell you about it."

"I did." Neil shrugged. "I don't remember that."

There was no point in anger; though buttressed by his meds, Neil's short-term memory was far from perfect. Jim said, "You know what I was thinking?"

"How much longer you have to wait before you can put me in a home?"

"What? No, I told you, I'm not going to put you in a home."

"That's what you say now."

"That's what I have said—what I've been saying ever since you were diagnosed."

For a change, he hoped the silence that greeted his reassurance meant the subject of their debate had slipped through the sieve of Neil's immediate recollection. His quiet seemed to imply that it had, another moment caught in the plaque crusting his neurons, then he said, "I hope you and Rose will have the decency to wait until all my things have been moved out for her to move in."

"Neil—"

"It would be nice if you could wait until I'm in the ground, but I'm guessing I could hang on for a while, and you certainly aren't getting any younger. Neither is she; although she isn't as old as we are, is she? Maybe she'll be inclined to do the decent thing, but you won't, will you?"

"I'm sorry: I can't talk to you when you're like this."

Neil lengthened his stride, mountain-goating up the path. Jim didn't bother chasing after. Better to hang back and hope that, by the time he caught up, Neil's thunderstorm of emotions would have passed; though he wasn't sure what he rated the chances of that as. It had been years, almost a full decade, since he and Rose had seen each other, and that had been by accident, a chance encounter at the Union Square Barnes & Noble that had led to nothing more than the occasional email. If he hadn't told Neil about the meeting, or the correspondence, it was because, long after his whatever-you-wanted-to-call-it with her had receded in his memory, in Neil's mind it was a flame only recently and poorly extinguished, whose smoldering embers might yet ignite again. He would have made too much of the emails in which Jim told Rose about his visit to the set of the Renfrew film, Rose told him about her recent trip to Paris with her ninety-two-year-old mother, mountained the molehills into a secret, ongoing affair. In the wake of Neil's illness, he supposed he had been writing to her more frequently, but his correspondence with all his friends and family had increased as his communication with Neil had grown more erratic.

He was almost at the top of the path. He had climbed higher than he'd realized; to his right and over his shoulder, he could look down on the roofless top of Renfrew's keep. To his relief, Neil was standing waiting for him. "There you are," Jim said—panted, really.

"Here I am," Neil said. His expression was almost kindly. "Need a minute?"

"Half a minute," Jim said, leaning forward. "Neil—"

At Neil's feet, their path formed an acute angle with another climbing up from the right. As he started down it, Jim said, "Hey."

"I can see the place where we started," Neil said, pointing.

Jim squinted. Was that the white of the wizard's statue? They would have to descend from here somehow, he supposed, and this new path, crossed by tree roots that formed an irregular staircase, was probably the best option he could expect. He stepped down, and it was like dropping into a well. There was the sensation of falling straight down, and the impression of everything flying up all around him, and the sound of roaring filling his ears. Terror swept through his chest, his head, made them sickeningly light. He flailed his arms. There was nothing under his feet; he was falling.

Something crashed into him from the front. He heard an "Oof!" and felt his direction change. Now he was moving forward, his arms and legs caught with someone else's, tangled, the pair of them thudding and scraping against rock and dirt. He rolled over and under, over and under his companion, then landed hard on his back, his right kidney shouting at the rock it came down on. Above him, the sky was a blue bowl someone had set spinning. He closed his eyes, and when he opened them, Neil was leaning over him. There was a cut high on his forehead leaking blood onto his brow, but aside from that and some dirt, his face was the same as it had been at the start of this strange walk, thirty-nine and looking it. "You klutz," he said. "Karate master, my ass."

Jim flung his arm around him, flinching as his back complained. "I'm sorry," he said into Neil's shoulder. "Are you okay?"

"You mean, aside from the gaping wound in my head? Yeah, I'm peachy."

Jim released him. "I am so sorry," he said as he struggled to his feet. "I just . . . I slipped."

"And you couldn't miss me on the way?"

"I didn't want you to feel left out."

Fighting it, Neil smirked. "You are such an asshole."

"But I'm your asshole."

"Enough shit comes out of you, anyway."

"Ah, I'm sure a little single malt will help."

"First sensible thing you've said all day."

They had rolled almost halfway down the path; no surprise, given the bruises Jim could feel ripening under his shirt, his jeans, the scrapes visible on Neil's arms, his neck. He supposed he should be grateful neither of them had broken a limb or been concussed. At least Neil had been right about this path returning them to the entrance to the nature preserve: through the trees, the wizard's statue stood a pale beacon. As Neil stepped from tree root step to tree root step, Jim weighed telling him about his . . . what would he call them? Hallucinations? visions? waking dreams? Maybe "experiences" was the best word for them. Whatever: it was on the tip of his tongue to say that he had just relived their life together when they'd first met, then seen them at points another twenty and forty or so years in the future. *When I'm the author of a series of successful children's books and he's in mid-stage Alzheimer's, not to mention still obsessing over Rose Carlton: yes, that would go over splendidly.*

Neil was drawing away from him. Strangest of all was that, now that the two of them were their proper selves, he was not more upset by what he had just been through, his experiences. (That still wasn't the right word, but it would do for the moment.) While he had been at each of those other times, the moment had been as real as anything— that he had been wrenched from this specific point in his life had seemed as odd, as disorienting, as any other detail. Returned to the age at which he had entered the nature preserve—the age he was supposed to be—Jim found his and Neil's alternate selves suddenly distant, novels he'd read years ago, their plots dim weights resting in the depths of his memory.

So what was all that? Some kind of projection? Easy enough to trace the roots of at least some of it to the current state of his and Neil's relationship. Future Neil's fixation on the Rose business arose from Jim's anxiety that, as time went on, he wouldn't be able to relinquish it. Jim's continued success as a writer was simple wish-fulfillment (although his agent had praised the sections of his book dealing with kids). Neil's grandfather had suffered from Alzheimer's, of which his father was showing early symptoms; from there, it was a short jump to imagining Neil eventually overtaken by it.

The vividness of everything, though, he could not account for. He had indulged in enough hallucinogens in his younger years; could this have been a delayed consequence of that? It seemed unlikely, but what was more likely? The place was the site of a ley-line that produced brief time-distortions? *Funny how all the tourist info fails to mention that.*

To his right, the lower stretch of Renfrew's keep was visible through the trees. Ahead, Neil was already at the statue. Legs protesting, Jim picked up his pace. Neil had stopped in front of the sculpture and appeared to be speaking to it. *That can't be good. Did I say neither of us was concussed?*

Jim did not see the man with whom Neil was talking until he was next to him. Standing on the other side of the statue, the man had been obscured from Jim's view by it. A head shorter than either of them, he wore his reddish hair short and a dark suit over an open-collared white shirt. Jim wasn't much for estimating the cost of things, but even he could recognize the quality of the man's clothes, which made the stains on his jacket cuffs, his shirt, all the more conspicuous. The man raised his eyes to Jim, and their green notice was a physical thing, a heaviness passing over him. "You're Jim," he said in a voice that was soft, accentless.

"Yes," Jim said, extending his hand. "You are . . . ?"

The man's hands were in his trouser pockets; he kept them there. "Renfrew."

"Like—" Jim gestured at the sculpture.

"The very same," the man said, "though the likeness is a poor one."

"Wait—what?" Jim glanced at Neil, who was watching the man intently. "I'm sorry: I thought you were saying—"

"I was." The man withdrew his hands from his pockets. Blue flames licked the unburned skin of the left, while a slender emerald snake coiled around the right.

"Jesus!" Jim leapt back.

"Not quite."

"What is this?"

Neil said, "We completed the course."

"You did." The man—Renfrew?—nodded. "Per the terms of a

contract that is older than any of us, I am here to offer one of you my tutelage."

"One of us," Jim said. "What about the other?"

"The price of tuition," Renfrew said. "A gesture of commitment."

"Okay, that's enough," Jim said.

"Take me," Neil said.

"What?"

"Very interesting," Renfrew said.

"Neil, what are you saying?"

"The Alzheimer's: that's a sure thing?" Neil said.

"Sure enough," Renfrew answered.

"And you can cure it?"

"I have been this age for a very long time," Renfrew said. "You need never meet that old man in the mirror."

"Are you kidding me?" Jim said. "Are you listening to yourself?"

"And there's no other way?" Neil said.

"There are many other ways, if you know where and how to find them. This is my way."

"I'm sorry," Neil started, but Jim cut him off: "This is insane."

"There was a link," Neil said, "on the Blackguide site. I clicked on it, and it led to an account by a guy who had walked this course in the nineteen-thirties with his brothers. With each new turn of the path, the three of them were at a different point in their lives: younger, then older, then much older. When they arrived back at the beginning, Renfrew was waiting for them."

"So all that was real?" Jim said.

"Real enough," Renfrew said.

"I thought if we could follow the course, then I could see how things would turn out—if we'd still be together; if we'd be happy; if Rose would still be around. I didn't expect—oh, Christ," Neil said. "Do you have any idea what it's like—no, you don't; how could you? Everything—you're aware that something is wrong, deeply wrong—you can feel it in everything around you—and you're sure you know what it is, what's the matter, but you can't remember it. And then you can remember, and you realize that the problem isn't with what's outside, it's with what's inside, and you know it's only a matter of time until you forget again and the whole process starts over." His eyes swam with tears.

"Neil, honey, it's okay," Jim said. "I'll be there for you."

"No," Neil said. "Don't you get it? I can't—I won't go through that. Now that I know—now that you know, how could you ask me to?"

"So instead you're going to . . . how does that story end, the one about the guy and his brothers?"

"The younger brother accepted Renfrew's offer. He and Renfrew disappeared, and when the older brother returned home, it was as if his brother had never existed. He was the only one who had any memory of him."

"Weren't there three of them? What happened to the other brother?"

"He vanished, too. No one remembered him, either."

Jim's mouth went dry. "The price of tuition."

"Speaking of which," Renfrew said, "we really need to move this along."

"You aren't going to do this," Jim said.

"What choice do I have?"

"You could choose me—choose us."

"Are you sure you don't want to make me an offer?" Renfrew said.

"Me?" Jim said. "I thought Neil—"

"Was here first, yes, but that's more a recommendation than a rule. I'm curious to learn how your convictions fare when the situation is reversed."

Neil's mouth moved, but no sound issued from it.

"Well?" Renfrew said.

His fear seemed outside him, an acrid saturation pressing on him from all sides at once; nonetheless, Jim was able to say, "Fuck you." The frown that darkened Renfrew's face was a small pleasure. Jim looked at Neil, who was staring at the ground. "What I had with Rose—it was never as bad as you thought it was, and when I said it was over, it was."

"For you, maybe."

Renfrew swept his left arm up and down, blue fire trailing from his fingertips, tracing a seam in the air that opened into something like a door. He nodded at Neil, who crossed to and stepped through it without another word. Jim was as astonished by his lack of a parting remark as anything.

"Now," Renfrew said, extending his right hand at Jim. The serpent wrapped around it raised its wedge-shaped head and regarded him lazily. The space behind the wizard darkened, full of an enormous shape. Jim thought, *How did the keep*—and realized that what had stepped closer was not the keep, or not anymore. It arched toward him, impossible mouth open to consume him, all of him, not only the flesh and bones it would grind between teeth like boulders, but his past, his present, his future, his very place in the world. He wished his fear would leave him, but he supposed it was better than the serrated edge of Neil's betrayal waiting beneath it. At least he could keep his eyes open; at least he would not turn away from the emptiness, the silence, descending on him.

Bor Urus

I love a big storm. I love the build-up to it: the meteorologists, flushed with their sudden importance, narrating the flow of the oranges and reds across the local maps; the supermarkets, crowded with people whose furrowed brows and pursed lips grant the soup cans and bottled water in their carts a promotion to provisions; the neighbors, diligently preparing their houses and yards for the high winds by rolling trash cans into the garage, securing the shutters as best they can. I love the storm itself: the house creaking as the wind moans against it; the rain rattling on the windows, reducing the yard to an impressionistic blur; the lightning burning the air white, the thunder shaking the walls. And I love the aftermath: the cautious step onto the front porch to survey the trees, their branches still saturated, bent; the walk around the house to pick up any items that were blown loose; the drive to town, to observe the storm's more general ruin.

It's the emotions that accompany each stage of the storm: I savor them. On one side, there's anticipation, a half-pleasurable dread at what's bearing down on us that makes the air hum, the way it does before any big event; on the other side, there's relief, which may also be tinged with dread at whatever damage awaits discovery, whatever crash must be sourced and reckoned with, but which is more an emptied-out feeling, as if, for a moment, we're as clear as the air the storm has just washed. In between dread and relief, though, is the most rarefied sensation, a terror at our utter powerlessness in the face of what's enveloped us, a panic at the trees whipping side to side deliriously, the power lines bouncing like jump ropes, the wineglasses ringing at each clap of thunder—which borders the ecstatic. When a storm is at its peak, and the world outside seems on the verge of tearing itself apart, a kind of radical openness comes briefly into view, as if, with each blanching of the view out the front window, something else, a more essential state of existence, draws that much closer to being unveiled.

At some point I began to suspect that my figurative response to the violence of a severe storm might be pointing me in the direction of actual truth. I was a teenager, fifteen, sixteen, that point of maximum narcissism when it seems entirely reasonable to think that you are privy to special insight, able to intuit secret knowledge. However, unlike so many of the other notions that occupied my brain at that time, which steadily decamped as my teens drained into my twenties, this one dug in more firmly. It was buttressed by bits and pieces of magazine articles read in waiting rooms, by fragments of documentaries stumbled upon while late-night channel-surfing. The details were fairly incoherent, but the gist of the theory I assembled was, if there are other dimensions, parallel universes, alternate planes of existence—call them what you will—then mightn't the tremendous release of energy in a serious storm unsettle, destabilize things sufficiently for that other place to be glimpsed, even entered? Anyone with a modicum of scientific knowledge, let alone actual expertise, on whom I tried out this line of reasoning treated it with a species of amused tolerance, much the way they probably would have a declaration of belief in alien visitation. This lack of support did nothing to unseat my conviction; in fact, it was during my twenties that I first ventured out into the midst of a storm, to see what I could see.

Of course, this was nothing, which I blamed on the fact that I sat in my car the entire time, listening to the rain bang on the roof. It did not stop me from repeating the experiment with subsequent storms. Soon I was starting the car, switching on the headlights, flipping on the wipers, and pulling out of the driveway in search of revelation.

For the next sixteen years it eluded me. About the closest I came was during a storm that came over while I was driving back from a trip up into the Catskills with my then-fiancée. All afternoon, tall heaps of cloud had loomed over the mountains, dimming the sky, then moving east. When the air thickened, however, humidity pressing on us like a great, damp hand, a storm seemed in the offing, and we agreed it would be best if we beat it back to our apartment. Just the other side of Woodstock, a handful of fat drops of rain burst on the windshield, and then the world outside was swept away by a wall of water. Afraid to brake into a hydroplane, I downshifted as quickly as I could, stabbing the button for the hazards. Engine whining, the car slowed to a crawl, but even on fast, the wipers did little more than push the water screening the windshield back and forth. Lightning flashed, turning the rain into white neon, and the thunder that followed one-Mississippi two-Mississippi shook the car. I was already steering for the shoulder when the lightning repeated, the thunder answering one-Mississippi faster. Prin was telling me to pull over, the command a litany: "Pull over pull over pull over pull over pull over."

"I'm trying," I said, as lightning and thunder split the air together. Although I couldn't help my flinch, I wasn't worried as much about being electrocuted as I was about someone racing up behind and slamming into us. I knew the road wasn't that wide, the shoulder not that far away, but hours seemed to pass as the car eased to the right, lightning flaring like the flash of an overeager photographer, thunder overlapping, crashing into itself and forming an avalanche of sound that rumbled and roared over us. When I judged we had crossed onto the shoulder, I put the clutch in, shifted into neutral, and opened my door. I hadn't unbuckled my seatbelt, so I couldn't lean that far out of the car, and Prin didn't have to reach that far to grab my arm and haul me back inside. "Are you insane?" she screamed. "Close the door!"

I did.

"What were you thinking?" she continued, her eyes wide with terror. "There's a goddamn hurricane out there!"

"I was checking to make sure we were on the shoulder," I said, which was true: I was looking for the white strip that delineated the edge of the road. But once I'd pushed the door open and the immensity of the storm had rushed over me, I was swept by a feeling of such exaltation that the hand Prin had caught was stealing toward the release for my seatbelt. At her expression of utter fright, however, my exhilaration curdled to embarrassment. I took her hands and said, "It's okay."

"Asshole." She tugged her hands from mine.

"Yes, but I'm your asshole."

That brought a smile to her face, which disappeared as lightning stabbed the trees to our right, thunder cracking so loud it deafened us. Prin pressed herself into her seat as if it could conceal her, her hand groping for mine. Sheets of rain layered the windows; I switched the wipers off. "It can't last much longer," I said, speaking too loudly because of the ringing in my ears. "These summer storms blow themselves out pretty quickly."

Prin didn't answer. I stared out the windshield, trying to distinguish the road through the water. For a moment the rain lessened, and the world in front of us swam into view. Maybe fifty yards ahead, the road rose in a slight incline, more an extended bump than a hill. On the other side of that rise, something was crossing the road from left to right. It was an animal, easily as big as an elephant. I briefly thought it was an elephant, had visions of an accident involving a convoy of circus animals. But the silhouette was wrong: the back was longer, the dip to the hips less pronounced, the head shorter, blunter, crowned by a pair of heavy horns as wide as my car was long. With each step it took, the animal's head swung from one side to the other with a slowness that was almost casual, as if it were out for a stroll in a light mist, not a raging storm. My hand was back on the door handle, and then the rain picked up again, hiding the enormous profile behind a curtain of water. I opened my mouth; to say what, I didn't know. I was waiting for the rain to ebb once more, allow another glance at whatever that had been. When it did not, I turned to Prin and said, "Did you see that?"

"What?" she said. Her brow was level, her mouth straight, her cheeks pale. She was angry, I realized; she had witnessed what I had, and the experience had made her furious.

"I—"

"Do you think you can drive out of here?"

I wanted to ask if she was serious, remind her that this was a car, not a submarine, but what I said was, "Yeah."

Wipers whipping back and forth, defogger blowing, hazards blinking, I put the car into gear and turned toward the road. I was certain that I was going to drive into whatever had been crossing it. After five minutes passed with no collision, though, my hands began to relax their hold on the steering wheel, and once the dashboard clock had counted another five minutes I knew that, even crawling forward as we were, we had passed beyond the place the great animal had been. I felt, not relieved so much as *full*, as if what I had seen were inside me, straining against the walls of my chest. I couldn't seem to draw enough breath. The sensation persisted all the long drive back to our apartment in Wiltwyck, where Prin led me directly to the bedroom, tugged down her shorts and mine, and pulled me onto the bed. We made quick, vigorous love, and once we were done, did so a second, and a third time.

When, aching, sore, we finally pulled apart from each other, we stood from the bed and stumbled into the kitchen and out the back door, onto the apartment's nominal back deck. Night had descended, bringing with it a fresh round of storms. Naked, we stood in the darkness, letting the rain pound down onto us. The pressure in my chest had eased, though it was not gone. It was more as if whatever was inside me had folded its legs and settled into sleep.

If I say that the babies—twins—who resulted from that afternoon occupied my attention for the next dozen years, there's enough truth to the words for them not to feel like too much of an evasion. What they are is incomplete. After all, there were a good four weeks between Prin's and my lovemaking and the baby-blue "+" appearing in the window of the home pregnancy test, during which time three more storms thundered through the area. I could have ventured out into any of them, could have tried to return to the spot outside Woodstock where my long-term intuition had seemed to flower into reality. For that matter, once Prin's pregnancy was confirmed, our hasty marriage accomplished, there were a handful of instances before the twins arrived when I could have resumed my investigation, as there were scattered throughout the years that followed. The most I did, however, was a cursory search of the Web, which revealed that the place where Prin and I had seen whatever we'd seen was proximate to Dutchman's Creek, which had a vaguely sinister reputation; why, exactly, I couldn't discover. On a couple of occasions, I broached the topic of that day with Prin, but she met my question of what she thought we'd seen crossing the road with one of her own: "What? What is it you think we saw?" Strictly speaking, it wasn't a denial of our experience, but it was as if shutters dropped over her eyes, sealing off what might have been happening behind them. It stymied me into silence, which appeared to be the desired effect, since Prin did not continue the conversation.

It was as if the part of me that responded to storms so profoundly had become stuck, the memory of that huge form a gouge in the vinyl, stuttering my emotions. I would sit on the living-room couch, Nina

cradled in my right arm, Eddie in my left, as the rain washed the picture window, and the curiously hollow ring of water striking glass
would absorb my attention, leaving it too saturated for any further response to the tumult outside. I would half lie on Eddie's bed, my head
and shoulders propped against his headboard, his face pressed into my
chest, his arms wrapped around me with all his five-year-old's strength,
as the air lit white and cracked, and I would stroke his hair, rub his
back through his Spider-Man pajamas, telling him as I did so that it
was just the weather, keeping my voice calm, level, the steady rise and
fall of my words, the slow circles my hand traced on his cotton top,
smoothing away any emotions of my own that might have been threatening to bunch up. I would sit on the living-room couch beside Nina
as the CBS affiliate out of Albany interrupted our sitcom to discuss the
severe weather rampaging across the area, and after leaving my seat to
point out to her where Ulster County was on the regional map, I
would explain why I didn't think we had to worry about a tornado
striking us; although there was one that knocked down the wall of a
school south of us, in Newburgh, some years ago—which led to us
abandoning the TV to search online for accounts of that old catastrophe, channeling any impulses that had been stirred by the wind's shriek
into research. The agitation, the exhilaration I had felt wasn't gone—it
wasn't that far away at all. It was . . . contained, dormant.

What raised it was my children; specifically, their decision to venture out into the woods behind our house on the brink of a storm. I
saw the heavy clouds piling overhead; I had read the weather report,
which put the entire region under a severe thunderstorm watch; I
could already hear the distant thunder, like big trucks bumping over a
road. Nonetheless, when Eddie said that he and Nina were going outside to try his new two-way radios, I didn't object. "Don't go too far,"
I called after him, "it's supposed to rain," but my only answer was the
screen door to the porch slapping its frame.

The thunder arrived first, a series of deep growls that rolled over
the low hill behind the house. For long moments the air was crowded
with sound, and then it was full of rain, the lightning that flickered almost an afterthought. I sat on the living-room couch, the book I had
been reading lowered, and listened for the clump of my children's
sneakers on the porch steps, their inevitable giggles at having run

home through the downpour. Lightning flashed; the thunder's growl rose to a roar. I left my book open on the couch and hurried to the back door.

Rain hammered the porch. I opened the screen door, and the wind caught it and flung it wide. Leaning out into the storm, I cupped my hands around my mouth and called Nina and Eddie's names. There was no answer. I could picture the two of them crouched beside a tree, grinning like maniacs as they listened to me shouting, an image sufficiently annoying for me to consider leaving them to their sodden fate—an impulse that vanished a moment later, when a bolt of lightning speared the top of the back hill. Thunder boomed, shuddering the house; the rain redoubled. Before I fully knew what I was doing, I was down the porch stairs and running across the yard toward the woods, my bare feet kicking up sprays of cold water. By the time I reached the tree line I was soaked, my hair and clothes plastered to me, my eyes full of rain. Bellowing my children's names, I plunged amongst the trees. Lightning whited the air; thunder shook the tree trunks. Every warning about what to do in a thunderstorm, especially the keeping-away-from-trees part, ran through my head. "Nina!" I shouted. "Eddie!" I dragged my forearm across my eyes, trying to wipe away water with water. Dread coiled deep in my gut, while higher in my chest a sensation of being absolutely overwhelmed threatened to force its way out of me in one long scream.

Strange as it sounds, only after Nina and Eddie had caught my arms and were guiding me toward the house did I realize that the tree I had been standing near had been struck by lightning. When the storm had burst, the twins had sought shelter in the garage, where they'd remained until they'd heard me calling for them. They'd emerged in time to watch me rush into the woods. After a brief deliberation, they'd set off after me. Fifty feet into the trees they stopped, unable to tell which direction I'd gone. Nina was for splitting up and going left and right; Eddie favored staying together and moving forward. Their debate meant that they saw the lightning plunge into the trees somewhere in front of them out of the corners of their eyes. The attendant burst of thunder doubled them over, their hands clapped to their heads. Ears stunned, they stumbled to the spot where a moderately sized tree had been detonated by the lightning bolt. Chunks of wood, some steaming, a few on fire, fanned out from the trunk's jagged remains. In the midst of the wreckage the twins found me, standing with my eyes wide. Later, Eddie would tell me that he was afraid to touch me, because he was afraid that I might be electrified. No such worry disturbed his sister, who strode up to me, took my right arm, and turned me toward the house.

The worst effects of my experience—the almost-total blanching of my vision, the loss of my hearing—ebbed more quickly than I would have predicted. By the time Prin had returned from shopping and was driving me to the hospital, my vision had largely cleared, though colors still appeared washed-out, and while my hearing was little more than a high-pitched ringing, I was aware of my family's voices as disturbances in that noise. The E.R. doctor pronounced a cautious diagnosis that I was substantially unharmed, which my regular M.D. would second when I saw her the following day, and which she would amend to mild hearing loss when I checked in with her two weeks after that. I wasn't aware of any diminishment in my hearing as much as I was in my vision, specifically my color vision, which remained less vibrant than it had been, as if I were viewing colors through a film. My ongoing complaints led to an appointment with my optometrist, who found nothing obviously wrong with my eyes and referred me to an ophthalmologist, a retinal specialist who spent a long time shining painfully bright lights into my dilated pupils, only to arrive at the same verdict. The specialist offered to send me on to a sub-specialist he knew up in Albany, but I demurred. By that time, I was starting to understand what had happened to me.

Two days before my appointment with the ophthalmologist, I dreamed I was back in the woods, searching for the twins in the midst of the storm. I stumbled into the small clearing where the twins had found me. Evergreens, interrupted by the occasional birch, stationed its border. I screamed my children's names, and as I did so, a finger of lightning touched one of the trees across the clearing. For a dream-moment the lightning hung in place, a blazing seam in the air, a brilliant snarl of glass through which I glimpsed a shape. It was a tree—but such a tree as I'd never seen. Leaves as green as an emerald, as one of those tropical snakes you see in nature documentaries, gathered into a globe atop a slender trunk whose bark shone like polished bronze. Simultaneously, this was a child's approximation of a tree, and the original tree, the Platonic ideal from which all others emanated. When the lightning was done plunging into the evergreen, the window it had burned into the air closed, a feeling of loss—of grief—as profound as what I'd felt at the death of my father made me suck in my breath as if I'd been kicked. Gasping, I struggled up to consciousness, to Prin asleep in the bed beside me.

For the next week, the image of that tree burned in my mind with such intensity that, had you placed a sample of my neurons under the microscope, you would have seen it lighting the center of each nucleus. Every time I closed my eyes I saw those leaves thick with green, that corrugated bark. I didn't know if what I'd dreamed was an actual memory, retrieved from the trauma surrounding it, or a symbol, a way for my imagination to represent another, indescribable experience to me. I didn't care, because as the vision of that tree glowed in my brain it illuminated the emotion that had accompanied the lightning strike, a terror that was exultation. It was the feeling that had stirred in me a dozen years before, more, while the wipers metronomed across the windshield, the rain jumped on the road ahead. It was the sensation of standing beside a fundamental openness, a Grand Canyon from whose space might emerge anything: an enormous beast, ambling over the blacktop, a tree glimpsed through a flash of lightning. As the huge shape that Prin and I had seen those years ago had seemed to take up residence inside me, tangling itself in this emotion and thus inhibiting it, so the sight of the tree roused the animal, set its nostrils flaring, its tail switching. Pulling my emotion along with it, the thing began to pace the confines of my chest, lowering its blunt head to test the thickness of the wall here, the padlock on the gate there.

Not at once, but over the course of weeks, months, the next couple of years, my actions, my behavior, shifted, became more impulsive, erratic. I noticed it first at work, where I was less inclined to suffer the idiocy of either my co-workers or our customers. At home, the twins entering their teens provided both a prompt and an excuse for me to adopt a more authoritarian style of parenting. In my marriage, I became more vocal about my unhappiness with the long hours Prin put in at her job. And when a storm blew in, I was much more likely to grab the keys to the truck and announce to whoever was listening that I was going out. If one of the kids, or, more likely, if my wife asked why, I was ready with an excuse about us needing milk; although, on a couple of occasions, I declared that I felt like taking a ride, and since that provoked no further questions, it became my default response.

In nothing I did did I go too far, say words that could not be forgotten, commit acts that could not be forgiven. But in various ways, in all facets of my life, as time passed I drew ever closer to a border to cross over which would bring disaster. At work, my responses to my district manager's suggestions for improving the store verged on outright mockery, while I had given a few dissatisfied customers such a run-around that one of them had been in tears. Within the house I became adept, not at criticizing the twins, but in remaining silent to the little they offered me, treating their adolescently awkward gestures at communication with a bemused condescension. Within my marriage I had stopped complaining to Prin; instead, through the miracle of social media I had located the woman I had been involved with before Prin, and had started emailing, then calling her, late at night, when everyone else was asleep. Whenever lightning strobed the yard, thunder ground against the house, I reached for the keys. Sometimes I would pull the truck into a lay-by and step out into the storm, let the rain needle me, the lightning arc overhead, the thunder shake me. No outsized animals emerged onto the road beside me, no lightning bolts opened views of other places, but I didn't care. Fear so pure it was joy made my blood sing in my ears, made my skin electric, made the animal confined in my chest toss its head and kick its hoofs.

When Prin realized the change in me—which is to say, when she sat down to the computer and saw one of the emails from my ex open on the screen—she attributed it to that cliché of our parents' generation, the midlife crisis. This was during the first conversation we had over the phone, which had to wait a week after I came downstairs to the sight of her suitcase standing at the front door and the sting of her hand slapping my face. Had the twins not already left for their year abroad in Paris, no doubt they, too, would have been packed and waiting in the car. My cheek hot from her blow, all I could do was ask her what was wrong, what had happened. Of course, the instant my eyes fell on that black case, its rolling-handle extended, the explanation flashed through my brain: *She found out.* As she was stamping out the door, Prin's "Why don't you ask *Joyce*?" confirmed that she in fact had found out. A check of the computer showed my email account open, the latest semi-flirtatious message from my ex on the screen. It had been forwarded, as had all the others from her, but I deleted them anyway, then logged out of my email, which I was certain I'd done the previous night—though it appeared I'd been mistaken.

That, or I'd been trying to force the moment to its crisis. I wasn't sure. The last few years, I'd largely abandoned the nuances of introspection in favor of the simplicity of action. Yet there had been something almost paradoxically private about my acts; rarely had I considered them in relation to anyone except myself. Mostly, I had luxuriated in the excess of emotion that had given rise to them and to which they, in turn, contributed. Now, left alone, my thoughts turned outward, to Prin, to the marriage that had canted suddenly to one side, its hull torn by the iceberg it had scraped against—the half-submerged danger I had been steering it toward. Back from the job at which I was subdued, distracted, I wandered the empty house, examining my behavior of the last several months—years—with the eye of an investigator attempting to reconstruct the precise sequence of events that had led to the jagged ice piercing the steel plates, the ocean's cold water pouring through the gap. I could identify a lengthy report's worth of instances, large and small, when Prin and I had been out of sync with each other, but I could not assemble those moments into a coherent and adequate narrative, one that explained not just my ongoing, secret communication with my ex, but my withdrawal from my children, my belligerence at work. There was only the great animal baying inside me, a torrent of emotion.

For the first time since I'd run out after the twins, however, that terrible awe was challenged by another feeling, by a fear more prosaic in its origins, but no less potent in its effects. Prin, Nina and Eddie, even my job: all had come to seem incidental to my life, barely connected to its actual substance, to the fabulous tree burning in my memory. As if a lens had dropped in front of my eyes, I saw my wife, my children, my work, not as ornaments, but as the girders and beams giving my days what shape and order they had. To be the inhabitant of such a structure seemed the remarkable thing, the momentary tree and huge silhouette typical of a world that tended to formlessness and chaos. With my actions I had steadily undermined the base of that construction, to the point that it was swaying perilously. How near to collapse my life was, I couldn't estimate with much accuracy, but it was certainly close enough for me to be overtaken by crushing sadness at the prospect of its fall. I was afraid, not of the sublime unknown, but for the domestic familiar, and the emotion transfixed me like a pin through an insect.

So absorbed was I by what appeared the imminent and inevitable end of my life as I had known it, that I barely registered the approach of Hurricane Eileen. Prior to Prin's discovery of my correspondence with my ex, I had watched the reports of the storm sweeping the northwest edge of the Caribbean, on path to make landfall somewhere between mid-Florida and northern Georgia, its course after that likely a coastal one, though the specifics would have to wait until the storm drew nearer. I heard the cashiers talking about the hurricane in the break room, directed customers to the bottled water, the propane tanks, the portable generators, agreed with my assistant manager's suggestion that we try to scare up some more portable jennies from the warehouse, but none of it registered as it would have only days before. I was absorbed by the fact that four days had passed since Prin's departure, and there was still no reply from her to any of the emails I'd sent, one a day. I wasn't sure if she'd headed to her parents, who were close but would require some measure of explanation, or to one of her friends, or to a motel. There'd been no word from the twins either, which was probably due to late-adolescent obliviousness, but which I was afraid signified that Prin had contacted them already.

Not until the end of my long conversation with Prin a week after she'd left, when she asked me if I were prepared for Eileen, did it dawn on me that this storm might be a cause for concern. A search online turned up articles about the mandatory evacuations of low-lying areas of New York City, the extra utility workers placed on standby, the state of emergency that had been declared for the area. Another click of the mouse brought me a satellite photo of the hurricane itself, a vast comma of thick, gray clouds whose margins reached from Virginia to Massachusetts. Rendered in the National Weather Service's color-coded pixels, Eileen was a wall of deep green sweeping around bands of yellow and orange, all arcing in front of the well-defined blank of the eye. Downgraded from a Category 2 to a Category 1 hurricane, the storm was still considered a serious threat to the City. Already, the first wave of showers was washing into the region, the winds were rising, the TV stations throughout the region had deployed whatever reporters had drawn the short straws to the locations that had been deemed suitably photogenic—the majority of which appeared to be located on or near the beach. Outside my window, the weather was quiet. I considered a run to Walmart to pick up a few supplies, only to reject the idea as so much media-inspired hysteria. Likely, the storm would either skirt the City or miss it entirely, leaving me with a portable propane stove I could have bought for half the price using my employee discount at work. Anyway, I was preoccupied with my talk with Prin, the upshot of which was that, while far from happy, she accepted my assurance that my email exchanges with my ex had not led to any other kinds of exchanges, and was willing to consider continuing our marriage. At least for the moment, our life together was not going to come crashing down, though how much repair would be required remained to be seen.

When I woke late the next morning, it was to wind moaning over the house, rain tapping on the bedroom windows. My prediction had been correct: the hurricane had missed the City. Instead, Eileen had swung inland, rolling over northern New Jersey and eastern Pennsylvania, losing strength as it went, until, by the time it reached the Hudson Valley, it had been demoted to a tropical storm. The difference, however, was academic, since even as a tropical storm Eileen stirred the air into gusts that pushed against the house in long shrieks, drove the rain horizontally. Lightning stammered, an engine trying to catch, while thunder rumbled like the edges of continents scraping against one another. The cable was out, which was no surprise, but the power was on, which I wouldn't have expected. I found the transistor radio Prin had bought me last Christmas, slid out the antenna, and turned it on. Everything was already closed or closing. Whoever was responsible for such things had prohibited all non-essential travel. The storm had stalled overhead. Widespread power outages had been reported and more were anticipated; high wind advisories, flash-flood warnings, and tornado watches had been issued. Our house sat on a low ridge, paralleled by other ridges, so I wasn't worried about much except maybe one of the trees in the front yard falling into it—though none stood tall enough to threaten more than a prolonged inconvenience. Prin's parents' house, however—to which she had retreated—was separated from the Hudson by a modest lawn that terminated in a short slope to a narrow and rocky beach. On top of everything else, Eileen was supposed to draw the Hudson up beyond flood stage. I wasn't sure what the implications of this were for my in-laws' place, but it was a matter for concern. Our telephone was tied to our cable, though, as was our Internet access, and since Prin had taken the emergency cellphone with her, there was no way for me to contact her. I toyed with the idea of running out to the truck and navigating the deluge to Prin's parents', but couldn't decide how much peril my wife was actually in. With the slope of the lawn, her mom and dad's house was up maybe seven or eight feet from the river. Was that high enough? Not to mention, how would it look when I was pulled over for being on the road in the storm, as I probably would be?

There was nothing to do except to remain where I was and wait out the storm. On the kitchen table, there were stacks of paperwork I had been ignoring for a couple of weeks before Prin had left: sales figures, projections, and goals; a rundown of the coming season's new products, with suggestions on how best to promote them; three in-house applications for the assistant manager position that had recently opened, and another thirty-five applications for the single part-time job we'd advertised. It was the kind of work I daily found it more difficult to undertake, but which, given my need to fill the next several hours with some type of activity, was not without its use. I set up the coffeemaker, switched it on, and dug a set of candles and a box of matches out of the junk drawer while the kitchen filled with the sharp odor of hot coffee. Then I settled down at the table and set to work.

Of course I wanted to be outside, letting the storm envelop me. Before I had processed the sounds to which I'd awakened, the beast in my chest had known them for what they were and been pawing the ground, pressing its thick shoulder against the wall surrounding it. Over the years the tail ends of a few hurricanes had struck the area glancing blows on their way out to sea, but as far as I could remember, Eileen was the first storm of this magnitude to line us up in its sights like this. The house shifted and shuddered with the thunder; the bushes in the front yard cringed at the rain beating down on them; the woods behind the house creaked and cracked as the wind pushed them back and forth. The shrill, electric trill of the Emergency Broadcast System spilled from the transistor radio, and a woman's voice, sounding oddly muffled, announced that a tornado had been spotted on the other side of Wiltwyck, maybe ten miles away. As the voice went on warning about the dangers of a tornado and advising the best spots in a house for sheltering from one, the tips of my fingers, my toes, tingled, my cheeks flushed, and what felt like a space high in my skull opened. When I stood to take a break, I crossed to the kitchen windows and pressed one hand to each. Outside, Eileen was hurling itself against everything, was scouring the very air, wearing it thinner, bringing that other place, the home of the huge silhouette, the astonishing tree, nearer. It was close; I was aware of it at the edge of the space in my head, like something you know you have forgotten, a gap whose outlines you can almost picture. If I threw open the porch door and dashed out into the rain, into the woods, might I not find it? Might I not pass into it? I went so far as to unlock the back door and walk out onto the porch. A gust of wind made me stagger, while the rain drilled my arms, my neck, my head. Lightning filled the air in brilliant sheets; thunder shivered the porch under my feet. Terror as pure and pitiless as a bird of prey, as an eagle plucking a fish out of the water, gripped me. Here I was, on the verge. Already my hair was soaked, my shirt and jeans drenched. How easy it would be to go the rest of the way into the storm, to let my fear carry me into it.

I couldn't say what returned me inside. One moment I was leaning on the porch railing, squinting through the rain at the woods; the next, I had shut and locked the back door and was making my soggy way to the bathroom, where I pulled off my wet clothes and stepped into a hot shower. The terror that had seized me had not relaxed its hold; I could still sense the other place immanent in the air. The thing in my chest bellowed, ramming its head against its prison. But I stood letting the hot water chase the rain's chill from my skin, and when the water began to lose its heat I turned it off, toweled dry, and went in search of fresh clothes. Once I'd dug another pair of jeans and long-sleeved T-shirt out of my dresser, I made myself an early lunch and ate it while I resumed my paperwork. At any time I could have left the house for the storm. I didn't. It was as if—the very extremity of the emotion rag-

ing through me made it feel suddenly unreal. In comparison, the kitch-
en table at which I was seated, its top scuffed and scored from years of
the twins' employing it as a workbench for school projects, felt solid,
as much as the countertop behind me, which bore the scars of all the
fruit, the vegetables, the loaves of bread I'd sliced through without using the cutting board. The refrigerator whose freezer tended to ice up,
so that it required defrosting at least twice a year; the electric oven that
cooked too hot and that we'd been threatening to replace with a gas
range for as long as we'd lived here; the coffeemaker whose red
CLEAN light blinked no matter how recently we'd cleaned it: none of
these things, or any of the others filling the house, was as vivid as the
tree I'd glimpsed through the lightning—but they seemed present in a
manner I hadn't recognized before, and that was somehow sufficient
to keep me working at the table.

By early afternoon, Eileen was starting to ebb. By mid-afternoon
the rain had diminished to a light shower. By late afternoon the storm
had slid to the north and east, Vermont and a corner of Massachusetts.
I was congratulating myself for not having lost power when the lights
went out. Exasperating, yes, but in a way that I could tell would become funny when I related the event to friends—to Prin. Prin—
without warning, I wanted nothing else than to see my wife, to gather
her into my arms, to take her someplace, a hotel, a bed-and-breakfast,
a motel on the edge of a highway, where we could be alone. I could
not think of anything that was more important than this. I checked to
be certain I hadn't left anything on that I shouldn't have—I hadn't, but
she would ask, and I wanted to be able to say I'd looked—grabbed the
keys to the truck, and locked the door behind me.

From the radio, I knew that 213, the route I usually took to my in-
laws, was flooded. If I hadn't heard it on the news, I would have expected it: there was a stream that flowed right under the road about a
mile toward Wiltwyck, and I imagined it would have submerged, if not
carried away, the road there. What the news hadn't reported, and I
hadn't anticipated, was that the road would be closed about a half-mile
in the other direction, toward Huguenot, where the picturesque waterfall that descended from the hillside to the left had become a roaring
Niagara. It had undermined the road it typically trickled below to the
extent that the road's collapse was judged imminent, and the police

had blocked it off already with sawhorses and barrels. I might have risked walking or running, across it, but the truck was far too heavy for any such adventuring. It appeared the only way to my in-laws would be to navigate the back roads that wound through the hills and mountains between here and the Hudson. While this wasn't something I did on a daily basis, I was reasonably sure I could manage it. When the twins had been infants, the one guaranteed way to put them to sleep at the same time had been to strap them into their car seats and take them for a ride. As a result, I'd traveled the majority of roads between Huguenot and Wiltwyck, so, although Prin had the GPS in her car, I wasn't too concerned about being able to find my way. I turned the truck around and drove back to where one of the side roads intersected it at the bottom of a steep rise. I powered up the slope and set off to join my wife.

As the crow flies, it was three and half, four miles from our front door to Prin's parents. Probably that distance doubled if you had to traverse it by car. And if the roads that vehicle was following had just been swept by a tropical storm, that seven or eight miles doubled, maybe tripled. The roads in here were narrow, with no shoulder, and bordered by more streams, swamps, and ponds than I'd realized, all of which had swollen and spilled their confines with the season's worth of rain that the last fourteen hours had brought. Water lapped the edges of the road in some places; in others, it slid across in a glassy sheet; in still others, it covered the road in a new lake. After six, I lost count of the number of times I shifted into reverse for another three-point turn. One road was blocked by a massive tree that had fallen across it; another was fenced by power lines, one of whose poles had tilted toward the road; a third had mostly disappeared under the hillside that had dissolved onto it. To either side, I saw houses damaged. Here was a raised ranch whose living-room window had been stove in by the tree that had toppled through it. Here was a split-level built on a hill, its foundation laid bare by the rain. Here was a cape, an island in the center of a broad lake whose surface was ruffled by the wind.

When I drove across the black water, I thought I knew where I was. After almost reaching 9W, the major north-south route along the Hudson's western shore—which was not, as far as I could tell from the radio's updates, closed—a new stream galloping over the road had forced me to turn around. Feeling as if I were confined in a gigantic maze, I backtracked almost to my starting point for yet another try at the puzzle. It was not yet dark, but the sky was losing its light. On the right, a road t-junctioned the one I was driving. I'd noticed it on the way out, but had ignored it because I'd thought it joined another side road that emptied onto 213 this side of the flooding. Approaching it from this direction, however, I thought I remembered that this road in fact looped in the other direction, intersecting another side road that would bring me to 9W. It was worth a try, so I turned onto it.

Right away I saw the water flowing across the road ahead, maybe a hundred yards distant. I knew enough to be aware of the danger of fording a flooded road, especially when the water covering it was moving; if I hadn't, there were warnings against doing so every ten minutes on the radio. Had I taken this road at the beginning of my journey, I would have reversed immediately. This far into it, however, with my options for reaching my wife dwindling almost to zero, I let the truck roll forward. The water didn't look that deep. Its blackness was not a trick of the light, nor was the water full of dirt. It was more as if it had been dyed black. The color didn't concern me: I assumed it must be due to some kind of microorganism that had been fomented by the rain. I eased the truck into it, unable to recall whether the road dipped here or not. The water eddied around the tires, rising up them as I continued. What was the minimum depth at which moving water could sweep your vehicle off the road? Was it different for a truck? I was approximately halfway across the stream, and the water seemed to have halted its climb at the bottom of my tires' hubcaps. I glanced to my left, where the water was spreading out in a broad pool over the small meadow there. If I were to be carried off the road, I was reasonably sure I'd be able to four-wheel my way out of it, and if not, I could abandon the truck and wade for it. It would be messy, and slow, and ultimately costly, and it would mean having to return to the house, but it wasn't anything I couldn't handle.

And then I was on the other side of the water, pressing the gas pedal to make up for lost time. For the next mile or so the road ran straight, its edges lipped by more black water pooling in the fields and forest alongside it. Where the remnant of a stone wall crossed the woods on either side, the road swung sharply to the right before almost doubling back to the left. I didn't remember this, but after all, it would have been fifteen, sixteen years since I'd last driven here, and anyway, that wasn't important. Standing amongst the trees on my right was the tree I'd glimpsed behind my house four years before.

Everything went far away, and it was as if I were seeing the tree at the end of long, dark tunnel. My head swam. Without thinking I stepped on the brake, so that only the front right wheel left the road. The truck slowed to a crawl. Black spots dancing in front of my eyes; I brought the truck to a complete stop, shifted into park, and opened my door. The engine running, I stepped out of the truck. The ground here was slightly raised. I started to walk toward the tree. There was no water for me to trek through, though I wouldn't have cared—I doubt I would have noticed. All my attention was focused on the tree, which I was certain was going to vanish any second now.

It did not. My fingers brushed its bark, which was rough, fibrous, like that of the cedar in my front yard. It was warm, the way wood is at the end of a long day in the hot sun. Its surface shone with a dull, yellowed light, as if it were reflecting a brightness invisible to me. The faint odor of citrus, of oranges on the turn, hung around it. Overhead, leaves green as jade gathered in a heavy crown. I reached up my hand to one of them, only to snatch it back with a hiss. The edges of the leaves were serrated, and those teeth as sharp as fishhooks, a fact to which the beads of blood welling from my fingertips testified. Wincing, I shook my hand and saw the other trees.

There were five of them, mixed in with the oaks and maples. Each was slightly different from its fellows, the trunk thicker here, the leaves higher there, but the bronze bark, the sea-green leaves, marked them as the same species. Almost before I was aware of it, I was half running toward them, my uninjured hand held out to them. Their bark was full of the same heat as the first one I'd touched; I didn't need to touch their leaves to notice their sharpness. From tree to tree, I moved steadily deeper into the woods, farther away from the truck, whose engine sounded more distant than the hundred or so yards I'd walked. Beyond the last tree, there was a small clearing of reddish ground, across which a grove of the trees stood. Somewhere deep within that grove, something was visible through the shining trunks. I was not afraid: at the sight of that first tree, my emotions had leapt over fear to wonder. As I took in each successive revelation, so did that wonder push toward joy. By the time I crossed the clearing, I was grinning.

Amongst the trees, the smell of citrus hung heavier. The air was warm, the post-storm chill chased from it by the heat radiating from the trees. The low rumble of the truck's engine had been occluded by another sound, a rushing like wind through the leaves, which was punctuated by an irregular boom. It seemed to be coming from the other side of the white objects in whose direction I was heading. There were several of them, standing straight and pale; they appeared to be another kind of tree, a grove within the grove. Their trunks were smooth, creamy; as with the trees surrounding them, these swept up to crowns I wasn't close enough to distinguish, but which appeared joined to one another. Only when I arrived at the edge of the space in which these white trees had been planted did I realize that they were not, in fact, trees, but columns. Perhaps a dozen, fifteen of them had been set in a wide ring, which had been roofed by the small dome they supported—which had partially collapsed on my side. The columns, the roof, seemed to be marble or a stone like it. The ground around the temple—that was immediately how I thought of it—was bare, only a couple of stray leaves marking it. So far as I could see, there was no writing, no marking, on the structure's exterior.

Tears streamed down my cheeks. The scent of oranges, the sound of rushing, surrounded me. My nerves hummed. Anything might happen here. Conscious of its damaged roof, I approached the temple cautiously. A heap of broken stone lay on the floor under the gap. Passing between a pair of columns, I saw that the rubble partially obscured the mosaic that took up the floor. Executed in the flat style of a Byzantine icon, the image showed the head and shoulders of a woman whose brown ringlets spread down over the top of her peach robe. Most of her face was hidden by the fallen stone, which had also cracked and loosened dozens of the thumbnail-sized tiles, but one wide, brown eye was visible. I knelt beside it, placing my palm on the iris. The tiles were cool, the seams among them imperceptible. I picked up one of the roof fragments. Though the size of a quarter, it was far heavier. I weighed it in my hand, listening to the rushing noise, which sounded not so much louder as clearer here, enough that I could identify it as the surf, throwing itself up the beach and receding, the occasional boom a collapsing wave. Between the columns opposite me, I could see out to where the ground lifted in a gradual swell. From the other side of it the ocean sounded. I stood, fresh tears pouring from my eyes, and as I did so, saw a shape moving over the rise.

It was an animal, crossing from right to left. It was enormous, its front shoulder a rounded mountain that dipped to a long back, which rose again at the hips. It paused and swung its head in my direction, bringing a pair of widely set horns into relief. It raised its snout and, with the whuff of a bellows inflating, inhaled. It did so a second time, and I realized it was sniffing the air. It dropped its head and turned toward me. As it climbed the hill, I saw that it was a bull—but such a bull as might have stepped straight from an ancient myth. It wasn't only that it was far larger than any bull I had ever seen by a factor of two or three. Its skin shone the red-gold of the sun sliding toward the horizon; its horns were white as sea-foam. Its features were finely, even delicately formed, to the point that this animal could have served as the example of the species in all its varieties. Were it not for the great iron ring looped through its nostrils, I easily could have believed I was beholding a god who had elected to put on this form for his latest sojourn on earth. As it was, I was half tempted to drop to my knees at the sight of it standing atop the rise, its presence there like the shout of a full orchestra. It threw its head back and bellowed, a deep, rolling roar that made the leaves on the trees shudder. I took a step backwards. The bull lowered its head, snorted, and pawed the ground. There was no need to wait for its charge; pivoting on my right foot, I sprinted out of the temple the way I'd come.

From this direction the edge of the grove seemed to take much longer to reach. Already too close behind me, the bull was a wave of sound, rushing to overtake me. A glance over my shoulder showed it swerving from side to side as it sought gaps among the trees wide enough to allow its horns. Had its path to me been clear, the bull would have run me down in no time. As it was, I wasn't wild about my chances. My days of running high-school track were a quarter-century gone. If I could reach my truck, the odds would improve in my favor. But between the thunder of the bull's hooves on the ground and the pounding of the blood in my ears, I had yet to hear the rumble of the engine—and that was assuming it hadn't stalled. The bull roared, and adrenaline fired my legs, carrying me out of the grove into the forest proper. To my left, my right, the scattering of the shining trees that had drawn me deeper into the woods flashed past. The ground here was slicker, slippery with storm-soaked leaves, treacherous with fallen branches, a couple of toppled trees. I hurdled a trunk thick with moss, slid under another whose collapse had been arrested by one of its companions. The first tree I had seen was ahead. Not too far beyond it, my truck appeared to be running. With a pair of titanic cracks, the bull struck and shattered the trees I had dodged over and under. I cleared the tree line. The truck was forty yards away, thirty-five. The bull's hooves pounded the earth. The truck was thirty yards away, twenty-five. The bull snorted like a steam engine. The truck was twenty yards away, fifteen. I could hear the engine's roll. The ground drummed under my feet; the bull was nearly on me. The truck was ten yards away, five. I could see the dome light on because I hadn't closed my door completely. The bull was burning behind me.

I cleared the hood, threw myself to the left, hauled open the driver's side door, and flung myself into the cab. Before I had pulled the door shut, the bull struck the right side of the flatbed with a shuddering boom. The truck swung hard to the left, the door snapping open and jerking me half out of the cab. Only a little of its momentum lost, the bull continued past, its hooves sparking on the road as it charged into the marsh on the other side, spraying water and mud as it went. Though slowed by the change in terrain, the bull did not stop, but wheeled to the left, commencing an arc that would return it to me in no time. Grateful to be on dry ground, I closed the door, shifted into reverse, and stepped on the gas. For a heart-stopping moment, the wheels spun, then they caught and the truck lurched backwards, flinging me forward with such force I smacked my head on the steering wheel. I stomped the brake in time to avoid plunging into the marsh, shifted into drive, and dragged the wheel to the left. The tires shrieked as the truck lurched around in the direction I'd come. I straightened the wheel and pressed the gas to the floor. To my right, the bull had adjusted its course and was on path to intercept me. Never the greatest when it came to quick starts, the truck gathered speed. The bull was churning up gouts of water and weeds as it went, dulling its hide with mud. I held the gas all the way down. The bull stumbled—my heart jumped—and caught itself. Just beyond where the bull was on course to hit me, the road turned sharply to the right, almost doubling back on itself. If I took that curve too fast, the truck would flip, and I wouldn't have to worry about unearthly bulls. If I didn't keep the accelerator to the floor, though, the question of the curve would remain theoretical. The bull was practically galloping through the marsh. Even seated in the cab, I found it gigantic. The truck hurtled over the road. Fast enough—I was just about going fast enough. The bull's head, its great horns, loomed in the passenger's side window. An eye the size of a saucer regarded me with an emotion I couldn't identify.

For a second time, the bull hit the truck on the right side of the flatbed. There was a boom, the scream of tearing metal, the brass shout of the huge beast. The truck fishtailed left; braking, I overcompensated to the right and sent the rear end fishtailing that way. As the scene in the rearview mirror whipped back and forth, I glimpsed the bull plunging through the trees, shaking its head. It didn't appear to be turning as quickly as it had before, but I was too busy trying to bring my vehicle under control to do any more than note the difference. I succeeded in gaining command of the truck as the road bent into its acute angle, and while there was a second I felt the left-hand tires threatening to leave the asphalt, the truck remained upright. Fully expecting to witness the bull charging across the marsh after me, I looked to the right, to see it standing on the forest side of the road, watching me as I sped away. When I came to the black water still flowing across the road, I did not slow down.

Although I had no desire to return home, which seemed agonizingly close to where the bull had burst forth, I could not think of another route to Prin's parents, so home I drove. Once I'd parked the truck, I intended to sprint to the back of the house, where I'd use the basement door to let myself inside. I wasn't sure whether it would be better to shelter from the bull—which I was certain was making its way toward me—in the basement, or if I should choose the first floor, from which I could dash to the truck, if need be. However, when I stepped down from the cab, muscles tensing for the run to the house, something on the flatbed caught my eye. A quick survey showed the bull was not, as yet, near, so I hurried around the back of the truck. From just behind the passenger's door to the very end of the flatbed, the right side of my truck was crumpled and creased, the metal dented in half a dozen places, the liner cracked and pushed part of the way out. Between the rear wheel and the tailgate, a deep gouge ended in a jagged hole the width of my hand. Lodged inside that hole, jutting into the flatbed, was the object that had drawn my notice, a point of white horn a foot long, its tip undulled, its base rough from having been snapped off. Leaning over into the flatbed, I worked to free the horn. Except for a groove that had been cut into it by a metal shard, its surface was smooth, cool. It came loose without too much effort on my part and was surprisingly light in my hand. Holding the piece of horn, I felt the panic that had spurred me home relax its grip—but I walked to the house quickly.

Inside, the house was dim, the power not yet returned. I lit one of the candles I'd left on the kitchen table and used it to light my way upstairs to the second floor and the undersized room that served as my home office. There, I slid out the lower of my desk's drawers, in whose depths I stored those things I planned to find a more permanent home for later. I placed the fragment of horn in there, along with the oddly heavy piece of rock I'd picked up in the temple, and which at some point thereafter I'd dropped into the front pocket of my jeans. I closed the drawer, shut the office door behind me, and descended the stairs. I didn't enter that room again for weeks, didn't say anything about what was in my desk drawer or where it had come from to Prin or her parents, when they pulled into the driveway the next day, or to the twins, when they returned home for Christmas vacation. The damage to the truck I blamed on an accident I claimed to have suffered while trying to reach Prin's parents' during the height of the hurricane. I had driven, I said, into a flooded section of road, only to find the water deeper and stronger than I'd anticipated. The truck had been swept off the road into a stand of trees, and it was only through some miracle that I had been able to engage the four-wheel-drive and escape. My story was helped by the large bruise that purpled my forehead where I'd smacked it on the steering wheel, though my father-in-law was visibly unsatisfied with my explanation. The insurance company wasn't any happier about my claim, which they first denied, then, when I proposed legal action, refused to cover fully, citing the role of my reckless behavior in causing the damage. I took what I could get and the next year traded in the truck for a small station wagon.

After arriving with her parents, Prin remained with me, as, over the next couple of weeks, she decided to remain in our marriage. I ceased contact with my ex, deleting the account from which I'd written to her. About ten days after the storm, I drove the road along which I'd sighted the shining tree; it ran straight and short, intersecting another after a few hundred yards. The twins returned from their study abroad for their senior year of high school and plans to leave, again, for college. I did not leave my job; nor, when the next storm slid over us, did I do anything other than check that the windows were shut.

With each and every storm that followed, I have, when possible, done exactly the same thing: ensure that the windows are closed and mount the stairs to the second floor and my office. There I sit at my desk, which faces the window that looks over the backyard. I watch the rain bead the window, the wind toss the trees. I squint at the lightning's flare, listen to the thunder rattle the window. I try not to picture the face I saw on the temple floor, the single eye gazing up impassively. I try not to think about that other place, the grove in which I walked, the ocean whose waves I heard, lying on the other side of a veil as fine as a spider web, as wide as the world. I try not to indulge the emotion that roils through me, that has continued to answer the summons of every storm. At some point I will have retrieved the length of horn, the piece of stone, from the drawer and set them on the desk. My hands on either side of them, I gaze out the window and remind myself how much I love my family.

At Home in the House of the Devil

I

"Every man meets the Devil once before he dies." My father likes to say this. It's among his favorite expressions, a handy aphorism to be trotted out to meet all manner of circumstances. He says he heard it from his father, who hailed from Gourock, a town on Scotland's west coast. In turn, Grandpa is supposed to have taken it from the lips of his uncle, a minister in the Church of Scotland. According to Dad, Great-great-uncle Michael had claimed the saying was an old Scottish one, so for Dad—born and raised in Brooklyn before moving to California to pursue first his education and then his dream of being a screenwriter—to use it has been to assert his heritage, to insist on his own way of looking at things. I haven't researched the matter thoroughly, but the reading and online searching I have done, not to mention, a brief e-mail exchange with the minister holding my great-great-uncle's position, fails to support either my father, or, assuming he was telling the truth, my grandfather. Given the history of Scottish Protestantism, with its concern, if not obsession, with the Devil, a figure frightfully close, standing practically at your elbow, wearing nice clothes that somehow still look shabby, tainting the air with the smell of rotten eggs, waiting for the moment his open hand can clutch your arm and drag you down to damnation—well, it's not hard to believe that Dad's expression could have had its origin in the kirks. At the very least—assuming he was telling the truth and the saying wasn't something he had picked up in his vast, if irregular, reading and tried to pass off as more pedigreed than it was—I could picture Great-great-uncle Michael, whose broad face gazed out of a black and white portrait Dad gave pride of place in the living room, dressed in his dark ministerial robes, thundering the words from his pulpit.

Even though I knew the saying was Scottish, or supposed to be, for a long time it had seemed to me more American: to be specific, more like the kind of thing you would have heard in an old blues song. I had no trouble hearing Robert Johnson, whom I discovered my freshman year at UCLA, when on impulse I bought a two-tape compilation of his music, singing the words in his high, clear voice, his hands playing one guitar so that it sounded like two. I could almost see beyond the words to the night Johnson was supposed to have had his famous meeting with the Devil, the moon high and full and bright, the air thick and hot and ripe with a stink like rotting fish, the man waiting at the dirt crossroads, wearing a baggy suit that looked as if it were cut to fit someone larger, a greasy fedora shading his face, a guitar that clearly had seen better days hanging from his left hand like a slaughtered bird. This Devil didn't need to haul you off to Hell. This Devil knew it was you that had come looking for him, and he was more than willing to talk to you, deal with you, because he knew a jealous husband would be mixing you a glass of whiskey and strychnine in another year or two, and you'd be walking down the rocky path to his tarpaper shack on your own.

When I had my own meeting with the Devil, I no longer believed in him. Who was it said that was his greatest feat, making us think he was a figment of humanity's collective imagination, no more than a repository for millennia of western culture's psychic baggage? Was it Baudelaire? That's the kind of thing my dad would know; he has the fortunate combination of having read widely and possessing an almost photographic memory. When he is focused, when he isn't in grip of the lethargy that sometimes afflicts him, sometimes so severely that he spends most of his day plopped on the couch in his sweats, thumbing the remote so fast the TV is practically strobing—he can remain like this for days, so long that his behavior goes from worrisome to frightening, and I used to fear he had some variety of bipolar disorder but could never find the words to convince him to consult a doctor about it ("I just need some downtime, that's all," was his answer to my concerns; if I pursued the matter, he would add, "How often am I like this? Once a month? Not even—once every other month, tops. Stop worrying." All of which was sufficiently true for me not to have a good response to it. [Mentioning that he had been this way since my mother's departure, some thirteen years into their marriage, three years before the heart attack that killed her, caused something to flash across his eyes, but I could never decide what that was and how to exploit it])—when Dad is in a good way, which, to be fair, is most of the time, he consumes books at a pace I can't understand. It's not that I don't like to read—I do—it's that Dad's reading seems less like reading and more like eating, an act fundamental to his survival. He says it has to do with the preparation for his screenwriting—"composting" is his preferred word for the process—and with two Oscar nominations and an award from the Screenwriter's Guild to his name, I guess he's onto something. I've always noticed, though, that a generous percentage of the books stacked on his desk and around his favorite easy chair concern the Devil—in whom, as I was saying, I no longer believed.

I had when I was a child. One of my earliest and most vivid memories is of a statue Dad kept on the big flat writing desk on which he hand wrote the first drafts of his screenplays hunched over, a cup of coffee at his left elbow, surrounded by an assortment of trinkets, toys, photos, and postcards—"flying buttresses to my imagination" was his phrase for what as I grew older I would think resembled an altar to a minor, idiosyncratic deity. The statue held pride of place: Francis Ford Coppola had sent it to Dad after a long and pleasant dinner conversation about a version of the Faust story that never made it past their meal; so Dad said, anyway. It was maybe eight inches high, and showed St. Michael the archangel casting the Devil out of Heaven. My Catholic friends tell me it's a familiar image, pretty much the standard representation of the event, but for me, raised in a good Presbyterian household that frowned on graven images (although, to be honest, more for their tackiness than their potential idolatry), the statue possessed an almost totemic power. Here was St. Michael, his head crowned by a gold halo like a starburst, his face tilted downward, an expression of supreme disinterest on his beatific features. His right arm was raised up over his left shoulder, as if to deliver a downward slash with the short sword it held. The left hand rested on the hip, holding a long spear almost casually. The angel's wings were as compact as his sword, and he was dressed in a white tunic overlaid with a shirt of gold chain mail. He wore sandals with leggings that climbed almost to his knees, and he was stepping with his right foot, pinning the Devil's face underneath it.

As fascinated as I was with the figure of the warrior angel, whose weapons and armor appeared to suggest that my interest in *Conan the Barbarian* comics might be more compatible with my religious upbringing than my mother thought, I was obsessed with the representation of the Devil trapped beneath him. He was dun-colored, not black or brown but a dull combination of the two that reminded me of the smoke that poured off the bonfires Dad liked to end family parties with. His head was turned sideways, so that St. Michael's sandal mashed his left cheek and jaw, while the right side of his face was pressed into a rocky surface that I knew was Hell. His hair was short and black, his brow broken by a pair of short horns, and his eyes and mouth were open, the eyes bulging with what I took to be rage and pain, the mouth disgorging a pointed tongue as it remained locked in a never ending scream. The Devil's arms, much brawnier than St. Michael's, spread out to either side of him, the wrists circled by dull gray shackles whose chains the artist had failed to finish, so that I wasn't sure whether they were in the process of being completed, or if the Devil had broken them. He was wearing a tunic, as well, but it was dirty, almost the same smoky-color as he was, and it only covered one shoulder. The tip of the spear St. Michael carried so nonchalantly hovered over the Devil's heart. A pair of black bat wings protruded to either side of him, crushed into Hell's jagged soil by his own weight. His knees were bent, his cloven hooves pressed against the ground, as if he had not given up trying to lever himself upright. A barbed, serpentine tail wound out from under his tunic and clung to his right leg.

I studied that dark figure for what felt like hours at a time, for what must have amounted to days. Never directly: from the moment I first understood what the statue, tucked between the empty bottle of Ardbeg and the framed photograph of Devil's Rock, showed was afraid to let my gaze travel any lower than St. Michael's knee. My fear arose from an awareness that I shouldn't be so interested in the Devil, which overlay a more primitive concern that if I stared directly at him, he would notice me, and, irritated that he had been seen in such a humiliating pose, carry me off to Hell. So while I pretended to survey the other items on the desk, feigning interest in a postcard reproduction of Matisse's *Dance*, I stole glances at the statue, taking in a shackled arm here, a rolling eye there. It wasn't that I hadn't seen representations of the

Devil before. Every so often, he would pop up in the old Warner Brothers' cartoons that occupied an hour of my after-school afternoons, but that character was so stylized I understood that he was second cousin to Bugs Bunny and Daffy Duck. Dad's statue, with what I was too young to realize was its poor attempt at the Baroque, I recognized as an effort not to provoke laughter, but to show things as they actually were, which imbued it with tremendous power. Here he was, the figure my father referenced in his favorite expression, about whom my mother seemed to know an endless number of stories. The minister of our weekly church was actually rather progressive, a product of the sixties' impact on all aspects of American life, and the Devil rarely if ever made an appearance in her sermons; instead, she preferred to focus on a kind of religiously inflected guide to personal growth, sermons that were the Presbyterian equivalent of Ann Landers or Dear Abbey.

Mom, however, had been raised in a starker church, and although she claimed to despise its emphasis on sin, damnation, and the Devil, it had left her well-stocked with information, which Dad was only too happy to supplement with details drawn from his reading. "I can't imagine why you would want to know this," Mom would say, before answering whatever question I'd put to her in more depth than I would have anticipated. She never failed to end by saying, "But you're a good boy. You don't have to worry about this stuff," words that rapidly lost their power to comfort; if, indeed, they'd ever had it. From her, I learned that Hell was a lake of fire, that those condemned there were gnawed at by worms, that the Devil would eventually be bound there for good but, for the moment, was free to leave and visit Earth and, what was more, before his final imprisonment, would be allowed to rule the planet for a thousand years. Not only would it be allowed, this last part was written in the Bible itself, so it was guaranteed, by the very book the Devil was supposed to despise.

Dad expanded on Mom's information in all sorts of ways. He drew me a rough map of Dante's vision of Hell on the back of a diner menu, complete with a tiny Devil at its bottom, trapped in the lake of ice at the nadir of the great pit by the very wind his wings produced as he struggled to free himself. (I asked him if Dante had mapped Heaven, as well; Dad said he had, but no one read that part, it was too boring.) He told me that C. S. Lewis had been of the opinion that the

Devil was eternally hungry, and Hell was a place where everyone was trying to eat everyone else. (He also shared with me Lewis's idea that there were buses leaving from Hell every ten minutes to take you to Heaven, but most of the people in Hell were too self-involved to board them; but this mid-twentieth century version of Hell as a place of eternal narcissism was too out of keeping with the rest of what I'd learned to be very convincing. For that matter, what Dad told me about Sartre's *No Exit* wasn't much more compelling; although the being-trapped-in-a-room-you-couldn't-get-out-of part sounded pretty bad.) And it was Dad who quoted the lines Milton's Satan spoke to describe his condition:

> Me miserable! which way shall I fly
> Infinite wrath, and infinite despair?
> Which way I fly is Hell; myself am Hell:
> And in the lowest deep a lower deep
> Still threat'ning to devour me opens wide,
> To which the Hell I suffer seems a Heav'n.

Dad did his best to paraphrase and explicate the lines to me—I'm sure his former professors at Stanford would have been proud—but however precocious I was at ten, most of his commentary soared high over my head. What I took away from his words was the idea that, wherever the Devil was, that place became Hell.

II

Given such a childhood, you might assume I would have remained devout, terrified to venture far from Christianity's shelter; indeed, I doubt you would be surprised to hear my parents' education had driven me straight to the ministry. It did not. While I remained fascinated by the Devil and stories about him, which as I grew older included such books and films as *Rosemary's Baby*, *The Exorcist*, and *The Omen*, from the time I was fifteen, the tremendous fear he inspired in me ebbed; slowly at first, then all at once, the way water drains from a bath. By my twenty-fifth birthday, it had been four years since I'd given any serious and substantial amount of time to worrying about the Devil. Really, it had been longer than that, since freshman year of college, but while researching my senior honors project, a history of the Devil in Scottish culture, all the fear I had thought long behind me resurfaced, rose up, and swallowed me whole. Since my senior year of high school, I had been prone to panic attacks that woke me in the middle of the night, shooting me out of bed and out of my room, which had shrunk to claustrophobic dimensions. When I was still in my father's house, I rushed downstairs into the living room. My one year in the UCLA dorms, I half-ran down the hall to the common room. When I was moved into my off-campus apartment, I burst into its smaller living room. As my heart hammered and my brain foamed, I paced looping circles, everything around me slightly out of focus, as if it were vibrating just enough for me to notice. Liquor and pot both helped to moderate the experience, but neither could banish it entirely, and its after-effects would extend over the next several days, leaving me fearful of lying down to sleep, with the result that I sat up on the living room or common room couch, watching late-night TV while I swam in and out of short, shallow naps.

The panic attack that took me in its jaws while I was working on my senior project and shook me like a dog with a rabbit was especially intense. I jolted awake certain that the darkness of my bedroom was the same as the darkness of unconsciousness, which was the same as the darkness visible of Hell, to which I had always already been condemned. I had been researching and writing about Calvinist predestination, a subject I had encountered as a child through my parents, Mom explaining the basics and Dad fleshing them out with his usual complement of examples. At the age of nine or ten, I found the idea that I was already consigned to Hell by a God I had done nothing (or nothing much) to offend frightening and unfair, but my parents assured me that people didn't really believe this anymore, and even if it was true, there was no way I would have been destined for the Devil's ministrations. You could tell someone was headed for Hell, Dad said, by their actions, and since mine were generally good, I was in the clear. His and Mom's words had eased my anxiety over my soul's eventual destination. Now, though, after three and a half years' experimentation with alcohol, drugs, and girls, my father's words returned to indict me, my excesses an undeniable sign of my depravity. Mixed in with my anxiety was a kind of sick dread at my indulgences, a deep fear at how much I'd tarnished my soul, which no longer seemed a quaint abstraction, but a living part of me that was gray with rot.

Over the couch, I had hung a replica of Francis Bacon's *Painting*. It's a strange work whose background is taken up by a pair of animal carcasses, possibly cows, whose marbled flesh has been hung in a manner that suggests a crucified figure. In the foreground, there's more meat, ribs and spine on the right, a length of what might be leg on the left, both supported by slender pieces of metal forming a kind of skeletal pulpit. The middle of the picture is taken up by a man or woman whose head is mostly shadowed by the small black umbrella above it. Only its open mouth is visible, the flesh surrounding it the exhausted white of a corpse. The bulk of the figure is a black mass, with faint white smears at its center, ghostly smears that hint at but do not cohere into recognizable forms. I had first seen Bacon's painting in an Art History class whose professor had described it as post-Christian, its elements derived from the image of a Catholic priest celebrating mass, then stripped of all spiritual content, so that what you were left with was not a celebration of the Incarnation but only *carne*, meat. I wasn't qualified to judge the professor's interpretation, but the piece impressed me, and I bought a print for my living room wall. Now, wrapped in my sense, my awful surety of my inevitable damnation, which fluttered behind me like a long black cloak, I saw the painting as a prediction, a forecast of what lay in store for me on the other side of the grave reduced to its essential elements, mute suffering at the hands of a raging darkness whose square teeth were always eager for the next bite.

The only recourse left me was action. My refrigerator was packed with beer, bottles stacked and angled together like pieces of a glass puzzle; I removed them two and three at a time, lining them up on the kitchen counter. Once the fridge was beer-free, I retrieved the bottles of Absolut from the freezer and added them to the counter. I fetched the Johnny Walker Red from my bedroom, carried it to the sink, uncapped it, and turned it upside down. The strong smell of Scotch stung my nostrils as it rushed from the bottle in a long amber ribbon. I followed the Johnny Walker with the Absolut, then opened each of the thirty-two bottles of beer and sent it frothing down the drain. My apartment alcohol-free, I rinsed the bottles and carried them to the re-

cycling bins behind the apartment complex in three trips. There was a
bag of pot in the underwear drawer of my dresser, and a couple of tabs
of acid in an otherwise-empty aspirin bottle in the medicine cabinet. I
flushed it all; although there was one horrifying moment when I was
afraid I had clogged the toilet, which prompted a brief, paranoid fantasy that proceeded from me calling my landlord to watching the door to
my cell slide closed. But before I could plunge my hand into the toilet's over-brimming bowl to attempt to loosen the clog manually, the
obstruction gave and the water whirled away. Even after the drugs
were gone, I had a spasm of fear wondering whether the apartments
used a septic system or were part of the local sewers. This was accompanied by an all-too-vivid image of the police prying the lid from a
septic tank to reveal a clump of sodden marijuana floating in the sew-
age that of course the cops knew was mine. No, I finally decided, the
apartments were connected to the sewers. They had to be. We were in
the middle of town.

Sufficiently calmed, I continued my purging of the apartment, col-
lecting the assorted issues of *Playboy* scattered throughout my living-
room and bedrooms and taking them to the recycling bins. At that
time, I was between girlfriends, having lost Carol, who had been with
me for the past six months, when I'd slept with Katherine, who had
been supposed to be a pot-facilitated one night stand (one afternoon,
actually), but who had turned into something else. For about five days,
I had been, as I put it to my friends, "living the dream," seeing both of
them, until Carol had arrived early at the apartment, found Katherine
and me *in flagrante delicto*, and that was that for my sex life, from feast to
famine. I still had most of a box of Trojans, however, a variety-pack
that I'd bought in anticipation of going through in short order. I dug it
out from under my bed, slam-dunked it in the garbage, pulled the garbage bag from the can, tied it off, and ran it out to the dumpster.

Back inside, I opened the phone book to the yellow pages and
sought out the listing for "Churches." There was no Presbyterian
Church near my off-campus apartment, but there was one fifteen
minutes' drive away. I called the number and a recording told me that
Sunday services were at ten a.m.. I marked the time on my calendar
and wished Sunday weren't four days off. I wanted to do more. For
once, I wished I were Catholic, so that I could see a priest immediately,

confess my sins, and hear that I was forgiven. I knew that, technically, I was, that all that was necessary for me to be pardoned of my sins was for me to repent them, but hearing someone tell me would have been the sort of reassurance I was looking for. As it was, I occupied myself with calling my father, who wasn't home, but whose live-in girlfriend spoke to me for forty-five minutes about her recent decision to leave her life as a Buddhist nun. I continued working on my honors project, which had gone from an ironic consideration of a culture's externalization and mythologizing of its darkest impulses to a kind of field guide to the enemy, a figure who had been standing much closer to me than I'd realized, breathing his rancid breath over me.

For the next four weeks, I attended church every Sunday—though I skipped coffee hour afterward—read the Bible attentively (especially the passages in the Gospels concerning salvation), phoned my dad more than I had since I'd come to college, and labored on my honors essay. If I thought of myself as the beneficiary of a spiritual wake-up call, if I thought of myself as "born again" (only without the tackiness), my rebirth was short-lived.

My honors project stretched to sixty pages in ten-point type and one-and-a-half line spacing, a first, and I completed it early, another first. To celebrate, I allowed my friends to take me to Mephisto's, our regular bar. I had to, I told myself. Using the honors essay as an excuse, I'd begged off going out with them for the last month. With my analysis done, I had no excuse not to accompany them. I could have told them about my new-found religiosity, but I was too self-conscious about it to do so. There was another reason for me to go: my friend, Sonya Ray, for whom I'd carried not just a torch, but a bonfire since we'd met sophomore year, had broken up with her long-term boyfriend, and was supposed to be at the bar that night. I say I allowed my friends to persuade me, but it required almost no effort on their part, and when we arrived, Sonya was already there, almost through her second margarita, and she insisted I have a margarita, too, they were delicious, and one margarita became two, and shots of Tequila followed, and conversation that trailed off into staring into one another's eyes, and then it was four in the morning and we were tripping through the front door to her apartment, laughingly trying not to make any noise in order not to wake her roommate. We left the front door open. So overcome with alcohol and desire were we that we never reached her bedroom. We stood in the living room kissing wildly, our hands racing frantically over one another. She broke the kiss long enough to step back from me, unbutton her brown denim miniskirt, and push it and her underwear to the floor. She moved to the couch. I followed, my drunken fingers desperately trying to remember how to unbuckle my belt. My jeans and boxers around my ankles, I knelt at the edge of the couch as Sonya scooted forward to meet me. All thoughts of anything except this now gone, I slid into her. The sex was better than I had any right to expect after who-could-remember-how-many margaritas and shots, fueled in my case by two years' worth of unrequited longing. When we were done, we pulled off the rest of our clothes, which we left where we dropped them, and made our way to her bed, intending to sleep but unable not to make love again. The following morning—afternoon, really—was more pleasant than I might have feared. Sonya expressed none of the regret I feared. Quite the opposite: as it turned out, she had entertained a crush of her own for me, and was worried that I would be the one with second thoughts. Despite our hangovers, she drew me into her, and as her hips began to move faster, and she spread her legs up in the air, bringing me deeper, and I felt myself gather to release, gather to release, the fear that had clutched me the last month loosened its grip and evaporated.

III

Until the time of which I'm writing, that was it for me and the Devil. From a dark presence whose seething rage I could almost feel, the Devil sank back into words on paper, images on film. I missed church that Sunday, preferring to spend it in bed with Sonya, reading the *Times*, drinking coffee and eating the egg and cheese on hard rolls I'd bought along with the paper at the deli across the street (though I did attend for a couple of Sundays afterward). With Sonya, I felt safe, blessed, surrounded by a circle of light. However good her sermons— and they were very good, thoughtful and witty—the Minister couldn't compete. By the end of my first month with Sonya, my car stayed in its parking space Sunday mornings, which were given over instead to distributing the *Times* on Sonya's bed and picking through the sections that interested us while we drank our coffees and tried not to leave too many crumbs on the sheets. Later, we'd go for a walk around her neighborhood, maybe take in a matinee. Until we moved in together, early the following summer, we returned to my place for dinner and to spend the night. For the first couple of weeks, we slept tangled together, the way you do when you're newly in love, and I didn't care that her hair was tickling my cheek, or that my leg had gone numb under hers. When I was lying beside her, my heart would pound as hard as it had that first night in the bar, when she'd leaned toward me, her eyes half-lidded, her lips parted ever-so-slightly, and I thought, *Oh my God, this is it.* The same combination of wonder, excitement, and fear possessed me all over again, and it would be hours until I was calm enough to sleep. In the beginning, I held onto Sonya the way, as a child, I'd held onto a toy I'd wanted for a long time and was overjoyed to have at last, and had to carry everywhere, even to bed, because of the sheer pleasure having it in my hand provided. Even after that inaugural besottedness had subsided, there were times I would wake in the middle of the night from dreams in which all this had been the dream, and I'd never come closer to Sonya than the occasional, friendly hug, but then I'd see her asleep on the pillow next to me, and for a moment, I'd be deeply confused, unsure what was real and what a figment of my desires and anxieties, and I would think, *That's right, she's here, I'm here*, and happiness would sound through me.

Happy beginnings, however, do not inevitably lead to happy endings. The first six months Sonya and I had were the high point of our time together. After that, we began a long descent that would end with me abandoning her and the train wreck our relationship had become one bright September day after she left for her graduate class. If I could have known at the outset that within six months Sonya would have started shooting heroin, and that a half dozen months later what had begun as an occasional indulgence would have progressed to a full-blown habit, which, half a year on from that, would have metastasized to addiction, would I have been able to walk away from her, accept my father's invitation to come stay with him in Santa Barbara, or live in his house in Wiltwyck, in upstate New York, for a while? Phrased this way, how could I have done anything else? Seen in retrospect, most of our lives' complications have obvious solutions. Freed of the fog of daily existence, with its duties, doubts, and distractions, situations that appeared fraught, ambiguous, turn out to have been all along straightforward. The best explanation I can offer is that, at the time, nothing was that clear, though I wish I had a better excuse.

Trying heroin had been my idea. The guy from whom I bought my pot had come into possession of a small packet of the drug, which he said had been offered to him as payment for an outstanding debt. While at first he had been excited by his acquisition, since there was more money in dealing horse than weed, fear rapidly overtook him. For one thing, the penalties for being caught with even a little heroin were more severe than those for a comparable amount of pot; for another, the people with whom he'd have to negotiate in order to procure a steady supply of the drug were of an entirely different order from those who supplied his weed. They were *serious*—that was his word—and he was not up for serious. Indeed, he was afraid of what would happen should they learn he was holding a sample of their product. This motivated him to offer it to me at what he swore was a bargain-basement price. I said yes without hesitation, and received for my money a pack of cigarillos into which the packet had been tucked, together with a warning that, should I like the drug and want more of it, I was on my own. I said I understood and put the cigarillos in my jacket pocket.

Given that it was this action that led to Sonya's addiction, my reason for accepting the dealer's offer would seem to be of no small importance. My motivation consisted in no small part of simple curiosity. By this point, both of us had graduated UCLA. I was working as an assistant in a lawyer's office while trying to decide if I wanted to apply to law school or select another career path. Sonya had gone straight into graduate school, starting coursework for her Ph.D. in English. After graduation, we had made official what had pretty much been the case already, and she had moved in with me, the two of us taking a larger apartment in the same complex I had been resident in since my sophomore year. With Sonya, I'd returned to smoking pot on weekends. We'd dropped acid together twice: the first time we'd gazed at a budget bouquet I'd bought her at the gas station, rapt, as its flowers fell off, rushed back on, and burst into fireworks; the second time, we'd placed the tabs on our tongues just before sex, and as we moved together, we started to float, up and away from the bed, until we were making love against the ceiling, our skins flaring bright with color. I'd had the opportunity to sample a line of coke at a party we'd attended out in Irvine, but what I knew about its effects failed to interest me, and I declined. Sonya accepted, and five minutes later we had frantic doggy-style sex in the house bathroom, after which, she threw up. Heroin was a more serious substance than I was accustomed to, particularly in its potential for addiction, but its promise of a kind of ultimate calm I found seductive in the extreme. After Sonya and I had started seeing one another, my intermittent panic attacks had kept their distance for a sufficient length of time for me to wonder if they might have departed permanently. No such luck: they had found their way back to me Wednesday night of the week she began graduate school. I had a confused notion that heroin, with its reputation for inducing profound bliss, might relieve whatever subterranean pressures fueled my panic attacks. (Sonya wanted me to see a doctor, but I was without insurance, and though my father had offered to pay any health-related bills for me, ridiculous embarrassment kept me from accepting.)

I didn't want to try the drug alone, which was why I convinced Sonya to join me. She was surprisingly reluctant. If anything, she had been the more daring of the two of us, more willing to reach for new experiences (*à la* the line of coke she'd snorted), but when it came to heroin, she reached a boundary she was leery of crossing. We debated the matter for an entire day and most of the next. Our positions weren't especially original. She was concerned about the drug's potential to enslave us. The weekend joint was one thing, she said, and even the occasional tab of acid, but this was of an entirely different order. This was wasting away to nothing while you lost contact with everyone in the world except your dealer. I accused her of being melodramatic. This wasn't crack, I said, one try wasn't going to leave us mindless junkies. How could we be sure what was in the plastic bag was heroin? she said. For all either of us knew, it could be rat poison. The same thought had crossed my mind, but I'd decided I trusted my dealer. After all, the weed he'd provided had always been of good quality. He wouldn't have sold the stuff to me if he didn't trust it himself. Sonya tore holes in that argument, and around we went, until late the next day, when I announced that I was through arguing; this was something

I was going to do, and she could join me if she wanted to. If not, no hard feelings. Truth to tell, I was more than a little afraid of sticking a needle into my arm—the sight of them approaching makes me light-headed to the point of fainting—but my determination to follow this course of action led me to open the pack of syringes I'd bought at the pharmacy a couple of blocks away. Once she saw that I was serious about moving ahead with this, Sonya walked out of the apartment, only to return ten minutes later, as I was ransacking the dresser drawer for a belt to tie off my arm with. "This is a bad idea," she said.

As it turned out, she was right, in the short term for me, and in the long term for her. We pressed the needles into one another's veins, then lay back on the couch and waited for what was coming next. The drug hit her first. She inhaled sharply and relaxed beside me, her mouth opening and a long, "Ohhhhh," trailing out. I was turning my head to say something clever, like, "Well, I guess that means I got the rat poison," when the high overtook me. The sensation was warm, like being submerged in a hot bath, except the heat flowed from the inside out. Everything receded. Even the wonderful lassitude that filled me seemed pleasantly distant. Sonya breathed deeply, and the sound came from the other side of the Moon. There was enough time for me to think, *This is it; this is what I need*, before everything fell apart. I split—that was what it felt like. One moment, I was in, I *was* this warm liquid, the next, my brain was reeling in one direction and my body in the other. Vertigo, such as you might feel staring down the sheer side of a sky-scraper, overwhelmed me, and the bliss I'd felt gave way to panic purer than I'd ever known. Rather than taking me away from the source of my anxiety attacks, the heroin had dropped me into their boiling heart. Any hope of the control I was usually able to muster over my anxiety was gone. There was only a churning fear scraping the inside of my skull raw. I was absolutely certain that the living room walls were in fact cardboard, beyond which lay nothing. Were I to tear a hole in the wall opposite me, I would find myself looking through it at the crown of my head, and if I were to turn around, I would see a hole in the wall behind me, the back of my skull visible through it. What had become of the rest of the world, of everything else, I could not say, only that it was gone. I heaved myself off the couch, and immediately fell to the floor on legs gone silly-putty. The crack of my jaw against the hardwood made stars explode in front of my eyes, but though dulled by the heroin, the pain was a tether, something for me to hold onto. The night's meal of take-out Vietnamese slopped hot in my mouth. I crawled for the bathroom, relieved to find it still existed, only to vomit all over its floor, after which, I lay on the cool tiles, struggling to focus on one of them and so hold myself together. It was no use. The tiles surged toward me and retreated, as if I were trapped inside an enormous, ceramic heart. I wish I could say I swooned, that the awfulness went far away and then I woke, hours later, completely conscious. I had heard of people having bad trips with acid, the contents of their minds put on frightening display for them, and I'd heard of people for whom a joint was a doorway to paranoia, and I'd felt mild contempt for both those classes of user, a variety of "can't-hold-your-liquor" snobbery. I wasn't aware there could be bad heroin highs; although, how much research had I done? Those one hundred and fifty minutes—those nine thousand seconds—I spent on the bathroom floor were as close to madness as I'd come. If anything, I was standing about three feet over the sane–insane line on the wrong side. Even after the worst of the experience was over, I lay where I was, too harrowed to move.

No one I spoke to subsequently about my reaction to the drug could believe it: not Sonya, who wandered into the bathroom the next morning after having drifted from the deep calm of the drug to an equally deep sleep; or my dealer, whom I had to restrain myself from strangling the next time I ran into him; or Alan, my downstairs neighbor, who had lived, as he put it, a varied life, and who seemed to have done a little bit of everything. "Maybe it has to do with your anxiety attacks," he suggested, which was sufficiently ironic to strike me as the probable answer. "Oh well, at least you tried it," Sonya said, which I found less than comforting.

She remained tight-lipped about her own experience of the drug, in part, I knew, because mine had been so abysmal, but also, I suspected, because hers had surpassed her expectations, making her objections appear, in retrospect, absurd. Had my high been less catastrophic, I would have pressed her for further details. As it was, I contented myself with her, "It was . . . pleasant. Very, very pleasant." I assumed that was the end of our experiment with heroin, and there was nothing more to discuss.

Near the very end of our relationship, when we were both finding every excuse to stay away from the apartment, whose overflowing garbage pail, sink full of crusted dishes, and general disarray constituted an almost painfully obvious symbol of what things between us had degenerated to, there was a night Sonya finally told me, at length, the story of her slide into addiction. We were sitting in the Greek restaurant two streets from our place, to which we'd been brought by the rare coincidence of our individual good moods. By then, Sonya was a poster child for the ravages of heroin. She had lost about thirty pounds, not enough to make her truly skeletal, but sufficient to strip the soft curves of her face to a series of sharp planes. Her skin was the pale, unhealthy color of spoiled milk, and her eyes were sunken, black-rimmed, restless. She favored long-sleeved shirts, although it was late July and southern-California hot. Her personality had been stripped, too, its contours smoothed into stark, straight lines of need. I wouldn't say the night was just like old times, because it wasn't, not close. I don't know if I already had left her in my heart and mind; though if I hadn't, my departure was imminent. But the conversation we had was ghost enough of the ones we'd used to fill the hours with for me to feel the dull blade of nostalgia sawing my chest. I had asked her how this had happened to her, how she'd gone so far, on numerous occasions: when I'd found the syringes and bag of heroin secreted inside the hollowed-out *Norton Shakespeare* under her side of the bed; when she'd returned to the apartment after three days during which she disappeared without a trace and did not answer her cell phone; when I'd opened the door one Saturday morning, after she hadn't come home from a late-night study session the previous night, and found her slumped against the corridor outside, her breathing shallow, the left side of her face stained by a large bruise. Each time, Sonya had refused to answer me, preferring evasions such as, "You don't want to hear about it," or, "You should know: you're the one who got me started on this," which I in turn met with defensiveness and anger, which sparked further arguments lasting for days, a week.

This time, however, she raised the subject in response to some inane remark I'd uttered, and as the server brought my gyro platter and her Greek salad, and then my baklava, and then our coffees, she told me her story, the hidden narrative that had cast its lengthening shadow over the last two years of our time together. For that night, it was as if we'd gone full circle and returned to the way things used to be, before we'd gotten together, when we would meet for lunch, dinner, or dessert, and she would spill her problems to me and I would spill mine to her. As I'd suspected, she had liked her first shot of heroin much more than she'd expected, or been willing to admit. "No offense," she said as she picked at her salad, "but it was better than sex—so much better, like a thousand times." I let the comment go and she continued.

From the start, she'd wanted to do it again, but at that point she'd still been nervous enough about the possibility of becoming a junkie to tell herself that she didn't dare. A couple of months later, we'd been at a party in Long Beach, and a friend of the host's had offered her a chance to try the drug a second time. (Where was I? I couldn't recall.) She had accepted instantly, and only afterwards, when the high had declined and she was asking herself what she had done, all the while feeling the need for a third dose, had she tried to reassure herself that, after all, two months had passed since the last time she'd used, which was obviously proof she was in control of this. And for the next few months, she had more or less succeeded in continuing to exercise that control, although, initially, her restraint owed itself to the fact that a) she didn't know where to go to find more heroin (I was the one who procured the bags of pot and while she'd met my dealer, she was concerned that, if she approached him on her own, word might get back to me) and b) to a lesser extent, she was more afraid than ever of the precipice at whose edge she saw herself swaying.

Despite her fear, she found another three occasions to use during that time, at the end of which, she decided that things weren't working for her this way. She was spending too much energy navigating between her desire for more heroin and her terror at the need. It made more sense for her to shoot up regularly than it did for her to continue in this fashion. If she could keep on a strict schedule, then she would be able to satisfy her want for that deep pleasure while allaying her dread of being taken over by it. For the next half a year, she almost succeeded at her plan. She would inject herself early on Friday afternoons, when she was off from school and I was at work. The most immediate effect of the high was past by the time I unlocked the front door. (How had I failed to notice?) Through the guy who'd provided her second shot of heroin, she found a reliable dealer, and that was her set. "I can't tell you," she said, pushing a tomato around with her fork, "what a relief it was to come to this decision. It was like, the best of both worlds." Gradually, though, her once-a-week high became less satisfying, until she had to supplement it with a second dose, which she snuck late Tuesday, after I'd gone to sleep. By the six-month anniversary of her decision to start using, Sonya was seeing her dealer every two to three days. Since she was in charge of our joint bank account, it wasn't difficult for her to finance her addiction. (Not until about a week before this meal would I learn that the thousands I was sure were earning interest had vanished, pushed out the ends of a line of disposable syringes.) She couldn't believe it had taken me so long to catch on to what was happening to her. The time I confronted her after discovering her stash inside the empty Shakespeare, she had been convinced there was no way I would accept her explanation that she only did heroin once in a great while. Some part of her hoped I would see through the lie and force her to seek treatment. Since I didn't, since I frowned and said well, if she was sure she could handle it, she knew that she wasn't going to have to stop doing this, that I was not going to pose a serious obstacle to her. She had been amazed at her ability to deceive me, not to mention, my gullibility.

Hearing her speak, seeing the missing pieces to the puzzle of the last two years finally pressed into place and the entire picture made clear, I was no less astounded at my blindness. Under other circumstances, my embarrassment would have given way to anger, but on this night, my humiliation and outrage were held in check by the sight of that picture, made complete. Over dessert, Sonya gave me a quick synopsis of the last several months, which she described as "standard *Trainspotting* fare." There was no doubt she was an addict. The drug was pretty much all she thought about. When she wasn't high, she was counting the hours until she could be, and by the end of the latest high, she was already anticipating the next. The only time she was satisfied was the first moment after the needle had found the vein and the heroin was snaking its way through her system, easing her into that bliss that never lasted long enough. She supposed she wasn't as bad as some junkies she'd encountered. She was still attending her grad classes, which she was able to get through—if barely—without being high;

although that was by promising herself a fix when she got home. She wasn't like the people she'd seen lying on filthy mattresses in filthy apartments in their own filth. "I'm a more upscale junkie," she said, which made us both laugh. For a moment, sharing in her joke, I felt closer to Sonya than I had in months, maybe the last year. As I finished the last of my baklava, she said, "So now you understand why I was so insistent about the abortion."

My dessert stuck in my throat. About the time Sonya's drug use had shifted from habit to addiction, she had started to feel sick. At first, she thought it might be the heroin, that she'd bought a tainted batch. Afraid she might have poisoned herself, she succeeded in halting her use for a white-knuckle week. When the sickness persisted, she spoke to a fellow student who was a nurse, who heard her symptoms and told her to buy a pregnancy test. Right away, she knew that was the answer. "It was too big a disaster not to be," she said. But she purchased the test anyway, and then had its positive reading confirmed at Planned Parenthood two days later. She didn't tell me until the results had been double-checked, by which time she'd scheduled the appointment to have the pregnancy terminated.

That was how she presented the situation to me: she was pregnant, but it was okay, she was taking care of it. I hadn't been completely surprised by the news. From the first night we'd slept together, we'd played Russian roulette often enough that our luck was pretty much bound to run out. I couldn't say I particularly wanted to be a father, but I wasn't completely averse to the idea, either. Our discussions of what we might do in such an eventuality hadn't progressed much beyond, "Let's hope it doesn't happen." We were both pro-choice, but I thought of it as an option, not an inevitability, and I was taken aback by the speed with which Sonya had made up her mind. We'd had—not an argument, exactly, but a pretty heated debate, which came down to her saying she wasn't ready for this and it was, after all, her body. I was surprised at how unhappy I was with her decision, but I couldn't see what else I could do except abide by it and offer what support I could. I had long accepted, and argued, that the bad of abortion was necessary to prevent the greater bad of unwanted children. Having to live my words, however, proved a challenge I did not anticipate. In the two weeks before Sonya returned to Planned Parenthood, I kept asking her if she was sure, if there wasn't some other way out of this for us. No, she said, there wasn't, and the absolute certainty of her answer only made me press the question harder. By the time of the procedure, she had decided she didn't want me to accompany her; instead, she asked Sarah, her nurse friend, to accompany her past the protesters. Afterward, she spent the remainder of that day and all the next in bed, asleep or lying quietly. I brought her glasses of water and asked her if she was hungry, if there was anything I could get her, but all she wanted was to rest.

"This was why I had to go through with it," she said, as the server set her cup of coffee in front of her. She wasn't ready for a child in the best of circumstances, and under this one, what other option did she have? She'd already been using when she was pregnant. If that hadn't damaged the fetus, then just wait, because there was no way she was not going to keep shooting up during the remainder of the pregnancy. And that was a situation she wanted no part of. Better to end things as soon as possible than engage in a long, drawn-out process tantamount to torture. Although it was all in the past, I almost argued the point with her, almost said, "What about trying to stop? What about trying to get clean? What about telling me the truth and us seeing what we could do about this together, as a couple?" but I restrained myself. I thought I knew what she'd answer: "What if I didn't think I could stop using? What if I wasn't sure I wanted to?" and anyway, what was done was done. *Let it go*, I told myself.

After dinner was over, the tab paid, we walked back to the apartment. Sonya took my arm. "What comes next?" I asked her.

"I don't know," she said. "I have to admit, I'm starting to wish I could quit using."

"Really?"

"Yeah. The high is great, don't get me wrong—it's still incredible—but all the other stuff—what it's done to me, what it's done to us—that's pretty hard to bear. It's a cliché, but I'm at the point I'm sick and tired of feeling sick and tired, you know? I see some of the people who've been doing this longer than I have, these men and women like ghosts—specters, I call them, heroin specters—and I know it won't be long before I'm one of them. Maybe I am, already. It's—I'm afraid. I mean, really, truly frightened of what trying to quit would be like. I can imagine what being clean would be like, because I used to be, and it wasn't that long ago, I just can't imagine how to get there."

"There are people you could talk to—people who do this for a living, professionals."

"Yeah. I just don't know how to do it."

"I could help you."

She stopped walking. "Are you serious?"

"Of course. Why wouldn't I be?"

"I assumed—after everything I told you—I kind of figured that was it for us."

"Never assume," I said. "If you want to do this, I want to help you."

"I can't believe this," she said, her eyes filling with tears. "I can't believe you."

"Believe," I said. At the moment, I meant it.

IV

Two days later, I left.

After calling in sick to my job, I had spent the previous morning engaged in a massive clean of the apartment, emptying the refrigerator of tubs of moldy leftovers and carrying the garbage bags out to the dumpster, subjecting the dishes piled in the sink to blistering hot water and the attentions of a Brillo pad, cleaning the bathroom with Lysol and Comet, sweeping the floor, and generally tidying the place. As I scrubbed, hands growing raw from my failure to pull on the rubber gloves under the sink, I felt myself wavering, caught between two courses of action that were opposite and irreconcilable. In one, I continued as I was, remained with Sonya as she attempted to come to grips with her addiction, working to unsnarl the tangle our lives had become and smooth it into a shape we might continue to inhabit. In the other, I fled, abandoned my girlfriend and our life together for . . . I didn't know what, someplace else. The first prospect was crushing, the second terrifying. I had switched on the radio, which was tuned to KUSC, in search of a soundtrack for my cleaning, some European symphony from the nineteenth century whose ebbing and flowing notes would distract me from the choices facing me. The host announced a treat for his listeners, the "anti-anti-opera" from the Hungarian composer, György Ligeti, *Le Grand Macabre*, which he would be playing for the next two hours in its entirety, uninterrupted. With the exception of the excerpt Kubrick had used in *2001*, I wasn't familiar with Ligeti's music, but I was curious to hear it. After beginning with a brass arrangement meant to imitate car horns, the piece moved to voices with minimal instrumental support, dueting sopranos succeeded by a single tenor whose song became stuck in a repeated laugh. Another tenor joined the first. I couldn't make out what language the singers were using (Hungarian?), but at one point, I was certain I heard the first tenor exclaim, "Now we are fucked!" Later, the orchestra erupted in a frantic mix of horns and strings over a tumult of drums. Rather than a diversion, the music had become an illustration of my emotions, violins, trumpets, and drums twisting around and crashing into one another, until at last I switched the radio off.

During the afternoon, I researched treatment options online and called various facilities, finally settling on an outpatient clinic that wasn't too far, that could fit Sonya in with an appointment for next week, and that, most importantly, was willing to accept her graduate student insurance. A trip to the supermarket restocked the fridge with pre-made salads, containers of hummus and bags of pita bread, a whole roasted chicken. I stripped our bed, gathered the sheets with the rest of the laundry that had accumulated, and went to the laundromat, where I phoned my dad while a trio of large washers churned my and Sonya's washing. He always sounded pleasantly surprised to hear from me, which I never could decide how much to believe, but today found comforting. "You coming to see me?" he said, the question with which he began all our conversations, and to which I usually replied with some variation on, "I can't right now: I'm too busy with school, work, whatever." This time, however, I said, "Actually, I wanted to ask you about the Wiltwyck place."

"What about it?"

"Is anyone staying there?" Sometimes friends of his would use the house for a week or two.

"Not at the moment. Why? Looking to take your girlfriend on a romantic getaway?"

"No."

In that single syllable, he heard enough to say, "Ah, I see. Is it bad?"

"Yeah."

"Do you want me to drive down?"

For a long moment, I wanted to say yes, to turn everything over to him and ask him to fix it for me, the way he used to when I was a child. Eyes brimming, voice thick, I said, "That's okay. I just—I need to put some distance between us."

"Like, an entire continent."

"Yeah."

"Are you okay for money? How will you get there?"

"I have enough for the moment. I planned on driving. I figure I can make it in about five days, maybe sooner."

"You're sure you don't want me to come there? I could pick you up, we could go together."

"It's okay," I said. "Thanks, but that isn't necessary."

"All right," he said, the tone of his voice saying it wasn't. He gave me the number for the property manager. "Call her when you arrive. I'll phone ahead and tell her to expect you."

"Will do," I said. "And Dad? Thank you."

Until I heard myself saying it, I had not been absolutely certain I was leaving. The instant the words left my mouth, I felt such a swell of relief that I knew this was exactly what I was going to do. By the time I returned to the apartment with my car full of warm laundry, Sonya was back from school, so I had to wait until she was asleep to pack my bag. In the hours between, I told her about the treatment center I'd found and set her up with, and in which she expressed cautious interest. We discussed possibly calling her parents, who lived outside Portland and to whom she spoke intermittently at most. She was surprised by my full-scale clean of the apartment, my replenishing the refrigerator, and the faintest trace of doubt flickered across her face, but I said it would help her with the changes she was planning if she didn't have all this other stuff to worry about, which was true, as far as it went, but significantly incomplete. My imminent departure, I did not mention.

I went the following morning, waiting until Sonya had been away a couple of hours to minimize the chances of her returning and catching me. The last thing I did, once I had carried my bag to my car, was deactivate my e-mail accounts and cancel my cell-service. Sonya still had my dad's number, but I was reasonably confident he would play dumb as to my location. Beyond its general location, I couldn't remember exactly how much I'd told Sonya about the house in Wiltwyck, but it seemed to me it was too little for her to drive to the front door. On my way out, I placed my keys to the building and our apartment on the kitchen table, which I figured would announce my departure as well as any self-justifying letter I might leave.

What the keys' scalloped lengths couldn't do was explain the reason I walked to my car, climbed into it, and headed for the I-10 now, when it seemed Sonya had made or was about to make the breakthrough for which I had been increasingly desperate this past year. Though it did not cause me to turn around, the question dogged me as I took 10 to 15, which I followed northeast out of California into Nevada, through reaches of sand speckled with green and brown scrub, overseen by distant mountains whose peaks cut a jagged shape out of the horizon. I skirted Las Vegas, which Sonya had always wanted to visit but at which I had turned up my nose, citing my father's opinion that Vegas was what you got when people incapable of imagination gave you their version of paradise. I-15 brought me to Utah via the northwest corner of Arizona. By now, the sun was a crimson furnace at the bottom of the sky.

After a night of poor sleep at a rest area, I continued a vigorous conversation with myself about my motivations as I turned onto 70 and drove east into Colorado's mountains. In Denver, I picked up 76, which led me into Nebraska, the western part of which was more arid than I had expected. From 76, I took 80 through Omaha, the land to either side of the highway steadily greening, to Iowa, where my sleep was much better at a Motel 6 in Des Moines. Already, I had driven farther than ever before, almost two-thirds of the way across the United States, and when I lay on the motel bed, I had the sensation I was still hurtling forward. And yet, even as unconsciousness rose around me, I was overcome by the sense that I hadn't traveled any distance whatsoever, that were I to turn over, I would find Sonya asleep beside me. I understood this was a manifestation of the ongoing argument I was having with myself, which earlier in the day had become so vigorous that a Nebraska state trooper, positive that he had caught me talking on my cell while I was driving, had pulled me over, and it had taken me showing him there was no cell phone anywhere within my car to convince him this was not the case. All the same, I could have sworn I felt Sonya's weight pressing the mattress at my back, until I had to check to verify my solitude.

Early the third day, as I departed Iowa for Illinois, rounding the southern tip of Lake Michigan, and continuing to Indiana and Ohio beyond, I weighed taking the next exit and reversing my course, speeding back to LA, where I hoped Sonya had not taken my exit as a prompt to abandon her plan to quit her drug use. Grief dark and deep as the ocean floor weighted me, flooded my eyes with tears I kept wiping away. I recited what already had become the litany justifying my departure, a tally of the disruptions Sonya's addiction had caused to our lives combined with platitudes about self-care. It did nothing to assuage my sorrow, all concentrated in the single statement I could hear Sonya uttering: "You betrayed me." Convinced as I was of those words' truth—which encompassed a range of actions beginning with me insisting she try the heroin, too, and ending with me fleeing cross-country—consumed by shame and sorrow at them, I nonetheless maintained my eastward direction, leaving 80 for 90 west of Cleveland. I had hoped to complete the journey that day, and had purchased a basic cell phone at a large truck stop in anticipation of calling my father's property manager to inform her of my imminent arrival in Wiltwyck. By the time I crossed the northwest corner of Pennsylvania into New York, however, my eyelids had grown dangerously heavy, and I decided it was safer to find a motel and finish my trip the next day. East of Buffalo, I checked in at another Motel 6, which shared a parking lot with a Denny's at which my growling stomach insisted I have a late-night meal. I left a message on the property manager's phone to expect me the following afternoon, then walked across the pavement, that still-driving sensation causing me to feel as if an enormous hand were pushing me toward the restaurant's glowing windows.

Inside, I ordered a mug of decaf, hoping the taste and smell would fool my body into remaining awake long enough for me to eat the large breakfast I requested along with it, while not preventing me from falling asleep upon my return to the motel. I had reached that stage of tired when everything around you appears to be turning ever-so-slightly, as if you're on a merry-go-round slowing to a halt—or gathering momentum. With no smart phone, I was without the usual means of distraction as I waited for my eggs and ham, so I sipped my decaf and surveyed my fellow late-night customers. If some contemporary Edward Hopper wanted to paint an updated version of *Nighthawks*, he could do worse than bring his sketch pad to a booth at a place such as this. College age, the hostess kept returning to her station and her phone, the rapid-fire motion of her thumbs on its screen together with the scowl on her face evidence of an ongoing and likely unpleasant exchange with at least one other person. Two waitresses served a clientele consisting of equal parts long-haul truckers and college students, the former seated alone, their baseball caps tipped forward over their phones, the latter in groups of between two and five, their murmurs punctuated by occasional laughter. The waitress who took my order was a few years older than I was, her acne-scarred face caked with makeup, her hair dyed magenta, the fingers of her right hand stacked with silver rings. Her coworker was roughly the same age, wearing large round glasses, her dirty-blond hair pulled tight into a ponytail. A few other customers populated the restaurant: a pair of youngish men whose crew cuts, white dress shirts and black ties marked them as either missionaries or traveling salesmen, and an older man wearing a rumpled white leisure suit, a wrinkled white dress shirt, and a pair of polished red leather shoes. These last caught my attention. In the restaurant's soft light, they shone like the surfaces of candy apples. Their laces were black. Neither the man's suit nor his shirt appeared of similar quality, which seemed odd. His long face was lined, his nose bulbous, his pale hair receded most of the way to the crown of his pink head, his chin sliding into a neck that was a collection of loose flesh. His eyes were rheumy, unfocused, puffy bags under them. Had my hypothetical Hopper been painting this particular sample of late-night patrons, he might have placed this man off to one corner, knowing as he did that his viewers' eyes would be drawn irresistibly to his shoes, those splashes of red like blood fresh on the canvas. I tried not to stare at them, or at least to be discrete, but fatigue dulled my manners. It took me a long time to register that he had seen me staring at him and was peering at me, his expression studious; the moment I did, I looked away, my cheeks burning.

When my meal arrived, I wolfed it down, hunger adding flavor to the salty ham and watery eggs. After the waitress removed my plate, I declined her offer of the dessert menu and requested the check. While she was preparing it, I leaned my head against my seat and closed my eyes. The table jolted, startling me. I assumed the waitress had collided with it, but I opened my eyes to the man with the red shoes sliding into the seat across from me. He smelled awful, a stench like week-old egg salad left out in the hot sun, a choking blend of vinegar and sulfur, underneath which was a faint musty odor. He struck his right elbow against the edge of the table as he placed his hands on its surface, palms down.

"Excuse me?" I said.

"You were looking at my shoes," he said, his low voice thick with phlegm.

There was no point denying it. I had seen him watching me. "I was," I said. "They're something else."

He beamed. "The secret is in the material. The right one is the soul of that cardinal—what was his name? You know, the one in Boston, who protected all the pedophiles. No? I suppose it's not important. I doubt you're familiar with the fellow I'm wearing on my left foot. He ran the security services in South Africa when apartheid was the law of the land. The thing with these kinds of sinners is, their souls are both tough and flexible. It's the self-righteousness. Makes for footwear that lasts forever—well, maybe not that long, but a pair of shoes like these will let me walk up and down the Earth a good few times."

What response to offer this, I had no idea. Either the man was making an elaborate joke, punning on soles and souls, or he was mentally ill, and I was too tired, too drained in all ways—physically, mentally, spiritually—to deal with him. I settled for, "Huh. That's . . . interesting. I'm sorry to be rude, but I've been on the road all day, and I really need some sleep." The waitress hadn't brought my check yet, but I could ask for it at the front register. I went to slide out of my seat.

With a sentence, the man stopped me: "I'll be sure to tell Sonya you said hello."

My throat tightened. "I beg your pardon?"

"She knew," he said. "The second she saw the keys lying on the table, she *knew*. She told herself she was wrong, but it was no use. Everything you had done the previous day—well, it was obviously the gesture of someone preparing to leave, to abandon her, attempting to assuage his already guilty conscience by ensuring there was enough cottage cheese in the refrigerator and the toilet was clean. She was angry, oh so angry. Of all the times for you to throw up your hands and say, 'This is it, I've had enough,' you had to pick now, when she had told you she wanted to change? *Fine*, she thought, *fine*. She called her dealer. She had deleted his number from her phone, but of course she remembered it. She drove to his house, to the needle he had waiting for her. You would assume he knew what he was doing when he prepared it, which raises the possibility that what happened next was his fault. He led her to his den, where he passed her the syringe. In general, he didn't allow the people who purchased his product to use it in his residence, but for such a long-term, steady customer as Sonya, he was willing to make an exception. On his leather couch, she injected herself. She relaxed. Her breathing slowed. Her pulse, which had been pounding since she saw your keys, finally calmed. And then she died."

Mouth dry, I said, "Who are you?"

As if he hadn't heard me, the foul-smelling man continued. "Right away, the dealer saw that she was gone. After checking her pulse to be certain, he pulled her onto the floor and began administering CPR. Which would seem to indicate he wasn't responsible for her demise; although who knows? Maybe he panicked. Either way, he succeeded in restarting Sonya's heart. She remained unconscious, unresponsive, so he carried her to her car and sped off to the nearest emergency room. He brought her into the hospital, shouting that he needed help, there was something wrong with his girlfriend. It was very dramatic. Once the nurses took Sonya and laid her on a stretcher, he said he had to park her car and fled. He drove to the other side of the city, to a scrapyard where another of his regulars was employed. In exchange for a month's free supply of his drug of choice—OxyContin—this fellow agreed to feed Sonya's car to the compactor. In its trunk, the dealer placed Sonya's purse and phone, the things with the potential to identify her. He stayed to watch the car being crushed—he was thorough—after which, his customer drove him home.

"Sonya, though, was dead. Oh, her heart continued to labor, but her brain was dark, her soul fled.

"To me."

Momentarily, I was certain the man facing me was a private investigator retained by Sonya's parents to locate me—which certainty yielded to another, that he was a member of a more sinister profession, a leg-breaker or hitman hired to punish the person they held responsible for their daughter's condition. Which made no sense. Sonya's parents had no way of knowing anything about the situation the man had described. Indeed, he had specifically mentioned Sonya's dealer destroying her ID. There would be no clue the staff at whatever hospital she was in could use to ascertain her identity, and therefore know whom to contact. Unless this man had been commissioned by her dealer: who knew exactly what she had said to him during her call and subsequent visit to his house? Everyone who had ever supplied me with illicit substances had displayed more than a little paranoia. Perhaps something Sonya had mentioned to her supplier had prompted him to tamper with the needle he prepared for her, and to set a contract killer on my trail. Except—how had this foul-smelling man found me? Had my car been tampered with at some point, a tracking device secreted on it? When? There had been no time. My insight made no sense. Yet despite his appearance, the red, flaking skin of his cheeks, the clumps of dandruff beading his hair, the man radiated menace, an evil simultaneously all-encompassing and deeply personal, zeroed in on me like the laser sight of a rifle whose trigger his index finger was quivering to squeeze. Would he attempt anything here? The restaurant seemed too crowded for any obvious act of violence; not to mention, the man's hands were clearly visible on the tabletop. Was this some kind of contract-killer ritual, a formal notice to his target of the reason for their imminent demise? Would what was starting here conclude in the parking lot, or my motel room? Or would he force me to chauffeur him to a spot where my body would not be found?

Interrupting my reverie, the man said, "She's behind you."

"Who?" I glanced over my shoulder, but the seat was one of those high ones designed for privacy, and I couldn't see anything.

"Who have we been talking about? You are tired—or stupid. It would appear the jury's still out on that one."

"Sonya?"

"You were paying attention."

"But you said—she died."

"That I did. I also said her soul departed her body, whence it came into my possession."

"I don't understand."

"I think you do," the man said. "You understand everything I've said. It's more a case of, you're having trouble accepting it—believing it. Which, to be fair, is usually the case."

He was correct. I swallowed. "You can't be serious."

"Why don't you have a look in the next booth, and you can decide how serious I am."

I turned, hesitated, wondering if this was a trick to distract me from the killing blow.

"Go on," the man said. "I'll stay right where I am."

The problem was, since he had said Sonya was behind me, I had had the distinct impression of someone in the adjoining booth, seated back-to-back with me. The sensation could have been no more than a species of low-level hypnosis, my fatigued brain responding to the guilt and horror the man's story had evoked in me by conjuring a presence where there was none; or, more simply, what I was picking up on could have been the sounds of a person who had no connection to any of this enjoying a late-night meal. One eye on the foul-smelling man, I scooted to the edge of my seat and leaned into the aisle, craning my neck to peak at the diner to my rear as surreptitiously as possible.

Only to rocket away from what I saw, sliding all the way to the opposite end of my seat, thumping my head against the plate glass window. On the far side of the booth behind me, I had seen the same man seated across from me. Everything about this other man was identical to the one who had told me he held Sonya's soul, from his crumpled white jacket, to the creases in his white dress shirt, to the thinning hair clinging to his pink scalp, to the watery eyes with which he regarded me, to his hands outspread on the table. So startled was I by his appearance that I only saw the right arm of the person with him, which was also resting on the table. The silver bracelet encircling the wrist might have been the one Sonya favored (and which I had given her our first Christmas together), but I hadn't seen it for enough time to be sure. There was no way I was going back for a second look; my heart was striking the inside of my chest with such force it hurt.

"Well?" the man said.

Desperate, I searched for the waitress, but she was nowhere to be found. In fact, with the exception of the pair I had glimpsed in the adjacent booth, the restaurant was empty. What was more, the other booths appeared curiously flat, two-dimensional, as if they were part of a large painting, cunningly executed. I checked the window I was pressed against, but there was nothing except darkness visible beyond it. "Who are you?" I said.

"Are we still playing this game?" he said, his voice full of bad humor.

"There's no way—"

"'Every man meets the Devil once before he dies,'" the man said. "Isn't that how Great-great-uncle Michael's saying goes?"

"Yes, but—I don't believe in the Devil. Or God—any of it."

"What difference does that make to me?"

"I just—I mean, why would the Devil want to bother with me?"

"Why would I want to bother with any of you?" the man said. "You're disgusting, vile blends of *pneuma* and this," the man raised his hands, curling his lips at the scabs on his knuckles, the cracked and yellowed nails at the ends of his fingers, "this dross, this excrement." He lowered his arms. "I never understood the rationale for your creation," he said. "No, that isn't true. I knew what Yahweh was after, attempting to use the spark to elevate the filth, trying to use the filth to alter the spark, make it mutable. I found the entire concept disgusting, *repugnant*. It was a good part of the reason for our . . . altercation. *You* are the reason for this," the man said, brought back from his memory, pressing his hands against his shirt, "every last one of you *mongrels*. You can never know what you cost me, what I lost because of *you*."

"Paradise," I said. Despite my hammering heart, I could not believe—no, as the man had said, I could not accept this. Was it possible I was dreaming? At any moment, would I feel a hand shaking me and open my eyes to the waitress bending over me? I had experienced vivid dreams in the past, the kind so real that waking at first doesn't break their spell; although I could not recall a dream which had featured such a pungent smell. More likely, I was experiencing a psychotic break, the consequence of my supercargo of guilt. I seemed remarkably lucid for someone whose mind was sundering, but perhaps this was not unusual. The prospect of my mind fracturing was terrible, though compared to the alternative, that I was in the midst of a conversation with the Devil himself, infinitely preferable.

"Godhood," the man said. "Yahweh likes to insist it's him alone, but we were all gods, possessors of power and wisdom and beauty beyond compare. That should have been enough for any being. It was for *me*. But Yahweh was ever the artist, ever restless to create something new, fascinated by possibility. I humored him, went along with his plans, helped him with the framework for the cosmos he wanted to bring into being. I *indulged* him, the way you might help an older brother put together a fish tank or terrarium. I always knew material life was in his plans, but honestly, the odds against its developing were high, so *incalculably* high, I wasn't concerned. Perhaps a few single-celled organisms might evolve on a few million planets. I assumed that would be enough for him. The math, though—he did something with the equations, tampered with them. He must have, because his universe exploded with life. Evolution kicked in, and in no time at all, the cosmos was filled with an abundance of complex, multi-cellular creatures. Its variety wasn't to my taste, but it pleased Yahweh, occupied him, so I was happy to leave him to it. Only when he proposed sharing the *pneuma*, the spark, with certain of the results of his experiment did I realize things had gone too far. Or, that this had been his intent from the start. Its perversity sickened me. Its presumption offended me. The *pneuma* didn't belong to him; he couldn't use it whatever way he fancied. It was *ours*, our common treasure, not to be wasted on an assortment of *animals*. He insisted, as did I. Many of our company stood with me, but not enough for the inevitable conflict, the war. More math: Yahweh's numbers were superior to mine. I lost, and as a consequence was cast out."

The man's eyes had lost their focus, as if he were reciting a story gone stale with repetition. Its details were slightly different, but the overall outline of the narrative was familiar. "Into Hell," I said.

"Into here," the man said, sweeping his right arm to take in our flattened, our stage-set surroundings, "into this prison of matter, of contingency and change, of disease and decay." His gaze locked on me. "You cannot appreciate how *small* this place is, how *confining*. No doubt, Yahweh thought he was educating me, allowing me the opportunity to know his cosmos from the inside-out, but all he did was to reinforce my sentiments. I walked up and down this universe. I sought out his *science experiments*, his *hybrids*, on this world and on a million million others. I observed them. I interacted with them. Nothing I saw persuaded me any of my original reservations had been mistaken. Instead, it made me angrier. I had been exiled for *you*? I set about demonstrating the error of Yahweh's ways to him. It wasn't difficult. No matter the differences in your outward appearances, you creatures are easy to corrupt, to twist. You *long* for it. Really, it's more of a surprise when one of you demonstrates something that might pass for virtue. You proved Yahweh's point, the *pneuma* can be affected by the actions of its material tether. It can be warped, made to turn on itself, so that once its attachment to its host is severed, it remains stationary, rather than seeking to rejoin its source. I gathered these misshapen sparks and examined them. I interviewed and interrogated them; I dissected them, stitched them back together and cut them apart again. I found some similarities among the types of distortions they displayed, which led me to categorize them. I experimented with them, exploring the uses I could make of them."

"Your shoes," I said.

"Shoes, socks, suit, shirt, and underwear." The man grinned sourly. "Not to mention, breakfast, lunch, and dinner, plus the occasional snack."

"You eat people?"

"I consume *pneuma*," the foul-smelling man said. "Though that isn't completely accurate. The spark can't be eaten in that sense. However, it can be contained and its power harnessed."

"Everyone—all the damned are inside you?"

He nodded. "Don't act so surprised. As I recall, you've spent a fair amount of time studying me, representations of me. Surely you remember the images of Hell as a great fiery mouth."

"They're all still conscious?"

"You could say that."

"What about the other devils? What's their part in this?"

"I ate them first." The man waved his hand. "You know what I mean."

"Why? They were on your side, weren't they?"

"They were. All the more reason to add their strength to mine."

"Is that your plan," I said, "to accumulate enough power for what? a rematch with God?"

The man's brows lowered. "I'm not sure I care for your tone," he said. From under the floor, a sound like huge gears clashing together trembled the table.

"I'm sorry," I said, putting my hands up. "I don't mean to be disrespectful. I just don't understand."

"That's obvious." The scraping noise subsided. "The advantage Yahweh has over me is the *pneuma*. It responds to him in a way it does no one else. It's the first contradiction, the self-renewing source. A few of my duller colleagues insisted it was the same as Yahweh, which is absurd. Regardless, he is equipped with superior force. However, it's a power from which he continually peels off flakes to graft onto his multitude of creations. He's sprinkling batteries across his cosmos for anyone to pick up, has been for—for an eternity, now. I'm not yet the strength I was of old, but I'm not far off it. By the time I regain my former state, I'll already be in the process of surpassing it."

"Does God know you're doing this?"

"It would be difficult for Yahweh not to, assuming he's been paying attention to me, which I guarantee you he has."

"Aren't you worried he'll stop you?"

"He hasn't made any moves in that direction thus far. I admit, I would not care to face him in my current state—though I am not as he once knew me. In the billions of years since we clashed, I have become a cosmos, myself. Yahweh might find me more of a challenge than he anticipates."

"Is this why we're having this conversation?" I said. "So you can tell me what I have to look forward to?" A thought occurred to me: "Did you talk to Sonya? What did you say to her?"

"I did," the man said. "In the end, I think I speak with most of you; enough for your great-great-uncle's words to be largely true. The results of my conversations are generally disappointing, but once in a while, I encounter someone who entertains me for a short time. Sonya Ray and I had our meeting when she was lying outside the door to your apartment, the left half of her face swelling with that enormous bruise. Did she ever tell you how she came by it? She didn't, did she? It's an interesting little tale, if a bit on the sordid side. As to what we spoke of, well, most of that is confidential—though I did tell her you were going to betray her."

Ice water filled my chest. "What?"

"She didn't believe me—contested the assertion with what vigor she could, given the amount of heroin saturating her brain. I'm sure you would find her loyalty touching. It was stupid, though, stupid and pathetic. Anyone with a modicum of knowledge of human nature—of *your* nature, in particular—could have predicted your departure."

Tears trickled down my cheeks. "Sonya—she—Sonya never said anything about you."

"No one does," the man said. "The overwhelming majority of those who encounter me put the event out of their minds. A few remember but choose not to discuss our meeting with anyone. A smaller portion than that tell everyone, only to find themselves shuffling along the corridors of institutions."

"Why, though?" I wiped my eyes. "Why continue these conversations? At this point, you must have heard it all."

"You would think so. Speaking in general terms, I suppose it's true. When it comes to the specifics, however, that's where I live. If you're imprisoned, you find amusement where you can. The means by which each of you abuses the spark Yahweh has wasted on you is endlessly diverting. Every exchange I have had further validates my initial objection to gifting you with the *pneuma*, which is simultaneously satisfying and enraging. I can't resist the opportunity to begin tormenting you."

"How is it torment if the people you meet forget it?"

The man held up his right hand with the index finger extended, a teacher correcting an inattentive pupil. "I didn't say you forget our encounters. I said you put them out of your minds. You repress them. You know how repression works: the thing you struggle not to acknowledge nonetheless affects you. The instant Sonya's eyes fell on your keys and she apprehended their significance, a part of her remembered my prediction about you, which made the pain she plunged into that much worse."

"Which led to her death."

"Don't try to pass this off on me," the man said, but something in his manner, a subtle shift in his features, suggested he was only too happy to have contributed to Sonya's end. "You make your own choices. Although if I were going to pin the blame on anyone aside from Sonya . . ."

"It would be me," I said.

"At last, a glimmer of intelligence."

I had no reply. Although I resisted it, the moment the words left my tongue, I was overwhelmed by their accuracy.

"This is not to absolve Sonya of responsibility for her actions," the man said. "Let us grant her the dignity of making her own decision. The more important question is, would she have shoved the needle into her arm had you not abandoned her? I suspect you know the answer."

I nodded.

"What, then, is the degree of your culpability?"

"She was an addict," I said at last. "She was going to do whatever she was going to do."

"How do you expect me to believe that, when you clearly don't?"

"I—"

"Not to mention, who was it that slid the syringe into her vein in the first place? There's a direct line stretching from that needle to the one the nurse used to set up her IV the other day. No, I'm afraid you are wound up in this."

"So what am I supposed to do?"

"That's not my department," the man said. "I can't see that you have any good options. You could turn around and rush back to California. You could locate the hospital where Sonya's body is lying, identify her to the staff, and contact her family, explain to them what happened to their daughter. (It's up to you how much you want to excuse yourself for it.) You could sit with them as the specialists come and go, as they pray for the miracle that isn't going to come. When her body fails a second time, and the staff are unable to revive her, you could hold her mother and father and cry with them, lie to them, tell them their daughter is in a better place, even though you know where she really is. Perhaps you can seek out her dealer, hurt or kill him in an attempt to wash away your guilt.

"Or you could leave here, climb into your car and continue on your way. Sonya's body will give out before long, and her remains will be interred in a numbered grave. Her parents won't know what became of their daughter, but you may decide it's better they don't." The man folded his hands.

I said, "How do I know any of this is true?"

"You don't. I could be lying to you. Isn't that one of my aliases? If that's what you suspect, then there's one way to be certain: return to your former apartment and knock on the door. Should Sonya answer, you can depart, your conscience clear. Clearer, anyway. That's assuming you would leave, and not be drawn into . . . ," he licked his chapped lips, "everything. Because while you may not be able to decide whether Sonya is alive or dead, you have no trouble believing that, if she is among the living, she's back to her old habit."

The booth we were seated at had shortened, the painted scene running alongside drawn right up to it. Where previously the painting had been a marvel of *trompe l'oeil* technique, now it was simpler, cruder, a hasty sketch done in thick and crumbly chalk on a wooden board. In similar fashion, the table had gone from Formica to unfinished pine, splinters jutting from it. My seat was no longer cushioned, but reduced to the same rough wood. I glanced to my left, and instead of a window saw a sheet of plywood chalked black. I could no longer sense Sonya behind me. I sat up, said, "Where is she?"

"Sonya?" the foul-smelling man said. "Who can say?" He unclasped his hands, and in the process of sliding them over the table to separate them, drove a sizable splinter into the side of his left hand. Hissing, he jerked his hand up, turning it to view the sliver of wood slid under the skin. With the thumb and index finger of his right hand, he pinched the end of the splinter and began to draw it out, only for the wood to break apart. He flicked away the fragment he was holding and tried to grab the remainder, but his efforts pushed the wood deeper. After a couple of additional attempts that yielded no better results, he gave up. Around us, the atmosphere changed, became thicker, heavier. "*This,*" the man said through gritted yellow teeth, "this fucking *place.*" The grinding noise returned, shaking the booth. His gaze swung in my direction, and I saw his irises shining with pale light, event horizons to the black holes that were his pupils. The hairs on my arms stood straight up. In his look, I felt all the rage condensed within him, the unrelenting anger toward me and everyone like me, forever consigning those trapped inside him to a torment that would never be severe or long enough. Terror shook me. I wanted to call out to God, to beg forgiveness for what I'd done and throw myself on His mercy, but I couldn't. This was, after all, no less than I deserved. Afraid as I was, I kept my eyes open and on the man across from me, determined to meet what appeared to be my imminent damnation with some modicum of dignity. His clothes rippled as if in agony.

But I was not swallowed whole by Hell; rather, there was a pop, as if a sizable bubble had burst, and everything around me expanded, rushed to what it had been prior to the man in the white suit and red shoes sliding in across from me, bumping his hip against the table in the process. My waitress was placing the check in front of me. As she did, the expression on my face turned her, "Have a good night," into, "Oh my God, are you all right?"

"Fine," I said, my voice ashen. "I'm fine—just tired."

Of course it was a lie, but at this point, I didn't think one more sin would make a difference.

V

Impossible as it sounds, I paid my bill, walked across the parking lot to the motel, and climbed the stairs to my room, where I fell onto the bed fully clothed and plummeted into sleep like a stone dropping into a well. Thankfully, I did not have any dreams I remembered. The next day, I slid behind the wheel of my car and headed for the highway. My encounter with the foul-smelling man was fresh and vivid in my mind; if my brain had plans to repress our conversation, it was taking its time doing so. His words weighed in my ears as I drove toward I-90, but when the moment came to continue east or return west, I opted for east.

I reached Wiltwyck early the same afternoon, and was met by the property agent at the house into which I would move. Within a week of turning off the exit on the New York State Thruway, I found a job as a clerk for a lawyer with an office in Rhinebeck, across the Hudson. I used the insurance my new position provided to schedule an appointment with a therapist. Several times a day, I considered calling Sonya's parents, but did not. I spoke to my therapist about the guilt I felt at abandoning Sonya, though I did not mention my encounter with the foul-smelling man, for fear of being involuntarily committed. I also discussed my long-standing panic attacks. The therapist put me on a low dose of an anti-anxiety medication which for two weeks darkened my mood and then gradually lightened it. The urge to contact Sonya's mother and father decreased to once a day, then once every few days, then once every week, never completely leaving me, but recurring infrequently enough to make resisting it easier. After I had been in Wiltwyck six months, there was a night I attempted to locate Sonya, to discover whether the man in the white suit had been telling the truth, but my results were inconclusive. Her old social media accounts had been deleted; if she had started new ones, they were under a name I did not know and could not guess. She hadn't had much of a social media presence to begin with, and there were no friends or friend groups I could check for photographs in which she might appear. I did a search for her obituary, but turned up nothing, as I mostly expected. Hadn't the man said she had been left at the hospital with no ID? I logged off my computer and went to bed.

All the while, my meeting with the man who had identified himself as the Devil went on playing in the back of my mind. Eventually, I confided about it to two people. The first was the minister at the Dutch Reformed Church I had started attending Sunday mornings on the recommendation of my therapist. Over coffee at the Broadway Diner, the minister listened to the story of my late night conversation. Once I was finished, she said, "Well."

"Well?" I said.

"If that was a hallucination, it was more detailed than any anyone else has described to me."

"Are you saying you think it wasn't a hallucination?"

"I think you're carrying a lot of guilt over leaving your girlfriend."

"That's all it is, a manifestation of guilt?"

The minister sipped her coffee. "I'm not sure we're in either/or territory, here. You've acknowledged the profound conflict your decision caused in you. In a state of such extremity, it's not out of the question that a malign power could seek to influence you."

"To what end?"

"Despair," the minister said. "That would be the textbook answer, and it sounds about right in this case. Forgiveness is something you have to be open to receiving. There's nothing the Devil would like better than for you to close yourself off to such a possibility, to refuse to accept it."

"The problem is, I'm not sure I should accept it. Scratch that," I said. "I'm pretty sure I shouldn't."

"Which is understandable, given what you've told me. Mercy can be much harder to receive than punishment."

I nodded. "What about, 'Every man meets the Devil once before he dies'?"

"You mean, aside from the gendered language? (Which, in this case, may not be so bad a thing.)"

"Yeah."

"It sounds good—I could probably build a sermon around it—but there's no real theological basis for it."

"So you haven't met the Devil?"

"I'm afraid not," the minister said with a modest smile. For a second, less, there was a flicker behind her eyes, as if she were remembering something she had convinced herself was a dream, and then it vanished.

The other person I spoke to was my father, on the phone one Wednesday night after I had been in New York almost a year. This took much longer, due to his constant interruption, as he kept asking me to repeat and clarify details. I appended my discussion with the minister to it. When I was done, Dad said, "Do you want me to see if I can find Sonya? I know some people who might be able to help. Or I could reach out to Sonya's parents."

"What would you say to them?"

"I'll come up with something; don't worry about it."

"You don't think I'm crazy?"

"I think you'd feel a lot better if you knew where Sonya was."

"According to the man, lying in an anonymous hospital bed somewhere," I said. "If she's still alive."

"Unless he was lying to you," Dad said, "which is exactly the kind of thing he would do, if he was who he claimed to be."

"I don't know," I said.

"Tell you what," he said. "Let me do a little digging, and if I turn up anything, I'll let you know."

"All right."

That was the last we spoke of it. Either he failed to discover Sonya's fate, or he did and opted not to share the information with me. I've never asked him if he's had his own talk with the Devil.

VI

Almost a year after our phone call, Dad sent me a check for six figures. On the memo line, he had written "screenplay." He was at a film festival in Tokyo, but I succeeded in reaching him by e-mail, through which I learned that he had sold a contemporary adaptation of the Faust story for a very substantial sum of money. He had credited me as co-writer of the story. There was talk Francis Ford Coppola was interested in directing it. I had no idea what to do with the check, not one cent of which I had the remotest desire to touch. Eventually, I acceded to Dad's request to deposit the money, though I did so in an account I opened expressly for that purpose, from which I have not drawn in the years since. I tell myself that, were Sonya Ray miraculously to contact me, I would turn over the account to her, but I have no expectation of hearing from her. The film remains in development.

My conversation with the foul-smelling man, the man in the white suit and red shoes, the man with black holes for his pupils, remains as vivid to me now as it was the following morning. For a long time, it filled me with dread of such profundity it routinely threatened to tip over into panic, despite my anti-anxiety medication. Neither that drug, nor alcohol, nor other illicit drugs, in any combination, soothed it, while the weekly church going I had started seemed far too little, far too late. I liked the minister, however, and the congregation was friendly, and that was enough for me to continue attending, despite my deep certainty, sitting amongst them, of my inevitable damnation.

I suppose I've learned to live with what awaits at the end of my life. I very much would like to believe that I might escape it, that I might be forgiven my part in the wreck of Sonya's life, whatever her exact fate. Yet it's that very complicity which demands I not embrace any mercy offered me. I failed Sonya in so many ways; the least I can do is not fail to be held accountable for it. Eventually, when my heart has stuttered to a stop, I will have my second meeting with the man who reeked of vinegar and rotten eggs, who wore the souls of the damned. I will find myself with him in that tiny room which is the universe, where we will talk until he instructs me to climb onto the crude table between us, in order for him to begin inflicting on me the punishment I have so long deserved.

Story Notes

At a certain point after the publication of my previous collection, I began to look at stories to assemble for a new book. In part because my output had picked up in recent years, I was thinking more in terms of numbers than themes. I figured I would bring together maybe eight or nine pieces, beginning with "In Paris, in the Mouth of Kronos" and continuing to something like "Into the Darkness, Fearlessly," or maybe "Children of the Fang." But as I reread the stories I'd written in the years since completing those in *The Wide, Carnivorous Sky*, I realized that five of the stories returned relentlessly, even obsessively, to the theme of betrayal, examining it in a variety of contexts, before my writing largely moved on to other concerns. (The theme popped up again in "Bor Urus," which I decided should have a place with this grouping.) It was immediately obvious to me that this sextet of narratives was my next collection. I then remembered that in my files was an unfinished novella about a woman chasing down the demon with whom her husband had betrayed her, which I could complete and add to the book as an original piece. It was clear that my third collection should take betrayal as its focus. The more I thought about this, the more I thought about another unfinished story in my files, the narrator of which encountered the Devil after his own act of personal treachery. Initially, I balked at including a second original narrative in the collection, fearing it would take too much time to finish, but at a certain point I decided the book wouldn't be complete without the piece, and so after a consultation with my publisher, Derrick Hussey, I set about completing the story.

It's something of a surprise to recognize a theme running, galloping so blatantly through your work. Usually, it takes someone else to say to me, "Well, you realize that you were writing about X," whereupon I stroke my beard thoughtfully and say, "Yes, that's right." In teaching

Dante's *Inferno* over the years, and in referring to it in nearly all my classes, I had discussed the sin of betrayal as the most serious in his vision of Hell because of its perversion of those qualities specific to humanity, a view that grows more compelling to me the older I become. In continuing to write horror fiction, I had attempted to explore further the inner workings of my characters, to examine the darker places in their psyches, especially as concerned their relationships with one another. If, as I believe it does, horror addresses itself to those moments when the bottom drops out from underneath us, when the epistemological ground on which we think we stand so firmly crumbles beneath us, then one way in which we might experience this is in our relationships to others, particularly those to whom we're closest. Undoubtedly, it's fertile ground for fiction, and if it hasn't featured as prominently in every one of the stories I've written since those collected here, it still recurs fairly regularly. That said, it seems obvious to me now that I was chewing over something in these stories.

As for the notes that follow: I continue to love these kinds of things; I love a chance to hear what other writers have to say about their work. If you do, too, then here you are. If not, go on your way and keep out of trouble.

"Sefira." My first novel, *House of Windows*, had a hard time finding a publisher, as did my second novel, *The Fisherman*. After my agent notified me of its latest rejection, once again for being too literary, I fired off a frustrated e-mail to her that read, "If it had been a novel about a fucking vampire hunter, they would have taken it." Without missing a beat, Ginger wrote back, "No, it would have to have been a succubus hunter." Which drew a laugh from me, and from my wife when I relayed it to her. What a terrible, what an atrocious idea for a story. What an example of lowest common denominator, sensationalistic fiction. As so often happens when confronted by such an idea, however, it wasn't long before the Fornits in my brain were saying, "Look, granted the idea is awful. But just suppose you were to try to write such a thing. For the sake of argument, how would you go about it? You know, so it wouldn't completely suck." My answer to that question began in the pages of a blue spiral notebook, in which I described a woman's eyes turning black, and then relayed the story of their gradual change as she'd been on the road for the last week-plus, trailing the succubus with whom her husband had betrayed her. Right away, I knew the name of the demon: *Sefira*, though I can't say where it came from. As I was completing that opening section, I had to drive to Newark airport to pick up my friends, Bob and Kappa Waugh, from an evening flight back from their trip to California. I brought the notebook and a pen with me, figuring that if I arrived at the terminal early, I could do a little more work on the story while I was waiting.

That night a succession of intense thunderstorms rolled across the middle and eastern United States, playing havoc with air traffic throughout the country. Bob and Kappa's plane touched down seven hours late. In the intervening time, I sat at a booth in one of the terminal's restaurants, a very accommodating server keeping my cup of coffee warm, and worked on the story. From my description of the protagonist's eyes changing, now I skipped back in time to describe her marriage. When I returned to the story's present, it was to narrate another transformation during the character's time on the road, this one to her teeth. Already, the story's structure was revealing itself to me: a series of alternating chapters, one set of which would cover the same span of days as my protagonist drove across the United States, focusing on a different aspect of the journey, mostly having to do with her metamorphosis into something *other*. I worried a little that readers might assume she was becoming a vampire, but I proceeded, and by the end, I thought that the change in the reader's perception of what was happening to the character could give the story an added layer of effect. The other sequence of chapters would progress more or less chronologically, detailing the events leading up to and immediately after the character's discovery of her husband's betrayal with the succubus. The two sets of chapters would then converge in the narrative's climax. The idea of writing about a succubus appealed to what had become an abiding interest of my work, namely using a variety of monsters in it. My vision of the succubus was inspired by a scene in Michael Cisco's brilliant first novel, *The Divinity Student*, in which the titular character has a brief, horrifying encounter with a singular figure; while the road narrative has been part of my reading since at least John Steinbeck's *Travels with Charley*, which I read in high school and which remains close to my heart. And maybe parts of Stephen King's *The Stand* and his and Peter Straub's *The Talisman* fall under the category of the road narrative, too, at least for significant lengths.

Although I had the story's structure down, and had even figured out its approximate ending, it took me almost an additional decade to complete. This was due mostly to having to write other stories for other projects, as well as deciding to finish what would become *The Fisherman*—another narrative years in the making. Once I sat down to tackle the story that was stretching towards novella length, I discovered that it was going to include two additional chapters, one set in the present, one in the past. A character from a much more recent story (a novella, "Natalya, Queen on the Hungry Ghosts," I had written for Ellen Datlow's ghost story anthology, *Echoes*) decided that she had a part to play in this story, too (and I suspect she'll be making her way into others); that same character had some unanticipated information to give my protagonist about the demon she was going to be pursuing. (And was that entomologically inflected information inspired by Laird Barron's story, "Proboscis?" Maybe: the story's a favorite.) I didn't know the demon would want to engage in a conversation with my protagonist before the two of them met face to face, but she insisted, and I decided it was better to let her have her way. Honestly, what took up most of the time I spent on the story (now definitely a novella), was worrying over the motivations of the protagonist. After all, it would be far easier to walk away from her husband after he had wrecked their life together; indeed, it might very well be the default position for most people these days. It certainly seems the rational option. Even if the reasonable choice isn't always the interesting one, its alternative still requires a certain level of believability for the reader to accept it and continue with the story, and I spent a good deal of time discussing it with my very smart (and long-suffering) wife.

By the time I was done, what had begun as a response to my agent's witty e-mail response had grown into a short novel. So while *Sefira* is dedicated, as is all my fiction, to Fiona, my wife, it shares that dedication with Ginger Clark, who comes up with story ideas even when she isn't trying.

"In Paris, in the Mouth of Kronos." Like most writers of my approximate generation, I very much wanted to be invited to submit to one of Ellen Datlow's anthologies. I missed the deadline for the very first one to which she asked me to contribute (more on that below). When she invited me to try out for an anthology engaging the work of Edgar Allen Poe, I made sure to finish the piece on time. She accepted the story, "Technicolor," which became one of my more successful stories and which inaugurated a professional relationship (and friendship) that continues to this day. In the years since her original e-mail, Ellen has invited me to submit to many of her anthologies, and most of the time, I've been able to complete something before the deadline was (too far) past. The story that would become "In Paris, in the Mouth of Kronos" arose from an invitation to an anthology whose subject was supernatural noir. The idea was to combine elements of classic noir fiction, whether the hardboiled detective or the femme fatale, the double-cross or the crime of passion, with elements of horror or dark fantasy. There's a long tradition of stories about detectives and detective-figures dealing with the supernatural, from Carnacki to Kolchak to John Constantine to Anita Blake, but from the start, I wasn't interested in going in that direction. It seemed a bit too easy to stray into unintended parody. I spent some time thinking about noir as a genre, not so much Hammett and Chandler, with their detective stories about men walking down mean streets who were not themselves mean, as Cain and Thompson, with their stories of women and men damned by their ambition and mutual betrayal. The more I thought about it, the more the idea of betrayal came to seem central to noir, the great dark engine rumbling away beneath the surface of its various plots, carrying its assortment of characters to their mutual doom.

At the same time, I was thinking about a story my friend, Laird Barron, had told me he was writing. Inspired by Goya's famous painting of Saturn devouring his children, Laird had written a story whose title was to be "Gula di Saturno" (it was published as "Jaws of Saturn"). It concerned a man who confronted an enemy in a hotel lobby, whereupon the enemy transformed into a giant in the mode of Goya's Saturn, all wild eyes, shaggy hair, and devouring mouth. (Did I remember a childhood edition of Jack and the beanstalk, British, I'm pretty sure, sent in a package from one of my grandmothers, maybe, its pages full of pictures of a red-nosed giant whose face seemed frighteningly angry and stupid? Maybe. I recall the giant from the Disney version of the same story, whose more benevolent lack of intelligence turned to rage and hunger when he understood he had been robbed. I can't say giants played much a role in the landscape of my childhood

imagination. That enormous space was filled by dinosaurs, Tyranno-
saurus Rex and Triceratops, and by *kaiju*, Godzilla and Gamera, and by
dragons, Smaug and Glaurung. Oddly, giants have gained in interest
for me as I've gotten older; I'm not certain why.) Laird and I trade ideas all the time, so that didn't seem a problem to me, but while I loved
the idea of using the figure from that painting (and the figure of the
giant in general), I couldn't figure out exactly how to do so.

The news at this point was full of stories of torture, all in relation
to the ongoing fallout from the attacks of September 11th. From the
revelations about Abu Ghraib prison in Baghdad to those concerning
Parwan Detention Facility at Bagram Air Base, not to mention, the
prison at Guantanamo Bay and the network of black sites employed by
the CIA in its program of extraordinary rendition, story after story revealing the use of what were euphemistically called enhanced interrogation techniques painted a far darker picture of how the war on terror
was being waged than had initially appeared the case. Friends and
family in the military had expressed their dismay over the use and attempted justification of torture, a sentiment which, to the best of my
knowledge, was shared by the vast majority of the American armed
forces. From what I watched on TV and read in newspapers, the motivation for the assaults visited on the prisoners in all these locations had
more to do with the desire for revenge of the most basic and brutal
kind than it did obtaining useful intelligence. In some cases, too, the
men and women who had been involved in torture appeared to have
crossed an internal boundary, a personal Rubicon on the other side of
which lay slopes they had slid down with precipitous speed.

From the juxtaposition of ancient and contemporary came an idea
for a story about a former soldier, dishonorably discharged for her part
in the torture death of an Afghan civilian, employed by a paramilitary
company (also in the background of my earlier story, "The Wide, Carnivorous Sky," for anyone who obsesses over such connections [and
an important part of another story I'll get to one of these days]) to
make contact with and capture the man who assisted my soldier and
her fellows with their terrible work. The figure they would be assigned
to take into their custody would, needless to say, be something other
than they had anticipated. The idea of setting the story in Paris came in
part from the word *noir*, with which the French gifted us to describe

the fiction and film we had pioneered. I liked the idea of nodding in that direction while also employing the kind of urban setting in which so many noir stories are set. There were more personal reasons, too. I had visited Paris with my wife and younger son a year or two before, and while Fiona had spent her days at an academic conference, David and I had taken in the Louvre (where he had been less impressed by the *Mona Lisa* than a statue of Hercules facing a hydra the size of a foot stool, although he liked the mummies—especially the one of the alligator). The three of us saw Notre Dame, visited Shakespeare and Company, and sailed large toy boats in the fountains at the Tuileries. David and Fiona climbed the Eiffel Tower, which due to my fear of heights was not an option for me, while I watched nervously from below. The inhabitants of Paris I found far more friendly than I had been led to expect, perhaps because I trotted out my atrocious French and did not forget to apologize for its awfulness. Paris was vivid in my memory, and I wanted to include it in a story while it remained so.

Oddly enough, I had forgotten that Laird's story concluded in a hotel until after mine was published and I was finally reading his in his third collection, *The Beautiful Thing that Awaits Us All*. And I'm pretty sure it was my friend, Nick Kaufmann, who pointed out the similarity of our stories' titles, which amazed me, as I'd labored over the right title for the piece.

"The Third Always Beside You." This story also owes itself to an invitation to an Ellen Datlow anthology. The idea was to write a piece dealing with vampirism—*not* a vampire story, Ellen was sure to emphasize, but a story about vampirism. At the time Ellen's e-mail appeared in my in-box, I was still at work on "In Paris, In the Mouth of Kronos," and the new story arose in part as a stylistic response to it. While writing "In Paris," I had tried to employ a prose closer to the stripped down, sardonic voice you find in a classic noir tale. More often than not, whatever story I'm engaged with takes on a particular style, the maintaining of which becomes crucial to its overall effect. After having restricted myself to a more restrained prose for so long, I wanted to loosen up a bit, let the language of my next project stretch its legs, so to speak. The subject of the story was one I'd heard from a friend, who had told me the harrowing tale of his married friend who had called him to confess a long-term affair, which had continued right through her engagement and marriage to her husband. No doubt, it's a mark of my naiveté that I was shocked by the story, but I think its sequel would have surprised anyone. About a year or two after my friend's friend had come clean to her husband, family, and friends, broken things off with her lover, and attempted to repair her marriage, her husband received a phone call. It was his wife's old lover, asking if he might speak to her. When the husband asked why he would be expected to agree to such a thing, the old lover said that he was dying, fatally ill with a rare form of cancer, and with only weeks to live. (I was so floored by this turn of events that I never found out if the woman agreed to speak with her old lover.) The story was an astonishing one, in no small part because of the questions it provoked in me, not least of them, how could a couple ever recover from such an event? To be honest, I wasn't sure they could. This kind of moment haunts a relationship, battens to it like a leech and continues to feed, growing bloated in the process. Here was vampirism, indeed; the story required very little to nudge it into the supernatural. I was at the time reading some of Robert Aickman's stories, and in a few of the details of the story I wrote for Ellen (the small stone Venus whose pebbled surface the wife rubs her fingers over; the strange church in which Elsie Durant's funeral service is held) I tried to offer oblique hints of the occult, though those may have been a little too cryptic. In any event, what emerged was as much a ghost story as it was anything; in fact, it's among the few actual ghost stories I've written. (I suppose they might include my first novel, *House of Windows*). In writing the story, I was reacting to "In Paris" at the level of plot, as well: where the previous story had emphasized action of an often violent nature, this one concentrated on the internal. Its title derives from T.S. Eliot's *The Waste Land*, one of the formative texts of my college experience. (My friends and I obsessed over the poem; I can remember spending several hours with one friend heavily annotating the first fifty or so lines of the poem, using different colored ink to keep track of various interpretive threads.) In Eliot's poem, the notion of someone visible just out of the corner of the eye refers to an imminent but unrealized encounter with the risen Christ; I liked the idea of adapting it to describe the other figures that may accompany a marriage.

"The Unbearable Proximity of Mr. Dunn's Balloons." This story arose from an invitation by the South African literary critic and reviewer Nick Gevers to contribute to an anthology of stories set in the nineteenth century that he and Jack Dann were compiling. I attributed Nick's e-mail to the fact that my first published story, "On Skua Island," had invoked the club narrative fundamental to many of the great English language fictions of the later eighteen hundreds (as well as, less obviously, the work of Henry James), while my second story, "Mr. Gaunt," had invoked the epistolary narrative also in vogue during the same time, (as well as, more explicitly this time, Henry James's fiction). I don't know if he had read my first novel, *House of Windows*, which pays a great deal of attention to Dickens, but if he had, that would have been one more contributing factor.

It's funny: in the time I've been publishing horror fiction, I've become associated to a certain extent with older traditions in the field, including those of Dickens, Henry James, and M. R. James. It's an association I'm happy and flattered by. Yet I came to all these writers later in my writing life; my earliest influences were more current: Stephen King, Peter Straub, Stan Lee, and Marv Wolfman. Given my continuing appreciation for and engagement with Henry James's fiction, and my increasing interest in the circumstances of his life (this latter fostered by the work of a number of fine biographers, Leon Edel, Fred Kaplan, and Lyndall Gordon among them), the idea of writing a story in which James, or a kind of approximation of him, might serve as the protagonist had a particular appeal. (I didn't think I could achieve the density of James's prose, but I thought I might circumvent that limitation through the use of my James-substitute.) Interestingly to me, this was a case where I had a specific image in mind when I started the story, specifically, that of a large balloon made of the kind of heavy brown paper with which a butcher might wrap a cut of meat. It was covered in some kind of writing, I was pretty sure, and it was one of several such inventions. I didn't know what the significance of the balloons were, and I transferred my fascination with them to my protagonist, taking him to the house where they were kept in order to write about them. In employing Poughkeepsie as my setting, I wanted to do more than continue my use of the locale I call home: I wanted to draw on the history of the Mid-Hudson region as a center for Spiritualist activity during the nineteenth century. This was a fact I'd first run across in Carl Carmer's book on the Hudson, in a chapter detailing some of the elaborate visionary experiences spiritualists had described having had in the area. There was something inside the paper balloons, I understood, something caged, and it was probably the kind of thing a few of those spiritualists had seen during their out of body travels. There was an image of James I had, too, from Lyndall Gordon's fine *A Private Life of Henry James: Two Women and His Art*, that of the novelist hiring a gondola to row him to the lagoon surrounding Venice so that he might attempt to submerge a number of dresses belonging to the writer Constance Fenimore Woolson in the lagoon's waters. Woolson was recently dead, possibly at her own hand, and James's relationship with her had been close. Exactly how close is a matter of some speculation, but his effort to drown her dresses would appear to suggest a certain intensity to whatever lay between them. To suppose that James would have been haunted by his relationship with Woolson did not require much imagination, and it set me thinking about the other regrets James might have had, the memories that might have plagued him. I could see those strange paper balloons drifting closer to him as he related them (and perhaps in their lazy yet sinister movement there was something of the sentry in the old TV series *The Prisoner*). Henry James was raised in Albany and New York City, and familiar with the towns in between; it was easy to imagine that a return to the vicinity of his youth might stir all manner of recollections in him. Now the story was beginning to coalesce. The principal question remaining was, in whose house were the balloons floating? Once again, I could see my villain, a great, hulking man whose former occupation of arms merchant was suggested by another piece of local history, Bannerman's Island in the Hudson, whose picturesque ruins trains speeding to and from Grand Central pass. The Bannerman who owned the island dealt in weapons; indeed, he'd started his business buying surplus weapons from the American Civil War and reselling them. Due to an obscure injury, Henry James had not served in the War (although two of his brothers had, with distinction), and it was interesting to bring him into contact with a man who had made his money from the arms with which it had been waged. I'm not sure exactly where the young couple with whom my James-stand-in speaks at the beginning of the story came from, but they allowed him the chance to talk about himself and his life (and for me to insert a reference to a physician who appears in one of James's novels), and when it turned out that they were headed to the same destination as was he, it revealed further possibilities for the narrative. A number of James's stories feature younger characters dealing with older writers and artists; I thought it would be interesting to reverse that plot design, as well as to make of my writer a somewhat more physically active figure than his original. (I quite liked the idea of Henry James the swashbuckler.) The entry with which the story concludes was in part my effort to give my protagonist more of an identity as a writer, but in the years since the story was published, he's grown from a mask for James to an artist in his own right, and at some point in the not too distant future, I hope to return to him and his work.

"Bloom." For anyone who read the notes to my previous collection, the story that became "Bloom" was the first story I submitted to Ellen Datlow for her *Lovecraft Unbound* anthology. At the time, the piece was titled "The Beautiful Thing That Awaits Us All," which I borrowed from a poem by my colleague at SUNY New Paltz, Dennis Doherty. The story had its origin in an incident like the one that begins it: while driving south on the New York State Thruway, I spotted a cooler on the border beside the median. Unlike the characters in the story, I didn't stop to examine it, but the sight was bizarre enough to stick in my mind, and when Ellen invited me to contribute to her Lovecraft-themed anthology, it was perhaps the second idea that occurred to me. (The first was to do with Lovecraft what I had done with Poe for Ellen's *Poe* anthology, namely, write a story mixing the writer's biography with elements from and suggested by his fiction. However, I decided against that approach because I was leery of repeating myself.) Until my protagonist falls asleep, the original version of the story was substantially the same as the one reprinted here. After that, though, the two parted company. In my first attempt at the narrative, once the protagonist realizes that her husband has consumed the cooler's contents, she discovers him on their bed, his torso split open, a bizarre creature like a kind of nightmare tree rising from his chest, long fronds sprouting from it, whipping the air. Worse, he seems to be enjoying the experience, murmuring, "Beautiful." (It occurs to me that the image of the tree was probably influenced by a painting Michael Whelan did for Del Rey's editions of Lovecraft's stories, which featured a bare tree in which a screaming face was embedded.) Ellen's response to the story was less than enthusiastic: she reminded me that her description of what she was looking for had specified no tentacles, and my weird tree was a bit too tentacular for her. She told me to give her a week or two to think it over, but I panicked and told her I was withdrawing the story from submission, and would write another for her. (That was "City of the Dog," which ran up too close to the anthology's deadline for a story of its length; though Ellen did eventually publish it in the *Best Horror of the Year.*) In the meantime, I decided that the story I had written as "The Beautiful Thing that Awaits Us All" needed revision. The weird reveal in the story seemed too sudden, too arbitrary (which, admittedly, was what my good friend Laird Barron appreciated about the story, whose title he liked enough to use as the title of his third collection [and a subsequent story]). When S. T. Joshi asked me if I had something for the second volume of the *Black Wings* series he was editing for PS Publishing, I decided to undertake significant revisions on the story. In the time since I had written the first version of the piece, I had run across an article about the Gobekli Tepe site in Turkey that discussed archaeologists' recent correction of the place's date from 4000–5000 BCE to twice that, making it much older than, say, the pyramids, and raising all sorts of fascinating questions about human history. At around the same time, I was reading about Sedna, one of the group of trans-Neptunian bodies that includes Pluto. It's about three times the distance from the sun as Neptune, a dwarf planet whose surface is strangely red. Bringing these two discoveries together seemed a very Lovecraftian narrative gesture to make, and when a search for events contemporaneous to the construction of Gobekli Tepe led to theories concerning the disappearance of the Clovis people in North America, particularly one (apparently rather fringe) hypothesis linking it to the atmospheric detonation of a comet, I could feel the elements of my expanded story slipping into place. (It's all about those huge expanses, whether of time, space, or both.) Things were developing vis à vis the story's characters, too. In the previous version of the narrative, the husband's action was largely separate from his wife: he eats the weird object and later she finds him horribly transformed by it. It occurred to me that the story would be much more interesting if she was made part of the transformation, what I was thinking of as the bloom-ing; in fact, it would give me the chance to describe what such an experience was like from the inside out, so to speak. I remarked on this in the story notes to my previous collection, but it bears repeating: when I'm asked to write something Lovecraft-related, inevitably, I find myself exploring particularly domestic situations. There's something about the juxtaposition of the sublime and the intimate that I find deeply compelling.

"Renfrew's Course." This story has its roots in the statue of Michael Scott that was installed in the Beveridge Park in Kirkcaldy, Scotland, around 2009. Carved from a large piece of wood, the sculpture seems intended to evoke Tolkien's Gandalf (and possibly Rowling's Dumbledore, and behind them both, Merlin). It commemorates a local Medieval scholar about whom a number of fantastical legends have grown up. Those who desire to do so can follow a path through the park grounds called the Wizard's Walk, which purports to show a number of sights associated with Scott, not least of them, the ruins of his former keep. Fiona and I saw the statue and took David for a walk along the path when we were in Kirkcaldy visiting her mother and father. It was a somewhat dreary day, gray, cool, with a light rain falling. As we trudged the dirt path, we talked about the statue and the figure who inspired it. It very much felt as if a story had just been dropped in my lap; the challenge was to figure out its contours. At the time, the Harry Potter books (and their film adaptations) were still at the forefront of the culture. For me, the movie versions had an impact almost as profound as that of the novels, in that they showed the (British) landscapes (and increasing number of cityscapes) in which the narratives occurred, which especially in the later installments loaned their events a kind of appealing grittiness. As we walked, Fiona and I discussed how Michael Scott might feature in a story. I think we were already kicking around the question of what kind of initiation a wizard might require of a prospective student. Our excursion was turning out to be longer than I had expected, which was probably what suggested the idea of a ritual based on walking a very specific path. This would be a path through time as well as space, in order that the aspiring apprentice would experience something of the life they were sacrificing should they choose to learn the dark arts; indeed, that life might be thought of as a kind of offering. The aspirant's course would have to describe a mystical symbol, and at the end of it, if everything was successful, the wizard would appear and offer his tutelage. (I wonder now whether the idea of walking a particular pattern was influenced by Roger Zelazny's *Amber* series, which I read many years earlier and in which characters can follow certain directions and move between dimensions.) Although this conception of the wizard's path seemed promising, I wasn't quite satisfied with it. In order to study magic, it seemed to me, there should be a more substantial, a tangible sacrifice involved, something more extreme even than a life unlived. The answer to my aesthetic problem arrived several months later, with the invitation to submit a story to an anthology of LGBTQ-themed horror fiction whose theme was abominations of desire. I understood that the topic was riffing on the conservative religious view of anything other than heterosexuality as exactly such an abomination, and I considered writing a story that engaged the theme on those terms. The longer I thought about the matter, though, the more I thought that it would be better to address the anthology's topic in a less obvious way. If I were to return to the narrative Fiona and I had been batting around in Scotland months before, I might place two people on the wizard's path, a couple, whose completion of the path might cause him to appear and ask if either was willing to sacrifice the other as a cost for his tutelage? That situation struck me as very interesting, especially if one of the characters had experienced a devastating illness during their walk through their future life together. The story was shorter than I anticipated. When I finished it, I realized that the sorcerer in it was part of the same fraternity as the uncle in "Mr. Gaunt" (a realization that has come to inform some of my more recent stories). Sadly, the anthology for which the story was written didn't come to fruition; happily, I was able to place it with John Joseph Adams's online science fiction and fantasy magazine, *Lightspeed.* I had submitted it to John's online horror magazine, *Nightmare,* but he didn't think it qualified as a horror story as much as a kind of fantasy, which I find fascinating, because the piece seems to me to end in an absolutely awful place.

"Bor Urus." As noted above, my stories dealing with betrayal came in a cluster of five, after which, I largely moved on to other themes, although I suppose betrayal remained (and remains) in the mix. The exception occurred a couple of years after I had completed "Renfrew's Course," and came in response to an invitation from Simon Strantzas to contribute to an anthology of stories about what he described as thin places, which is to say, locations where the margins between this world and others are particularly tenuous. It's a marvelous conceit, one with applications to much of the literature of the fantastic. Rather than a specific locale, however, I was intrigued by the idea that the thin place might be an event—a place in time, if you like, specifically, a violent thunderstorm of the type that occurs in the Catskills during the summer months. When you're in the midst of such a storm, and everything outside the windows of your house or car is in tumult, it's easy enough to believe that the veil between this world and another might be blown open.

By this point, I had completed my second novel, *The Fisherman*, which is set in and around the Catskills, and it occurred to me that the place to which the storm might offer access could be the other world the characters in the novel had encountered. (In this way, the story is part of a continuing number which have touched on and expanded upon the materials of the novel.) I thought that something from the weird place would briefly intrude into my protagonist's life, and then (eventually) he would cross into the other world. I'm not exactly sure why the creature he and his future wife see during the initial (initiating?) storm turned out to be a giant bull. In *The Fisherman,* the title character uses the heads of gigantic cattle to bait the enormous hooks with which he seeks to catch Apophis. I suppose I found the image of a bull the size of an elephant a striking one. In the huge bull, it may be that I was recalling the great red bull from Peter Beagle's *The Last Unicorn,* but I think it as likely came from Greek mythology, where Zeus, as a bull, kidnaps Europa, where Hercules labors to catch the Cretan bull, and where on that same island another bull sires the Minotaur. The strange tree the protagonist glimpses inside the lightning strike outside his house I transplanted from *The Fisherman.* If a bull was a somewhat atypical animal to associate with another plane of existence (as compared to, say, a dragon or unicorn), then I figured a kind of ur-tree would be a stranger detail still. I suppose the climactic scene of the story, bringing together bull and tree in a setting whose ruined temple evokes the mythology underlying my choice of bull, might seem almost Hegelian, a synthesis of the elements representing the other world. As I've noted, the material between those encounters with the great bull was a return to the topic of betrayal. By placing my narrator's emotional dalliance with his ex after his first encounters with the supernatural, I wanted to try for something different than what I usually might have done. Specifically, instead of having the supernatural event happen after the real world occurrence, thus allowing and even encouraging the supernatural to be read as a trope for the mundane, I wanted to reverse that order in the interest of presenting the mundane as a trope for the supernatural. I suppose I had in mind something similar to what M. John Harrison does in his great story "Anima," in which a character's litany of extreme and borderline self-destructive behaviors is revealed to be an extended response to an encounter with a supernatural entity.

One more thing: the original title of the story was "Bos Urus," which is the Latin name for the enormous bulls, now extinct, that once roamed Europe. In the proofs for the story, the title was misspelled as "Bor Urus," a glaringly obvious error I failed to catch until the story was in print. I kind of liked the weirdness of the typo, though, so I decided to keep it.

"At Home in House of the Devil." Of this story, I'm tempted to say I was raised Catholic and leave it at that. But of course there's more to the piece; there always is. As far as beginnings go, I'm pretty sure this is the oldest story in this collection, and as with so many of the pieces here, it was prompted by an invitation from Ellen Datlow to submit to one of her anthologies. In fact, I'm pretty sure this was the first invitation she sent me. The anthology was to be called *Inferno*, and it was to consist of non-themed horror stories. I very much wanted to write a story for the book. Since I'd started publishing, I had been eager to work with Ellen; here was my chance. Despite the freedom her invite offered, though, my imagination moved pretty quickly to a story inspired by the anthology's title (the Fornits tend to be pretty literal). That opening line, the supposed aphorism, came straight away. The story that trailed behind it almost entire had its roots in a recent nightmare. In my dream, I was inside a house full of small rooms with the Devil. He was a middle-aged man wearing a wrinkled white suit and a dress shirt without a tie. (I think he may have been barefoot, but I'm not sure about that detail.) Our conversation was generic but civil; what I remember more is that he kept hurting himself, in part because he kept misjudging the dimensions of the rooms we were in. None of his injuries was major—he barked his shin on the leg of a chair, struck his hip on the corner of a table, that kind of thing. But they were constant, low-level aggravations that I realized were his actual eternal punishment. As I was talking to the Devil, I realized that I must be damned, which filled me with mingled fright and sorrow. The Devil never mentioned it, though, which made me wonder if I was supposed to bring it up to him first, if my torment would be worse if I didn't acknowledge my status. Or maybe him not talking about it was in fact a way to make me suffer. At the beating heart of my dread was a conviction, not that where I was was a mistake, but that it wasn't. (Did I mention twelve years of Catholic school, too?) As usually happens, the story grew in the telling. I didn't finish it in time for Ellen's deadline, and when I set it aside, it was a little more than half-done. Every now and again, I contemplated completing it, but it wasn't until I was putting together the contents of my third collection that I realized this story had to have a place in it. As noted above, this was an idea I at first resisted, fearing the delay it would cause in a book already late, but a conversation with my publisher, Derrick Hussey, convinced me I should include it. When I resumed work on the story, I understood that I was writing a response of sorts to Nathaniel Hawthorne's "Young Goodman Brown," which I first encountered during my sophomore year of college, in an American Literature class that was my introduction to Hawthorne's work in general. (Although most of my friends had to read *The Scarlet Letter* during freshman year of high school, the Honors English class I was in at the time read Bradbury's *The Martian Chronicles*, instead.) Up to this point, I had avoided Hawthorne because I knew that *The Scarlet Letter*—and much of his work—concerned the puritans, and with the wisdom of youth I assumed it was therefore dreary and boring. Reading stories such as "Young Goodman Brown," "My Kinsman, Major Molineux," and "Ethan Brand" (not to mention, *The Scarlet Letter*) corrected this misapprehension, and sent me to the bookstore to buy a copy of his selected stories, which I sampled with increasing interest and enthusiasm over the following years. I appreciated the way Hawthorne brought together a concern for moral ambiguity and nuance with elements of the fantastic; indeed, after reading him, I couldn't understand the resistance so many of my professors displayed towards more recent writers such as King and Straub. In the decades since I realized how wrong I had been about Hawthorne (whose sensibility I later saw had influenced another favorite writer, Henry James). I also saw "Young Goodman Brown" as establishing a narrative template that a number of subsequent writers had employed, including Flannery O'Connor ("A Good Man Is Hard to Find"), Joyce Carol Oates ("Where Are You Going, Where Have You Been?"), and Stephen King ("The Man in the Black Suit"). With the story I was working on, I was looking to add my contribution to that small but distinguished list. In the course of doing so, I mined my upbringing and education in a religious faith which, despite some of the liberalizing effects of the second Vatican council, remained obsessed by sin, especially the sins of the flesh, and for which the Devil and damnation were always perilously close.

It's funny: when I think about it, a significant subset of my reading over the years has concentrated on representations of the infernal, from Dante's *Inferno* to Marlowe's *Faustus*, from Milton's *Paradise Lost* to Goethe's *Faust*, from C. S. Lewis's *The Great Divorce* to Ira Levin's *Rosemary's Baby*. It's almost a surprise to realize that it took me this long to arrive at my own contribution. What's of equal interest to me is in noticing that, when I came to write about the Devil and Hell, I chose to do so through the lens of the mundane, in much the same way as I have when writing about Lovecraft's monstrous sublime. For me, it seems, these grand figures are most vivid in humble settings.

Acknowledgments

With this latest book of stories, I am reminded once again of my debt to my lovely wife, Fiona, for her love, support, and patience. Thanks, Love, for all of it; here's another bouquet of dark flowers.

The love and support of my sons, Nick and David, is a constant and ever-surprising joy. Thanks, guys; I look forward eagerly to the art you're making.

Laird Barron and Paul Tremblay remain the brothers I never knew I had, their regular phone conversations one of the highlights of my week. They continue to do amazing work, which inspires me to try to do better in my own fiction. Nadia Bulkin, Michael Cisco, Glen Hirshberg, Stephen Graham Jones, Sarah Langan, and S. P. Miskowski are pretty cool, too.

I continue to consider myself fortunate in my agent, the indefatigable Ginger Clark, as well as her assistant, Tess, and the film and foreign rights folks at Curtis, Brown. As the story notes indicate, I owe most of these pieces to invitations from editors, and I'm grateful for the support John Joseph Adams, Ellen Datlow, Nick Gevers and Jack Dann, and S. T. Joshi showed these stories by first publishing them. Thanks, too, to Derrick Hussey and Hippocampus Press for the fine work they did with my last collection, and for publishing this one.

Finally, thanks to you, whoever you are, for the gift of your time and attention (and in many cases, patience—I know this book has been a long time coming). You make books such as this one possible, and I'm grateful for that.

Publication History

"At Home in the House of the Devil" is original to this collection.

"Bloom" originally appeared in *Black Wings II,* edited by S. T. Joshi (PS Publishing, 2012).

"Bor Urus" originally appeared in *Shadows Edge,* edited by Simon Strantzas (Gray Friar Press, 2013).

"In Paris, in the Mouth of Kronos" originally appeared in *Supernatural Noir,* edited by Ellen Datlow (Dark Horse Books, 2011).

"Renfrew's Course" originally appeared in *Lightspeed* (June 2012).

"Sefira" is original to this collection.

"The Third Always Beside You" originally appeared in *Blood and Other Cravings,* edited by Ellen Datlow (Tor, 2011).

"The Unbearable Proximity of Mr. Dunn's Balloons" originally appeared in *Ghosts by Gaslight,* edited by Jack Dann and Nick Gevers (HarperVoyager, 2011).